CW00530072

GETTING ORLANDO

A Novel

Anthony McDonald

Anchor Mill Publishing

Getting Orlando

Anchor Mill Publishing

4/04 Anchor Mill

Paisley PA1 1JR

SCOTLAND

anchormillpublishing@gmail.com

First published 2011 by BIGfib Books

For Tony Linford, who has been my Oliver ever since the days when I had Orlando's youth and all his silliness, if never quite his magical good looks.

.

Acknowledgements: The author would like to thank Kate Akester, Olivier Cuperlier, James Simpson and Joachim Vieritz – for more than mere help with research for a book.

.

ONE

The boy – or young man – was perched on the low rail in front of the station buffet. A few of the other waiting passengers were perching near him, but Oliver did not give them a glance.

When the train came in, Oliver climbed aboard and took a seat. The young man, who had entered behind him, came and sat directly across the gangway. Oliver thought the seating arrangements couldn't have been better if he'd planned them himself. People of that age – twenty-one, twenty-two? – could be wonderfully unaware of the interest they awoke in people of Oliver's age, which was thirty-eight. Oliver aimed his gaze over the young man's shoulder as if he were fascinated by the landscape jogging past the window on the other side of the train: the receding view of the flyover that carried the Eurostar tracks, and of vast weed-grown sheds – which had once been Ashford's railway carriage works – peeling away as the branch line curved right, bearing the train and its passengers across the Romney Marsh.

First there was his hair. That deep dark red had been the first thing to catch Oliver's attention on the platform. Neither short nor long, it framed his face, and arranged itself around his ears, in close waves that were almost curls: the copper coils and windings of a clean electrical machine. Eyes were brilliant, kingfisher blue, quite large – full of intelligence, Oliver decided; empty of cynicism and hurt. Nose small, short and straight: the kind that

Oliver found cute; he had something of the sort himself. A sensitive mouth: lips full but not to overflowing. He was not gabbling into a mobile phone, nor were his ears wired for sound. He was simply gazing across the gangway, over Oliver's shoulder, mirroring Oliver's attitude, though from more innocent motives no doubt.

Oliver was sure they would be travelling together as far as Rye; almost everyone on that train usually did; but the boy disappointed him by getting up after a few minutes and leaving the train at its first stop, which was called Ham Street. Oliver watched him through the window, striding along the platform: slightly taller than average height, slim, a little broader in the shoulder than at the hips.

'He sounds the acme of ordinariness,' was David's adjudication, after Oliver had described the nine minutes' wonder later that evening. 'Slim without being skinny? Not off-puttingly muscular...? Come on. Except for the hair, perhaps, you've just described every normal-looking kid of that age.'

'I don't know,' said Zara, David's wife. 'Oliver made him sound very appealing. Maybe ordinariness and perfection are more closely connected than we tend to think.'

'Intriguing,' said David. 'But enough. We've got an appointment at the Rose and Crown. Remember?' To Oliver, 'There's someone would like to meet you. I said nine o'clock.'

'Someone wants to meet me?' Oliver meant to sound sardonic, but actually came over as surprised and flattered.

'I don't think it's for romantic purposes,' Zara said.

David, who took pride in finishing his wife's sentences, added, 'But rather a little job offer. If you're interested, that is. Just a one off. Three hundred quid, if you want it, for sitting on a plane for a couple of hours. Tell you about it in the car.'

Oliver was staying the weekend with old friends. He had known David the longer of the two. They had been at university together sixteen years ago, at which time David had been something of a boy's boy. Now though, the fact that he had been married to Zara for nine years told Oliver as much as he needed, or had any right, to know. When they had all lived in London Oliver saw them rarely, Putney and Kilburn being as remote from each other as Land's End and John o'Groat's. But two years ago Zara's mother had died and they had moved into the cottage she left them, full of atmosphere and beamed ceilings, in a village called Beckley, on the border of East Sussex and Kent. They both had offices in London still, but now also worked from home two or three days a week. Oliver had spent a number of weekends here with them, and already knew their local pub. He was interested, intrigued even, by the prospect of making an easy three hundred pounds as a result of his visit there tonight. But he was surprised to find the buoyancy this gave to his spirits tempered somewhat. Because Beckley was some sixteen miles from Ham

Street, where the handsome boy had got off the train, there was no realistic chance of bumping into him again in the Rose and Crown.

'Actually,' David said in the car, 'the job was offered to me first. This chap I know slightly – in a pub sort of way – asked me a few days ago, out of the blue, did I want to be a courier for a day? I thought he was joking. Laughed the idea off. But he said he was serious – his name's Donald by the way. He said did I know anyone... Well, I thought of you and said you'd be down at the weekend. I hope that was OK. No harm done?' He looked round into the back seat enquiringly.

'No harm at all,' Oliver reassured him. He guessed that David had understood the enquiry to mean: did David know anyone who was really short of money and had an open enough schedule to be able to hop on a flight at a moment's notice. Well yes. Oliver, unfortunately, fitted the bill rather well just now. Unlike David, who was a quantity surveyor in a big London firm. Unlike Zara, a busy actuary. On the time-is-money conversion scale they could be placed towards the cash-heavy time-light end while Oliver, who had lost both his job and his partner during the last eight months found himself very much nearer the other.

They reached the pub. You could sense its surroundings of copses and open fields even in the darkness of a February evening. It was a cheerful place to enter, an old building with low overhead beams and bracket lights on the walls. A log fire burned in the wide hearth. There were people sitting at the bar with whom

Oliver remembered exchanging nods and hallos on previous visits. Perhaps he had even already spoken to the man he was now going to meet.

Then an anxiety struck him, as David went to the bar to order drinks. He turned to Zara, who was looking about her with the deepest concentration for a table for them to sit at; several were unoccupied but it seemed that she was in search of the one that most nearly corresponded to the Platonic paradigm of what a pub table ought to be. Oliver said, 'You don't suppose it's drugs or something? You know, I don't think I'd want to…'

'…Swallow condoms full of heroin and have them all burst inside you?' Zara's blue eyes were laughing, though she delivered the thought deadpan. 'I don't know. You'll have to ask.' She looked around them, at the cosy room with its horse brasses, and the beam above the bar festooned with last autumn's hop bines for Sussex luck. 'Though I must say, I doubt it.'

'Child porn? There's no way…'

Zara laughed. 'Do you always think your way out of doing new things before you've even started?'

'No,' Oliver said with sudden resolution. He was not a timid man, and he did not consider himself a scrupulously moral one, but he had managed to clock up his thirty-eight years without any involvement in what most people call crime. 'If it's anything else, anything else at all, I'll do it.'

'Good for you,' said David, arriving at just that moment, landing pint mugs of Harvey's on the table. 'White wine's coming,' he told his wife.

A few minutes later David's acquaintance, Donald, came into the bar and David waved him over to join them as soon as he had got himself a drink. As introductions were made, Oliver found himself oddly reassured by the fact that the new arrival bore a resemblance to the one-time leader of the Labour Party, Michael Foot. He had the same straight white, unkempt hair, the same way of screwing up his eyes behind thick spectacles and nodding and twisting his head as he talked. Actually, Oliver thought, Donald looked more like the Spitting Image puppet of Michael Foot than the man himself, but then, in a strange way, so had the original. In any case, Oliver decided, there was no possible danger or risk to be imagined as a consequence of associating himself with a man who looked like that.

'Tell you what it is.' Donald even sounded like Michael Foot. 'I need a set of pub games delivered to some friends in Funchal, middle of next week. Up to now I haven't found anybody with the time to spare. Think you can help me out?'

'Funchal?' Oliver recognised the name but for the moment couldn't place it.

'Capital of Madeira. Island in the Atlantic. Just north of the Canaries. Nice climate. Takes about three hours.'

'And you want to pay a special courier to deliver a set

of pub games?' Oliver coloured his voice with a tinge of worldly scepticism. He would stay polite but he didn't want to be thought a complete mug.

Donald took a slow steady swallow of Guinness, then peered fixedly at Oliver through his extremely thick spectacles. He might have looked quite intimidating had it not been for the moustache of white froth that now adhered to his long upper lip. 'That's right. I do. Draughts, dominos, shove-halfpenny. All the old-fashioned things. You can inspect the cargo yourself. Look inside the boxes.' Donald's face relaxed into a cautious smile. 'Don't want you to think I take you for a fool. Give you my word there's nothing illegal about this. Although you'd agree that in different circumstances, if there *was* anything … *unusual*, let's say, about a certain consignment, it might be better if the courier did not know until after. Right?'

Oliver looked at Donald open-mouthed for a split second and then began to nod his agreement. But at the same moment Donald burst out laughing and, looking round at the others, said, 'Nearly had him there, didn't I? He was almost on the point of taking me serious.' Then the others, first David, then Zara, and finally Oliver himself, joined in the laughter, if a bit faintly. They had all been on the point of taking Donald serious.

But Donald's joke – if it had been a joke – had done the trick for Oliver. With the veiled suggestion embedded in that one phrase – *an unusual consignment* – Donald had hooked Oliver like a fish, had jerked him out of his humdrum present existence, the life of a redundant civil servant whose lover had left him, and into a new dimension: a dimension that encompassed who knew what. Excitement? Adventure? Risk?

'I *think* I'm your man,' Oliver said, with a little show of hesitation. 'But I'd like to know a little bit more about the arrangements.' His cautious mien was only a charade though. Oliver knew that he was up for this, come what might.

*

Oliver's weekend in the country passed pleasantly enough. There was a trip to Hastings where they bought fresh fish on the beach beneath the cliff, among the hauled-up boats and those strange tarred weatherboard towers, the net sheds, while being dive-bombed by the raucous gulls. There was Zara's classy cooking, and a walk in the dormant woods where the first optimistic primroses were opening in sheltered places among last autumn's fallen leaves.

When it came to bedtime, Oliver didn't waste too much time regretting that David belonged to Zara, not to him. Ten years ago he might have done, but not now. In any case his mind was too preoccupied with the impending new adventure that life, in the shape of Donald, had thrown his way. He would be flying out from Gatwick on Tuesday around midday. His hosts were conscious of his state of preoccupation and occasionally, though very gently, teased him about it. But some of the excitement that surrounds any mystery had rubbed off on them too; Oliver guessed that, though they would never have admitted it, both of them felt the faintest stirrings of envy when they talked about what he was going to do.

They drove him to the train at Rye on Sunday evening. *Appledore will be the next stop,* announced the recorded on-board voice. What brilliant names the stations had round here. It was only after Appledore, when the same even female tones reminded everyone that the following halt would be Ham Street, that Oliver, with a jolt, remembered the beautiful young man. As the train slowed to a stop, Oliver's eyes swept the length of the platform. Only two passengers were waiting to get on, neither of them the red-headed youth. Irrationally, because he hadn't given the boy a moment's thought since his meeting with Donald on Friday night, Oliver felt a pang of disappointment. Involuntarily he looked across the gangway where the seats were empty. He was surprised at how readily his inner eye now pictured him sitting there. Above the radiant blue eyes his eyelashes were thick and dark brown, not ginger pale like those of most red-haired people. Oliver was unaware he'd even noticed that. And then his clothes. Light blue jeans, plain white trainers and – white socks. Oliver had worn that combination when he was very young. Fashionable then. But Oliver had gone on dressing the same way ever since. He glanced down. He was dressed that way today. Perhaps white socks were back in fashion again. He doubted it. More probably the boy just didn't care: wore his tennis socks or whatever came tumbling out of the drawer first. He would never find out. There were many trains in the world: even at Ham Street one in each direction every hour. There was no reason why he should ever cross paths with that particular pair of elegant ankles again. But ten minutes later, when Oliver had left the Marsh Link service at Ashford International and was waiting for his mainline connection to London, his spirits rose. A Eurostar train came exploding out of its burrow on the other side of the tracks and raced like a firework up onto the ramp that spanned the junction: a fizzing line of lights and sparks on overhead wires that quickly vanished at two hundred miles per hour. In twenty minutes that vanishing streak would be in France. Abroad. Two days from now Oliver would follow it. Not to France. But abroad. To somewhere other than here. Oliver smiled to himself and gave a silent, inward cheer.

TWO

Oliver took the number sixteen down the Edgware Road and got off near Paddington station. He was to collect his consignment from an address in Praed Street. He found it easily enough: a number above a door, a bell, a fuzzy *come on up* from the entry-phone, then uncarpeted stairs that led to an office, a cubby-hole really, above a shop. It might have been the headquarters of a mini-cab company, to judge from the paperwork on the walls and desk, but Oliver missed the usual row of seedy-looking drivers waiting for their next call-out. But, as if in compensation, the sole, pensionable-looking, occupant of the room looked seedy enough for four.

'Donald sent me,' Oliver said. 'For the pub games.'

The man grunted and reached under his desk. He dredged up a black plastic rubbish sack, which had been wrapped round itself to form a medium-sized parcel, and handed it to Oliver without comment. It was not heavy.

Oliver part unwrapped it and glanced inside. He saw boxes of board games, scuffed and well-used, that might have come from a flea market or an old pub that awaited the demolition ball. 'Thank you,' he said.

'Take care of them,' said the man. Oliver nodded, gathered the top of the sack in his fist and a moment later was back in the street. He felt a sense of amazement at the disorienting ordinariness of the encounter – the handover, was that what you called it? – and also at the fact that he held in his hands something which, for reasons unknown to him, was valuable enough to warrant his making a trip abroad with a return plane ticket and three hundred pounds of somebody else's money.

The arrangements were simple. Electronic ticket. He had only to show his passport at the Gatwick check-in. Once he arrived at Funchal airport he would take a taxi to the address Donald had given him. It was the address of a bar in the Old Town, run by friends of Donald's. Friends? Oliver asked himself, and tried not to think the word *accomplices*. He would hand over the boxes and they would hand over three hundred pounds in cash. They would also – and this was the astonishing bit – put him up for the night, or two nights if he wanted. Donald had given him the option of any return date he chose, though he couldn't say whether his friends would be prepared to put him up indefinitely. Oliver had thought for a moment and said that two nights would do fine. If he didn't fancy staying with Donald's' friends'he could always find somewhere else for a night or two. A two-day holiday in a balmy climate seemed about right. Whereas to blow the whole three hundred quid on a week in a hotel would have defeated the object of his going. Besides, he only had Donald's word that he was doing nothing illegal, and it seemed prudent not to hang about too long within the jurisdiction of the Madeiran customs and police. Finally Donald had surprised him by fishing in his wallet and producing seventy euros to cover his taxi fares while he was on the island.

At each stage Oliver was braced for the discovery that either the whole thing was an elaborate joke, a hoax, or that he was being set up in some way: that there was a real crime going on somewhere and he was going to be the fall-guy. So it was with a sense of near disbelief that he found there really was a ticket waiting for him when he arrived at Gatwick the following morning; and that nobody challenged him when he claimed it; nor were police lurking, ready to pounce. But when the check-in girl, attaching a cabin-baggage sticker to his battered hold-all, asked him, 'Did you pack your luggage yourself? Did you leave your bag unattended at any time? Did anyone give you anything to carry for them?' and he answered a breezy yes, no and no – though lying in the third instance – he finally had to accept that it was all for real and there was no going back now.

Lunch was served as they crossed the Bay of Biscay, and coincided neatly with a bout of high altitude turbulence. The airline had provided a stew of squid as a main dish and, in Economy at least, plastic cutlery to eat it with. The cutlery was only marginally tougher than the squid pieces and so the passenger cabin soon became a battleground of knocking elbows, muttered apologies, airborne chunks of mollusc, and snapping knives. But this actually had a beneficial effect on Oliver: his feelings of nervousness were wonderfully overcome by a series of urges to giggle. After which, a glance through the window surprised him with the sight of the Portuguese coastline all covered in snow, sliding slowly away to the east: a line of blue and white icing-sugar mountains that sparkled in the afternoon sun, like a

Portuguese tiling frieze.

His first glimpse of the island of Madeira was less inspiring. Holes in the cloud showed the Atlantic now looking cold and dark, with rocks like black teeth emerging from it. But a minute later, with the cloud cover finally left above them, everything changed. A vista of green terraced hills appeared and they descended among orange-roofed hillside farms, to land on a runway that jutted out over the sea at both ends, coming to rest among flowers and palm trees. When Oliver stepped out through the cabin door the air that met him was warm and soft.

He was almost clear of the customs hall, and beginning to feel he'd made it safely, when a man in uniform stepped into his path. 'You come this way, please?' Oliver wasn't entirely surprised. In a perverse way he thought he would have felt let down if he hadn't been stopped. The awakened interest of the customs men meant that he still maintained an aura of danger, of youth, about him. They had seen a man, travelling alone, who had the appearance of someone in his early rather than late thirties: a little smaller than the average, but stocky and fit-looking, not running to fat; with hair still curly, dark and thick; and bright brown eyes that peered alertly out at the world from an intelligent, still boyish-looking face. Someone who (the customs men were not to know this) was often told that he had a nose like Matt Damon's. It meant he didn't strike them as totally safe and unthreatening. In their eyes he was not yet neutered by middle age. All the same, their picking him out for special scrutiny signalled the start of a potentially very awkward encounter indeed. If they opened his case, perhaps they would see only what he had seen himself: boxes of games that you might play at home or in the pub. On the other hand, might their trained eyes spot something that his own had missed?

But it wasn't trained eyes he had to fear, as he quickly discovered; it was a trained dog. Oliver was escorted to a small room which was entered at the same moment from the other side by a German shepherd towing its handler on a leash. 'Sit please,' the customs officer told Oliver. 'Baggage on floor. You put it flat. No move.' The dog slowly circled him, sniffing both him and his hold-all with great thoroughness. Oliver sat quietly and wondered apprehensively what would happen next. That the dog would stand up, perhaps, and make an accusation in human speech? But the dog didn't even growl or bark; it simply walked away and its handler went too. Whatever it was trained to detect and whatever was contained in Oliver's luggage clearly did not match up. 'Thank you,' said the customs officer. 'You can go.'

Oliver stood up. He almost felt like blurting, 'Aren't you going to look inside?' Instead he said, 'Thank you,' and wondered as he did so why he had not thought to find out what *thank you* might be in Portuguese. Or *please*, for that matter. Or *yes* and *no* – and how to tell a taxi driver where to take him to.

Fortunately the taxi driver understood his English and spoke it well enough himself. It dawned on Oliver that he had come to a place where probably almost everybody did.

The road into town ran through a series of tunnels round a headland, with a mountain rearing up on one side and with plunging views to the sea on the other. Then, emerging from the last tunnel, Oliver was confronted with the sight of the whole Bay of Funchal laid out below him and above like a vast amphitheatre. Harbour and town centre occupied the arena, while terraces of neat villas rose tier upon tier till they gave way to thick forest, that seemed to climb almost vertically through sunshine and mauve shadow, disappearing finally into mountain cloud. Down below, beyond the harbour mole and all the way to a distant, sharply drawn horizon, the sea was an uncompromising blue.

The taxi took him winding down through narrow ways that were as steep as stairs into the Old Town, shadowy with plane trees and tucked away behind the big market building, and there deposited him at the address he had been given, in – at least, this was Oliver's quick first impression – an eerily cobwebby street. But there was a bar at this address and it was open. The Bar Zarco. You went down a few steps into it and found it full of beams and old-style lantern lights. It was late afternoon and only a few customers propped up the bar. But the woman serving welcomed him with a smile and Oliver again relaxed. He said, 'Oliver Watson. I think you may be expecting me.'

'That's right, we are. I'm Maggie. My husband's Joe. Somewhere about. How was your trip?' Across the counter she held out her hand. She was slim, had a pleasant face and was neatly dressed. Probably about Oliver's own age. She had a South African accent, he thought. So far there was nothing to dismay or alarm him. No sign of any trap. 'Come through.'

Oliver stepped through a bead curtain and found himself in a meticulously organised mini-kitchen. He imagined the galley of a submarine would be something like this. 'Parcel for you,' he said, and pointed to the hold-all he was carrying.

'And cash for you.' She said this quite matter-of-factly, still with a smile, as if this was the kind of transaction she handled every day, like paying the man who arrived with the meat. She turned away to get the money from somewhere. From a coffee jar perhaps. Oliver didn't see the source of the banknotes that she handed to him a few seconds later, as he had bent down to undo the hold-all and take the plastic sack out. It was somehow strange to see it again, in different circumstances, in a different climate from February London's. With precision timing, sack and money changed hands. 'Count it,' Maggie said. 'I won't mind. Donald said you might want to stay a night or two. Do you?'

'It might be...'

'Let me show you what's on offer before you make up your mind.' She left the sack of toys on a worktop in the kitchen and led him up narrow stairs. She showed him a put-u-up in a windowless corridor of a room that also

17

contained crates of spirits, stacked up chairs, bottles of bleach and all the other paraphernalia that went to equip and maintain a bar. 'It's not much of a bedroom, but it's the best we can do. No charge, obviously.'

Oliver decided he would say yes. 'It'll do just fine. And, thank you, by the way.'

'Grub's on us. Tonight anyway. Just pot luck in the bar, nothing fancy. Guess you'll be buying a few beers over the bar before you go. Fair?'

Oliver smiled and shrugged. 'Sounds fair to me. Meantime, where's the...?' Maggie pointed up the next twist of the uncarpeted stairs.

The remaining hours of sunshine found Oliver exploring the nearby streets. They had their own distinctive colour scheme. Ochre, cream and chocolate were the livery of the old houses, while the smarter shoppers, of both sexes, wore amber or mustard tops above bronze, or coffee, or old gold. Even the buses were butterscotch. And as he continued to puzzle over the nature of the cargo he'd brought with him in a seafront bar, Oliver found those same colours reflected most pleasingly in the glasses of Madeira wine that were placed in front of him.

Finding his way back to the Bar Zarco wasn't as easy as he expected to since it was now dark, and he took a few wrong turnings among the alleys of the Old Town. The area, which he had dismissed at first sight as cobwebby and asleep had now woken up. Bars and restaurants, eyebrowed with strings of coloured lights, had opened where only inscrutable dark brown shutters had lined the cobbled streets before, and some hundreds of tourists had descended from their plate-glass hotels up the hills behind the town to dine and drink and party.

At last he saw *Zarco* in bright neon and made his way back inside. In the bar a tall, well-built man was serving. Red-faced and sandy-haired, he looked jovial enough but also as if he would not stand for any nonsense if any were to be offered. 'Are you Joe?' Oliver asked. The big man squeezed his hand. 'Doctor Watson, I presume?'

Nearby a clientele that consisted of roughly equal numbers of British ex-pats, tourists and locals were already getting to grips with draughts and shove-halfpenny. Oliver saw no sign of the dominos, however. Later, after he'd been served a supper of fish and vegetables with crème caramel for afters, and was feeling emboldened by the beers he'd washed all this down with, he said to Joe, 'It was the dominos, wasn't it?'

'What was the dominos?' Joe asked, poker-faced. Then he laughed. 'Come here,' he said, with a jerk of the thumb. Oliver passed through the bead curtain and entered the galley-sized kitchen for the second time. The three boxes of dominos stood like books in the corner of a shelf, next to a food processor and some chopping boards. Joe took down one of the boxes and opened it up. He scratched at one of the tiles with a thumbnail. Black paint flaked away easily. Underneath was creamy white.

'Ivory,' said Joe. 'This game's called Beat the Ban.' He saw a startled expression take over Oliver's face. 'Nothing illegal, mind. This is all old ivory. Sliced off a block of tusk from an elephant that died half a century before the ban came into effect. But how do you prove the provenance? They didn't go dating it in those days, or tagging stuff, like just in case someone was going to clamp down on the trade a generation or so later. That's what makes the game a difficult one to play. That's why your contribution's been so useful.'

'Yeah,' said Oliver, 'but I don't see...' He was going to say something like –why couldn't Joe or Maggie or Donald have done the courier bit themselves and saved the three hundred quid that had been paid to him? – but Joe stopped him.

'There's nothing to see. Nothing else, I mean. Especially if you want to make this kind of work a regular thing. Could be a nice little earner for you if you played it right.'

Oliver decided he had asked enough questions for the time being.

The Zarco bar offered two kinds of draught lager: Coral and Super-Bock, the second being the more expensive. They tasted much the same after you'd had a few, Oliver decided. He guessed the principal difference would lie in the quality of the hangover you could expect in the morning.

He regretted for a moment that he hadn't done any

research before leaving home: checking with acquaintances or looking up Spartacus perhaps. But in the end he told himself he hadn't come here for sex and he might as well accept the situation and end the evening where he was. The people in the bar were friendly enough.

He learned that the Queen Mary 2 was due to dock at Funchal in the morning. Someone contradicted this, saying that the harbour was too small to take her. And he remembered hearing – as he finally staggered away to bed – some other person, whom nobody quite believed, saying that she was too big for any harbour in the world except Southampton, and was obliged to anchor offshore at every port she put in at.

*

He was awoken at sunrise by the sonorous siren-blasts of the Queen Mary 2. The huge ship was confounding all doubters, docking at dawn in the harbour. But a couple more hours passed before Oliver surfaced and made his way out into the sunshine. Then there was no escaping the sight of the vessel. A small piece of her black hull blocked the view at the end of each street, and her towering white superstructure seemed to hover above the roof line like a mass of cumulus cloud.

A cable car was in operation, its bottom station just two minutes from the Zarco bar. It was scooping up passengers in threes and fours in a never-ending series of shiny blue capsules and whisking them over the rooftops of the town and up to some invisible destination on the wooded mountainside above. Oliver forked out for a return ticket – a minor extravagance – and climbed into his bright blue bubble. Above the orange roofs of the Old Town he flew, high above the hairpins and tunnels of the approach roads, close in to houses on spurs of rock where terraced gardens grew lemons and oranges, among eucalyptus trees and pines and palms. He passed over spreading trees with crowns of red flowers, big and bright as scarlet poppies. Pigeons and pursuing falcons raced below him, crossing gaping wild ravines. The ground swept up once more. A woman stooped to cut a gourd or pumpkin just twenty feet beneath, in a handkerchief-sized garden prudently walled to stop it disappearing into the abyss.

'Does it make you want to live here?'

Oliver had paid no attention at all to his three fellow passengers. They were an elderly tourist couple: Scandinavian, he thought, guessing from the impenetrability of their brief exchanges. But it was the other one who had spoken. Oliver focused his eyes on him for the first time. He was a young man, dark-eyed and dark-skinned and not at all bad-looking. In any other situation Oliver would have noticed him at once. 'Do you live here?' Oliver asked him. It was a reasonable enquiry.

'Yes,' said the other. 'This is my journey to work.'

'Lucky you,' said Oliver. 'You really make this trip every day?'

'No,' said the native, and laughed. 'It's expensive. I take the bus, but it's very slow. I only take the cable car if I'm late, or feeling rich.'

'And which are you today,' Oliver asked flippantly, 'late or rich?'

The other continued to smile with his eyes. 'I'm never rich. I only said I sometimes felt it. Late though…' He laughed. 'Quite often.'

'I live in London,' said Oliver and was startled by the bitterness he heard in his own voice, 'but at the moment I have no work. We have nothing like this in London.' He gestured around them – their three hundred and sixty degree view encompassed green valleys, mountainsides and distant cliffs, with a sparkling ocean below. 'At least not in February.'

'Don't be too jealous,' the young Madeiran cautioned him. 'London's big. Lisbon, even Porto. Opportunities. But here…' He shrugged. 'I cook in a hotel.'

'You could do worse,' Oliver said. I could do worse, he was thinking.

'I'm a graduate in economics.'

'So am I,' said Oliver. 'And I don't have any job.'

The young man struck his forehead with the heel of his hand theatrically. 'I'm sorry. I'm also stupid. You told me that. Forgive me?'

Oliver forgave him and would have liked to show his

forgiveness in the form of a hug at least, but in their present setting it was out of the question. Their cable car entered the gleaming steel and glass perched structure that was its upper terminus. It was in a place called Monte – with some lack of imagination, Oliver thought: the name could have been applied equally well to every other place in view.

'I go this way.' Oliver's short-time companion pointed up some steps. Then he indicated a broad path among the woods. 'The tourist bit's along there. But Hotel Splendor's where I am.' He looked again towards the steps. 'Come up for a cocktail some time. Oh, I'm Ricardo. I should have said.' He pronounced it the Portuguese way: *Hicardo.*

'Oliver. I should have said. Oliver Watson.' He held out his hand and they shook.

What was the point of that? Oliver asked himself after they'd parted. Giving both his names. They'd never meet again.

What Monte had was position. Lots of it. And lots of vegetation. But not much else. A fine church, up a mountain of steps, and a few hotels and cafés in a leafy, forest garden setting. But the vertiginous view down to the town of Funchal and sea was what people came for. Even the Queen Mary 2, though still filling the harbour, was reduced to the size of a rather pretentious bath-time toy. And the ear-popping journey down, even without Oliver's companion of earlier, was almost as good as the journey up.

By evening Funchal was full. Everybody on the island who had a car had driven into town to see the great ship, and was trying to park or double park. Police were making an effort to control the crowds. The chestnut sellers and beer kiosks on the sea front could hardly cope. Zebra crossings surged with arriving hordes like Cannon Street in the morning rush. Men in their sixties were clambering over the crush barriers. Youngsters vaulted.

'Come on,' Maggie said. 'We can see this better.' She marched him three blocks inland and up the hill to a hotel that was seven storeys high. 'One of the waiters here, João, used to work for us.' They were let up onto the roof. It was half past six and the sun was starting to sink behind the distant cliff of Cabo Girao. They were just in time to see the ship sail. João was an appealing looking man in his early twenties. Oliver would have liked to ask him what time he got off work but, aware that lack of interest, like a refusal of credit, often offends, decided not to. A few years more and he would probably be expected to pay for it. He went suddenly hot at the thought that he might even be expected to pay for it now.

The low sun picked out the ship's three rotating radar scanners and made them flash in a complex sequential pattern as if they were signalling messages in code. Black hull, white superstructure, red funnel; brown smoke drifted on the light south-westerly breeze.

'Big boat,' said João, his smile sparking across the gap between them. Oliver guessed that his English, though probably very limited, could cut right to the heart of any matter.

Slowly the floating city left its berth and, after one turn at the harbour entrance, headed in a straight line towards the open sea. Her extending wake was a snail's trail upon the mirror-smooth surface. The sea had been changing colours all day: from black, to mercury and turquoise and back again. Now it was the colour (and, you could imagine, the texture) of blue paint: thick navy-blue paint that had been poured into a tray – a tray whose sides were the green headlands to the east and west. Sunset-lit, they shone terra-cotta and white where houses stood, emerald and ochre where terraced hills were not yet built on, the whole spectrum merging in the last few seconds of sunset into a dizzying red-brown and purple blaze. The sky was a sheet of copper, apricot and flame. Oliver was suddenly conscious of the nearness of João at his side. Then, unexpectedly, he thought of the young man in the cable car earlier in the day and, along some chain of association, there came back the memory of the beautiful creature with whom he had spent nine minutes on a train just five days before.

The ship's siren blew long farewells to Madeira that echoed in the stairwells of all the houses for a mile or two inland. And all the smaller ships, the tankers, dredgers, coasters, tramps, and yachts and smaller boats, sounded their sirens in return. *Remember me,* blew the siren of the Queen Mary 2. *We will remember,* signalled the sirens of Funchal's boats. No-one, thought Oliver, who saw that sight in Funchal that cobalt-canopied evening would forget it, ever.

'It was a beautiful sight just now, wasn't it?' he said to no-one in particular.

'Beautiful boat,' answered João.

THREE

London was wearing its February face when Oliver saw it again the next day. It was the same face the city had been wearing when he had left: wind-chapped, drawn and grey with the cold. But seeing it now, Oliver found his discontent sharpened: thrown into relief by his three-day visit to Abroad – a three-day package of sun and new horizon. The experience had been spiced by the element of adventure, almost danger even, that had flavoured at least the beginning of the trip. He still didn't know whether he'd been a party to something quite legal and above board or an unwitting accessory to something much more shady. Joe and Maggie had given nothing more away by the end of his visit than Joe had already divulged: that the dominos were solid ivory, and would be sawn up and used in the restoration of an antique piano that was in the collection of one of the big Madeira wine families. They had waved him off, smiling, on his day of departure, when he set out for the taxi rank just round the corner, en route for the airport.

He was glad that he had not, in the end, attempted to proposition the barman, João, while under the influence of a carnival atmosphere and a beautiful sunset. He would almost certainly have been met with a rebuff, or worse, and in the unlikely event of a positive outcome his last evening as a guest of Joe and Maggie's would have become unpleasantly complicated. And yet... Oliver always experienced a degree of regret on the occasions when he allowed his head to overrule the promptings of his heart and cock.

For six years London had been his home with Adi. But Adi – short for Adrian – had gone back to his native Germany when their storm-tossed teacup of a relationship had finally foundered. Shortly after that, though there was no connection between the two events, his job had gone too, in a cull of Home Office civil servants that had been much applauded by almost everybody else in the country and hailed as long overdue. Now London was simply the place where he had a flat and signed on. It had never got into his bloodstream the way it did for so many other people. He had no family there. Friends, yes, but after six years with Adi those friends had tended to be the friends of both of them: they were friends of someone called Oliandadi; and when that someone had split in two – like Czechoslovakia, as one of those friends had said – there was some awkwardness among them as to whether the spirit of Oliandadi now resided in the eastern or the western half of the divided entity.

Oliver let a few days pass and then phoned David and Zara in Sussex. Partly to reassure them that he had not been arrested for gun running or drug trafficking. But more importantly, he wanted to know if they had had any more sightings of Donald. David said yes, he'd seen him once in the pub and Donald had said something like, 'Your friend's mission seems to have gone off all right,' but hadn't volunteered more on the subject. Oliver said that, next time David saw Donald, he could tell him Oliver had enjoyed doing his little job for him, and if any more work of a similar nature to the Funchal trip was on offer, he would take it.

Meanwhile Oliver had a more prosaic errand to run. It was his god-daughter's birthday in a few days'time, and as his god-daughter was also his niece, the daughter of his elder sister Jenny, he knew it would be a long time before he heard the end of it were he to forget the occasion. He had been to Hamley's and was just coming out of the store with something he hoped might be vaguely suitable – it would at least keep Jenny off his back – when a male voice hailed him from a traffic island in the middle of Regent Street. 'Oliver!'

Oliver turned and looked at the figure who had called him. The figure itself was about thirty per cent wider than it had been at university, and the face that went with it was correspondingly older and plumper too, but they both belonged unmistakeably to a person called Stuart – a person to whom he had barely given a thought for fifteen years. Yet Oliver was surprised at the way the name came so quickly to his lips, apparently bypassing mind and memory to get there. 'Stuart.'

Five minutes later they were sitting over pints of Young's at a scrubbed oak table in the Guinea in Bruton Place. Ten minutes more and they had exchanged their stories of those last fifteen years. How quickly they got this done! How different from the first time they had sat in a pub together... No, it couldn't have been the first time. It must have been the third or fourth. Then the pints of beer, or rather the signals that had been exchanged over them, conveyed by looks and tones of voice, had led on to a *my place or yours?*, to a bottle of wine, and a night of enjoyable and abandoned sex. But that had never been repeated. For some reason. Oliver had no memory of what that reason was.

Stuart was in London for a business meeting. Unusually, this had lasted less time than expected and that accounted for his being here, wandering in the West End, on a weekday afternoon. He was dismayed to hear that Oliver had lost his job.

'We got a reasonable settlement, of course,' Oliver told him. 'But that won't last for ever. I'm thinking of going abroad.'

'To do what?' Stuart was interested.

Oliver shifted slightly in his chair. 'I don't know yet. Have to think of something.' He told Stuart about his courier's trip to Funchal. 'Not that I could count on that for the long term.'

'Or even for the short term. A friend of mine moved to Madrid a few years ago. Survived by teaching English. A couple of years later he got a post at the university. He has a great time there. They've got an ex-pat footie team together. It's called Real Ale Madrid.'

Oliver laughed at that. He began to toy with the idea of inviting Stuart back to his flat in Kilburn – by way of an experiment. See what might happen. True, Stuart had not neglected to mention his wife and children in Basingstoke during the eight minutes it had taken them to exchange their news of the past half-lifetime, but you never knew. As an old friend of his had liked to say: you didn't miss a slice off a cut loaf.

The possibility must have been in Stuart's mind also, because Oliver saw it floating between their eyes across the beer glasses, just as he had seen it in the same circumstances all those years ago. But to wake sleeping dogs after nearly twenty years... No, it was not a good idea. As Oliver reached that conclusion he could see from Stuart's face that he had thought better of it too. They drained their glasses, and exchanged address cards with promises to keep in touch, which both knew would never be kept.

So Oliver was alone at home when the call came from Donald. With only the sound of his voice to pick up on, Oliver had a stronger than ever impression that he was being addressed by the Honourable Michael Foot. 'So glad to hear you're interested in doing something else for us,' the voice began. Oliver noticed the' us'. It had just been' me'before. 'Originally got the feeling you weren't too keen on this kind of work. But ... well, it seems you are, so, good for all of us. Wondering now if you'd like to deliver a picture for us. Same terms, same procedure as last time.'

'A picture?' Oliver had a vision of himself staggering through the green channel with something huge in a massive gilt rococo frame: a Titian perhaps, or a Rembrandt. 'Where to?'

'Cologne,' said Donald and then casually, as if he was habitually a party to Oliver's thoughts, 'Don't worry. It's not a Rembrandt. Quite small actually. Go in a suitcase. One day next week would be best. Not sure if we can offer accommodation this time though.'

Breezily Oliver said that he wasn't worried about that. Yes, he would agree to do the job. Then he listened while Donald spelled out the details.

The picture was to be collected from a framer's shop near Shepherd Market. Oliver would be travelling from Stansted this time, picking up his boarding pass when he got there, just as before. The money would be a little better than the last time in view of the fact that Donald would not be seeing him in person and so would be unable to give him cash up front for taxi fares. Would that be OK? He would receive his fee, as Donald called it, when he delivered the painting.

Oliver thought that Cologne in February would not have the appeal of Madeira at the same time of year and he thought wistfully, why couldn't it be somewhere else with a balmy winter climate? Cairo, say, or Marrakech. But he welcomed the thought of another mini-adventure – almost as much as the cash.

He was thinking about his pending mission a few days later as he walked along Piccadilly looking for Shepherd Market. He was on the north side of the street, roughly opposite the Ritz Hotel and heading west, when he was suddenly jolted out of his thoughts by the sight of a figure walking towards him: one figure among crowds. It was a slim young man, rather taller than Oliver, dressed in dark trousers and a smart black winter coat.

There were any number of young men in the crowd who were dressed in almost identical fashion; what caught Oliver's attention was the colour of this one's hair: a brilliant copper red. And then there was the face. Those intelligent blue eyes, the neat small nose and generous mouth... Oliver had no doubt whatever that here was the same young man he had admired across the aisle of the Marsh Link train a couple of weeks ago. He peered as closely as he dared into the face while it first came towards him and then disappeared as the boy walked past; it was replaced by a view of red curls above the turned-up collar of his black coat: a transformation as mysterious and poignant as the change in pitch of a train's whistle as it hurtles past. Oliver had an urge to run after the boy and accost him: 'I saw you on a train...'

He discovered that he had in fact turned round and was now moving in the same direction as the young man, towards Piccadilly Circus and Eros. But the object of his interest was doing anything but loitering; he strode rapidly along the pavement: someone with a purpose. Oliver had a shrewd idea what that purpose might be: to walk, or catch a bus, to Charing Cross, there to take a train to Ashford and change onto the Marsh Link service for Ham Street – where presumably he lived. He carried no luggage with him, not even a brief-case. Was he an office worker after all? For no particular reason Oliver had imagined that he was someone who worked outdoors. Maybe that was wrong. Smartly dressed. For a job interview maybe?

Oliver had to ask himself the question he always asked himself on sighting an exceptionally beautiful man. But in the present instance Oliver could gain no hint of an answer. Though he could be certain of one thing at least: in whichever direction the boy's sexual interests might lie in general, he was definitely not expecting to be stopped and propositioned in the middle of Piccadilly by an older man on this particular afternoon, nor would he be very pleased if Oliver were to do just that.

Reluctantly Oliver allowed the fleeing vision to gain on him, as it strode eastwards without a nod of those glorious curls to left or right. Oliver watched the back of the head as if it were a receding light. There were many of those in Piccadilly: the brake lights of all the cars and buses in multiple queues, stopping and starting as the traffic bled slowly through the gauze of traffic lights and crossings; but Oliver had eyes only for this one: a head of hair that carried light and power as surely as one of Monet's haystack paintings, ablaze with the setting sun. At last the glow faded and went dim among the crowds. Then, feeling that he was doing it in very slow motion, Oliver turned back again and resumed his walk towards Shepherd Market.

It was not difficult to find the picture framer's shop. Oliver had looked up the street name in the A to Z before setting out. Just as well, he thought, since he seemed to be functioning on automatic pilot, or even existing in some other, unreal world. His second encounter with the red-headed boy had knocked him off balance, and left him unable to focus on any other thought for more than a second or two before his mind returned to that dizzying moment; it would give to whatever happened to him next, minute by minute, or even in the next days as he lived through them, a profound sense of otherness.

So he was immune to surprise of any sort when he entered the shop, which did photocopying and printing as well as picture framing, asked for someone called Mr Evans, and was immediately beckoned from across the shop by a bald man in a suit, then asked to step into the back office. Mr Evans – presumably this was he – opened up a safe that stood, bolted to the floor, between filing cabinets in a corner, and took out a large parcel, about eighteen inches by twelve, wrapped in brown paper. He handed it to Oliver. It was surprisingly light. The nature of the contents was pretty unmistakeable. Oliver could feel bubble-wrap through the paper, and through that the hard rim of the frame, the solid back of it, and the taut, bouncy empty space at the front that indicated where the picture itself lay back in its recess.

'Am I allowed to ask what the picture is?' Oliver said.

'Yes of course,' said Mr Evans brightly. 'It's a nineteenth century mini-portrait of no great value – except sentimental, as the subject was a member of the owner's family. But the frame's the original one.' Mr. Evans gave an undertaker's smile. 'In my opinion it's probably worth more than the painting. Though that's strictly between you and me. The frame had got damaged over the years. We've simply restored it – to the best of our abilities – to its former state.'

Oliver glanced out through the open door of the office into the back of the shop. There were upright racks of hardwood mouldings in two-metre lengths, a couple of mitre-boxes on a work-bench, saws and screwdrivers, boxes of silvery frame-clips, and panes of glass in stacks against the wall. There was no evidence of the kind of highly sophisticated restoration facilities that would justify the sending of a piece of antique woodwork all the way from Germany. Still, one never knew what was in the basement, and Oliver did at least know by now at what point to let his line of questions drop.

He left the shop with the picture in the small battered suitcase, a relic of his student days, that he'd had the forethought to bring with him. Some instinct of self-preservation had argued against using the same hold-all that he had taken on the Madeira job. He would keep the picture overnight at his flat. He had asked about the insurance situation. Mr Evans told him that that was all looked after. He just had to take normal precautions: locking the street door; not forgetting the suitcase in a pub. Oliver thought he could manage that. Nevertheless, he slept that night with the suitcase, now also containing overnight things and a change of clothes, right up against his bed. Just in case.

In the morning he took the Bakerloo line from Kilburn Park down to Oxford Circus and changed onto the Central line for Liverpool Street. It seemed to take for ever. How could two places in the same capital possibly be so far apart? Still, he had allowed himself plenty of time so had no need to rush across the station to get onto the Stansted Express.

Collecting his boarding pass and declaring with a smile, for the second time in a fortnight, that he had packed his luggage himself and that nobody had tampered with it, he began to feel that he had done this job a few dozen times, not just two, and was very much the seasoned professional. Professional whatever it was. Courier of course. He was working as a courier, albeit an unofficial, paid-in-cash kind of courier. He imagined himself saying, if he were stopped again and found himself having to answer any awkward questions, 'I really don't know. I'm just a courier.' He was even quite relaxed about the possibility of having to face sniffer dogs at Köln-Bonn. Nobody would go hiding drugs inside a framed picture. Or would they? Maybe that was exactly what they would do. The truth was that he had absolutely no idea. He was a complete innocent in whatever game it was that he'd chosen to go on playing. An unquestioning pawn. In the main he thought it was best that way, but a small interior voice whispered to him from time to time, telling him he owed it to himself to be more responsible.

It was Oliver's first arrival at Köln-Bonn.He took a deep breath as he passed through incoming customs control, but nobody bothered him or even appeared to notice his arrival; the passport check had been perfunctory. Out in the open air he felt himself exhale loudly and long, as if after swimming underwater. Had he actually been holding his breath all this time? Unfamiliar with the bus routes, Oliver took the easier option and joined the taxi queue. He told the driver the address he had been given, then sat back, and was pleased to recognise the landmark twin spires of Cologne's cathedral in the distance as the taxi crossed the Rhine.

They drove through the smart centre area of the city before plunging into a quarter that was noticeably less attractive. The street, or alley, in which the driver finally deposited him (with an air of puzzlement, did Oliver detect?) ran alongside a line of railway arches under which were installed car repair workshops and other small businesses whose nature was not easy to make out. On the other side of the alley a line of derelict properties was boarded up, awaiting demolition. The number he had been given was hand-painted next to a small door cut in the boarded front of one of the railway arches. With a vague feeling of apprehension in the pit of his stomach, Oliver rang the bell beside the door. He waited for a very long minute while nothing happened, except that a van drew up at the adjacent arch and a man there took a delivery of what looked like coffins. Then the door opened and a small wiry man appeared. He might have been Oliver's age.

'Oliver Watson. Delivery. *Lieferung – ein Päckchen aus London.*'

The man did not invite him inside. Instead he gestured to Oliver that he should put his case down on the ground and open it there and then. With a grunt that the man could interpret as displeasure if he wanted to, Oliver crouched down and opened up his case on the uneven pavement.

The man reached down and took, almost snatched, Oliver's parcel. He said, without smiling, *'Warten Sie hier,'* and disappeared back inside his shabby premises with a gesture that indicated, in case Oliver had not understood the *warten Sie hier*, that he was not to be followed. The door closed behind him. Oliver now had another wait of about two minutes – which was a very long time when you were wondering where you had come to, and whether or not you were going to collect four hundred pounds. Oliver supposed the man was unwrapping his parcel and inspecting it to see that he'd got his money's worth. Meanwhile he tried to relax himself by counting the coffin-like objects that were being carried into the workshop next door.

The door reopened. *'Herein,'* said the man, still unsmiling, but he only let Oliver take half a pace inside the doorway, just sufficient for the handover of cash to take place out of sight of any curious eyes in the alley. Oliver only just had the presence of mind to count the notes before he was bulldozed out onto the pavement by the closing door. He heard the lock click as it was pushed to.

The alley in which he stood was one that you could take a taxi to get into, but not the sort of place where you could expect to find a taxi to get you out again. Oliver regretted for a moment that he hadn't asked the driver who'd brought him here to wait. But then to take him where? Oliver had arranged with Donald that he would fly back to England the following morning, but had not done anything about finding somewhere to spend the night. He felt he could afford to leave it a little longer before looking for a hotel. It was still afternoon and not yet dark. Learning from his failure to do the appropriate research before visiting Madeira, he had taken the trouble this time to look up an old Spartacus guide, where he had read that there was a whole area of cafés and bars near the cathedral. And from where he stood he could see the twin spires, looking not too distant, rearing above the rooftops of nearer buildings. He decided to set off towards them on foot. He might have looked a bit odd, carrying his ancient suitcase, but it was not at all heavy, containing little more now than a toothbrush, spare socks and a shirt.

But epic-size buildings always look nearer than they are, and Oliver's walk took him half an hour. During which time he found his thoughts kept straying back to another street much nearer home, and the vision he had seen there: Piccadilly, and the young man with his luminous head of hair.

Now that he'd seen him twice, Oliver had an even clearer picture of him in his mind. Although fair-skinned and blue-eyed, his face had not had that translucent, alabaster whiteness that many redheads have when young. Rather, his complexion looked slightly weather-tanned, as if childhood freckles had reached an accommodation with the realities of life and merged and faded into an even skin-tone. Perhaps that was why Oliver had at first presumed that he did outdoor work. He tried to imagine him on a building site but couldn't quite; there was an elegance in the way he moved, but no swagger: he was too much of a racehorse to fit that particular niche. Oliver, chunkily muscular and built like a half-size rugby player, had an envious grass-is-greener fascination with taller, slimmer physiques. Having seen him now in two locations sixty miles apart, Oliver found himself looking around him in the streets of Cologne, almost expecting, or at least willing, him to be here. With him. Sharing Germany with him.

Germany had taken Adi away from him. He felt the place owed him something in return. On sober reflection the possibility that it might be the reappearance of the copper-haired beauty was altogether too far-fetched. (And even if that improbability were to be realised, what would Oliver be able to do about it? Attract the boy's attention with a wolf whistle?) But maybe Germany could still offer something else.

Oliver reached the grid of streets near the cathedral that he'd been aiming for. Without looking at his watch he decided it was time for a beer. He chose a bar at random and went in. Seating himself on a stool near the bar he ordered himself a Kölsch. There were perhaps half a dozen other people in the bar. Oliver guessed that they were tourists or visitors to the city, like himself. He knew, from Adi and his circle, that in the normal run of things German people did not venture out to their local *Kneipe* until later in the evening.

Nobody else was perched at the bar. Oliver made one or two routine remarks in German to the barman, but it was like applying lit matches to damp paper: none of them took. After a minute or two he lapsed into silence. Then a man came in and perched on one of the stools. He was a man of roughly Oliver's age, and he gave Oliver a friendly smile – but also, Oliver noticed, a practised, brief as a blink, look-over – as he sat down. He ordered a Königspilsner. Oliver nodded courteously and said, *'Guten Abend,'* and was surprised, especially after his discouraging experience a moment ago with the barman, to find that the stranger seemed in the mood to begin a conversation with him almost at once. He hadn't seen Oliver here before. Was he just visiting? His eyes dropped towards Oliver's suitcase as he said this. Oliver, a little carefully, said yes, he was: just a tourist, just passing through. The other, detecting a slight accent, asked Oliver which country he came from and, when Oliver said England, switched language abruptly. 'We can speak English then. Good training for me.' Oliver thought that continuing to speak German would have been equally good practice for himself, his German having grown rusty since his break-up with Adi, but he didn't say so.

The newcomer was attractive. He was tall and well-built, quite handsome in a cosy sort of way, with large grey eyes, set off with strong black lashes, that laughed whenever his mouth and voice did. There were pinpricks of silver in his thick dark hair, but the same went for Oliver too. They had already exchanged a few polite sentences about the city and the weather, which did not have to be repeated in English. Oliver's new acquaintance introduced himself instead. 'I'm Bernd.'

'Oliver.' They shook hands.

'What do you do now?' Bernd asked.

Oliver was slightly taken aback. 'I'm between jobs actually.'

'It means out of work?' Bernd queried and then answered his own question in an undertone, as if another person were talking, 'Right, I see.' Resuming delivery at normal volume he tried to make himself more clear. 'No, but I wanted to say… I mean, here, Köln, now. After.' Again he looked down at Oliver's unlikely-looking luggage.

'OK, I get you,' Oliver said. Then he realised that he could do his companion a small favour by explaining the nuance. 'It's clearer if you ask: what are you doing now? Or after, or later.' He felt the little glow of satisfaction that rewards the doer of a good deed. If Bernd was in the habit of picking up English-speaking people in bars, the correct formula would save time and confusion in the future.

'Yes. Thank you. Now I see. So…?'

'I don't have any plans at the moment,' said Oliver. 'I'm flying back to London tomorrow.'

'And you arrived…?'

'Today.'

Again Bernd glanced down at the suitcase. It did look a bit big for an overnight stay. 'Are you here to sell something?' Case full of samples perhaps.

'No, no,' Oliver tried to keep it vague. 'I had something to deliver, that's all.'

'Where do you spend the night?'

Oliver didn't correct him a second time. Years of living with Adi had taught him there were only so many times you could do that. 'I don't know just yet. I'll look for a cheap hotel I suppose.' He grinned. 'Later.'

Bernd smiled back. 'Maybe I could help you there.' Pause. 'Who knows?'

'Who knows indeed?' – brightly but with an edge of caution. 'Anyway, what do you do?'

'I take photographs,' said Bernd. 'Freelance.'

'What kind of photographs – if I may ask?' Oliver enquired.

'Different kinds. I travel with journalists when they do magazine interviews. I make travel photography. And…' Bernd had given himself time to size Oliver up and thought he could say this safely now. 'And I take pictures of young men. For calendars and, you know, special magazines.'

'Erotic photos, you mean?' Oliver said this with an amused chuckle which didn't quite mask the interest in his voice.

'I could show you if you want. My studio's near here.

Maybe we have one beer more first?' Bernd was clearly aware of Oliver's growing interest: it was visible in Oliver's trousers.

Bernd ordered two more beers. They drank them quite slowly, not saying very much but each catching the other's eye from time to time, and sharing a cautious little half smile when they did so.

'If I come to your studio, am I expected to buy an expensive picture?' Oliver wanted to know. 'I think I told you, I don't have a job. That means I'm not especially rich.'

'There is no – how do you say? – there is no obligation to purchase. There is actually no obligation to do anything.' He looked meaningfully at Oliver. 'Not for you, not for me. You do what you want. We do what we want both. If we want. OK?'

'Sounds OK to me,' said Oliver.

They stood up, paid, and left the bar. Bernd led Oliver around two street corners, then fished in his pocket for keys as they approached a door which was recessed between two shop-fronts. He turned to Oliver as he unlocked it: 'It's up two floors,' he said. 'No elevator. You not too old for stairs?' They both laughed, and Bernd ushered Oliver inside before leading the way up the staircase.

With another key Bernd led Oliver into a large and airy flat. Though part of an old building, it had been beautifully modernised. Old beams showed here and there in walls and high white ceilings, but the space had been opened out: there were few doors, and so you passed seamlessly from living space to studio, to bedroom and kitchen. Only the bathroom was modestly secreted behind a door. Oliver felt a twinge of envy at once: the apartment was so much better than his own.

'The dark room's in the basement.' Bernd explained. He must have caught a momentary look of alarm on Oliver's face, because he added, 'Don't worry; we don't have to go there.'

The studio itself was much as Oliver had expected, with two cameras set up on tripods, bright lights and reflecting screens, and photographs, mounted and un-mounted, on the walls, and in stacks everywhere. The most prominently displayed were landscape scenes, in colour, featuring – Oliver guessed – northern Italy or Provence. Italy, Bernd told him: a project of the previous summer. 'Beautiful place.' More startling was a portrait-sized picture of Gerhard Schröder, his face thrown into unexpectedly angular relief by the shadows from a desk lamp. 'Not to be understood as a political statement. Only I was pleased with the way it came out. I kept a copy.'

But cheekily appearing between and behind the landscapes and newspaper shots of the famous were glimpses of male nudes and semi-nudes, in every pose imaginable – with the proviso only that each one had elegance and grace. Oliver said, 'Hey, you've been busy,' pointing to one particular stack of thoughtfully posed nudes whose subject particularly caught his eye, and Bernd was only too happy to drag them out and let him have a better look. Then Bernd smiled mischievously and said, 'Take a look at these.' He reached under a table, on the top of which Oliver could not help noticing lay a packet of condoms. Perhaps the studio's uses were not exclusively photographic. Bernd re-emerged from under the table with half a dozen shots of an impressively built man of perhaps thirty, in progressive states of sexual arousal. 'It was a few years ago, mind,' he said modestly. For the pictures were unmistakeably of Bernd himself.

'I'm sure a few years haven't altered the quality of the original,' said Oliver quietly, and placed a hand on the front of Bernd's jeans as if to check. The veracity of his assumption was immediately confirmed as his fingers made contact with a substantial and resistant ridge of hardness through the fabric.

Bernd was a big man in all departments, as Oliver was able to verify with all his senses when they moved through into the sleeping area a few seconds later. But Oliver knew he would be able to surprise Bernd when he presented his own naked form for inspection a few more seconds after that. Bernd let out a sort of low, respectful whistle. *'Eindrucksvoll,'* he said. Impressive.

For all his sturdy muscularity, Oliver was built for the most part on a smallish scale – pint-size rugby player. But his cock would not have looked out of place on a man of twice his bulk, especially when, as now, it was under maximum tension in the excitement of a situation in which he had not found himself for some time. Bernd said, 'I'd like to photograph you, if you permit. But later.' He pressed his naked body up against Oliver's and enfolded him in his big arms. There was more urgent business to attend to first.

Oliver was, both by temperament and in practice, a giver and a receiver in equal measure. But he also knew the effect he had on people of his own age: they tended to expect him to go on the receiving end, at least first time round. Something to do with his still boyish-looking face perhaps. Anyway, he was quite sanguine about what happened next, allowing Bernd to lay him on his back, and happy to let Bernd coax him off by hand while Bernd climaxed exuberantly somewhere deep inside him. If time allowed and the opportunity arose he would return Bernd's compliment later.

Later in the evening Bernd did take Oliver's photo. ('I'm thirty-eight,' Oliver protested bashfully. 'It doesn't matter,' Bernd replied. 'So am I. And you look just fine. Anyway, you'd be surprised at the market.') He did a series of shots, with Oliver dressed in nothing but a pair of work-boots with his own trademark white socks spilling over the tops. Oliver, to whom Bernd had administered two glasses of schnapps before the shoot started, insisted that if he was to be naked then Bernd had to be too; and Bernd, with no show of reluctance, obliged. He said he would call the series *British Workman*. Getting Oliver into the right position for each shot required quite a lot of physical contact between them, and it was no surprise to either of them that the session ended with both of them massively excited and, like smouldering volcanoes, ready to erupt a second time. There and then, on the floor of the studio – no time to get to the bedroom but only to reach for the packet on the table – Oliver, boots and all, gave Bernd as good as he'd been given earlier.

After that they dressed carefully and went out for something to eat, sitting decorously opposite each other in a pasta restaurant. 'So tell me about this delivery job that brought you here today,' Bernd said. 'And that *ausserordentlich* suitcase.' Oliver felt relaxed enough in Bernd's company to give him a more complete account of his business in Cologne.

'Four hundred pounds,' said Bernd. 'That's very nice for you. But do you really believe what they told you? I'm in this business. I know about picture frames and what things cost. Nobody in this country, I tell you nobody, sends a nineteenth-century wood frame to be restored in England. No rudeness to your English craftsmen. It's just that we have hundreds of specialists here in Germany, and several even in Köln.'

'That is rather what I suspected all along,' Oliver admitted. They both laughed.

On the way back to Bernd's apartment they stopped at a couple of bars for a beer or two. *Schlenderschlücke*. Nightcaps. Neither of them expressed any wish to go on into clubbing mode. They had found a kind of sufficiency in themselves as a pair, at least as far as this evening went, and were completely relaxed and at home in each other's company by the time they returned to spend a quite energetic night in the now familiar territory, to Oliver, of Bernd's bed.

*

The alarm clock failed to go off. When Oliver awoke there remained only an hour and ten minutes before his plane was due to leave. He shook the slumbering Bernd awake, saw in so doing that his new friend had a magnificent erection, had to accept with regret that there was no time to do anything about this, and hopped in a state of panic into his jeans: no time to waste looking for underpants. Bernd had very soon done the same and said, very decently, that he would drive Oliver to the airport himself. Oliver rinsed his face and armpits, gave his teeth a five-second scrub and threw his paraphernalia into his case. Together they ran down the stairs.

Then they were out amongst the morning traffic, Bernd weaving and changing lanes with the bravura and speed of a motor-cycle courier, the only difference being that he was actually in charge of a car. They parted outside the terminal with an ultra-brief hug and kiss. They had exchanged contact details the night before. There were just twenty-one minutes left before take-off. Oliver ran in, arriving at the check-in desk seconds before it closed. By the time he'd got through passport control and the security scanner and, breathless, reached his departure gate, passengers were already on their feet and filing out to board the aircraft. Oliver joined them.

German and English newspapers were available just inside the plane's entrance door. Oliver picked up an

English one as he passed – it happened to be the
Telegraph – and found his seat, sliding into it gratefully,
only too aware that he'd come within seconds of missing
the flight. He scanned the paper as the plane was pushed
back and then started its engines. There was nothing
much to take note of. No major events or disasters had
occurred in England or the world at large in the previous
twenty-four hours. He turned the pages, only half
attentive. Then something caught his eye: a small item
near the bottom of page five. *Art Theft* was the terse
headline. Oliver began to read. *A painting belonging to
the National Gallery was last night discovered missing,
and is believed to have been stolen. The painting, a
Nativity scene by the early German master Lucas
Cranach, was due to have arrived yesterday in
Manchester where an exhibition…*

Oliver found that he couldn't go on. He began to feel
the sensations that herald the onset of food poisoning:
sickness, dizziness, and a kind of nervous depression of
his system that reached out down his legs and along his
arms to his fingers'ends – the experience of waking in
the small hours to the realization, too late, that you had
eaten a bad oyster. He flapped the newspaper shut and
found himself swiping at it with his hand as if trying to
extinguish a flame, or crush some dangerous insect that
was crawling among the pages.

He really did not want to know any more about the
stolen painting. He was glad he hadn't been tempted by
curiosity to take it out of its wrappings and inspect it
while it was still in his keeping. He didn't want to read

about how or where it had disappeared, nor of any theories about where it might have gone to, nor did he wish to know the painting's value. Above all, he did not want to know the picture's dimensions. Lucas Cranach was no more than a name to him: he couldn't tie the name in with any particular works or style of painting. He found himself fervently hoping that the artist's output consisted of the kind of painting that filled an entire gallery wall, like Titian's, perhaps, or Tintoretto's.

With a roar and a sudden ripple of power, Oliver's homebound plane sprang forward into its take-off run.

FOUR

Back in London Oliver called David. Zara answered. 'Hallo,' she said. 'How did the job go?'

'Fine,' Oliver answered. 'All neat and tidy and I got my money. Cologne's nice. Probably more so in the summer.' Had it been David on the other end he would probably have told him about Bernd, but he wasn't on quite such intimate terms with David's wife. Instead he went on, 'Listen. How well do you – does David – know Donald?'

'Donald Faircross, your new boss? Well, not all that well actually. He's just a pub acquaintance really. Though I suppose we've known him in that capacity, or David has, about two years – maybe three.'

'What does he do for a living? If anything.' Oliver remembered Donald's very white hair. 'Maybe that should have been' did'.'

'He's retired now,' Zara said. 'I think he used to have his own company. A haulage firm, I think. Do you want me to find out for you? David's out at the moment or I'd put him on.'

'Ah. No. Well, yes, but short of asking him directly. Maybe though – no – well, just if David has anything more to add I'd be very interested.'

'You're not in trouble are you?' There was concern in

Zara's voice. 'I mean about this work you're doing for him.'

'No. Nothing like that at all. Only…'

'You sound as if you're having second thoughts. About working for Donald I mean.'

'Not even that. It's just… Look, it's nothing. Maybe one day we can have a laugh about it over a drink.'

'Come down and see us again soon,' Zara invited. 'David would like that. Say, next weekend, or the one after?'

'I'd love to,' Oliver said. 'Can I ring you in a few days? Only there's something else that may be in the offing and it may affect my schedule if it comes off. But I won't know for a few days if it's going to happen or not, and I don't want to talk about it now in case it doesn't. Does that make sense? Love to David.' Oliver rang off.

*

Oliver again found himself walking up Piccadilly. This had nothing to do with his recent visit to Shepherd Market. He had wanted to give the picture framer's shop and its surroundings a wide berth, but now found that it couldn't be all that wide: he was on his way to an interview at an address in Piccadilly, and as he neared it he realised that he was getting closer to Shepherd Market as well.

Coincidence, he thought. Couldn't be helped. Perhaps making a lazy connection between one coincidence and another, he started looking among the crowds, though not very seriously, for the handsome redhead – in roughly the place where he had last seen him, opposite the Ritz. The young man had by now established himself in Oliver's mind as something of a fixture, something almost totemic, though his thoughts shied away from the idea of exactly what he represented. But looking for him now, on his way to an interview whose outcome might have a major bearing on his future, Oliver felt like someone who has seen a single magpie and is now looking around anxiously for a second. That analogy wasn't perfect though: Oliver had already seen the boy twice. Three was for a girl, *four* for a boy.

He arrived at his destination: a fine converted Georgian mansion overlooking Green Park with, he guessed, Shepherd Market about one block away at the back. He made his way up steps under a striped awning and into the building, having notched up no sighting of the redhead. Still, he hadn't seen a magpie either.

The place was a rabbit warren of corridors and staircases; young people from all over the world swarmed through it, speaking a babel of languages. Oliver was conducted to a small room in the basement.

'You interview very well,' said the fiftyish-looking woman who was dealing with him. 'I think we can be confident that you'd cope perfectly well with the demands of the course. My only doubt is…' She lightly shook a mane of greying hair. '…Well, frankly, you'd be more than ten years older than the average participant.' Oliver drew breath to speak but she carried on. 'I'm not saying you wouldn't be able to handle that. It's simply that the financial rewards of teaching English as a foreign language are not that great. At least, not at first. The four-week post-graduate course is seen only as an introduction, you know. The Certificate will get you your first job or two. But if you did decide to make a career of it, you'd need to clock up at least a couple of years'practical experience before working for a diploma.' She looked at him steadily with pale blue eyes. 'Not everyone of your age is prepared to go through that – especially someone who's been used to Civil Service salary scales – for very limited financial reward.'

Oliver looked back at her equally steadily. 'Thank you for being frank with me,' he said. 'I appreciate that. But right now I don't have any brighter ideas about what to do with my future. Do you?'

His interviewer regarded him in silence for a moment, perhaps trying to decide whether she could risk a collusive laugh at her profession's expense, but in the end deciding against. 'The next course for which we have places available is not till the end of May,' she said, and immediately saw Oliver's face fall, like a child's. She gave a half smile and went on, 'However, we've had one person drop out from one of the courses starting next Monday…'

'I'll do it,' said Oliver, adding hastily, 'If I'm accepted, that is.'

'There are some tasks to do before the course starts.' She handed him a sheaf of papers.

'I'll do them over the weekend,' said Oliver, sounding like a teenager who's been picked for a top sports team. 'Stay up all night if I have to.'

The woman smiled properly this time. 'That sounds like a good beginning.' Shepherd Market seemed a long way away.

*

Monday morning found Oliver back in the basement of the training college, though this time in a large room that was the canteen, in a milling crowd of about sixty people. Looking around him, he could see that his interviewer had been right: almost everyone was in their twenties; yet there was a reassuring scattering of grey heads, maybe four or five, that belonged to people who were ten – maybe even twenty – years older than himself. The earliest arrivals had filled all the seats around the tables, as well as the stools at the serving counters; others, including Oliver, stood lining the walls. The principal of the college, a suave looking man with swept-back grey hair, made an entrance and an upbeat speech of welcome. All those present – or most of them – would in a short time be setting out across the globe, exporting a very precious commodity: the English language . Precious because it was the preferred language of international business worldwide. Precious because it was the language of one of the world's richest literatures. Precious in economic terms too: it was

Britain's second largest invisible export...

Oliver didn't want to be reminded of the export of precious commodities, invisible or otherwise. He had heard nothing further about the missing Lucas Cranach, perhaps because he'd avoided looking at the newspapers and, busy with his pre-course language tasks, had managed largely to miss the radio and television news as well.

The speech ended. Names were called out. The crowd of people was divided into groups of fifteen. Oliver wove his way towards the place where his class were being assembled by a young female trainer. She led them down a narrow corridor, up broad stairs, then finally into a magnificent first floor room with a painted wood and plaster ceiling, chandeliers, and French windows, opulently curtained, which opened onto a balcony overlooking Green Park. Classroom chairs, each one fitted with a flap-over work-surface, were arranged in a semi-circle facing the trainer's desk, and in the corners were two coat-stands. Everyone was either wearing or carrying a coat, and everyone had some sort of backpack or briefcase. There was general uncertainty as to whether to make for one of the coat-stands first or whether to make a priority of bagging a seat, and there was some nervous laughter as people wove their way around each other. Oliver hung his coat up first. And then froze. Six inches away from him, hanging his own coat on the other side of the stand, was the red-haired young man. The redhead of Piccadilly and Ham Streeet, and of the inside of Oliver's head.

Oliver said, 'Hi,' without thinking. It came out as a sort of gasp of surprise. The redhead said, 'Hi,' and smiled.

Oliver turned away, his mental processes paralysed, his heart thumping in his chest, overcome with shock. His astonishment was the greater for the fact that he hadn't spotted the boy in the canteen. Perhaps he had been hidden by someone bigger and taller, perhaps he'd been standing round a corner, out of sight, or directly behind Oliver himself. Oliver dithered for a second about where to sit; others were doing the same. The trainer took the matter out of their hands. 'Before you sit down,' she said, 'or if you have sat down, get up again – I want you to find whichever person in the room has the birthday nearest to your own. Not date of birth: birthday. Then sit down with them and find out from them…' She switched on the projector that stood on her desk and a list of questions appeared on a screen. Name, home town, ambitions...

Oliver found himself wandering around the room announcing the date of his birthday, September the twenty-third, to fourteen total strangers, all of whom were grinning madly at him as they replied with their own. Oliver supposed he was wearing the same mad, nervous grin himself. March the second. July the twelfth. A tall young blonde woman had September the fifteenth. Suddenly Oliver was face to face with the redhead. He heard his voice a second time, but uttering now a string of syllables: 'September the twentieth.'

'September the twenty-third,' Oliver replied, then

threw himself down into the nearest seat with the desperate urgency of a child playing musical chairs, and motioned to the younger man to sit down next to him. No way was he going to allow anyone to rob him of this extraordinary chance. If anybody dared to arrive with a spoilsport birth-date of September the twenty-first or - second he would send them smartly on their way. But nobody did. A moment later almost everybody was sitting down. Oliver and his new companion exchanged the awkward smiles of people forced into unexpected proximity by the demands of a training exercise, although Oliver's smile was also born of more complex causes. 'I'm Oliver,' he said. 'Oliver Watson.'

'Orlando Kidd,' said the other. 'I suppose we ought to be writing this down.' He had been carrying a sports bag which he had placed at his feet. He bent and rummaged in it. He would have to have a name like Orlando, thought Oliver, feeling a pinprick of irritation, although simultaneously realising that he would have been disappointed had the boy been common-or-garden Michael or John. As he came back up with a pen and an A4 notepad block, Oliver reached into his own backpack for writing materials of his own.

'And you come from Ham Street,' Oliver said, mischievously matter-of-fact.

A wide-eyed stare of surprise. Brilliant blue-gentian eyes, long chestnut lashes. 'Newchurch, actually, but near enough. How do you know?'

'I saw you on a train recently. You got off at Ham

Street. I was going on to Rye. For some reason I remembered you.' Oliver wasn't going to spell out what the reason was. Orlando would hardly need telling why Oliver remembered him; he must be used to it.

'Well,' said Orlando, his eyes returning to their normal size, which was not all that small. 'And what about you?'

They went through the list of questions. What work did Orlando do? If he wasn't still in full-time education? Oliver doubted that: he had asked the question in a spirit of teasing politeness. Now that he saw him close-up and had heard him speak, he realised that he was a little older than the twenty-one years he had at first given him. But age was not on the list of questions.

'I'm an actor,' said Orlando. 'At least, I thought I was.'

Oliver chuckled sympathetically. All over the room, similar confessions were being similarly received. But Oliver was impressed nevertheless. It was not what he had been expecting. 'Oh right. Would I have seen you in something? TV?'

'Hardly. A bit part in Monarch of the Glen once. Mind you, there was an ad I did for the Post Office a year ago. Turned out to be the pinnacle of my career, though I didn't know it at the time.'

'Of course,' said Oliver. 'I remember now. Remembered your hair.' He found he could say that now. 'Probably why I spotted you on the train.' So today was the fourth time he'd seen Orlando, after all, not just the third. *Four for a boy*. Today he was wearing his blue jeans again, and the white socks and trainers, just as he had been on the train. Just as, once again, so was Oliver himself. Oliver wanted to know more about the acting career, wanted to know all about him. He felt a great surge of hunger for him, a complex emotion, rooted in curiosity and lust, but with finer feelings as well among its tangling branches. But this was not the time to explore such things or even indulge his curiosity, if such a time would ever come at all. They had to go on with the questions. Last holiday. Ambitions.

The trainer reclaimed the centre stage. She asked everyone to introduce their neighbour to the group, using the information they had gathered. The backgrounds of Oliver's classmates were varied. There was a retired lecturer in economics. An office temp. A Territorial Army volunteer who had just returned from a tour of duty in Iraq. A painter.

It was Oliver's turn to speak. 'This lad's name is Orlando Kidd. He comes from the Romney Marsh originally, but lives mostly in London. He speaks fluent Spanish and a little French. Oh, and English of course.' Titters of politeness. If it hadn't been the first morning, those would have been groans. 'He's an actor mostly. Remember the redhead in the Post Office ad?' A bit of a risk, that, Oliver realised, but most people did remember, and there were ohs and ahs of surprise and recognition. 'His last holiday was in Greece, and his ambition, which remains unaltered, is to play Hamlet.' Oliver delivered the last item with a straight face, daring anyone to laugh. Nobody did.

Next up was a girl called Lorraine. 'But everyone calls her Quiche.' General laughter. Then a young man who had trained as a geologist. Then it was Orlando's turn to present Oliver. Oliver listened, with a feeling of disbelief – that this couldn't actually be happening – as the vision which had materialised in front of him twice before today, and had had such a powerful effect on his emotions and imagination when it had done so, began to introduce him to his new peers.

'The guy next to me is called Oliver Watson.' Orlando had an educated voice but it had a just noticeable sheen of rural accent on it: it was not that he spoke like a character from the Archers, but you could imagine that his parents or grandparents had done. And it was probably only noticeable to Oliver: nobody else in the room was listening to him with the same rapt attention; nobody else had already been half in love with Orlando for four weeks and three days. 'Oliver grew up in Banbury but has lived in London for the last twelve years. He speaks fluent German and can get by in French, Spanish and Italian. I put that down to too many holidays. He's a graduate in economics and till recently worked for the Home Office. As a – a what was it?' He turned to Oliver.

'Statistician.'

'Statistician. His ambitions? A life in the sunshine, and sunshine in his life.'

Oliver started, visibly perhaps to the people nearest him. The last few words had been Orlando's, not his own. He would never have expressed himself like that to a person he had only just met, though he had mentioned wanting to work abroad. Yet Orlando had found a phrase that encapsulated exactly what Oliver did want. Had he made a shrewd and accurate guess as to what was missing in Oliver's life: picked up vibes, or read it in his face and manner? Was Oliver as transparent as all that? Or was he simply making a play on words to amuse the class? Oliver supposed that he would never know.

Some people had brought sandwiches for lunch. Oliver had not. He found himself buying a salad and, against his better judgement, a small beer in the basement canteen. He joined a table where other members of his group, including the girl named Quiche, were already installed. He looked around for Orlando but he wasn't there, had probably gone out for some fresh air. Perhaps that was as well. Oliver didn't want to give him, or anyone else, the impression he was clinging to him. They had been sitting next to each other for most of the morning and Oliver had had time and opportunity to form a more detailed impression of his new acquaintance. His contributions to the group discussions had shown him to be intelligent and articulate, and as likeable and friendly as Oliver had judged him during the first minutes of their meeting. All this was a relief to Oliver. Having lived for the last few weeks with the gilded image of Orlando's face and figure etched on his mind, he would have hated to discover that in reality the boy was a boor, or a snob, or an idiot.

That evening Oliver phoned David and Zara. Again it was Zara who answered. He asked: could he take her up on her invitation this coming weekend? Since they had last spoken, some amazing things had been happening, he said. He told Zara how he had applied to go on a course and was now, to his own surprise, already on it. The other thing was – did she remember him talking, during his last visit, about a remarkably good looking red-haired boy he'd seen on the train?

Zara certainly did. She thought that if his meeting with Donald hadn't intervened to take his mind off the subject, Oliver would have gone on about him all weekend.

'Well, believe it or not, he's on the course too. Not only that but we're going to be in the same TP group.'

'TP group?' Zara queried.

How quickly you picked up the jargon of a new working environment and made it part of you. 'Teaching practice. It's a very hands-on course. We get put in front of a class of real students on the second day. Three teams of five to work together, each with a different class to teach. They divided us up this afternoon. You, you and you. I didn't get to choose.' He felt it necessary to make that clear. He went on, 'So we'll be thrown together rather a lot. We spent most of this afternoon together, preparing tomorrow's lesson. He was full of good ideas. Not just a pretty face, you see. But I think I'd guessed that all along.'

'You do sound a bit… besotted, I must say,' said Zara. 'He doesn't happen to be gay, does he?'

'Orlando? I shouldn't think so for a moment. He hasn't given any sign of it anyway.'

'Have you?'

'Well no, I suppose not. At least, not intentionally. Anyway, red-haired men hardly ever are gay. It's a fact of life. There used to be a saying among gay men, a sort of warning not to waste your time pursuing them:' Ginger beer, seldom queer'. Anyway, I may be able to give you a more definite answer at the weekend.' They arranged to meet at Rye station on Friday evening.

The next morning it was snowing heavily. Hyde Park, which Oliver observed from the top deck of the number sixteen bus, was turning steadily white, the mauve and yellow crocuses that ringed its trees disappearing into the monochrome like fading hopes. Oliver got off near the Hilton and cut through the side streets to Piccadilly. He was more than half an hour early. He went down to the canteen for a coffee. There were only a few people there, none of whom he knew. Except that when he looked round a corner, there was Orlando, sitting alone at a table, nursing a coffee of his own. Oliver got one for himself and joined him. By coincidence they had both responded to the weather conditions by dressing in big white cable-knit sweaters. They both registered this coincidence, not with a remark, but with an exchange of glances: a little baggage carried by their initial smiles of greeting, a bonding step. And Oliver noticed, with a little frisson of pleasure, that Orlando's smile this morning was less like an acquaintance's, more like a friend's.

'Ready for the ordeal?' Oliver asked him.

'You mean this afternoon? First crack at teaching? Sort of.' Orlando frowned down at his coffee cup. 'This clothes-shopping dialogue I'm going to do. Well, I've written it. But I can't decide whether we say' try on clothes'or' try clothes on'.' He looked back up at Oliver. 'What do you think?'

'I've never thought about it,' said Oliver. 'I think we say both, don't we? But maybe one of them's supposed to be wrong.'

'In which case,' said Orlando, 'sure as hell they'll tell us.'

*

After that first teaching practice – a baptismal hour as defining as a first bungee jump or parachute drop – there was a feedback session, mediated by the group's tutor, which lasted longer than the lesson had. And after that, the exhausted group of five headed, urgently, for the nearest pub. Apart from Oliver and Orlando, the group consisted of the girl called (Quiche) Lorraine, and two other women, who were slightly older than the others – Oliver excepted, of course.

The pub, it turned out – it had to be – was in Shepherd Market, just doors away from the picture framer's shop. Oliver, already light-headed with decompression, the natural after-symptom of the intense experience of the afternoon, now had an additional sense of vertigo as he glimpsed the shop doorway along the street when they turned to go into the bar. He took a deep breath and told himself to get a grip. He had no reason to suppose that any stolen art treasure had been inside the package that he had delivered in Germany. Even if it had been, Oliver could truthfully say he had been told that the parcel's contents were a nineteenth-century portrait of no great worth. Beyond his own suspicions – he tried not to dwell on Bernd's sceptical reception of the official story – he had no connection with any crime whatever.

As the oldest person present and a male to boot, Oliver found himself asking the others what they would have to drink. But at once Orlando intervened and said, 'Let's split it.' He clearly had old-fashioned sensibilities, in this regard at least, and that pleased Oliver. He also plumped for a pint of Young's Special, just as Oliver had done, when it was his turn to choose. That made Oliver remember the football team that had been called Real Ale Madrid, which had been at least a little bit responsible for his signing up for the training course and for bringing him here now. For a vain, fond moment he imagined himself and Orlando playing together for that mythic team. Oliver would probably be consigned, at his age, to keeping goal. But Orlando… He pushed the thought away.

They were all in a mood of mutual congratulation. Together they had faced a class of Chinese, Brazilians, Romanians and Poles, dividing the hour into five twelve-minute solo slots. And, while they had been only too eager, at the feedback session, to impress their tutor with their trenchant criticisms of each other's performances, they were now as one: bonded as a team and united in their support for each other's efforts. The tutor was relegated to the role of absent other.

The focus of the group had divided. Quiche was turning her attention mostly towards Orlando, the handsome boy of her own age, while Oliver continued to bandy compliments with the two slightly older women, both of whom he found he actually liked. But after twenty minutes or so he decided to be the first to leave. Better that, at his age, than be the last. He drained his glass and, after a few words with everybody about their collective lesson plan for the next day, left the pub. Let the younger people sort themselves out as they liked. When he came in sight of Hyde Park a few moments later he saw that the morning's snow had gone.

*

'Pity you couldn't have stayed,' Orlando said. 'We all ended up having a meal in Chinatown.' For the second time Oliver and he were the early birds in the canteen.

'Well, I had things to do at home.' Quite untrue. Oliver had had nothing to do beyond preparing his solitary supper, getting his next day's lesson ready, and watching television. 'Anyway, I didn't want to cramp your style.'

'Whoa there! Me and Lorraine do you mean? Quiche to her friends. Great person but to what you're thinking, no, no, no.'

'I've got a girlfriend, thank you,' was what he might have said, Oliver thought, clocking the fact that he hadn't. Instead, Orlando changed the subject. 'Where do you live?'

'Kilburn,' Oliver replied. 'North west. Up the Edgware Road a mile or two.'

Orlando nodded. 'I'm dossing with friends near Kentish Town. It's actually a flat I used to share when I was based in London. Now I sort of half-share it. Sounds a bit complicated, but people come and go on a casual basis and it works out OK.'

'Are you sure it's a flat-share and not a squat?' Oliver teased him.

'Ha-ha. Yes, I think so. One of the guys – I was at drama school with him – actually owns it. You got your own place I suppose?'

'I suppose I have,' said Oliver. 'I used to have a boyfriend to share it with. But we split up, and came to an arrangement about it.' He made an ironic grimace to show that this was neither a sob story nor an invitation. It was quite easy these days to tell people that you lived with another guy. It was much harder, Oliver had discovered, to tell them that you didn't.

Orlando nodded sympathetically, said, 'Tough, that one,' and gave a quick smile before deftly manipulating the subject without too crassly changing it. 'House or flat?' At least Orlando hadn't been fazed by the announcement, but if Oliver had expected any reciprocal disclosure about Orlando's love life it seemed that he would be disappointed, at least for now.

'Flat,' said Oliver. 'A house in the bit of Kilburn where I live would put me in millionaire territory.'

'Only a paper millionaire, though,' said Orlando. 'My friends tease me about that.'

'But you're not a millionaire, are you?' Oliver asked, then, uninvited, donned the mantle of friend to tease him gently too. 'One TV ad for the Post Office?'

Orlando made an oh-very-funny expression and said, 'Not me. My family. My dad's a farmer. Owns a farm in other words. Down at Newchurch. Hundred and twenty acres. Mostly sheep, being in that part of the world, though there's some arable too. But a farmer's never rich until he's dead. Believe me.'

'A farmer?' That made sense, though. The lean but athletic figure, the slightly weather-tanned complexion, the burred edge to his educated voice.

'You sound surprised,' said Orlando, who possibly hadn't guessed just how much his origins, together with everything else about him, preoccupied Oliver. 'What does your father do, then?'

Two other members of their class, clutching cups of coffee, were crossing the canteen to join them. Oliver saw them out of the corner of his eye. 'Bit of a long story. I'll tell you some other time.' He looked up. 'Hallo there.' Both men greeted the new arrivals.

*

Some other time came two days later, on Friday afternoon. Oliver had told Orlando that he would be travelling through his part of Kent on his way to Rye and Beckley for the weekend. And Orlando had said, with every sign that the prospect was a pleasant one, 'Then we may end up on the same train. I'm going that way too. Weekend with dad …and my brother.' He made no mention of his mother, Oliver noticed.

There was no way they wouldn't have ended up on the same train – unless they had deliberately tried to avoid each other – finishing teaching practice at the same time, as they did. They walked together to Charing Cross. Oliver would have hopped on a bus or taken the tube if Orlando had suggested it, but he didn't, and Oliver found this cheering. He himself thought nothing of a thirty-minute walk through London, even on a chilly March afternoon: it was his preferred way of getting around the city, though it was hardly a preference that everybody shared. But now it appeared that Orlando did share it. They had a beer in the station bar and then boarded the Dover and Ramsgate train at platform six.

'You were going to tell me,' Orlando said, when they'd settled themselves in facing window seats, 'about your old man. And we got interrupted.'

Oliver was touched. Orlando had not only remembered

their interrupted conversation, but had waited till now, when they were alone and quiet together, to return to it. But he also knew that Orlando would not be disappointed by what Oliver had to tell him. He drew breath importantly and looked him straight in the eye. 'My father – wait for this – my father was a monk.'

'Oh my God!' Orlando guffawed. 'I'm sorry. I didn't mean to laugh. It was just so unexpected. Is he... I mean, is he now...?'

'You're allowed to laugh. Everybody does when I tell them. I told you it was a long story. But I'll tell you straightaway that my father's dead. He's been dead some years. And, he wasn't still a monk when he fathered me. He had been one earlier in his life, for a couple of years, in a monastery in Leicestershire. But then he decided it didn't suit him, so he left.'

'Can they do that?'

'It's not all that easy, but yes, during the early stages. It's not the same as being a priest. Of course anyone can simply walk out of the door, like with a job, but in fact they do a sort of trial period of three years. After that they can leave, quite officially, if they don't want to commit for keeps. And that's what my father did. He retrained as a social worker, met my mother, they got married and had me – after a couple of trial efforts: namely one brother, one sister.'

'I suppose that makes you a Catholic.'

'By upbringing, yes. By persuasion, no. Is that a

problem?' He smiled as he asked the question, to show that he was joking.

'Of course not,' said Orlando, smiling back. 'We're not in bloody Belfast. So, one brother, one sister. Youngest of three. Same as me.' His face became serious again. 'My mother died last year.'

'Oh. I'm sorry.'

'She got quite religious in her last few years. Used to do the flowers in the village church... OK, sorry, I don't mean that's in the same league as what your dad did. Funny thing was, it wasn't as if she had any inkling she was going to die – at just over fifty. She didn't have cancer or anything.'

'Tell me.'

'It was some kind of tumour on the brain, completely undiagnosed and no symptoms. She just died one perfectly normal evening last summer. I wasn't there. My father and brother were. But you know what? My grandmother had only died the year before. She'd been gaga for some time and my mother had had her come to live with us. My mother looked after her like a saint. Drove everyone else mad.'

'My father used to say that saints always did.'

'When my gran finally died, everyone said that would be great for my mum and dad: that they'd have time to be together again. But it didn't work out that way. It was just a few months.'

'Do you get on with your dad?' Oliver probed gently.

Orlando wagged his head from side to side. 'Yes and no.'

'Like the rest of us.'

'And your mother?' Orlando asked. 'Is she still alive?'

'She died about ten years ago. The big C. I'm over that now. But in my experience you're never without parents for very long. In my case my brother and sister seem to have appropriated the roles fairly comprehensively.'

They talked all the way to Ashford, though mostly of lighter things. Oliver found himself answering Orlando's inevitable question: What does a statistician do? A lot of it was fairly mind-numbing, Oliver explained, collating and interpreting numbers and facts, though in his case it had been reasonably well paid. 'You acquire a few skills along the way,' he told him. 'Though being good with numbers to begin with helps. So, for instance, if you give me a number in feet and inches – or kilometres or pints, I can usually give it back to you in centimetres, miles or litres as the case may be.'

'Let me try you then,' Orlando said. 'Two miles.'

'Too easy. Three point two four kilometres. Give me a harder one.'

'Let me see. Four thousand six hundred feet.'

'That's more like it. That's about – approximately – er – fourteen hundred metres. But you'd need to check in a

76

table to see how near I was with that one.'

'Sounds good enough to me,' said Orlando, not sounding as if he wanted to waste his time checking up. 'I guess you must have a great memory for figures.'

'Phone numbers and addresses too, which comes in handy.' Oliver was beginning to be afraid that he was presenting himself as weird and nerdy, but the uncomplicated pleasure his companion seemed to be taking in their conversation reassured him. Nevertheless he took care to move quite quickly after that into less anorakky areas.

Oliver never had the feeling, which he had with some of the other youngsters on the training course, that the years between them presented any kind of obstacle to mutual understanding or the appreciation of each other's company. Perhaps Orlando was not so firmly rooted in the mores of his own generation as the others were. He remembered how he had been struck by his non-dependence on iPod or mobile phone when he had first set eyes on him: perhaps that was symptomatic. That was fine by Oliver. If it made it easier for the younger man to relate to him, so much the better. Oliver had no ulterior ambitions with regard to Orlando just at that moment. Simply talking to this pleasant, attractive young man, alone together on a train for an hour or so, was quite good enough.

They got off at Ashford and crossed by subway to platform one to await the Marsh Link. Oliver found his eye roaming to the metal guard rail on which he had first seen Orlando uncomfortably perched. He didn't mention it.

'How old are you?' Orlando suddenly asked.

Oliver was tempted to knock a couple of years off, but he had done so in the past once or twice and been caught out, so he came clean. 'Thirty-eight. And you?'

'Twenty-four.' Their grunting diesel train arrived and they climbed onto it.

'One of the new ones,' said Orlando. 'They only came on last year. Until then they had incredibly old diesels that my father remembers being introduced when he was a kid himself. When there were leaves on the line they sometimes didn't make it up the hills at Doleham and Ham Street. Mind you, my dad remembers the steam trains.' They squeezed into side-by-side seats and the train started off, peeling away from the main line that ran straight on to Dover, crossing the river flats where houses were being built across the green fields with what seemed almost indecent haste, then climbing towards the modest ridge that, according to Orlando, had defeated the old trains when the leaves fell.

It was Oliver's turn to ask a personal question. 'Does everyone call you Orlando, or do people shorten it?'

'Well, some people used to call me Orly – like the airport near Paris. Of course at school I did end up with the obvious nickname...'

'Marmalade Cat?' hazarded Oliver.

'*The* Marmalade Cat, if you don't mind. Yes, that and The Marmalade Kid, and sometimes just The Cat. I rather liked that one. You can call me any of those if you want to – or invent one of your own. What about you?'

'Nothing so interesting. I got called Fidget at school, but I'd rather you didn't call me that. My friends call me Oli. You're welcome if you want.'

'Thanks. Hey! We're slowing down for Ham Street. Gotta go, …Oli.' He stood up.

'See you Monday,' Oliver said. Neither of them had suggested meeting over the weekend. It would hardly have occurred to Orlando, when the villages they would be staying in were more than fifteen miles apart, and as for Oliver, he had disciplined his imagination sufficiently well for this not to appear a realistic possibility.

'Yeah. Have a good weekend.' Orlando smiled and half waved a hand as he made towards the door. Then he was out of the train and striding along the platform. The train started off and overtook him a few seconds later. He looked briefly in at Oliver as the train passed him. Smiled, half waved again. Understated gestures which Oliver demurely returned.

But as soon as Orlando had disappeared from sight Oliver experienced a sense of loss and longing as powerful as if he had been parting from a lover. It was as if a hole was opening up inside him, or that a hole was opening up around him and he was falling into it. He was shocked by his own reaction and cross with himself for letting his emotions ambush him in such a way. He was old and experienced enough to know how to deal with his feelings in cases like this. Orlando by no means represented the first younger-man scenario he had had to work his way through; he thought he'd learnt all those lessons by now. Perhaps you only ever learnt what not to do, though –

not what not to feel.

FIVE

Zara met Oliver at Rye station and drove him up the startlingly abrupt hill that led out of the town and along the ridge to Beckley. 'So, this red-headed boy of yours – what's his name – what's the latest?'

Oliver was slightly shocked at her directness, but not unpleasantly so. 'He's hardly a boy of *mine*, as you put it. I don't actually think he's anybody's boy right now, though we've never discussed those things. I've let him know I'm gay, nothing more; he took that on board but he hasn't told me anything about himself, and I'm happy to leave it that way. We did travel down on the train together just now.' He couldn't help sounding pleased with himself as he said that. 'He got off at Ham Street. His family farm near there.' They were passing a pub whose unusual name Oliver half remembered: the Peace and Plenty.

'It sounds as though you've made a friend of him at any rate,' Zara said. 'Next time you come down, bring him along and introduce us.'

'Ha-ha,' said Oliver, though perhaps Zara was being serious. He wasn't quite sure how well he knew her.

'You need to be careful with redheads, though,' Zara said. 'They can be slightly mad. My parents had a red setter once. Beautiful dog it was. But inside it was completely screwed up, all the wires were crossed. It had to be put down in the end.'

'You're not serious,' said Oliver. 'This is a person, not an animal. And if he were an animal he wouldn't be a dog. His name's Orlando.'

'Like the marmalade cat?'

'Exactly. Why do people always imagine that if people are exceptionally beautiful on the outside there must be something very wrong with them on the inside?'

'Interesting,' said Zara, taking no notice of the thirty-mile-an-hour sign as they zigzagged through Peasmarsh. 'I'd always thought that was a fact of life, but maybe it's just a comfort myth designed to make the rest of us feel better. David had to go out but he should be back before we are.'

'He won't be if we keep on at this speed,' said Oliver. Zara's foot relaxed its pressure on the accelerator infinitesimally. Three minute later they arrived at Lilac Cottage. Lilacs weren't out yet but forget-me-nots and primroses bordered the brick path up to the door.

David greeted Oliver with a bear-like hug. Was it Oliver's imagination, or had David's hugs grown cooler, warier, since the break-up with Adi? Until this one, which seemed to be once again at full strength. Like his wife, David wanted to hear about Orlando before anything else. Again Oliver had to explain that there was really very little to tell. It was his own fault, he thought, blurting things out over the telephone when in reality he had nothing to report beyond a couple of coincidences. 'Anyway,' David eventually changed the subject.

'There's something else. Donald wants to see you.'

'Donald wants to see me?' Oliver echoed, in the tone of voice that a much younger Oliver might have used on hearing that he'd been summoned by the headmaster. For a day or two he had almost managed to forget about Donald, what with the demanding newness of the training course, the comet-like reappearance of the redhead, and the metamorphosis of that apparition into the real person who was called Orlando. Yet Donald, or at least Oliver's desire to talk to David about him, was the original reason why he had been keen to visit Beckley this weekend. Intermittently he had been reminded of his anxieties on that score by the proximity of his training college to Shepherd Market – it was impossible to forget this if he went to the pub with his group after teaching practice – and there had been moments when he had imagined himself bottling out altogether and saying to David: could they perhaps *not* visit the Rose and Crown this weekend, since he didn't particularly wish to confront Donald face to face? For the last couple of hours, cocooned in his train with Orlando, he had put Donald out of his mind altogether. And now, like a blow in the stomach, came the dismaying news that Donald wanted to see him. 'Why?'

'Ask him,' said David. 'I met him in the pub a couple of days ago, that's all. I imagine he wants you to do another little job for him, but I don't know for certain.'

'Oh hell,' said Oliver. 'And I'm not sure if I want to.'

'I told you,' Zara said to her husband, 'Oliver's having

doubts about working for him.'

'Well I'm sorry if I've put my foot in it,' David addressed both of them. 'He was perfectly friendly and relaxed when we spoke. I told him you were coming down, Oli – you didn't tell us not to – and he said he hoped I'd be bringing you to the pub.' Be nice to see him again.'Those were his exact words. He didn't sound as if he wanted to bite your head off or send you on a gun-running mission to Outer Mongolia.'

'The last job I did for him,' Oliver began cautiously, 'was to carry a small framed picture to Germany. The dates coincided – I won't put it more strongly that that – with the theft of a German old master from the National Gallery.'

David frowned. 'I think I read about that. Did you … did you take a look at the picture you were carrying?'

'I chose not to.'

'Perhaps you were wise.' David was still looking thoughtful. 'Look, we don't have to frogmarch you to the door of the Rose and Crown if you'd really prefer to cut your ties with the man. I can tell Donald you didn't come in the end. If I tell him anything at all.'

'Let me think about it for a bit. After all, we don't have to go this minute.'

David took the hint and poured them all a gin and tonic, without asking Oliver what he wanted. He knew him very well.

Zara and David wanted to hear all about Oliver's training course. 'You, a teacher,' said David. 'I can't get my head round it.'

'Sometimes, neither can I,' said Oliver.

'And then this guy from the Red-Headed League. Are things looking up on that front, perhaps?'

'Don't read too much into what I told Zara on the phone,' Oliver said. 'I may have got a bit carried away with surprise. It's one thing for me to be attracted by a pretty young face. It's hardly likely that it's going to work in reverse. So I'm not going to do anything silly, or even think it.' Oliver sat back in his armchair and took a gulp of his gin and tonic. *Oh but you already have,* he told himself. When it came to thinking silly things, in this particular case, the malady was far advanced.

'Well I don't know,' said David, with a twinkle in his eye that Oliver felt he had known for ever. 'I'd been thinking it was about time you got yourself a new boyfriend.'

Oliver looked at David, still handsome in his late thirties. He thought: *a couple of worlds ago I used to imagine that boyfriend was going to be you.* Then he thought, there would be no harm in just meeting Donald in the pub and being civil to him. If he offered him another job he could easily say no. It would be something to tell Orlando on Monday: they could have a laugh about it. Of course, if he liked the sound of the job – if it sounded safe and above board in other words –

then another three or four hundred pounds would be very welcome. He imagined himself telling Orlando that he had a weekend job flying around Europe delivering mysterious packages, and tried to guess Orlando's reaction. Any twenty-four-year-old would be impressed, wouldn't he? As he was hardly likely to be by Oliver's modest good looks and youthful physique. It was one thing to be considered physically attractive by Bernd, who was his own age, but Orlando was a very different matter.

Oliver remembered the young man on his training course – his name was Mike – who had just come back from a tour of duty with the Territorial Army in Iraq. That rather put his own apprehensions into perspective. As David had just said, Donald was unlikely to send him to Outer Mongolia. 'OK,' he said. 'We'll go along to the pub later. I am up for it. I'll talk to Donald. Or let him talk to me. See what he wants.'

Once he saw Donald in the flesh, peering benignly through thick glasses, sitting in a wheel-back chair amid the brass and pewter and the beamed cosiness of the Rose and Crown, a pint of Guinness in his hand, Oliver's residual anxieties drained away. The theft of a picture shortly before his trip to Cologne was certainly no more than a coincidence; it could be dismissed from his mind.

Donald left his seat and his conversation at the table when he saw them come in, and made his way up to the bar where David was about to order drinks. 'Let me get these,' he said. He turned to Oliver, smiling warmly. 'Good to see you again. I was hoping to catch you when you were next down. We'll talk when you've got a pint in front of you.' He gestured to the barman and began the serious business of ordering the round.

They all stayed at the bar while they drank. No discreet table or whispering in corners. It made Oliver feel very safe. 'What it is,' Donald said, 'as you may have already guessed, is that I want you to do one more job for me.'

'Thank you for thinking of me,' Oliver answered. 'The fact is that I'm a bit busier now than I used to be. I'm actually in the middle of a training course. I don't know what kind of a timetable you're working to.'

'But you're free at weekends, aren't you? I mean, here you are, away from London on a Friday night.'

Oliver smiled. 'That's true.'

'The money would be a bit more,' Donald said casually, as if he'd just remembered that. 'What about next weekend?'

Oliver had already guessed that beneath Donald's mild manner there lurked a character that expected to get what it wanted. 'Tell me what it is,' he said.

'You know your way to Málaga, I suppose?' Oliver nodded. 'Well, I need someone to pick something up for me there. A little flat parcel, light as a feather. Nothing to it. You could go out on Friday night if you wanted, come back Sunday evening – have a weekend in the sun.' Donald's benign expression changed for a moment. He looked sharply into Oliver's eyes, examining them for his inner thoughts as he waited for him to say yes or no.

A parcel. From Málaga. In Oliver's mind that could only mean one thing, even when the parcel was described unthreateningly as flat and light as a feather. He thought of the sniffer dog at Funchal. He must remember to tell Orlando that story too.

'Seven hundred pounds,' said Donald matter-of-factly. 'Is that beer all right for you?'

'It's fine,' Oliver said, trying not to show his startlement at the seven hundred pounds. 'And I'll do the job for you.' He saw David and Zara's heads nod almost imperceptibly, as if in support of his decision. Around them the copper and brass-work winked their reflections of the lantern lights among the dark beams. 'The money's fine too,' he added. 'I wasn't going to say no.'

*

There was only one occasion during the weekend when Oliver and David were alone together for any length of time: they took a walk in the cold sunshine of Sunday morning up the lane towards Methersham Farm, and then down where the landscape opened out across the flat Rother valley and its reed-beds, with the Isle of Oxney on the other side, Wittersham church tower poking up among the trees, and the broad vastness of the Romney Marsh in the distance. Perhaps, Oliver thought, if you knew exactly where to look, and had eyes like a goshawk, you could see all the way to Newchurch. 'I had a crazy experience in Germany,' he said. He started to tell David the whole story, including his encounter with Bernd and the photographic session, without stinting on the details. For all that David was now a fully paid-up member of the heterosexual community, he would want to know exactly who did what and how. Oliver knew that about him.

'He sounds OK, this guy,' David said. 'And German too, which is on the plus side when you think how many years of practice you've had. Have you been in touch with him since you got back?'

'He hasn't been in touch with me.'

'That's not what I asked. But obviously you haven't. I think you should.'

'I think I would have done,' said Oliver slowly. 'Only…'

'Oh I see,' said David. 'I get it now. Something that happened on Monday?' He caught hold of the back of Oliver's head and rumpled his hair. 'You dissembling bugger, you. Zara was right all along. You've got it bad. This Orlando kid.'

'Funnily enough, that's his name,' said Oliver. 'Orlando Kidd.'

*

He was in his usual place in the canteen, the first of their class to arrive, on Monday morning. 'I looked out for you on the train yesterday,' he told Oliver casually. 'I guess you were on a different one.'

'I was on the one leaving Ashford just after five,' Oliver said, trying to sound equally casual. Yet it was far from casually that he had scanned the empty platform at Ham Street, and looked down the station approach road as far as he could see along it – ready to jump up and press *Door Open* should he glimpse him, a hurrying late arrival – then swept with his eyes the crowded platforms at Ashford International. How absurdly despondent he had been to find that they wouldn't be travelling together. And how absurdly happy it made him to be here, talking to him, holding a monopoly on his interest, now. He envied the ease with which Orlando could say, 'I looked out for you on the train.' Those were words he couldn't have brought himself to utter if he had been tortured with rack and thumbscrew.

'I caught the one an hour later,' Orlando said lightly. 'Pity. We should have synchronised our plans on the way down.' As Oliver had so much wanted to do. And not dared.

Orlando's jeans looked immaculate and bright blue like his eyes. Who did the weekend wash on the farm now that his mother was no longer there? His father? Sister-in-law? Orlando himself? He had his trademark blue denim jacket on, and the usual trainers and fresh white socks. The cable-knit pullover had gone, for the weather had turned milder, and a snowy white sweatshirt took its place. His eyes were their most piercing blue and his hair such a blaze of copper and flame that it seemed almost too much for eight o'clock on a Monday morning. Yet imagine waking up each day and seeing that.

'I've got that phrasal verb lesson to do this afternoon,' Orlando said, momentarily sounding a bit less confident than usual. 'I'm not sure it's going to be all right.'

Orlando might have been apprehensive about the lesson he was to teach that afternoon, but he turned out to be the star of the morning's training session. The class explored stress and intonation – the systems by which meaning and nuance are conveyed by the pitch and rhythms of the voice. Everybody knew there were rules of grammar, but it was a new discovery to many in the class that there were rules for this as well. But Orlando, as the only trained actor among them, was aware of this already. When they were given sentences to say in as many different ways as possible, changing the meaning through accents, pauses and pitch changes, it was he who came up with more alternatives than anybody else, and he made the class, and their trainer, laugh by adding one or two of his own, which he remembered from his drama school days. 'What is *this* thing called, love?' Another was: '*Who* is? *Sylvia?!* What! *Is* she?!'

In the pub at the end of the day he was still the admired focus of attention, even though, as he had feared, his afternoon class had not gone particularly well. So it came as a surprise to Oliver to find the two of them finishing their pints alone together after the others, one by one had left for home.

'I liked that thing you did this afternoon,' Orlando said. 'You know, that vocabulary thing.' The mutual compliments session was still very much a part of the winding-down ritual after the bruising experience of teaching practice.

'Oh I don't know,' said Oliver, in the same spirit. 'Your lesson wasn't nearly as bad as you imagined.' We're like monkeys, he thought: comforting each other, picking out fleas. 'And you were brilliant at handling Miguel.' Miguel was the difficult member of their practice group. He came from Argentina and had acquired the rather obvious nickname of Argy Bargy. Oliver thought back to Orlando that morning, impressing everyone with his verbal skills. But they couldn't go on for ever exchanging compliments, so Oliver's next remark, though not unrelated, was a little different. 'What made a horny-handed son of the soil like you go and become an actor?'

Orlando gave a small laugh of surprise. 'We weren't entirely a family of yokels, you know. My mother was a floor manager for the BBC before she got married. But marrying a farmer means marrying the farm as well. I suppose I got it through her. I acted a bit at school. Well quite a lot, actually. But... New Romney Comprehensive... It wasn't exactly tops as a theatrical experience. Then, when the others were applying for university places, I started writing off to drama schools. Auditions here and there. I finally got a place at Birmingham. Became a Brummie for a few years.' He did a passable imitation of the accent at this point. 'And the rest you more or less know already.' He looked keenly into Oliver's face. A starburst of blue eyes. 'You ever do any acting?'

'Me? No. Well, not in the same way. But...' Oliver said this shyly as people do when they reveal something about themselves that they haven't told anybody for a long time, '...I used to do light opera when I was at university. You know, Gilbert and Sullivan, Offenbach, that sort of stuff.'

'You sing. Hey!'

'Not that brilliantly. And not at all now.'

'Pity. Be nice to hear you.'

'Get away. Only other thing I did in that connection was a bit of backstage work in the local theatre. That was Nottingham, where I went to uni. I just did it sometimes, when they needed some casual labour for big shows – opera and ballet.'

'You're full of surprises, you are,' said Orlando. Another flash of blue. 'And yet you're not in a way. When I met you I sort of knew you'd be full of surprises.' The kid couldn't imagine the effect he was having on him, Oliver thought. He'd never seen this childlike side of Orlando before – naïf and eager for surprises, and yet why should he have done? They still hardly knew each other.

'There was another thing,' Oliver said, 'talking of

surprises. Surprised me anyway. A ballet company was in town, doing a new ballet on the subject of Othello. One of the extras, the walk-ons, was off sick one day. They asked me to go on in his place. No rehearsal. Just like that. I was jammed into the costume of a medieval halberdier and sent striding on stage to go and arrest the principal male dancer. I was petrified I'd go on and arrest the wrong person.'

'But you didn't.'

'Fortunately not. And fortunately I didn't have to do a single dance step.'

'That probably was fortunate,' said Orlando with a sly smile. 'There was a time when I thought I might do ballet. When I was a teenager. Probably just as well I didn't go far along that road. The kids at school thought it was weird enough my just wanting to act. As for what my father would have done... It'd have been Billy Elliot with Kentish accents. Anyway, so we've both worked on stage. That's something.'

They looked at each other in silence for a moment, neither of them able to think how the conversation could go on. The silence became awkward. Desperately Oliver broke it. 'Tell you something else, if you're still interested in being surprised by me. I've been offered a bit of work next weekend. Courier work. Not unlike being an extra in a show in fact. I'm getting paid to fly out to Málaga and pick up a parcel. Funny thing is, I don't know exactly what sort of show I'm appearing in.'

'Meaning?'

'I'm not supposed to know what's in the parcel.'

Orlando gave him a look of intense curiosity mingled with a little caution. 'Do you do this regularly? Are you a – a drug-smuggler?'

'I don't think I am,' Oliver answered, savouring the moment. He would remember this conversation for the rest of his life. 'But neither can I be quite certain that I'm not.'

Orlando was shaking his head and half laughing. 'You take the fucking biscuit, mate. Boy, I'm glad I met you. Now you've got to tell me everything. Everything you do know.'

'I'd better get us another drink in that case,' said Oliver. He got up and walked to the bar. His legs felt as wobbly and remote from him as a convalescent's.

Oliver came out with the whole story. Meeting Donald in Beckley. The trip to Funchal and the sniffer dog. The German adventure. Though not the Bernd episode: Orlando still kept the subject of his own love life conspicuously absent from their conversations, and unless that should ever change, Oliver was going to do the same. But he told Orlando his suspicions about the missing Lucas Cranach. Then the arrangements for the forthcoming trip: collect ticket at airport, find a cheap place to spend a couple of nights in Málaga, meet a Spanish guy at the main rail station, return with unspecified package, deliver it on Monday morning to –

wait for this – the picture framer's shop just a few doors away from the pub they were now sitting in. Orlando was almost speechless. Oliver had accepted the Málaga job mostly – and rather pathetically – in order to have something to tell Orlando that would boost his standing in the younger man's eyes. So far – and almost as pathetically – the plan had worked astonishingly well.

Orlando suddenly remembered something. He felt at his wrist for his watch, found he was not wearing one, and had to ask Oliver the time. 'Shit,' he said. 'I'm supposed to be cooking tonight. Couple of nights a week we all eat together – or most of us do – and take it in turns to… Tonight it's me. Look, I'll have to go.' He drank the last of his beer quickly. 'There's a supermarket near the flat. I can nip in and get some things on the way. Something simple.' He paused and looked at Oliver, his mouth hanging half-open for a second. Oliver saw, as plainly as if there were a thought-bubble suspended over his head, that he was considering asking him to go back to Kentish Town with him for communal supper. But the invitation didn't materialise; the mouth shut again. Oliver could not guess whether Orlando had felt he ought to ask Oliver out of politeness and then realised that he didn't really want to; or whether he had actually wanted to invite him but then felt shy about doing so: perhaps he had decided the ensuing social situation would be awkward. Probably it was the former, Oliver the realist told himself. 'Sorry to desert you in such a rush,' Orlando concluded, picking up his jacket from the empty seat next to him. 'See you tomorrow.' Then his breath came out in an involuntary chuckle and he shook his head. 'You're cool.' He walked out of the pub.

Oliver finished the last of his pint slowly. He had got past the age of enjoying student suppers in shared flats that were little better than squats. Over-cooked pasta with bottled tomato sauce, Parmesan cheese that wasn't Parmesan at all, tinned pineapple chunks...

When he got home, and after he had eaten his own supper of pork chop and salad, Oliver remembered to check his emails. There was one from a Bernd Müller. Oliver had to think for a half a second who that could be, though no longer than that.

Hi Oliver! Remember me? I must come to England next week for my business. Maybe we can meet us? But only when you want that. You must tell me. Tschüs. Bernd

Oliver emailed Bernd back. He would be away at the weekend, and busy during the day, but his evenings were more or less free. If Bernd needed somewhere to stay, Oliver could put him up. In any case, Bernd was to let him know which day he would be coming and he would suggest a time and place to meet. Oliver wrote this laboriously in German. He could use the practice.

*

'How was the meal?' Oliver asked next morning. Usual time, usual place.

'I should have invited you,' Orlando said. He wasn't

smiling, Oliver noticed.

'No, come off it. I'd got things sorted for myself.' Oliver brushed the subject aside with a laugh. It would be embarrassing if it became an issue.

But Orlando didn't seem to see the need to let it go. 'I did pork chops in the end. In cider. With rosemary and capers. And mashed spuds with celeriac.' He saw something like a smirk on Oliver's face. 'What's funny?'

'Nothing. Just I had a pork chop too. Without the trimmings.' Was there to be no escape from the subject of last night's supper?

Perhaps Orlando picked up on Oliver's discomfort. He said, 'So you nearly an opera star and me nearly going to be a dancer – and you end up in a bloody ballet. Funny old world.'

Oliver couldn't quite pick the meaning out of the muddled syntax. Had Orlando been mulling over their yesterday evening's conversation? He looked into his face but could read no clues in the trusting, candid blue eyes. To look deeply into them always hurt somehow. Out of self-preservation, Oliver tried not to do it too often.

Then Orlando said, 'You know this trip you're going on. This – er – package trip to Málaga. I don't suppose you're allowed to take a friend.'

Oliver managed a faint laugh as a cover for his

confusion. 'You mean you? You're joking, aren't you?' He didn't dare to think otherwise.

'Maybe I am,' Orlando said, but Oliver saw from his face – almost to his disbelief – that he hadn't been joking at all: there had been a flicker of disappointment there that Orlando wasn't quick enough to hide. Suddenly Oliver found himself at one of those junctures in life where the stakes become unimaginably high – when an instant before there had seemed to be no stake at all. It was as if he had unexpectedly hooked a prize fish on an inadequate line, or was leaping for an awkward one-hand catch in cricket.

'But if you aren't joking,' Oliver said boldly – there was no alternative to boldness just then – 'I'll see if it's possible.' He was rewarded by a look of relaxation – not yet a smile – appearing on Orlando's face. He pressed home his advantage. 'It would be good to have company.'

*

Oliver phoned Donald during the morning break, his heart thumping. He had a friend, he told him, who wanted to come with him to Málaga for the weekend. Would Donald have any objection to that? He'd fix up the additional ticket himself, of course... He waited, anticipating a volcanic refusal. But to his great surprise, Donald said, why not? He even added that Oliver's chances of getting a second ticket were quite good: even though the weekend coincided with the start of Semana Santa in Seville, the flights were not yet full – at least they hadn't been when he had booked for Oliver. He reminded Oliver of his flight numbers and take-off times from Gatwick, and from Málaga on Sunday. Oliver rang off, hardly able to believe he'd got this far. Immediately, before his courage had time to fail him, he dialled up a telephone flight sales company; he'd used it before; the number was stored in his phone. He reeled off the data. Was there any chance of an extra return ticket for the same flights? There was, but his was a relatively late booking. The price was not far off two hundred pounds. Oliver recited his credit card number like a hymn of joy. It wouldn't have mattered if it had cost two thousand.

He slid into the classroom a few minutes late for the second morning session, mouthed, 'Sorry' to the trainer and took the only vacant seat which, as it happened, was nowhere near Orlando. Still seething with impatience to impart his news, he was reduced to writing, like an infatuated schoolgirl, *Flight sorted, all OK, Oli,* on a piece of paper, then folding it, putting Orlando's name on the outside, and having it passed childishly around the room till it got to him. He watched its progress until he saw it reach Orlando, who frowned as he unfolded it, then read it and looked up and across the room at him with an uncomplicated smile of pleasure.

They went to the pub together when the day's work was done, but this time, by unspoken agreement, they chose one that they had not visited with the others in their group. 'It's great,' Orlando said. 'That you've fixed it, I mean. I can hardly believe it's happening.' He took a gulp of beer, noisily. He seemed very excited by the prospect. He went on, 'I used to speak quite good Spanish. When I was seventeen I did a swap with a Spanish farmer's son for the summer. He came and worked for my parents, I went out there and worked for his. It was a great place, in the north, near Logroño.'

'Rioja country?'

'They didn't make the stuff themselves, they were just outside the area. But they were near enough; there was plenty of it around.' He grinned. 'I've kept thinking about Spain. I always said that if acting didn't work out I'd go back there. Said to myself, I mean. Now, doing this course, I'd sort of decided that I'd take off there, look for a job – teaching, I suppose, assuming I get the qualification, but ready to take anything that came along.'

Oliver had actually been thinking along very similar lines although he hadn't formulated the idea as an action plan even to himself. But now, hearing it articulated by an excitable twenty-four-year-old, it sounded dismayingly half-baked.

Orlando had paused in his flow for a moment. Now he said, 'Sounds as if I'm admitting the acting hasn't worked out, doesn't it?'

And why would that be? Oliver asked himself. When he's got looks to die for, intelligence and – to go on his performances in the classroom – an enviable degree of talent. But he said, in an even tone, 'It's always good to have a plan B.' Then he thought: what do I sound like?

Senior statesman. Teacher with bright pupil. What on earth could Orlando be thinking of, wanting to latch onto him? Free plane ticket, perhaps.

Orlando chose that moment to say, 'I haven't asked you the price of the ticket yet. It won't make any difference: I'm coming anyway. But tell me what I owe you and I'll settle with you at the nearest cash machine.'

Oliver just had the presence of mind to say, 'It's a hundred and eighty-five, I'm afraid, but we can sort it out later.' He thought that if he'd said, 'Don't you worry, I'll take care of it,' he would have been lost for ever.

For the same reason he resisted the urge to invite Orlando home with him that evening or on the two that followed. Friday night was going to be a bizarre enough experience anyway without doing anything to pre-empt it. If this crazy little episode in his life, with himself as an object of fascination for this most exceptional young man, was going to come to an abrupt and unceremonious end – and Oliver had to suppose that it inevitably would – at least let it last till the weekend.

He also resisted the temptation to phone David and say, *guess what?* They might hear from Donald that he was taking a friend to Málaga, and though Donald wouldn't know the colour of his companion's hair, David and Zara between them might make an intelligent guess. But Oliver didn't want to give hostages to fortune by crowing publicly about the surprising new turn things had taken: he would keep it to himself.

He found an email from Bernd awaiting him when he got home that night. He could probably have been forgiven, in the circumstances, for forgetting that he was expecting one. *I come to London next Tuesday. I need stay for two nights. If it's OK I stay by you. Thank you. We meet in London Downtown Tuesday evening? In a pub maybe? You say me where and what time. I'm there. Tschüs.*

He emailed back, naming a pub near Piccadilly Circus that would be easy for Bernd to find, and set the time for six o'clock. Oliver saw no point in telling Orlando about this arrangement. The Málaga jaunt would be over by next Tuesday and Orlando's interest in Oliver would almost certainly be at an end.

Next day they returned to their habit of joining the rest of their group for a quick drink together after TP, and discussing their battle plans for the next day. The tasks expected of them had grown in complexity as the course advanced. The things they had done in their first week now looked easy in retrospect, whereas ten days ago the mere fact of standing in front of a group of foreigners and' managing their learning experience'for a period of ten minutes had seemed daunting enough. Quiche said, 'All this preparation we have to do. We've all been to school, and teachers all over the world must always have been doing this, and I bet none of us ever thought about it before.' There were nods of agreement all round. Neither Oliver nor Orlando mentioned the impending trip to Málaga.

Thursday morning and they met as usual in the canteen

before class. It was the only time they were ever really alone – but Oliver made sure they had that time together, and had been doing so now for several days, by catching a bus twenty minutes before the one he strictly needed. Orlando was in tail-wagging mood. Proud of his relative fluency in Spanish, he had volunteered to arrange somewhere for them to stay while they were in Málaga. They would be arriving late in the evening, the more so when they took the hour's time difference into account. There was a copy of the Rough Guide to Spain at the flat where he was living, he had told Oliver, with phone numbers of *hostals* in it. He was pleased with himself now because he had found them a room at rock-bottom price in the centre of Málaga's old town. 'Always get a room near the cathedral when staying in a strange town,' he explained. 'First, because it's easy to find your way back late at night if you're pissed. Second, because you don't need to take an alarm clock for the mornings.' He took a slurp of coffee and grinned up at Oliver.

SIX

Oliver had some trouble getting to sleep, assailed by last minute doubts and fears about what the morrow had in store. Orlando's eagerness to join him on his potentially risky adventure worried him. It was quite uncharacteristic of any straight man of his age: wanting to wander off for the weekend with an older man who was gay. Not very typical of a young gay man either, come to that, even supposing Orlando *was* gay – something for which he had no evidence at all. He wondered if Zara's absurd suggestion that the boy wasn't quite all there had something in it after all. Then it even crossed his mind that Orlando might be working for the police, tracking him across Europe in order to get hold of a real criminal network. But Oliver dismissed that as being too fantastic, even as he became awkwardly aware of having divulged to Orlando rather a lot of the kind of information that a real policeman might have been interested in.

He told himself Orlando had just as many good reasons to mistrust him: a man he'd only known ten days, travelling to Spain with a story about a mystery package. In the end, he decided, they would both simply have to make an investment of belief in each other. You had to do that with people or life would grind to a halt.

He felt more positive when Friday dawned, although a veil of unreality seemed to lie over the morning. He felt the way a child feels when setting out on a holiday: that sense that, though the day will begin ordinarily enough, the ending is un-guessable. He didn't try to communicate this to Orlando when he met him in the canteen: it would have sounded foolish, especially if Orlando was feeling nothing of the same sort. On the other hand the mere sight him sitting there with his coffee, giving Oliver his usual smile of greeting, allayed his fears of the previous night as nothing else possibly could. He just said, 'Got your passport?' at which Orlando pulled it out of a pocket and waved it in Oliver's face, then asked in his turn, 'Tickets?'

'E-ticketing,' Oliver answered. 'I've got a reference number.' And that was that. Moments later the others were arriving and they began to talk about their lesson preparation for the afternoon. Oliver still didn't tell any of the others where he was going that evening or who with. He noticed that Orlando didn't either. It had become The Secret That They Shared, and Oliver liked that. The fact that they both had fuller backpacks than usual attracted no comment. It was a Friday and many of the others had bulging backpacks too. The day passed. Oliver's teaching was markedly below his usual standard in the afternoon: he was having trouble concentrating. But he noticed that Orlando's part of the lesson showed similar signs of divided attention. Their tutor was not slow to pick up on it either. 'Bit Fridayish, Orlando? Oliver too? I'll say no more. Only I don't want to see anyone Mondayish on Monday.'

Then there was the usual general move to the pub. 'Not coming?' people said to Oliver and Orlando on the pavement as they showed signs of heading in a different direction.

Then Orlando did come out with it, after a fashion. 'We've got a train to catch.' A mysterious smile appeared on his face, which was then faintly reflected on Oliver's.

'We?' Somebody picked up on that, and one or two faces showed signs of surprise but they were quickly extinguished out of politeness.

'We can walk, can't we?' said Orlando, turning to check with Oliver.

'I thought you'd say that,' Oliver replied.

They crossed Green Park in the last of the daylight, rounded the front of Buckingham Palace, and a few minutes later were installed in the Gatwick Express.

For all his misgivings about Donald and about the nature of the errand he'd been sent on, Oliver felt a sense of lightness as they presented themselves at the South Terminal check-in and were waved through passport control into departures. He told himself it was because he was not carrying any unusual cargoes with him this time and that he might be feeling very different on the journey back. He tried not to think that it had anything to do with the fact that he was flying off to the sun with this particular young man, whom he had noticed when they were two strangers on a train and had expected never to see again.

'Reckon we deserve a pint, don't you?' Orlando said. They went up the escalator and chose one of the cafés at the top, where they sat looking out over the aircraft stands and down the runway. The lights of incoming planes were lined up, seemingly motionless, pinned like jewels against the dark sky. They had time for two pints before their flight was called. Oliver hoped his bladder wouldn't inconvenience him too much on board the aircraft or – still worse – if there were to be a delay at the departure gate. He'd been caught out in that way more than once over the years. But he decided to set his anxiety aside for the moment. And Orlando gave no indication that he was worried on that score himself. His tongue slightly loosened by this time (two inches down into his second pint) he was telling Oliver all about the dogs on his father's farm: the sheepdogs, retrievers (one was called Arabella), a terrier for the rats – the usual farm complement. Orlando was clearly very attached to them. For his own part, Oliver did not care overmuch for dogs. The barking they made produced the same painful sensations in his teeth and skull as if he had bitten off a square of chocolate only to find he'd bitten into the silver paper as well.

They had been served their drinks by a pretty, petite Hispanic waiter, whose liquid eyes and long dark lashes had caught Oliver's attention. He was on the point of mentioning this to his companion as he would automatically have done to Adi in years gone by. But as he turned back to Orlando and found himself looking directly into his trusting blue eyes, just a foot from his own, it seemed a singularly inappropriate thing to do.

It was a clear night and they flew under the light of a full winter moon, which picked out the rivers of Sussex below them like broken capillaries of mercury. After a few minutes it was highlighting the pinprick billows of the English Channel. Orlando pointed all this out to Oliver who had to lean over his shoulder to see. Orlando had the window seat; Oliver, mindful of his bladder, had thought it prudent not to sit too far from the aisle. Orlando approached the experience of flying with the wide-eyed wonder of someone less than half his age. ('There's Brighton. Look at the lights. Hey! Wow. The pier.')

Oliver ordered them both a gin and tonic, without checking to see if Orlando liked that. He would drink what he was given: Oliver was pretty sure by now that he usually did. But Orlando surprised him by going one stage further, leaning over and collaring the steward on his return journey: 'Do you think we could have another one of those while we're waiting for our tea?' And the steward found one for them both without a second's hesitation, waving aside Orlando's wide-eyed offer to pay.

'It always works,' Orlando said, through the *phut* of his opening tonic can.

'For you I'm sure it does.' It was the first concrete proof for Oliver that Orlando was conscious of the effect his beauty had on people, and that he knew how to trade on it. It was also the first time Oliver had ever addressed a remark to him that might have been considered even remotely camp. He was rewarded by a chuckle of surprise, almost a giggle, and something that might have been a blush, though Orlando's face was already rather pink from the gin.

After that, Oliver was quite unsurprised when, along with the in-flight meal, two small bottles of the red wine they had asked for were handed to each of them instead of the customary one. The only thing that did surprise him was how soon they found themselves fastening their seat belts in readiness for landing at Málaga. Their plane turned slowly over the sea, doubling back on itself to make its final approach and causing the lights of the Costa del Sol to revolve beneath them like the night sky on time lapse film. 'Jesus, look at that,' said Orlando. 'Just so beautiful.'

Oliver suddenly realised that he hadn't given his bladder a thought for over two hours, and at the same time remembered thankfully, first, that they'd already booked a room for the night, and second, that neither of them was going to have to drive.

In the arrivals hall they both had to scramble for the gents. Don't look at him, Oliver ordered himself sternly. But a moment later he relaxed that to, don't let him see you looking. But all he saw was a high-pressure horizontal jet of water, such as might have been released by a fire extinguisher, or a race horse. His own stream, he noticed, was of similar amplitude.

There was a train, they both knew, which ran from the airport into the centre of Málaga. It was very easy to use, provided you got onto the right platform. Failure to do this would result in your being whisked off in the opposite direction, to Fuengirola. People with a good sense of direction were the most apt to make the mistake. The railway line made an S-shaped bend around the airport, with the result that trains arrived in the station pointing in almost the opposite direction to the one in which their destinations lay. 'It's under the tunnel to the further platform,' Oliver told Orlando, 'even if your instinct tells you the opposite.'

'Tunnel, what tunnel?' Orlando answered. 'It's over the bloody footbridge. How long since you've been here?'

'Ten years or more,' Oliver had to admit.

'I'd have been fourteen,' was Orlando's inevitable reply.

'You still are,' Oliver said. They were almost on the bridge now. Oliver clapped an arm around his companion's back for a second. Nothing had to be read into that. Straight people did it all the time. 'Kid,' he said.

The platforms were raised above the surrounding land: airfield to one side, reeds – or was that sugar cane? – to the other. Crickets chirped in the darkness and a frog croaked. The wind blew warm. Veering for a moment it brought a trace of aircraft fuel to the nose. 'I love Spain,' Orlando said. 'It's good to be back.' There were only a few other people on the platform. Oliver wanted to throw his arm around Orlando a second time but restrained himself. This wasn't going to get easier, he thought.

The train took them into the centre of town, diving down underground for the last mile or so. They stopped beneath the main railway station, though they were not getting out here. This would be Oliver's place of rendezvous tomorrow with the stranger called Jorge who was going to hand over the mysterious package. Orlando caught his eye. 'Nerves?' he said, and pulled a face of mock apprehension. It was the first time today that either of them had referred to the original purpose of the expedition. They left the train at its terminus and headed up steps to street level. They were in the Alameda, the town's wide boulevard. Trees and grass sward ran down the middle of it, while the old buildings of its two sides, yellow ochre in the lamplight, were kept far apart by lanes of traffic, broad pavements and yet more lines of trees. 'I remember a bar near here,' Orlando said, turning his head from side to side as if trying to scent it on the breeze.

'You would do,' said Oliver, though he thought he knew it too. 'Do you mean the Antigua Casa?'

'You're right. It was called something like that.'

'It's over there.' Oliver waved an arm towards the other side of the Alameda. 'Behind those trees.'

They were soon standing at an old mahogany counter and topping up their levels with glasses of the sweet local wine, drawn from one of several black barrels high up on a rack behind the bar. The counter was spread with plates of prawns and mussels: treats for those on expense accounts, expensive traps for the unwary backpacker. Around them, caramel coloured walls were studded with sepia photographs of the sedate, more upmarket Málaga of a hundred years ago, with horse-drawn carriages among the palm trees on the sea-front *paseo*.

'Reckon we should find our *hostal* soon?' Oliver put this in the form of a question, though he meant it as a piece of elder-brotherly advice. 'We can go out again later if we want.'

They set off again along the Alameda. Orlando dived into a shop at one point and emerged with two bottles of wine. 'You never know when you're going to need one,' he said. 'Screw-top,' he added. 'I made sure. Hotel bedroom. Wine bottle. No corkscrew. Been there. Dire.'

Five minutes brought them to a turning near the cathedral; they had heard the dull clatter of its bell striking eleven – as if in vindication of Orlando's plan of campaign. Flights of stairs, almost dark. An entrance buzzer. A grille sliding back. '*Reservado?* Mister Keed?' They were shown to the door of a room and left to unlock and inspect it by themselves. Now was the moment Oliver had tried not to think about all day: Orlando and himself alone in a bedroom. Though in fact not thinking about it had not been so difficult: it was something his imagination had been unable to tackle. But the reality, now, was something else. An enormous double bed. They faced each other across it.

'Look,' Oliver began uncertainly, 'it's not a problem for me but you might prefer...'

'It was the only room they had when I booked,' said Orlando. 'So I don't think we'd get far if we asked to change now. Anyway, no problem.' He smiled mischievously. 'I can take care of myself.'

He probably could, Oliver thought. Though his build was slender and coltish, he was not far off six foot and used to manual work. They moved on to easier territory: checked out the bathroom. 'Two glasses,'said Orlando. 'Good.' Then they examined the view from the shuttered window down into the narrow street. 'We go eat?'

Late though it was, restaurants were still lit up and serving customers. They found one just a few minutes'away and ordered plates of Malaguena fried fish, which came fresh and sea-tasting in crisp gold batter, with a lemon half and crusty bread – plus the necessary bottle of red wine. Outside, the rubbish cart went by, clearing sacks and bins, though it was gone midnight. 'Málaga never sleeps,' said Oliver.

'Who needs sleep?' asked Orlando. 'Bed's another thing.'

What did he mean by that, Oliver wondered? To his surprise he didn't feel at all drunk: his senses were exceptionally keen and alert. He wondered if Orlando felt the same. But he wasn't surprised by what Orlando said next: by now he could almost see it coming. 'When did you first know you were gay?'

Oliver had a stock response to that one: he used it now. 'When did you first know you were straight?' It was quite a good tactic for sorting the serious thirsters after knowledge from the teases. Over the last few hours Oliver the statistician had narrowed the possible explanations of Orlando's behaviour down to three: he was gay and always had been, though he hadn't wanted Oliver to know that up to now; or, he wanted to turn the weekend into a lifestyle experiment, using Oliver – a presumably safe older man – as his guinea pig; or else, as Zara had suggested, he was quite simply a nutter.

But Oliver's question failed to flush Orlando out. He didn't answer it at all, but looked embarrassed by it or even hurt. Oliver immediately regretted having asked it – with hindsight it sounded unsubtle in the context of the relationship he seemed to be developing with him – and when Orlando changed the subject and began to talk about his time in the north of Spain near Logroño, was happy to go along. He would have to be patient, he told himself. Whatever game Orlando was playing, he would find out in the end.

He didn't have to wait long. As they began their walk back from the restaurant, along the lamplit street, Orlando asked teasingly, 'What's the difference between a straight boy and a gay one?'

'Don't know,' said Oliver warily. 'What is the difference?'

'Two pints of lager,' said Orlando. 'Here's another one. What's the difference between straight boys and gay ones?'

'Tell me,' said Oliver. He hoped Orlando didn't have twenty of these up his sleeve. It would make for a tedious end of the evening.

'They all go to bed with other boys but the straight ones hate themselves in the morning.' Then he swung round towards Oliver as if he were going to punch him in the chest – and Oliver's heart skipped a beat as he thought for an instant that that was exactly what Orlando was going to do. The boy was seriously deranged; or else he'd planned this all along: lead him on, get him drunk in a foreign town, then beat him up and leave him for dead in the street, taking cash and credit cards with him. But Orlando actually kissed him on the lips – not very gently. Because of his intoxicated state it was more of a head-butt, and it jarred the back of Oliver's neck. He threw his arms around Oliver at the same time and Oliver, barely able to believe what was happening, hugged and kissed him back, though a bit more tentatively.

When he could speak, Oliver said gently, 'And are you going to hate yourself in the morning?'

'Possibly,' Orlando said. 'But there's a first time for everything, *n'est-ce pas?*'

It was a first time for Oliver – to find himself walking through the back streets of a southern town, hand in hand with another man. He had been quite open about his sexuality for many years but even he would have drawn a prudent line at this. He kept the other fist half clenched just in case there should be any trouble. One or two people did indeed turn their heads to look at them, but only for a second or two of passing interest, and no challenge came.

They regained the safety of their *hostal*. And then, for the second time, they were alone together with a bed. And a figurine of the Virgin Mary, which Oliver now noticed for the first time, regarding them from on high, above the headboard.

'Open a bottle of wine,' Orlando commanded. Then, more doubtfully, 'You don't tie people up or do anything weird, do you?'

'No I don't,' said Oliver. He'd been right in one of his guesses at least.

'Good,' said Orlando. 'I thought you weren't that sort.'

'Just the normal things, I guess. You said yourself you knew how to take care of yourself. I don't think you'd let yourself get forced into anything you didn't want. Your muscles look good enough for action, from what I can see of them.' He reached out and playfully felt Orlando's left bicep through his shirt.

'Muscles can only do so much,' Orlando said. 'They're no good against guns and knives.'

'Guns and knives?' Oliver laughed out loud. 'You think I might be carrying a knife or a gun? Hand baggage only, remember. Checked at the airport. Post

117

nine-eleven. Come on.'

Orlando looked back at him with a serious expression. 'You thought I was going to go for you in the street just now. You didn't think I'd noticed that, but I did. We're just both being careful with each other, that's all. It's good.' Then he smiled and held out his hand, and Oliver absurdly kissed the back of it as if Orlando had been a dowager and the time two centuries ago.

Then they did pour two glasses of wine. They drank them leaning out of the open window, side by side. Street lamps lit the pavements a dull orange down below. The cathedral clock clanked one. They leant in towards each other, shoulders touching, two nests of wavy hair buffering together like springy cushions. Each could hear the other's breath, and feel his warmth.

Oliver made the next move. If he didn't, he thought, perhaps Orlando never would. They'd both removed their sweaters on the plane and stuffed them into their backpacks. Oliver now had only a T-shirt on, Orlando a broad-check shirt. Oliver stepped back from the window and pulled his T-shirt off. He'd always known he looked OK without his clothes on and, added to that, his recent photo and sex session with Bernd had given his confidence an extra boost. He might not be as young as Orly or as tall, but his chest was muscular and his stomach firm and taut.

'Hey, you're good,' said Orlando. And then – Oliver knew this was coming next – 'You don't look thirty-eight.'

'Now you.' Oliver nodded towards the buttons on Orly's shirt, and he obediently bowed his copper head and undid the buttons one by one. Then, with an extravagant gesture he might have got from drama school, released his arms and torso from the shirt and flung it to the floor.

Oliver couldn't help showing his reaction in his face. No wonder the kid had been called The Marmalade Cat. His chest was ornamented with a swirling pattern of fine bright hair that was nevertheless quite neat and symmetrical, fountaining up from his navel from a line that disappeared teasingly behind the waistband of his jeans. In the dull light of this bedroom the plumage looked almost orange. 'That's so beautiful,' Oliver said. 'I think I meant to say, you are.' Slowly he reached out his hands and laid the palms flat on Orlando's chest, just brushing his erect nipples with the forefingers and feeling the spongy bounce of that brilliant copper hair. He followed the pattern back to its source, the single orderly line arrowing straight down – save for a minimal detour round the navel's left-hand rim – into his jeans. 'Hey wait,' Orlando objected when Oliver's fingers began to push down inside. 'That's not fair. You've got to take something off next.'

They kept the game up a few minutes longer. Trainers next, then socks. 'I hope my feet don't smell,' Orlando said. Oliver assured him they did not. He wouldn't have cared a jot, though, if they had. Oliver unbuckled, then removed, his jeans. 'Good legs too,' Orlando said, as if he'd expected less and been agreeably surprised. 'Do you work out?'

'I used to,' Oliver said. Till Adi left him, that had been, but recently he'd let the routine drop. He thought that for the boy who now stood before him he would willingly train six days a week.

Slowly Orlando undid his belt, un-popped his fly studs and let his own jeans fall to the floor. He paused for a second – he was well practised at this, Oliver decided – then stepped out of them. His was no bodybuilder's physique, for which Oliver was somehow grateful, but there were serviceable farmer's-boy muscles attached to his coltish frame, including a well defined pair of calves, low-slung at the back of his legs like elongated ripe plums – and worn proudly like those of teenagers who have only recently acquired them. Like his arms they were spangled with fine gold light-catching hairs. He looked back at Oliver and said, 'I didn't know anyone wore knicks like that any more.'

'And I'd never have imagined you wore dreadful ones like that.' They both laughed. But they could not have been less interested in each other's choice of underwear. Simultaneously they each made a grab for the other's last claim to modesty and yanked the fig leaves down. Neither of them was laughing now.

'My God, you're big,' said Orly. Oliver had been expecting that. His secret weapon – metaphorically speaking.

'And you're pretty well hung yourself,' Oliver

delivered the only acceptable answer, though in Orlando's case it was quite true. He nudged this newest discovered treasure with the backs of his fingers. 'A real redhead,' he added. 'Marmalade Cat even down to here.'

They broke away from each other. Orlando refilled the wine glasses. They sat side by side on the edge of the bed, sipping from the glasses that each held in one hand, occasionally exchanging them through linking arms and raising them to each other's lips, each fondling with his free hand what had been kept secret from him up till now, and exploring the soft warm inner surface of the other's thighs.

The wine was finished. Orlando's legs were shaking, one knee tapping up and down. 'Your engine's running,' Oliver said.

They were lying tangled together on the bed without knowing how they'd got there, exploring everywhere with lips and fingers and tongues. 'Can I fuck you?' Oliver whispered close to Orly's ear. He was long past believing this might be Orlando's first time.

'I think so,' Orly whispered back. He sounded doubtful. 'No wait.' His body tensed. 'We haven't got a thing.'

'There's one in my backpack,' Oliver said, sounding a bit shamefaced.

'You planned it all along.'

'I swear I didn't. Cross my heart. It's just that I always

keep some there.' Already he was reaching over the side of the bed, groping in the backpack which was on the floor, while trying not to lose contact with Orlando with his other hand. Orlando, compliant as Oliver had never in his wildest dreams even dared to hope, turned half away from him, on his side. Dear God, Oliver thought as he quickly sheathed himself, he even has beautiful feet. They were long and narrow, the second toes an elegant few millimetres longer than the first ones. Oliver gave himself one more moment to admire Orlando's thighs and calves before accepting the invitation that lay concealed between his smooth buttocks, and easing his way in. He came quickly, for all the quantity that he had drunk, and Orlando made contented quacking, grunting noises – probably something to do with being brought up in a farmyard, Oliver thought facetiously – while Oliver worked him to his own climax with his hand. He came extravagantly, noisily; then Oliver kissed the nape of his neck as his gasps and spasms died to quiet. A few moments later they were both asleep, still joined, as it were, at the hip or – to be more prosaically literal – a few inches further down.

SEVEN

By morning the pair of them had somehow disentangled themselves, unconsciously found their way in between the sheets, and were lolling out of opposite sides of the bed like a long-married couple. Earlier they had been lying on their backs, both snoring contentedly. Oliver was the first to find himself properly awake. It took him a few minutes of awestruck contemplation to reassure himself that what he remembered of last night, what he was piecing together in his mind like some miraculous jigsaw, was not some teasing dream. When the first intimations of waking life began to come from Orly a few minutes later, Oliver reached out experimentally for his cock. It was semi-hard, but Orly's hand brushed Oliver's away. Oliver was neither offended nor surprised. As the Kid himself had said, straight men hated themselves the next morning. And if Orlando wasn't straight – and it seemed highly probable on last night's evidence that he wasn't – well, as Oliver knew from his own experience, a lot of gay men hated themselves the next morning too. What else could Oliver expect, after the unexpectedness of last night? Even if, in hindsight, there appeared to be a kind of magnificent inevitability entwined with that very unexpectedness.

He remembered an occasion at university, when a straight friend of his had been confiding in him about his love life and the progress he'd been making with a girl he'd been chasing. The friend had said – and Oliver remembered it word for word, even after eighteen years

– 'I've screwed her of course, but where do I go from here?'

Oliver had had no answer to that. Unless it had been: marry her and have lots of beautiful children. But that was not the answer his friend had wanted to hear, he was sure of that. Now, putting the same question to himself, he still had no answer. He wasn't going to marry Orlando. Nor, which was more to the point, was the Kid going to marry him. They would not be having lots of beautiful children with marmalade hair and forget-me-not eyes. What they *were* going to do, on the other hand, was spend a weekend in Málaga together, without any other company, and after that there still remained two weeks of a training course to finish, working together on teaching practice every afternoon. Oliver's heart began to sink.

A voice, almost a groan, came from the other side of the bed. 'My head's killing me.' And then, 'How's yours?' Which cheered Oliver slightly, like a cold chink of light on a winter morning.

'Not great,' Oliver said. 'Stay there. I'll get you some aspirin.' He crawled out of bed and fished in his backpack. He looked down at himself to make sure he wasn't grotesquely still wearing last night's condom. He wasn't. It was on the floor beside the backpack. He must have thrown it there, asleep or drunkenly, during the night. How these things happened was always a mystery. A minute later he was at Orlando's side of the bed with a glass of water in one hand and three tablets in the palm of the other. 'Take these. You'll be OK.'

Orlando opened his eyes and studied the gifts with what looked like incredulity, though he was probably simply waking up. Then he jacked himself up on one elbow and put the tablets in his mouth, washing them down with most of the water. Half in, half out of the bedclothes, he still looked beautiful to Oliver, even in his present wrecked state. But Oliver was not going to be so foolish as to tell him so right now. Instead, surprisingly, it was Orly who spoke. He looked into Oliver's eyes as steadily as he was able to. 'I did pick the right man, didn't I? For my crazy drunken experiment. One who travels with aspirin in his luggage. You're probably used to all this.'

Not exactly, thought Oliver. He said, 'And do you hate yourself this fine morning?' Sunshine was streaming between the shutters on a tide of southern warmth.

Orlando considered for a moment. 'Maybe,' he said thoughtfully. Then, 'I don't hate you though.'

Yes, but it's himself he's got to live with, Oliver thought. He said, 'Go back to sleep if you want.'

'I need to piss,' said Orly. 'Rather painfully.' He hauled himself awkwardly out of bed, using the naked, crouching Oliver's shoulder as a handhold, the way an infirm person might have used the bedside locker or a Zimmer frame. Slightly to Oliver's surprise Orlando ruffled his hair before moving away to empty his bladder into the wash-basin – with some difficulty, as he now had a very full erection. Oliver stayed where he was. By chance his position relative to Orlando and his reflection in the basin mirror afforded him the unusual spectacle of his recent bed-mate's back and front views at the same time: in the mirror, his forward-bending head, the face almost masked by the radiant curls; the bright hair of his chest and all the way down; the long and plump penis that Orly was only intermittently managing to keep pressed down and pointing in the right direction; and from the rear, the square shoulders, neat firm buttocks, shapely thighs, and those luscious calf muscles that made Oliver want to take a bite out of each of them. In a way, and despite all the hideous embarrassments that would now have to be lived through by both of them, last night's adventure might have been worth it just for this.

*

Oliver's rendezvous with the man called Jorge was scheduled for the early evening. This was just as well given that it was nearly midday before Orlando and he felt well enough to emerge from their room, showered and dressed, though still feeling as delicate as butterflies newly hatched from their pupal shells. Oliver fully expected that Orly would want to go off on his own and spend the day hating himself quietly, without the nagging presence of Oliver to keep reminding him of why he was doing so. But he showed no sign of wanting to go off on his own. 'We need to find coffee,' he announced instead. He was wearing dark glasses: something which he had had the forethought to bring and which Oliver hadn't.

The streets were filled with warm air and sunshine.

When there was a rare lull in the noise of the traffic, sparrows could be hear chattering in the trees. They had coffee on the pavement, under an awning, in the Calle Alcazabilla, watching the world go about its business, and began to feel slightly better. Oliver was relieved that Orly hadn't suggested they begin with a beer; that would have had him worried. On the table in front of them was an ashtray emblazoned with the bull's head logo of Osborne's sherry. Oliver found his eyes kept going to it. It was as if he read in it a message addressed to himself. Bull by the horns, it said. Oliver took a deep breath and said it. 'We can get separate rooms for tonight if you want. You don't have to be stuck with me.'

'It's OK,' Orlando answered non-committally. 'I don't need to change – unless you do.'

'I don't have a problem,' Oliver said, his tone similarly neutral.

'Only I'd rather treat last night as a one-off, if you don't mind. If that's possible.'

'It's possible,' said Oliver, feeling absolutely flattened. Knowing in advance that that was what Orlando would say was no protection. 'I wasn't expecting anything other. You want to draw a line under it. Naturally you do.' He found he was unable to look at Orly as he said this, but gazed at the ashtray as if it held immense fascination for him. 'If you can, I can.' But his heart was still sinking. Sharing a bed chastely with Orlando had been a difficult enough prospect yesterday evening, when he had had no intimation that Orlando was going to leap on him and kiss him in the street. Tonight, after all that had happened in the meantime… Well, he simply couldn't imagine how it was to be done. But, 'No worries,' was what he said.

A young gypsy woman approached the table, dressed entirely in black, and holding out a single red rose-bud towards Oliver, as if expecting him – having taken and paid for it first of course – to present it romantically to Orlando. It seemed at that moment a particularly cruel joke on the part of the gods. *'Nada,'* Oliver said. 'Go away.' But Orlando took pity on the young woman with the shining dark hair and eyes, and gave her two euros in exchange for the crimson flower. When she had gone, he twirled it in his fingers. 'What the fuck do we do with this?' he said. He looked for a second as if he was going to poke it playfully through one of the open button-holes of Oliver's shirt, but then clearly decided it would have been grossly inappropriate at that particular moment. He tucked it into one of his own instead.

*

Even when seriously hung over Orlando still liked walking, it appeared. And Oliver had no objection to being dragged off on a tour of the town on foot. 'You know, people hardly ever visit Málaga,' Orlando mused. 'People like us, I mean. We arrive by the planeload and are either bussed down the coast to the resorts or head off inland to Granada and Seville. But it's a good little town.'

Oliver, though, couldn't help comparing it with the last

southern town he'd been to: Funchal, a month ago. In comparison with the Madeiran capital Málaga seemed seedy and rough; even its beautiful buildings had a brooding, watchful air about them, as if they had seen an unwelcome abundance of the cruelties of life and expected to see plenty more. Oliver imagined himself showing Madeira, one day, to an admiring Orlando. In your dreams, he told himself. Still, it was pleasant enough just to be here in the spring sunshine. With Orlando. Enjoy the moment, he thought. This moment, this man. Who knew what nightmares even tomorrow might bring, from arrest at Gatwick on drug-trafficking charges to Orlando's coming to hate him? Of those particular two prospects, the second, Oliver found, was decidedly the worse. For now, though, he had no more complaints about the company he was in than he would have had about winning the lottery on a roll-over night.

They wandered around the gardens and fountains of the old Alcazaba, the eleventh century fortress of the Moors, and then climbed up the cypress-grown hillside to the ruins of the Castillo de Gibralfaro. A few rough looking individuals lurked among the trees; whether their purposes were sexual or piratical was unclear; but Oliver and the Kid were neither mugged nor propositioned. Perhaps that was simply because there were two of them. The climb was more than worthwhile. They had expected panoramas of the town beneath, the port and the sparkling sea, the sierras on the landward side. Quite unexpected was the additional sight of the Rock of Gibraltar, thirty miles along the coast, looking like a beached, dark, hump-backed whale. And then, on the distant horizon, the faint blue trace of Africa: a line of mountains that looked as small as a row of silhouetted teeth.

It was late in the afternoon by the time they felt ready to put food into their stomachs, and descended the hill to go and find some. Even then they didn't feel like taking any alcohol with it, but contented themselves with omelettes and salad, washed down with liberal quantities of Coca-cola, outside a small café near the port.

'You don't have to come with me to this rendezvous,' Oliver told his companion. 'After all, it's me that's getting paid.'

'Would you rather go on your own?' Orlando asked.

'Not specially,' Oliver answered.

'Then I'll come with you,' said Orlando, exactly as Oliver had hoped he would.

Why had he been so keen to come to Málaga with Oliver in the first place? Oliver still had no answer to that, even after the events of the previous night. Perhaps it really had been an experiment with his own sexuality, perhaps even a sort of test, or a bet with himself. (I can prove I'm straight: I can share a bed with a gay man and nothing'll happen to me.) If that were the case then Orlando had spectacularly lost. Perhaps Oliver would ask him one day. But not today. Not here. Not now. And whatever Orlando's motivation, Oliver felt more than a little honoured that the Kid had chosen to carry out his experiment with him.

'I'll come with you if you like,' Orlando repeated.

'Sorry. Of course I'd like. Very much. So please do.'

They set off round the sea-front promenades towards the railway station. As they walked, Oliver explained the arrangements: something he hadn't done before, as it was a sensitive matter and, until now, there had been no need to go into it. 'We meet in the cafeteria, or one of them. I spread a map on the table in front of me...'

'So do any number of arriving tourists, I'd imagine,' Orlando interrupted.

'Ah, but they'd have maps of southern Spain. Mine's a map of the north, something you'd only notice if you peered at it quite closely. There won't be too many of those.'

'Blimey,' said Orlando. 'It's like a fucking spy movie. Gets better and better.'

'I hope you're right about that,' said Oliver a bit grimly. 'Anyway, what's supposed to happen next is this. He – Jorge is his name, I have to keep remembering – comes up to me and asks me where I'm going. I'm supposed to say' Granada'while pointing clearly to Burgos on the map. Then he knows he's found the right guy and hands me the famous parcel.'

Orlando, walking alongside Oliver in the sunshine, was shaking his head in a pantomime of disbelief. 'Incredible,' he finally said. The station, a vast barn of a building, appeared before them as they turned a corner at the end of a long straight street.

Under the arching canopy of the concourse were rows of seats, placed as though the arrival and departure of trains for all over Andalucía were spectacles in their own right. To one side was a newspaper kiosk, to the other the cafeteria and bar where the handover was scheduled for seven o'clock. The station clock now showed twelve minutes to. 'At least we can have a beer while we're waiting,' Orlando said.

Oliver peered at him through the suspicion of a frown. 'Are you quite sure you ever want to look at a beer again after last night?'

Orlando stared seriously at him for a second as if trying to choose between a number of possible answers to a question that had included those thorny words *last night*. But he clearly decided to deploy none of them. Instead, his face relaxed into a grin and he just said, 'Come on. My shout.'

They collected their beers from the counter and went to sit at a table some distance from it, in the most sparsely populated part of the big room. Oliver reached into his backpack, pulled out the map of northern Spain and spread it on the table in front of him as if laying out some sort of bait.

Minutes passed. It was difficult to drink slowly. And then a young man came sidling up; he was swarthy faced, with unkempt clothes and hair, and a moustache the size of a large mouse. He peered over Oliver's shoulder. *'Donde van?'* he said.

Oliver felt as if he were acting in a play. He felt as he had done when he was an extra in the ballet and had found himself rushing out onstage to arrest Othello. Now, just as theatrically, using his whole arm for the gesture, he tapped his middle finger smartly on the city of Burgos and said, 'Granada,' exactly according to the script.

'Bueno,' said the young man and went on in Spanish, 'Can you take this with you?' He took off his own backpack and placed it on the table, right on top of the outspread map. Oliver experienced a frisson of apprehension as he waited for the contents to emerge. And then they did. Jorge pulled out exactly what Donald had told him to expect: a very flat parcel indeed. It consisted of two sheets of strong cardboard, not much bigger than A4, sandwiched together and taped all around the edges. Whatever was between them could be little thicker than a piece of paper.

'You understand Spanish?' the young man asked as he handed the thing to Oliver. Oliver nodded diffidently, but Orly said, in such a capable, confident way, *'Si, si, seguro,'* that the other turned and delivered the rest of his instructions to him. 'It's a picture for framing. It goes to the shop in London that you know already, or so I was told.'

Orlando glanced at Oliver, then said to Jorge, 'Yes, the one in Shepherd Market. We know it.'

'That's all,' said Jorge gravely. 'Payment will be made on delivery. Please do not try to open the package. It's very carefully packed and could be damaged by being handled. It's very special. Keep it with you at all times, even when you sleep. On the plane, hand baggage.'

'I'll handcuff it to my wrist,' Orlando joked, and Oliver smiled, having more or less understood what he had said, though he wouldn't have been able to say it himself in Spanish. He admired Orlando's ease in the language.

But Jorge was not amused. 'Be serious,' he said, his tone becoming quite nasty for a second. 'Now, *adios.*' He picked up his bag, abruptly turned and walked quickly away from them and out of the door onto the concourse.

Oliver and Orlando gazed at each other blankly for a moment, then Orlando said, 'Wow. That's a scene I might have expected to play on telly or on the stage one day. Never thought I'd get to do it in real life.'

'Nor me,' said Oliver.

Neither of them had given a thought to how they might spend the rest of their evening: the whole day had been a lead-up to the handover and now that that had been safely accomplished they found themselves at a loss. They left the cafeteria and headed, slowly and aimlessly, back up Calle Cuarteles towards the Alameda and the centre of town. 'So,' Orly eventually came to it. 'What do you think it is?'

'Your guess is worth as much as mine, I should think,' said Oliver. 'You know as much as I do about the last time. That was a painting in a frame, this one looks like a painting without a frame – just as he said. And my last trip coincided with an art theft... So who knows what we're going to read in the newspapers when we get back?' He paused for a second's reflection. 'If we get back.' A thought struck him. 'Oh my God.'

'Oh my God, what?'

'Nothing. Nothing at all. I just remembered something. A friend of mine's supposed to be staying at my place on Tuesday and Wednesday. I'd forgotten all about it. That's all.'

Orlando was interested. 'What sort of friend?'

'A German one. His name's Bernd. He's not – I mean, he's nobody that special. Just someone I happened to meet when I was in Cologne.'

'I see,' said Orly, and he obviously did. He changed the subject back again. 'So are we going to steam the tapes open and see what we've got?'

'You can if you want,' said Oliver. 'But I'm certainly not going to.' And Orlando understood the subtext of that answer just as clearly as he had the previous one.

They were back on the Alameda now, and the open door of the Antigua Casa was signalling to them from across the way as clearly as if it had been a lighthouse, beaming out its welcome of distant chatter and light.

There was no longer any doubt where they were going next.

Talking your own language with a friend in a foreign bar or restaurant, you imagine yourself in a cocoon of safety, incapable of being overheard or understood. But the reality is almost the opposite. Your conversation becomes a homing beacon for anyone within earshot who shares your native tongue or can speak it tolerably well. And so it became for Orlando and Oliver now. After all, they were in relatively cosmopolitan Málaga, not in some lost village of Tibet. A man approached them as they stood near the counter, sipping their second beer of the day, among the sepia photographs and the cool azulejo tiles. He was about thirty years old, with thick dark hair, was stockily built though not especially tall, and, though hardly handsome, had a pleasant enough face. He said, in confident if Spanish-accented English, 'Hallo, I heard you speaking English. I wonder where you from.' Oliver experienced a vague sense of déjà vu, half expecting to find himself receiving a second parcel for delivery to London. At least the new arrival was holding a fairly full *copita* of something in his hand, so it was unlikely that he had come over in order to cadge a drink.

'England,' Orlando beat Oliver to it. 'What about you?'

'Córdoba,' the other answered quickly. 'Know where that is?'

'Of course,' Orlando said. 'And I've been there.'

'Me too.' And Oliver added the expected, polite cliché, 'A beautiful city.' But he was careful to keep his tone polite rather than rapt. He wasn't sure if he wanted to prolong the conversation.

'Tourists? Up from the resorts?'

'Something like that,' Oliver answered, still cautious.

To Orlando's ears that sounded suspiciously as if they had something to hide. He added quickly, 'We're also looking for work, sort of.'

Their new acquaintance laughed. 'We're all doing that. That's what I'm doing here. At least I'm looking for sales. I sell furniture.' He caught sight of looks of alarm on the faces of the other two and said, 'Don't worry. I sell to restaurants and bars, not to the people I meet in them.'

Oliver relaxed suddenly and saw that Orlando had too. Curious how the discovery that a stranger has a purpose to his existence that is unconnected with yourself could allay that initial feeling of *what does he want with me?*

Orlando carried on. 'We'll both be looking for work soon, if we aren't already. We're just about to qualify as English language teachers. We'll probably be looking in this direction for our first jobs.'

What Oliver said next he said tritely, without thinking; it was a conversational reflex. 'Though not necessarily together.' But as the short phrase came out a silence fell on the other two, and to Oliver it seemed that the silence extended to the whole of the busy bar. It was as if, with those four simple words, he had dropped a pebble down some deep dark hole or chasm and it was falling towards a vast unseen lake that was his future life. He didn't want to catch Orlando's eyes at that moment but by some accident he did. And what he read in them was the information that the now irretrievable pebble was heading for another unseen lake as well, the one that was Orlando's future. The impact waves would go on rippling out across both those lakes as far as the furthest shores.

Orlando broke the silence. 'Who knows?' He tossed the remark away with a brittle laugh.

The stranger had caught something of the significance of the moment, but only a faint trace. He had no idea of the hinterland of that brief exchange; he knew nothing of any relationship that might or might not exist between them. He said, 'Well, if you are looking for work in Andalucía, I know someone who could, maybe, help you. Only maybe, of course. It's always only maybe.'

'Any leads are welcome,' said Orlando. 'Grateful for any contacts you can offer.' He was careful, Oliver noticed, not to say who would be grateful. No *I* nor *we*, no *us* nor *me*.

'Someone I know in Seville. He has a school. He employs people like you. British and American I mean. If you wanted to contact him…'

'I'd like to, anyway,' said Orlando, not looking at

Oliver. 'Do you have an address? A phone number? Er…'

'My name is Felipe,' said the stranger. He began to rummage in a pocket while Oliver and Orly gave him their own names. Felipe fished out a small, battered address book. 'Guttierez, Guttierez,' he muttered a few times as he riffled the pages. 'Eduardo Guttierez López. Yes, here.' Orlando then had to rummage in his own pockets for something to write on and with. The best he could come up with was an old London bus ticket. Oliver helped him out by producing a biro from a side pocket in his backpack. He was quite glad not to have to open up the main compartment, to reveal its precious cargo to curious eyes.

'If you decide to go and see him, or phone him,' said Felipe, when Orlando had finished cramming name, address and phone number on the back of the bus ticket, 'tell him I gave you his name. We're old friends.'

'Felipe who?' Orlando asked.

'Suarez Villacarillo,' Felipe answered, and so Orlando had another long Spanish name to cram into the tiny space. Oliver, now standing about with nothing much to do while Orlando accomplished this, asked Felipe if he'd like another drink.

It was hardly surprising that Felipe had homed in on them, especially if he was gay – as Oliver thought he probably was. Right from the beginning Oliver had noticed the glances that were aimed in Orlando's direction, usually by women but sometimes by men too, when he entered a public space with him. On these occasions he felt as if he were being bathed in the reflected light of Orlando's beauty, as people who find themselves in the company of the extremely beautiful often do. Oliver had mixed feelings about this, since he had no *a priori* objection to being a focus of admiring attention himself. But in Orlando's company he felt as if he were escorting someone with the recognition factor of a Jude Law or a David Beckham, rather than a bit player in a Post Office commercial. He had noticed that Orlando generally seemed unaware of the attention he received. Perhaps he was just so used to it. He couldn't really be unaware though: Oliver had not forgotten his shameless behaviour on the plane, trading on his physical charms in order to obtain double rations of gin and wine. But he also remembered how he had first studied Orly's face at extremely close quarters on the Marsh Link train, and how oblivious the boy had been – or seemed to be – to his attention back then.

As the second drink led to a third, Oliver began to wonder if they would have Felipe's company for the entire evening. He was a pleasant enough man, but Oliver had recently been getting used to having Orly's company entirely to himself, and with a bittersweet sense of impending loss, was expecting this evening to be the last ever occasion on which he would have this privilege. It also crossed his mind that, if Felipe was gay, he might want to try and take Orlando off him. He thought, with grim resolution: let him try. Conversation was flowing easily between the three of them, mostly about general things – Spanish wines, the cost of living in London – and mostly in English, though Orlando did drift off into Spanish from time to time, presumably in order to show off his prowess in the language. Oliver wondered whom he most wanted to impress by doing this: Felipe or him?

Then, quite suddenly, Felipe announced that he would have to leave them now, as he was meeting people later on. He gave Orlando his phone number before he went, but extended his smile to Oliver also as he said, 'Call me when you're back in Spain. We'll have a drink or something.'

When Felipe had gone, Oliver turnd to Orly. 'Well, you certainly collect them. Moths to the candle flame.' He'd intended to be humorous, but was dismayed to find himself sounding bitchy. Almost camp, almost bitter.

Orlando brushed the question aside. 'I don't think about it.' His tone was almost as sharp. Annoyed. Oliver could only think of one possible reason why Orlando might be annoyed with him. It had to do with what he had said when Orlando mentioned looking for jobs in Spain.' Not necessarily together.'Had he – incredibly – been miffed, disappointed even, by that remark? Oliver didn't dare let himself think it: it was far too flattering. In any case there had been their conversation this morning. One-night stands were one-night stands.

Felipe had given them the address of a good fish restaurant at a place called El Palo, on the outskirts of Málaga, and almost on the beach. He also told them the number of the bus that would take them there and where to catch it. They found the restaurant easily after their short bus ride: it was a simple no-nonsense place that catered more for locals on their Saturday night out than for tourists. Oliver was glad of that. It meant that no-one raised an eyebrow at his arriving with a backpack and insisting on keeping it with him, under the table, one of his legs firmly planted through one of the straps. If or when he needed to visit the loo it was arranged that Orlando's leg would take over in his absence. They ate bowls of mussels and then various plates of fried fish, garnished with extravagantly large lemon halves. Oliver enjoyed food like this, though not everybody he knew shared his taste. It was a bonus to discover that Orlando did.

Over their second bottle of Marqués de Cáceres Oliver returned to the subject of Orlando's acting career. 'You wonder why I haven't made more of a go of it of course,' Orly told him candidly. 'Everybody does. I guess the main thing is, which may surprise you, there isn't a limitless demand for red-headed men. There was Robert Redford, of course, whose name almost tells you redhead. Now, in England anyway, there's Damian Lewis who scoops all the ginger parts on TV. Next it'll probably be Sam Aston.'

'Who?'

'He's still only a child. Plays Chesney in Coronation Street. You'd know the one. Then there's the name. There's usually only room for about one Orlando in the market at any given time. And Orlando Bloom happened

142

to get there first.'

Oliver was dismayed. 'You're blaming your bad luck on Orlando Bloom, and a kid who won't even be playing adult roles for another ten years? That sounds terribly defeatist. You can always change your name. I've had actor friends who did just that.'

Orly shifted in his seat. 'I suppose it's not just those things. There was something else. I took some bad advice once... I don't really want to go into it all. But the upshot was that I started doing' extra'work when things began to flag. I mean working as an extra for TV and so on. And the trouble with that is that you find you've blown your cred as an actor. Nobody wants to know you any more. It paid me a bit of money, it was better than bar work, but that was it.' He smiled at a memory. 'I grew my hair real long at one point – even had a bit of a beard. Played Vikings in the background of one or two crap films.'

'Pity I missed them. You must have looked great,' Oliver said without thinking.

Orlando laughed. 'Not as good as all that. I looked more like a Somerset cider-head than a Viking, truth be told.'

When the bill finally came it was much bigger than they'd been expecting, but Oliver gamely paid it, refusing Orlando's protesting offer to pay his half. He pointed out that it was he who was getting paid for the trip and had had the free plane ticket. But he knew that wasn't the real reason.

Typically it was Orly who said, 'Let's walk back, it's only a mile or two.' And you couldn't get lost provided you kept the sea on your left.

They walked along the beach itself, although they realised that they would have to leave it at some point before they reached the eastern mole of the port, which they could see extending into the sea about a mile ahead of them. Despite rocks and other obstructions the walk along the shore was not hazardous because the moon was still practically full and such clouds as hung about it were mere silver wisps. There were few sounds to be heard, but those that there were came to Oliver with great distinctness. There was the regular breathing of the sea: its long rhythmic sigh of withdrawal, the pregnant silence that followed, then the gentle slap of the next incoming wave. From the landward side came only an occasional human voice, raised in an angry shout, or a dog abruptly barking. Ahead of them sporadic bangs and crashes came from the hidden docks where, under arc lights, work was clearly going on all night. Lastly, there was the sound of Orlando's jeans rubbing together at the thighs, scritch-scritch, as he walked. Presently Oliver would be sharing a bed with Orlando and his thighs – and somehow not having sex with him. He still couldn't imagine how it was to be done.

As if he had heard Oliver's thoughts, Orly chose that moment to throw an arm around Oliver's shoulder.

'Now listen, Marmalade Kid,' Oliver said, 'I won't

have you flirting with me. We have an agreement about tonight, right? So don't start making it difficult for me. I mean, making it more difficult.' Orlando withdrew his arm without comment.

They continued to pick their way along the beach in silence for a minute or so. The sea sighed and slapped at intervals: a metronome set to its slowest tempo. Then Orly said, 'Supposing I change my mind?'

'About what?' Oliver's tone was huffy, though he could hardly have had any doubt about what.

'About tonight. About what I said this morning.'

'Look.' Oliver stopped and turned to face him, suddenly angry. 'Whatever kind of a prick-tease are you? Supposing you change your mind? Supposing you don't? Supposing I change my mind? Supposing we did the wrong thing last night? Supposing we didn't? How do you think you're making me feel? And then you go and get all sulky on me in the Antigua Casa – when you're talking about coming here to work. What are you fucking playing at? I don't know how I'm supposed to make sense of you.' The storm abated as suddenly as it had arisen. 'Sorry.'

'I didn't mean it like that at all,' said Orly in a crushed voice. 'There's things you don't know about me. I only meant, if I change my mind – I mean if I have changed my mind – would you think less of me? Would you think me a complete fucking idiot?'

'No,' said Oliver carefully. 'That's about the one thing

I wouldn't think.'

Orlando's next remark took Oliver by surprise. 'I suppose you'll be sleeping with this Bernd character when he comes to stay with you next week.' He delivered this flatly as if not really wanting an answer.

'I don't know,' Oliver said. 'Maybe yes, maybe no.' Then he quipped bitterly, riskily, 'Depends if I get a better offer. No, but seriously now. Since yesterday I haven't actually been thinking very much about next week – not about Bernd, not about anything else. Does that surprise you?' There was no answer from Orlando, who was looking down at the rocks beneath his feet, his face lost in shadow. Oliver continued. 'I don't know what's happening next week. I don't even know what's happening tonight. Or what's happening now.' He discovered that he was close to tears.

'Yes you do,' said Orlando. 'We both do.' Then he replicated his gesture of the previous night, though more elegantly, less drunkenly, abruptly looking up, taking the single necessary pace towards Oliver and drawing him into an embrace, kissing his mouth. They both heard the quiet knock of a wave, then its long withdrawing sigh.

They didn't have sex on the beach in the end. It wasn't that comfortable, and they were too uncertain of their environment. At that time of night would there be people, unseen but seeing, above them on the raised promenade and the hill behind? They had heard the occasional dog. So they made their way back along the beach, climbing off it finally to skirt the port area and regain the centre of town. Orlando, in a perverse spirit of bravado, insisted they dive into a late open bar for a nightcap. It was a rough place, crammed full of Spanish sailors and stevedores, and Oliver and Orlando – especially the fair-haired Orlando – stood marked out as the unwelcome strangers they were. It was not a comfortable experience and even Orlando, despite his initial bravado and fluent Spanish, was not keen to linger for more than one quick drink.

In the *hostal* bedroom, and undressed, this time it was Orlando who reached into Oliver's backpack for a condom and – after courteously asking permission – fucked Oliver. He did this rather roughly and without much finesse: something which surprised Oliver, since he had found gentleness to be one of the hallmarks of Orlando's nature. He would have to talk to him about it should the experience ever be repeated – though Oliver was fairly certain that after this weekend it wouldn't be. On the other hand, Oliver was no longer able to sustain the illusion that sex with another man might be something new to Orly. He'd still thought that might be the case as recently as yesterday night, even tried to start believing it again during their conversation – the' last night was a one-off' conversation – of earlier today. Oliver was not going to start believing that little pretence again even if Orlando were to fall on his knees and swear on the tomb of his late mother. Not that he really thought Orly would attempt to deny his sexual orientation now. Oliver gave him credit for that at least. He had said on the beach, 'There are things about me you don't know.' Well obviously there were: they'd only known each other two weeks. One of those things was clearly the fact that he was used to having sex at least, if not actual affairs, with men. Oliver wasn't bothered which. If Orlando wanted to tell him he would do so in his own good time – if more time together was something they were going to have.

'Something I haven't told you.' It was Oliver speaking, as he mopped at his chest with the corner of the sheet. 'Before I knew you – though it was after I'd first seen you on that train – I followed you once in Piccadilly.' They were lying side by side now, on top of the bedclothes. Oliver, once he considered himself clean and dry, turned the attention of his fingers to Orly's nipples and marmalade chest hair. As he stroked him he recounted the Piccadilly incident in detail, even to the smart coat and trousers Orly had been wearing. 'It would have been about the third week in February. I guess you'd have just had your interview for the course.'

'That's right,' said Orly, his voice registering flattered surprise, if not wonder. 'I'd had no other reason to be in Piccadilly before that for months.' He half sat up, propped on one elbow, to look Oliver in the eyes. 'And you followed me because, because you'd seen me on a train? Wow. I don't know quite what to say.'

'If I'd known then what I know now I'd have asked you back to my flat. But you weren't exactly loitering. I'm not quite so brazen as to proposition handsome young strangers who are hurrying purposefully along a street to catch a train.'

'Now I think about it,' said Orly, 'I must have some memory of that. Not that you followed me, obviously, I couldn't have known that, but that you passed me in the street and that I'd seen you on the train.'

'How do you mean?'

'Just that if you remembered me, I must have remembered you.'

'Get off,' said Oliver realistically. 'Gay men of thirty-eight remember men of twenty-four. It doesn't work the other way round.'

'Well maybe at a subcutaneous level then.'

'Subconscious, you pillock.'

'I meant subconscious.' They both laughed. 'Yeah, but when we met that Monday morning, it was nice to see your face, to be sitting talking with you rather than with any of the others. Like I'd always known you. So you see, I probably did remember.' There were crumbs of comfort for Oliver in that. 'You know what?' Orlando sat up on the bed.

'What?' said Oliver.

'I think we should crack open that other bottle of wine.'

*

The cathedral bell tolling for mass on Sunday morning set the pattern for the day. It was to be a day of tolling

149

bells, of ticking clocks, of countdowns. Countdown towards the flight back, to the potentially dangerous encounters with authority at Málaga airport and at Gatwick. Both of them were conscious of this as they energetically pleasured each other on waking and then took their morning showers.

There was the countdown towards the end of this weekend fling: to the moment when – if they weren't both in the hands of the police before that moment was reached – they came to the parting of their homeward ways at Victoria station and said … what?' See you in the morning, then'?' Come back to my place'? Oliver tried not to think ahead to that particular moment.

Countdown to the moment they resumed their roles as training course participants on Monday morning. Tomorrow. Oliver's imagination balked at that completely. And then the countdown to Tuesday, to Bernd's impending visit and the imponderable complications of that. Bernd. You waited months for a bus to come along and then two arrived together. Oliver refused to allow himself the thought: Orlando and I are having an affair. Still less: Orlando and I are destined to become an item.

The day was already very warm by the time they tumbled out into it. The clock was propelling them inexorably towards their afternoon flight. There was only time for a short stroll along the Paseo del Parque before lunch, which ended up being a paella, colourfully garnished with red peppers and green peas, that they ate standing up at the gleaming steel counter of a new bar in the Alameda. Then it was time to head for the train that would take them back to the airport. They talked of inconsequential things, too nervous about the coming journey to talk of that, and as for anything that might happen after clearing customs at Gatwick, well, that was off-limits as a subject for conversation for both of them. There were too many ticking time-bombs that Oliver didn't want to explode prematurely. Perhaps the same ones were ticking for Orly. Or perhaps he had time-bombs of his own to deal with.

'Hand luggage only,' they said as they checked in. Orlando gave the woman behind the desk a blue-eyed, little-boy smile and said, *'Con una ventana? Se puede?'* And after a little juggling on the computer, was awarded a window seat.

Passport control next. Then the terror of the scanner. They both passed through the arch, unchallenged by bleeps, and Oliver wondered what the X-ray was making of his mystery parcel. Did the scanner simply film it from the side? In which case it would reveal only the edges of pieces of cardboard and paper or canvas. Or did another camera take shots from above or below? Revealing in all their glory the cartoon outlines of a missing masterpiece? To his horror Oliver saw the backpack seized and himself beckoned to it. He was made to rummage through it. His hands and face went clammy with sweat; they'd see that surely. They'd hear his irregular nervous breathing, feel his pounding heart. He could hardly believe it when, as if waking from a dream, he realised it was his electric razor that had aroused their curiosity. Satisfied that that was all it was, they waved him past.

'Thank God for that,' said Orlando when Oliver joined him a half second later. 'I thought I was going to wet myself. Come on, let's get a drink.'

'Well don't take too much liquid on board,' said Oliver archly. 'We've still got the other end to face.'

Oliver's advice did not stop Orlando from downing two beers in the short time available, nor, once they were airborne, from putting his good looks to work in getting them both an extra gin and tonic and a second quarter bottle of wine apiece with their in-flight sandwich. Oliver gave in and joined him, drink for drink. If they were going to be marched out of Gatwick in handcuffs there would be no advantage in being sober at the time.

They landed just as the sun was setting. 'Brace yourself,' said Orlando as they filed out of the plane. They had no need to hang round the carousel waiting for luggage, but they did break their journey with a prudent visit to the gents'. This time Oliver made no secret of his interest in watching his friend recycling his liquid intake. It might be the last time he would ever see that particular sight, he thought, as they both zipped themselves up. A minute more and they were walking through an eerily deserted green channel. It was a short enough walk but Oliver was acutely conscious – as if he were walking down a snipers'alley – of accomplishing, first a quarter of it, then a half…

A customs officer appeared. From behind a partition? From nowhere? He pointed authoritatively at Orlando. 'You, sir. Yes you. Can you come over here please?'

At which point Oliver took one of the bigger gambles of his lifetime. Laying an affectionate hand on Orly's shoulder, he treated the customs man to a brilliant smile that was worthy of Orlando himself and said, 'It's all right, officer, the Kid's with me.'

EIGHT

Stony faced, the customs officer stared at them for the half second it took him to register what Oliver had said. Then his professional mask crumpled into an involuntary smile. 'Lucky you,' he said to Oliver, and suddenly laughed. 'All right, get along with you.' He made a gesture with his thumb towards the exit, a gesture that said something like, now get out of here before I change my mind. Oliver thought he had never been so lucky in his life. But that was a thought he had been having rather frequently in the last few weeks and days. Days especially.

'I can't believe you just did that,' Orlando said as they passed out through the wide doors of the green channel and walked along the crowded crush barrier of the arrivals hall, as if on identity parade, in front of the massed ranks of meeters and greeters, and taxi drivers with people's names on sticks.

'*I* can't believe I did it.' Oliver's spirits were suddenly soaring, borne aloft on a rush of adrenalin and alcohol and manifold success. They had been delivered from the clutches of the airport authorities as surely and as spectacularly as if the Red Sea, not just the green channel, had opened for them. Oliver's gamble had been rewarded with Orlando's awestruck admiration. He had been rewarded with Orlando, full stop. Orlando had been making nearly all the running up till now, deciding day by day, or even hour by hour, what was going to happen to them next. But now had come the moment, if ever there would be one, for Oliver to seize the initiative for himself. Whatever the consequences might be. Whatever the risks. He said, 'Stay with me tonight.' Then, like someone who has lit a firework, or pressed the launch button of some dangerously unpredictable weapon, he had nothing to do but wait.

Orlando did not reply at once. For Oliver it was one of the longest moments of his life. Then he saw Orly assume a serious, troubled-teenager face and guessed that he was getting ready to say something polite like, 'I think perhaps I need a bit of time to think.' Or, 'Don't you think a cooling-off period might be in order?' or even, 'I would, only I need to get some washing done.' In anticipation Oliver felt his soaring spirits fall, like bright-plumed birds shot down during their dizzying ascent above the mountains and now about to disappear into an abyss. But that was how it had to be. Oliver had asked for it.

'What's the matter?' Orlando queried, for some reason reaching out with a finger to touch Oliver's cheek. 'I'd like that more than anything. Only you took me by surprise. I didn't think you were going to ask that.'

'I took *you* by surprise?'

Somehow Orlando steered them towards some seats against a wall, next to a cash dispenser. He half pushed Oliver into one of the seats, the precious cargo in his backpack in danger of being crushed in the process, and crouched down beside him, his hands on Oliver's knees.

'Of course I'm coming home with you. I'm glad you want that.'

The throng of passing travellers, trailing their cases and pushing trolleys, looked quickly at them, looked away, then glanced curiously back again before continuing on their journeys, wondering what they had just been witnessing, and what it meant.

*

On board the Gatwick Express they played at making anagrams of each other's names. 'Yours is simple,' said Orlando. 'It's what you say after a heavy night on the sauce. O liver! Of course it's also a self proclamation. I, lover. Like I Claudius.' Oliver simply nodded, having worked those two out years before. 'It could also be a smarmy vicar of course – the Rev Oil.'

Oliver found his new lover's name less amenable to the anagram process, and had to write the letters down on the back of his ticket. 'Roo-land?' he offered doubtfully. 'A new way of talking about Down Under? Or – but you'd have to change the D into a T – there's Ortolan. A kind of lark, isn't that, that the French eat?'

Orlando grinned. 'I never thought of that one. I think it's a kind of finch, actually. They used to cook them in butter till they were nearly bursting, then sit and eat them in top restaurants, sitting shrouded in dust sheets. I saw a photo once. They banned it.'

'I remember,' said Oliver. They were sitting opposite each other, each looking at the other's sprawled legs,

Oliver thinking – in some amazement – he's mine, at least for tonight; that territory's all mine. The thought was a humbling one. He tried to guess what Orly was thinking, then found he didn't dare.

They reached Victoria. Oliver shepherded Orlando onto the sixteen bus. It was a short walk from the stop in Kilburn High Road to Oliver's flat in Oxford Road. Had he left things tidy? That was his first thought as he turned the key in the door. And, what would Orlando's judgement of the place be? Three weeks ago Oliver had compared his flat unfavourably with Bernd's in Cologne, but Orlando, arriving at Oxford Road – where Oliver occupied the first floor of a well-kept Victorian terraced house – seemed delighted by everything he saw. Perhaps he really does live in a squat, Oliver thought, before remembering that he'd been brought up in a presumably well-appointed Kent farmhouse. So Oliver took comfort from Orly's reactions as he explored the place, examined the motley collection of pictures, prints and posters on the walls, peered at titles in the book shelves, nodded in silent approval at the double bed in the main bedroom (Oliver noticed with relief that he had at least made it before leaving for Málaga) then turned his attention to Oliver's collection of CDs.

'You really are an opera buff, aren't you?' Orlando said.

Oliver, for whom Mozart's Magic Flute represented the gleaming pinnacle of human achievement, said something non-committal. Orly might be a candidate for conversion at some future date – if fate should permit such a future – but it wouldn't be tonight. Exposing impressionable young men to the glories of opera on their first evening at home with you tended to put the kiss of death on things, as Oliver, over the years, had learned to his cost.

They ordered in a Chinese and ate it with a bottle of wine in the kitchen. The heating had been off for two days, and the kitchen always warmed up faster than the other rooms. The backpack with its precious contents lay importantly, unignorably, on the floor beside them. 'So are we up for Seville together?' Orlando asked, spooning out the contents of aluminium foil boxes.

'Wait a minute,' Oliver said warily, the wine he was pouring into Orly's glass stopping in mid-flow. 'We need to think about this. You're talking about what you said to Felipe last night – about going out on spec and looking for something.'

'And what you were so rude about – saying we wouldn't necessarily go together.'

'Well, if you remember, at that stage you were planning never to have sex with me again. It wasn't an unreasonable assumption to...'

'Only last night. Doesn't seem possible.' Orlando shook his head as though his own behaviour was a mystery to him. Then he looked at Oliver brightly. 'We wouldn't be going out on spec, though. Not exactly. Felipe's got this friend, remember, who I'm going to call. I'll do that. See what happens. And if there's anything doing we go together, right?'

'And if I say no,' said Oliver, suddenly flat and despondent, 'you go on your own?'

Orlando looked upset. 'I wanted to go with you all along, back when I thought we were just going to be two buddies. When I stupidly imagined we could ever just be that. I want it even more now things have changed, not less.'

How had things changed? Oliver asked himself. And what were those things that had changed called? A one-night stand became a fling if you repeated things the second night, that was an easy one, a question of maths. But when did a fling metamorphose into an affair? At what stage did an affair become a relationship? And how long could even one of those be relied upon to last?

'What's the matter?' Orlando asked.

The man. The moment. Take them minute by minute, Oliver told himself. 'I'll have to think about it,' he said. 'There's practicalities that would have to be dealt with. The mortgage on this flat for one thing.'

'Rent it out.'

'That takes time to organise. What about your flat anyway?'

'It's not an issue. I'm there on a temporary basis, remember. To be extended after the course or not, depending. I've decided not to stay. I'll tell them. D'you want some more prawn thingy?'

'OK,' said Oliver. 'So I find a tenant for this place.' Involuntarily he looked about him, round the kitchen. 'And we go to Seville. If it doesn't work out you've got your father's place to go back to. What about me? With my flat let to strangers. I don't see your father giving houseroom to someone he's never been introduced to. Especially not under those circumstances.'

'You've got your sister. Brother.'

'Oh come on!'

'Then don't go presuming I can just easily run back to the farm. I'd be in exactly the same boat as you.'

This ran on for some time, with arguments and objections being volleyed back and forth across the beef and green peppers, though in a good-natured enough way. Oliver ended it by saying, 'OK. Go ahead and make your phone call. See what happens. In the meantime I'll think about it. But no decisions yet, all right?' They left it there.

*

Hi Bernd! See you Tuesday if you still want to. But I have to tell you something. I'm no longer living alone. A young friend seems suddenly to have become a bit more than that. He seems to have moved in with me. Can't say how long this will last, but he says till Tuesday at least. That's why I've written' if you still want to'. It would be great to see you, but if you decide to change your plans

I'll understand. Love, Oliver

Orlando read Oliver's email standing at his shoulder, glass of wine in hand. That was what living together meant, Oliver remembered.

'What do you mean,' Can't say how long this will last'?' Orlando objected.

Oliver half turned. 'It's true, isn't it? It's always true. Whatever people want. Whatever you and I might both want. Nobody knows the future. People get run over by buses.'

A little taken aback by Oliver's vehemence, Orlando changed tack. 'Do you not want him to come?'

'I don't know. I like him, and last week I was looking forward to seeing him again. But then – well you know what happened. On balance I'd prefer it if he took the hint and cancelled – at least for now. But what about you? What do you want?'

Orlando took a thoughtful sip of red wine. 'He can come if he wants. I'll be interested to meet him.'

Not half as interested as he'll be to meet you, Oliver thought. But he kept the thought to himself. He reached out with one hand and laid it on Orlando's bottom. 'Time for bed,' he said. With the other hand he clicked on *Send*.

*

When the other trainee teachers came to college on

Monday morning they found the first two arrivals were, as usual, Orlando and Oliver, sitting hunched over cups of coffee in the canteen. Nobody had ever asked themselves which of the two usually arrived first: it was not remotely interesting. In the same way it would have crossed nobody's mind this morning that the two of them might have arrived together. The rumour had gone round that the third week was going to be immensely tougher than the two weeks that had preceded it. And so, when mid-morning break came and neither of the pair joined the others in the canteen, nobody noticed that either; nor that Orlando, who for some reason did not possess a mobile phone, had borrowed Oliver's and stayed in the classroom with it, while Oliver himself left the building on his own with his backpack.

Oliver was a minute or two late back from the break; he mouthed his apology at their trainer and plonked himself down next to Orly.

'You got the money?' Orlando hissed at him as soon as the people nearest them were sufficiently engrossed in their discussion about modal verbs.

'No,' said Oliver, a bit breathlessly. 'The man wasn't there. I have to go back again at lunchtime.'

Orlando looked alarmed. 'You didn't leave the package, did you?'

'Course not. I've got it here.' Oliver flapped a hand against the backpack which he had laid down beside his seat.

'You reckon it's a trap?'

'I don't know what it is. How can I?'

'Did anything look suspicious? Police about or anything? Never mind. Whatever happens, if you go back at lunchtime the Cat's coming with you.'

'But…'

'No argument. If you go, I go. Simple as that. Seville's sorted, by the way. Tell you all about it lunchtime.'

But when lunchtime came, the priority was clearly to get hold of the seven hundred pounds. They set off up the narrow street into Shepherd Market. Orlando was looking all around him for the telltale signs of a trap that were familiar to him from films and television: square-shouldered detectives with upturned coat collars, parked cars with people sitting in them; he even glanced up to the roofline from time to time, as if looking for snipers, but would then look down again with an embarrassed smirk, as if ashamed of his imagination. 'If we don't get the money this time,' he said, 'we'll simply hang on to the picture or whatever it is. We'd probably stand to make a lot more by selling it ourselves.'

'Careful,' warned Oliver. 'Don't let all this go to your head. We may be working for a bunch of crooks but we're not going to start turning into crooks ourselves. Keep hold of that.' But privately he wondered where exactly the dividing line lay and whether he, at any rate, had already crossed it. They reached the door of the shop and marched in, exactly abreast, which made them look a bit Hollywood themselves, and a bit threatening to the staff in the shop. One of them, a young woman whom Oliver had seen earlier that morning, went running into the back room. They could just hear her saying, 'Mr Evans.'

Mr Evans appeared in person, still reassuringly bald and wearing the same suit as when Oliver had first met him. 'Sorry I wasn't here earlier,' he said, smiling disarmingly. 'Come through.'

Oliver walked into the back room, again finding Orlando side by side with him in the doorway so that they nearly jammed in it. Oliver took the parcel from his backpack and placed it on the desk. Mr Evans glanced at it, then opened the safe and took out a bundle of notes which he kept in his hand. From the desk he picked up a Stanley knife and, rather clumsily because he was trying to avoid chopping into the bank notes, slit the tape that held the two pieces of cardboard together. He glanced at whatever was between them, without letting either of the others see, then handed the money to Oliver. 'Count it,' he said, and Oliver did, while Orlando looked around him, a little disappointed at seeing only the accoutrements of a print shop and picture framing business, and Mr Evans, still keeping the thing masked from their view by the pieces of cardboard, looked again and more carefully at his new acquisition.

'Fine,' said Oliver and turned to go. Orlando also turned and, this time, followed him. Behind them they heard Mr Evans say, in his permanently cheerful tone, 'There was no need to bring your bodyguard with you.'

'Brilliant,' said Orlando as soon as they were out of the shop.

'Half of it's yours,' said Oliver. 'I've decided.'

'Bollocks you have. It was your job. Your risk'

'You shared the risk...' They went on in this Claude and Cecil way for a minute or so but finally compromised, with Orlando accepting only the recompense for his plane fare to Málaga and back. Oliver's ticket had been paid for by Donald as part of the deal. They agreed to divide up the cash once they were no longer in full view of everyone in the street.

'Let me tell you about Seville,' Orlando said. 'I spoke to Felipe's friend, Eduardo Guttierez. Direct line. And Felipe was right. He's expanding his operation and looking for two new people. I told him about you and me – I don't mean *that*, obviously – simply that we'll be two newly qualified people within a fortnight. He said he could use us starting in three weeks. If we turn up, say the Thursday before, he could show us the ropes. And there's a flat available too. Some teacher who's moving out. A bit small, he says, but the rent's peanuts.'

The rent Orly went on to quote sounded absurdly cheap. The whole proposition sounded too easy, suspiciously so. People in the real world didn't just dish out jobs and flats. But seeing Orlando's eager face Oliver didn't have the heart to say so. And perhaps it was he who was wrong – with his civil servant's cautious attitude to work and jobs. Perhaps Orlando's instinct, honed in the world of the freelance actor, was the right one to trust. 'Let's take it a step at a time, though,' he said. 'We've got to get our Certificates yet. There's my flat to think of.' He thought, there's the question of our relationship also. Will it actually last the next three weeks? Is it even going to survive the next two days? It's all happening too quickly, he wanted to caution Orlando, but he couldn't bring himself to.

'I'll need to go back to Kentish Town this evening, though,' Orlando said. 'Get a couple of changes of clothes.' Oliver could see the point of that. Orlando had come to college this morning in shirt, socks and underpants belonging to his new lover. But as the underpants were invisible to their colleagues, the socks plain white like Orlando's own, and the shirt mostly hidden by Orlando's pullover, nobody had noticed.

'I suppose you'll be staying the night there,' said Oliver, trying to sound as if it didn't matter.

'No, no. I'll be back. Back for bedtime.'

'Will you want something to eat?' Oliver heard himself say. Dear God, he thought, I sound like his mother.

'That'd be nice,' said Orlando. 'You offering to cook?' They were heading up the front steps of the college now, about to descend to the canteen in search of a sandwich.

'I'm offering to organise something. It *might* involve cooking – or it might be a takeaway.' He grinned at Orlando, then changed his expression and said with mock severity, 'You'll eat what you're given.'

*

The weekend in Málaga wasn't alluded to by anyone in the pub that evening; there was an awful lot of shop to talk. But then Orlando left early and said breezily to Oliver, 'See you later. I should make it by eight or eight-thirty.' For a moment Oliver thought, with a frisson of mixed horror and delight, that Orlando was going to kiss him as he left the bar, but he didn't, and then Oliver felt let down because he hadn't. After he had gone there was a strong feeling in the air that somebody ought to say something by way of clarifying what had changed in the nature of Oliver's relationship with Orlando but nobody dared to – and especially not Oliver. Whatever anyone might say could only sound crass. Everybody simply looked uncomfortable for a moment, shifted in their chairs and then started talking about something else.

*

He won't come, Oliver told himself. Once he gets talking to his flatmates and they tell him he's gone mad, getting involved with a much older man, he'll come to his senses. He'll show up at college in the morning and say he got delayed.

Oliver did nothing about shopping for a meal or cooking anything. He didn't want to give hostages to fortune. He could do his lesson preparation thoroughly, then go out for a takeaway before bed, when he'd finally given Orlando up for the night.

He was almost shocked when the doorbell rang just before nine and it turned out to be Orlando. 'Do you have such a thing as a spare key?' Orly asked as Oliver let him in. 'I forgot to ask.' Then, more cheekily, 'Dinner ready?'

Oliver looked at him without smiling. They were standing just inside the street doorway. 'I haven't done anything about dinner.'

Orlando's face fell, uncomprehending, desolate, like a child's.

'I'm sorry,' Oliver said, and found that he was crying. 'I didn't think you'd come back.'

'Not come back?' Orlando shut the door behind him, kissed Oliver and took his hands as if Oliver were now the child. 'Why ever not?'

'Because you're a kid, Kidd, and I'm an older man. You'll understand one day.'

Orlando pulled Oliver down with him till they were kneeling, face to face, at the foot of the stairs. Orlando had his hands, with Oliver's beneath them, against the front of Oliver's thighs. If Oliver's downstairs neighbours chose this moment to...

'I love you,' Orlando said quietly. His face too now ran with tears.

Oliver pressed and pulled at Orlando's head, which was now in his lap. Almost soundlessly he said, 'I love you, I love you, I love you.' It might as well be said three times, if it was going to be said at all. 'Sorry,' he added.

'Why sorry?' They had pulled themselves to their feet and were beginning to climb the stairs.

Oliver quoted, 'He's mad that trusts in the tameness of a wolf, a horse's health, a boy's love…'

'King Lear,' said Orlando. 'But you can trust me. When the Cat says he's going to do something he does it. When he says he loves you he means it. So of course I came back. Got my gear.' They went into the living room and Orly unburdened himself of his backpack. 'And a bottle of wine. Only I didn't …get any food.'

'I said I'd organise that,' said Oliver, 'and I will. There's a good Spanish place about fifteen minutes'walk away. Up for that? I'm buying. To say sorry for doubting you. And for a bit of a better reason than that.' If Le Gavroche had been just fifteen minutes'walk away he'd as happily, if bank-breakingly, have taken Orlando there.

It was an unpromising walk. A footbridge over a busy road, then zigzag through a tower-block estate with patchy street lighting. But then, rather unexpectedly, you came into a little Victorian street lined with small restaurants: Indian, Chinese, Caribbean. Their window lights spilled generously out onto the dark pavement. The Spanish one was called Mesón Bilbao, not that you'd have known it from the outside: the proprietor deemed it far too well known to need the name written up. Inside, Oliver and Orly felt abruptly returned to Spain again, as they took their seats at small dark wood tables – where candles pushed into bottles made individual inroads into the gloom, and under beams where strings of dried red peppers hung like paper chains.

They chose octopus and, to follow, T-bone steaks. Rioja to accompany, of course. T-bone steaks were like maps of South America, Oliver thought as they were placed before them: Brazil and Argentina down one side of the bony mountain chain in the middle, and Chile down the other. Oliver began sawing at the continent with his serrated knife.' I love you'was something that you said to someone before you knew almost anything about them, he thought: before you found out whether they could ride a bicycle, or had any money in their bank account. He looked across the table. 'Can you ride a bike, Orly?'

Orlando looked astonished, as well he might. '' Course I can. And ride a horse. Drive a tractor, car and even trucks. Why?'

'What I said earlier – what we both said…'

'You mean you think it wasn't true? Because what I said…'

'No, I don't mean that,' said Oliver. 'Far from it. Just, I hadn't meant to say it quite so soon.'

'I understand,' said Orlando. 'I hadn't meant to either. At first I didn't want it to be true. Then I didn't want to make myself vulnerable by saying it. But now we both have, so there.' Orlando had his fists on the table, immobile, knife and fork pointing upwards. His eyes were dark blue and wide in the candle light.

'Yes, but it's something else,' Oliver went on, suddenly experiencing a lurching change of mood, feeling depressed and anxious. 'People like me are always falling for kids younger than themselves. We're supposed not to let ourselves get carried away. Because the younger person never…'

'You think I don't know what I'm talking about? That I'm wet behind the ears? I told you there were things about me you don't know.'

'Well, obviously…'

'I lived with another bloke for two whole years. He was older than me too. He said he loved me, I said I loved him.'

'What happened?' Oliver asked tentatively. He wasn't sure he wanted to hear.

'Long story. And not important tonight. Tell you another time. Enough to say we both got hurt. When I met you I didn't want it all to happen all over again.'

'Insisting on coming to Málaga with me was a pretty funny way of avoiding the occasion of sin, then.' More gently, 'If you both got hurt, perhaps I'll need to know, some time, in what way – especially if you're afraid of it happening again. Maybe there's other things about you

I'll need to know some time. That you're living with Aids, maybe? Or you're an under-cover cop?'

They both managed to laugh at that. 'Neither of those at least,' said Orlando. 'I pick my nose sometimes. And I might end up voting Tory at the election.'

'I did suppose you might,' Oliver said. 'Being a farmer's boy. I might have to just live with that. But I'm relieved about the others.'

A troubled look came over Orlando's face. 'The only really bad thing – from your point of view, though mine as well since the last few days – is that I may not actually be gay.'

Oliver groaned. Why did they all have to say that?

Orlando seemed to feel that more was required. 'I've had affairs with women too.'

'Most people have,' said Oliver suavely. He himself was one of the few gay men he knew who hadn't, but he wasn't going to share that with Orlando just now. He went on, 'But you seem quite gay enough for me.' To his surprise he found he was smiling as he said it. 'I really don't need you to be any gayer.' He went on. 'But if you thought you weren't, why on earth did you come to Málaga with me? Why did you put yourself – put both of us – in that position?'

'Maybe,' Orlando said slowly, apparently wondering at his own words as he heard them, 'it was meant to be a kind of exorcism. That I could spend a weekend, share a bed even, with an older gay man who I trusted, and nothing would happen.'

As I guessed, Oliver thought. He said, 'Then your plan didn't really work out, did it?'

'Not as intended, I agree,' said Orlando. 'But the unintended results, so far, have been brilliant. *Verdad? Non?'* He took a slug of wine and grinned across the table at Oliver.

*

Somehow, next day everybody knew. It was in their smiles, in little looks; it went mostly unsaid. Though one or two people did mention it. Mike, the veteran of Iraq, obviously not afraid of confronting things head on, came up to Oliver with a broad grin. 'Done all right for yourself there, mate. Copping off with our friend from the Post Office commercial. I may look like a boring straight guy to you but even I can see he's got it: looks, charm, the lot. Mind you, you're quite cute yourself. Jesus, what am I saying?' He slapped at his head with the heel of his hand. 'Been on active service too long. I'll be on the turn myself next.'

Lorraine said, 'Good on yer, Oliver! I suppose we'd all sort of seen it coming – well, half seen it, but, anyway… Hey, wow!' All the world loves a lover.

But this evening there was Bernd to deal with. After teaching practice they made their way on foot to the pub where they'd arranged to meet: Oliver had chosen the Glassblower because it would be easy for Bernd to find.

Orlando, for all his breezy agreement to this meeting two days ago, was now looking as nervous and apprehensive as Oliver felt. 'What exactly is he coming to London for?' Orly asked.

'It's some kind of international conference of freelance photographers. Sounds kind of high-powered, don't you think?'

'Hmm,' said Orlando.

When they entered the pub Oliver saw that Bernd had got there first. The place was furnished with high tables and high stools with backs and arms to them, all made of blond wood, and there was Bernd, perched at one of them. But – and this was an eventuality that neither Oliver nor Orlando had remotely considered – he was not alone. A bespectacled, serious looking man of about thirty sat with him, dressed, as they all were, in jeans and a big sweater, except this his jeans alone had ironing creases down the front. He and Bernd had just-started pints of lager in front of them. Bernd looked entirely at ease. He jumped down, out of his cage-like stool (Oliver thought of the driving-cab of a crane), kissed Oliver's cheek and shook hands with Orlando. If he felt surprise, or anything else, at Orlando's beauty and Oliver's apparent good fortune, he had the good manners not to show it. He introduced his companion. 'Hans is at the same conference as I. Also from Köln. He is not gay but many of his friends are, which is good.' He saw doubts and uncertainties scudding across the faces of the Englishmen. 'Don't worry. We don't disturb your domestic arrangements. We will find a cheap hotel for the night. But nice to have a drink together first.'

It must have been the sheer relief of finding Bernd not alone, and thus the potentially explosive situation largely defused, that made Oliver say, without stopping for thought – 'No, you're welcome to stay. Both of you. London's not like other cities. There's no such thing as a cheap hotel here, unless you want to doss with ten backpackers. I've got a spare room. Only, one of you'd have to have the put-u-up in the living room.' He stopped, realising that one stage in the invitation process – a new and lately unfamiliar bit of protocol – had been missed out. He turned to Orlando. 'Sorry. Would that be OK?'

They ate, the four of them, just a block or two away, in Chinatown, then had a couple more drinks in Old Compton Street, where Oliver deliberately chose a venue – and he did *not* consult Orlando this time – that would not find Hans too eye-poppingly out of his depth.

Back at Oxford Road, one tube journey later, Hans seemed even more interested in seeing Oliver's home for the first time than Bernd was. The reason soon became clear. 'Next month I will come to work in London. Teaching photography in an art college. I need to find a flat but it will be difficult, everyone says.'

Orlando, sitting beside Oliver on the sofa, gave him a nudge. 'Go on, say it.'

'Say what?'

'That you're thinking of letting this one.'

'Jesus Christ, Orly,' Oliver said. He felt unacceptably pressured. 'You really do…' But he stopped himself from saying something they might both have regretted. Instead, he made a joke of it. 'Kidd's running my life for me now. Did you notice? Sorry, Hans. I haven't decided to let it yet. – I mean rent it out. But maybe in a few days I will.' Then, rather uncharacteristically, 'Can I ask how much you were expecting to fork out?'

NINE

Hans was a perfect gentleman. Having exchanged phone numbers with Oliver he went straight off to bed in the spare bedroom. Bernd and he had tossed a coin and Bernd had won the living-room put-u-up. This gave Bernd, sitting enthroned on the sofa that would later metamorphose into his bed, an opportunity to ask Oliver a question he hadn't wanted to raise in front of his travelling companion. 'Your delivery of a picture frame to Köln. What exactly happened with that?'

'Nothing exactly,' Oliver said, but then he told him how he had read of the theft of the Lucas Cranach, minutes after saying goodbye to Bernd at the airport. Bernd raised his eyes and eyebrows at that, but before he could say anything, Orlando brought the story up to date by recounting the Málaga adventure – shorn of its bedroom scenes, but in dramatic detail in all other respects – including its satisfactory conclusion in the picture framer's shop. Bernd shook his head and smiled to show he was impressed. But he said, 'Are you not thinking: here we are playing with thin ice?'

Orlando, facetious and just a little drunk, said, 'Or even skating on hot coals,' and Oliver groaned at him as if they'd been lovers for a lot longer than three days. Oliver then answered Bernd,

'Yes, it could be a dangerous thing. We really don't know. But we've taken as many risks as we're going to.

No more courier jobs to Málaga or anywhere else. And we're going to have nothing more to do with this Donald character. He who sups with the devil should take a long spoon.' And he translated the proverb into German for Bernd.

Orlando found an unfinished bottle of red and refilled everybody's glasses. Then Bernd shot a glance in the direction of the portfolio case that was resting against the wall alongside his backpack and said, 'I've got some pictures to show you, Oliver.' He rolled his eyes mischievously in Orlando's direction. 'Is he allowed to see them?'

It took Oliver a second to cotton on to which pictures Bernd might mean, then he realised. 'He may as well see them. Now that he's seen the original.'

Bernd fished in the portfolio and drew out a file. It had a printed label on the outside: *British Workman*. If Oliver was astonished at how good the photographs looked – at how good Bernd had made him look – then Orlando was even more so, though much of his astonishment was due to the fact that the photos existed at all. 'My God,' he said. 'You look even bigger and better than in life. Look at this last one. You look like you're just about to ejaculate.'

'I was,' said Oliver as matter-of-factly as he could, and Orlando looked from Oliver to Bernd and back again while he digested the implication, feeling perhaps a little uncomfortable with it.

'I think I may have a buyer for them,' Bernd said.

'You're kidding,' said Oliver.

'No, absolutely. And if I make a sale, you get a cut. OK?'

'OK,' said Oliver. 'But … wow.'

There was a second's silence and then Orlando said, very quietly, 'I did a shoot like that once. Modelling for an erotic magazine.'

'Straight?' asked Oliver. 'Or gay?' He was actually only a little bit surprised.

'Gay,' said Orlando, making it sound the more embarrassing of the two possibilities.

'Without clothes?' Oliver was interested for a number of separate reasons.

'In some shots, yes. It was something someone talked me into doing once.'

'Who?' Oliver naturally wanted to know.

'Someone I mentioned yesterday. But I don't want to talk about him now, if that's OK.'

'It's OK with me,' said Bernd, smoothing out the sudden crumple in the conversation. 'I'm sure you must have looked fantastic.'

Oliver had an even clearer idea of how Orly might

have looked, and even as the idea took pleasing shape in his imagination, a half memory stirred alongside it. Had he in fact seen those very pictures in a magazine a year or two back? Did he – did he – still have them in the bottom of the cupboard in his bedroom?

Bernd looked at Oliver, amusement twinkling in his grey eyes. 'Your friend's a man of secrets.'

'I know,' said Oliver. 'And I've only learnt two of them up to now. It worries me.'

'I can imagine it does,' said Bernd.

It was not until the second evening that Oliver found himself briefly alone with Bernd. Hans and Orlando were cooking omelettes together in the kitchen. 'He's a beautiful boy, your new discovery,' Bernd said. 'And charming too. I'm not surprised you fell in love with him. But...' Bernd's face made a frown of concern. 'Are you sure it's a good idea to be going off to Spain with him in two weeks?'

'I'm not surprised I fell in love with him either,' Oliver answered. 'Surprised only that he seems to have fallen for me too. As for Spain, I haven't finally made up my mind. But it does seem to be happening rather of its own accord. Orly getting us both jobs – and now Hans ready to take on the flat...' For a moment Oliver found himself wishing he was considering a future life with Bernd instead: someone his own age, whose outlook and behaviour would be informed by a similar experience of life to his own. The comforting security of that prospect.

Bernd's nice flat in Cologne. Oliver could have taught English there as easily as in Seville – and for better money, beyond any doubt.

'He drinks more than we do,' said Bernd. We. Already Bernd talked to Oliver like a very old friend rather than merely the other party to a recent one-night stand. He could have said, 'Come back to Germany instead,' but he was wiser than that.

'I don't know that he does,' Oliver said a bit uncertainly. 'I drink quite a lot myself.'

'And so do I. And I'm not talking about last night: it was a social evening and he drank the same as the rest of us, no more, no less. But he seems to have – how to say this? – an enthusiasm for it that most people don't.'

'You're imagining it,' said Oliver, though he had actually, reluctantly, been forming the same opinion himself. 'But, hell, I'll just have to keep a watchful eye on him when we get to Seville. If we go there. I still haven't decided, mind.'

'Oh, I think you will,' said Bernd.

Next day they parted early in the morning: Oliver and Orlando turning up the road to catch the bus to Park Lane, the two Germans heading down to Kilburn Park and the tube that would take them out to Heathrow and their plane. 'One day I'll photograph Orlando, if he'll let me,' Bernd said.

'Or if I will,' Oliver said, laughing. He and Bernd gave

each other a peck on the cheek as they parted on the pavement of Oxford Road, and Oliver wondered if they would ever meet again.

*

Easter was upon them, and now Orlando did absent himself, for three nights. He wanted to take a few of his belongings back to his father's farm and would need to say his goodbyes down there. The more Oliver reminded him that he hadn't finally made up his mind about the Spanish venture, the more Orlando behaved as if no such doubt existed. He would bring a few other bits and pieces to Oliver's flat, if that was OK, to leave in a cupboard until they were back from Spain – presumably when the summer vacation began. He left for Kent on Good Friday afternoon.

After he was gone, Oliver had an energetic root around his bedroom cupboards for himself, and was only half surprised by what he found. Then he called David in Beckley and was pleased that, just for once, it was he and not Zara who came to the telephone. 'Are you going to be in London at all this weekend?' he asked him. 'There's stuff I'd like to talk to you about.'

As it happened, David was planning to be in London the following morning. They could meet somewhere for a bite of lunch. David suggested the Lido café in Hyde Park and then asked, 'Are you getting married again?'

*

They risked an outdoor table in the hazy sunshine. The

Serpentine rippled just a foot away, on the other side of a miniature guard rail that appeared to have been made of overlapping croquet hoops, painted dark green. On the far side of the lake, the willows and hawthorns were beginning to be a blur of emerald. Nearer at hand, ducks and geese and grebes of all kinds swam and displayed to each other, with half an eye to their partners and half to the appealing prospect of thrown food. Over pints of lager and baguettes of chicken with salad and mayonnaise Oliver told his news.

'Quite a story,' said David when he had been brought up to date. 'But I'm not at all sure what you want me to say. You know the saying, of course, that when the gods wish to punish us they begin by granting our desires. But you won't thank me for reminding you of that.'

'You think I'm making a fool of myself, don't you?'

'No I don't,' David said. 'Nobody's a fool for loving another person.' He stared at the copy of the Guardian that Oliver had plonked on the table next to his lager when they sat down. 'What have you got wrapped in that?'

Oliver opened the paper up and showed him. 'Jesus,' David said in startled recoil. 'Is that the kind of thing you people read in bed?' He looked round to see if the people at the neighbouring tables had registered the appearance, in broad daylight, of a glossy porn-mag back number among the sandwiches and glasses of chardonnay.

'The sequence starts there,' Oliver said, flicking open the page. David seized the magazine and held it aloft, still shrouded in the Guardian, with his back carefully turned towards the water so that only the ducks and dabchicks would be in a position to see over his shoulder. 'That's him.'

'He doesn't leave much to the imagination, does he?' said David, slowly turning pages. 'But I have to admit you're right. I mean, that he's extremely beautiful. What about the ones of you?' Oliver had forgotten he'd told David about the photo shoot in Cologne. 'Have they been printed yet?'

'They're at home,' said Oliver. 'I didn't think you'd particularly want to see them.'

'Oh I don't know,' said David lightly.

'The thing is,' Oliver returned to more pressing concerns, 'I'm serious about him and that's one thing. But can he really be serious about me? Supposing he's just happy to have sex with me and to tell me he loves me when he's drunk? Maybe he has a coke habit and I've failed to notice. People say cocaine makes you want to bed the first thing you see – like Titania and the ass.' Oliver's only drugs of choice were alcohol and aspirin and even those never taken in combination. For information about the others he relied on hearsay.

'Only for an hour or so,' said David. 'Not for a week at a time. And if he was using that much you couldn't live with him and not notice.'

'I suppose you're right,' said Oliver, finding comfort in that.

'It's the age thing, of course,' David went on. 'And a problem with self belief. If he wants *you*, there must be something wrong with him. It's that, isn't it?'

Oliver nodded.

'And then you devalue him in your own eyes in turn, and start to think he must be a nutter or a freak. I know.' He refolded the Guardian and its surprising colour section and replaced them on Oliver's side of the table. He looked steadily into Oliver's eyes. 'People our age fall in love with people their age every minute of every day. It usually doesn't work out.' He tapped a finger at a headline in the newspaper that announced another glitch in the arrangements for the imminent marriage of the Prince of Wales to Camilla Parker-Bowles. 'You only have to look at Charles'first marriage.'

Oliver's gaze travelled a few yards to where the Princess Diana Memorial Fountain was being remodelled for the umpteenth time – turf all dug up and concrete in turmoil – for the benefit of people who couldn't see the difference between an art installation and a paddling pool.

'Another thing.' David had hit his stride. 'It seems you're embarking on two risky ventures at the same time and turning them into one. Flying off to a new job you know nothing about – you've nothing in writing, not even an email – *and* falling madly in love with a kid, however beautiful… To an outsider, I'm afraid it does look like asking for trouble.'

'I know,' said Oliver. 'I want to hold on to Orlando, and I can see that going to Seville with him may well be the worst possible way to do that. But if I put my foot down and say I'm not going, what then? Either he'll go on his own, in which case I've lost him for ever, or else he'll agree to give up the idea, stay with me and then hold it against me as a grudge until it – or something else – tears us apart. But then I think, what did I go and do a teaching course for if not to go abroad, take a risk and have an adventure? – And now, of course, I seem to have a tenant for my flat.'

David looked at Oliver. 'It doesn't look like you wanted my advice at all. Your mind seems pretty made up to me.'

'It was good to hear what you thought,' Oliver said, slightly apologetically.

'Last time we met,' said David, 'I said you might do better to try making a go of it with this Bernd character. A safer bet altogether. And he obviously still wants to keep in touch. But clearly…'

Oliver shook his head. 'I sometimes think that. But thinking doesn't always work, does it?'

David smiled. 'Maybe you'll be lucky with the kid. Prove the exception to the rule. You haven't lost your own good looks yet anyway.'

'Neither have you,' said Oliver quietly. They looked at each other in silence for a moment.

'Anyway,' David resumed, 'listen. I've got something else to tell you. Complete change of subject. Exceptions to the rule reminded me. You wanted the lowdown on Donald. This is what I've got. He appeared on the scene about three years ago. Everybody in the pub knows him and yet nobody does, if you see what I mean. He says he was the owner of a haulage business; that he sold up and retired to Sussex. He has a cottage, he and his wife do, between Beckley and Northiam – the next village, you know. But he rents, he didn't buy a place, which makes him a bit unusual in a village like that. They have a place in Spain too, apparently, and he's always disappearing off to it, sometimes for months at a time. Hardly anyone ever sees the wife, by the way. She's Spanish. Maybe her English isn't so good. People think she spends more time abroad than he does.'

'Where in Spain?' Oliver asked warily.

'That I don't know,' said David, relaxing back in his chair. 'I've pretty well told you everything I do know.'

'Well, that's quite a bit to be going on with. The Spanish connection makes sense of a few things.'

'Hmmm,' said David. 'Have you actually looked at the newspaper this morning?'

'Not really,' Oliver admitted. 'Except the front page. I couldn't really let it fall open on the bus.'

'Of course,' said David. 'Well it'll be on an inside page somewhere. Small item. Not the National Gallery this time. An old Flemish painting's gone missing from a collection in Madeira. It was in store in a basement.'

'When?' Oliver discovered that he felt no surprise, just a slow, sinking feeling of disquiet.

'Discovered two days ago during a security check. They don't know exactly when it was taken. Naturally I thought of you.'

'Naturally,' said Oliver. He pinched off a piece of bread from his baguette and threw it in the direction of an astute looking mallard.

*

Oliver decided that he would go ahead with the Seville venture if two things happened. One, that Orlando returned from the weekend still set on the idea himself. Two, that Hans remained serious about renting the Oxford Road flat. He did not phone Orly over the weekend, though Orly inhabited his thoughts all the time, like a second self. He thought it a good idea to let the boy have a bit of space. But Oliver did telephone Hans to check that his interest in the flat had not faded on his return to Germany. Hans told him he still wanted Oxford Road if it was available. Oliver said that he had almost made up his mind, and that he would let him know finally on Monday night.

Orlando was back in Kilburn at seven o'clock on Easter Monday evening. 'You're early,' Oliver said as he opened the door to him, trying to keep both the joy and the anxiety out of his voice. 'That's nice.'

'I thought I'd better be,' said Orlando, his accent sounding very farmer's boy – perhaps it was the country air that did it. 'I didn't want you to be upset again like last time.'

'You're a lovely boy,' Oliver said, and took him in his arms. 'I couldn't get you out of my head the whole weekend.'

'It was the same for me,' Orlando said, with something like wonder in his voice.

'So, then.' It was Oliver who came to it first. 'Are we off to Spain?'

'I am if you are,' said Orlando.

'And if you are, I am,' said Oliver. Hesitantly he touched the bright curls of his lover's head, as if he doubted they were real.

'It sounds like an exchange of vows,' said Orlando.

'It is,' said Oliver.

*

'I found this,' Oliver said once they'd got upstairs and inside. He plonked himself down in an armchair and gestured towards the magazine, lying on the sofa and now demurely closed, in which the naked Orlando so prominently featured.

'Oh my God!' Orlando seized it, laughed, and opened it up. He turned pages and gazed at the pictures of himself for a few seconds. 'Oh well.' He closed the magazine and put it down again on the sofa where he installed himself next to it. 'Not too bad, was I? Maybe that's why you recognised me on the train the first time. Nothing to do with the Post Office ad. I'll tell you about it sometime.'

For the moment, though, Oliver was more interested in knowing what Orlando had told his father about going to Spain. Had he mentioned Oliver? Did his family know that he was – well, not entirely straight?

'I said I'd been offered a job in Spain, starting in two weeks and that I'd be back in the summer. It wasn't that big a deal. It's not like I'm leaving home for the first time.'

'And me?'

'I said I was going with a friend I'd made on the course. If you're asking, did I tell him we're also screwing each other, well, no. I've never told him that about anyone, girl or boy. I've always let him work it out for himself if he wants to.'

'And let me guess,' said Oliver. 'He usually works it out when it's been a girl, and fails to when it's a bloke.'

'Probably.'

'Well, I suppose that's his problem, not mine,' Oliver said. He thought, not mine yet.

'We went hunting on Saturday,' Orlando changed the subject nonchalantly.

'Hunting?' The announcement had given Oliver a jolt. 'I thought that was illegal now.'

'It's only illegal if you let hounds actually kill a fox – *and* that that's premeditated. Riding to hounds is still allowed. It still goes on. It's a good day out on horseback.' Orly looked challengingly at Oliver. 'Do you have a problem?'

'I'm a bit surprised, that's all,' said Oliver uncomfortably. 'I sort of didn't imagine you doing something like that.' He realised as he spoke that he had no reason to be surprised. Orlando was a country boy, a farmer's son. And, love each other as they might, they hardly knew each other yet.

Orlando shrugged. Then a challenging look appeared in his eye. 'I sort of didn't imagine you as a smuggler of stolen art treasures when we first met, but there you go. Some foxes have to be killed. Now we have to do it by shooting. But hunting used to make a sport out of a necessity. Good idea, surely?'

'It doesn't feel good to me, that's all.'

'Yeah, but what you don't know...'

'I do know, Kidd,' Oliver said. 'I've listened to all the arguments – on both sides – so you needn't go on.' He thought, perhaps when we get to Seville he'll want to go to the bullfight.

But Orlando did go on. 'The ban was totally hypocritical. And vindictive. Dreamed up by people who don't understand the countryside and don't even want it to exist.'

'Oh come on…'

'Nobody raises a finger because terriers are used for catching rats in the London Underground. Bet you didn't even know that went on. They use peregrine falcons to kill London pigeons. And nobody's banned from keeping a cat to catch the mice in their kitchen. The government doesn't give a flying fuck. But because it's something people in the country do…'

'OK,' Oliver said firmly. 'Can we just drop it? Maybe my logic isn't too consistent, but it's something people feel strongly about.'

'On both sides…'

Jesus, thought Oliver, are we about to have our first row – *about fox hunting?* 'Anyway, what happened? On Saturday I mean.'

'Two foxes got shot. We all had a nice ride out in the sunshine. I hadn't ridden for a while.' His face broke into a shy smile. 'I didn't fall off, if that's what you were hoping.'

'I do love you,' Oliver said quietly.

Orlando got up and kissed him on the forehead. Then he looked at Oliver's watch. 'D'you think it's too early for a gin and tonic?'

*

Oliver telephoned Hans to tell him he could have the flat, and promised to prepare a written agreement that they could both sign in a few days'time. He told his friends of his imminent change of country by blanket email. There wasn't time to go through everything repetitiously by telephone. Even David and Zara had to make do with the email. But he did make an exception for his sister. She was not impressed, and far from ready to wish him well. She asked – rather presciently, Oliver thought – how old his new companion was, and was then predictably horrified when he told her he was only twenty-four. He told her he would give her his address in Seville as soon as he had one, and that he would be giving her phone number to Hans, then rang off. He had been thinking of phoning Bernd, but this negative reaction from his sister made him think again. In the end he took the easy way out, and Bernd got an email like everyone else.

*

The end of the training course came towards them with a rush. And the final day of the course brought with it an even greater degree of tension and nervous excitement. The day acquired an epic, fever-pitch quality as the hours passed. Some of the reasons for this were unconnected with the ending of the course. It was April Fools'Day. And in bizarre juxtaposition to that, Pope John-Paul II, who was on his deathbed, was widely expected to pass away during the afternoon. In fact he didn't, but this impending end-of-an-era happening lent an epic quality to the ending of teaching practice, as if a seldom played drum-roll were unexpectedly shadowing the concluding bars of a familiar symphony.

The course ended with a rowdy celebratory meal in Chinatown. People pledged eternal friendship through a haze of tears and wine, and swapped indecipherable scrawled addresses with promises to keep in touch that might or might not be kept, before spilling out, fledglings in a new world, into the midnight streets, all separating to go their different future ways. The Bakerloo line was still running and it took them anticlimactically home.

*

The few nights they had spent alone at home together had all been busy with the demands of their coursework, and they had made do with snacks or takeaways. But on the suddenly peaceful Saturday that followed, Orlando decided to show off his prowess as a cook, and served up a dinner of prawns in garlic oil, Spanish style, followed by wedges of salmon baked with orange slices and Dubonnet. He said this was a seventeenth century Franco-Scottish recipe, though Oliver objected that if that were the case the Dubonnet could hardly be totally authentic. Orlando said robustly that all good cooks modified the classics as the centuries passed, and in the end Oliver found he had no complaints.

After dinner, the Pope's death was announced on the

news. Which prompted a question from Orlando. 'Tell me about your father who was a monk.'

'My father who was a monk?' said Oliver. 'As opposed to my other fathers who weren't?'

'Whatever. But seriously. Did he stay a believer right to the end? I mean after he quit his monastery. Would he be believing the Pope's gone straight to Heaven and all that stuff if he were alive now?'

'Not right to the end, no. He was still a believer when I was born, I think. He had me baptised, after all. Though later he said jokingly that it was a kind of hell-fire insurance. He did send me to a Catholic school to begin with, but I think he was pretty much an agnostic by then. I ended up in an ordinary comprehensive, like you. As you know.'

'So… I mean, did he think the whole thing – the whole experience of giving up life for so long – had been a waste?'

'No, far from it.' Oliver took a sip of wine, a gesture that Orlando, sitting on the chair opposite, unconsciously mirrored: something that Oliver found absurdly flattering. 'My father thought the Bible was the best book that had ever been written. And that if you stopped trying to think it had been ghost-written by God it was all the better. What did he use to say…? That if it was divinely inspired, the Old Testament was pretty obscure and unsatisfactory, but if you looked on it as an iron age attempt to get a handle on life and make sense of the world as they saw it, then it was brilliant.'

'And the Jesus bit?'

'He thought much the same about the New Testament too. He came to think it didn't matter too much who Jesus was. Whether he was a travelling preacher who'd somehow made it to India and come back all fired up with Buddhist teaching, or whether he was some Jewish sect's dreamed-up answer to the Stoics. But Dad reckoned Saint Matthew's Gospel was the best template for life that anybody had ever come up with, no matter where the ideas had come from. He thought it was a waste if it was going to be kept, like restricted information, for the diminishing number of people who still believed in God and Heaven.'

Orlando looked back at Oliver and frowned suddenly. 'What would your father have thought of us?'

'Good question,' said Oliver. 'Especially as in terms of living life together we've hardly started. He'd have liked you though, no doubt about that. And that's quite a good beginning, don't you think?'

*

On Monday the date of the Pope's funeral was announced, an arrangement that obliged poor Prince Charles to postpone his wedding for twenty-four hours. And in the evening Oliver got a rare phone call from his brother Lawrence.

'I've heard from Jenny,' Lawrence began. 'And I

could hardly believe it. That you've picked up some loser of a kid who's half your age, and you're running away to Spain together – to fail even more comprehensively.'

'It's not running away,' Oliver barked back. 'And we're not going to fail. We've got jobs to go to. And we love each other. That's all there is to be said.' Oliver was well used to rowing with his brother and knew that he had to stand his ground.

'It won't last. You know it won't. It didn't last in the end with Adi and at least he was your own age.'

'With Adi it was six years – nearly seven. OK. Could have done better. But even six years was longer than your first marriage, to Annie. At least when Adi and I got together you didn't all have to fork out for wedding presents.'

Orlando, who had been hovering at Oliver's side, winced at that. He rested a hand on the nape of Oliver's neck for a moment, then withdrew to an armchair on the other side of the room. The phone conversation continued a few minutes longer in similar vein, ending only when Oliver banged the phone down.

'Families,' said Orlando. 'They're all the same.'

*

Oliver slit the envelope with an urgent forefinger. Pass. Grade B. A formal certificate and report would be sent on in a few weeks'time. They had to make the trek over to Kentish Town to pick up Orly's result. It meant a trip on the thirty-one bus to Camden Town and then a bit of a walk. Oliver asked Orly about the other people at his flat.

'Nobody that special,' Orlando replied. He named them. 'They come and go rather, same as me. Tim and Bluey were at drama school with me – they now do other things.' Orly fleshed them out with a few additional sentences; he didn't make them sound all that special.

'So, then,' probed Oliver carefully, 'who was your Svengali character? The one you lived with for two years and who got you into porn modelling.'

'Clever of you.' Orlando's eyebrows became two rainbows of surprise, then knitted down into a frown. 'How did you know it was the same guy?'

'Just an inspired guess,' said Oliver.

'Jeremy. He was one of the teachers at drama school. Ten years older than me – so you see, you do have antecedents. Fell for me in a big way. And I with him, I have to admit. The attention … that was part of it, I suppose. I moved in with him. It didn't go down at all well with most of the others.'

'I imagine not.'

'When I left, he left too. Set himself up as an agent, taking the best and brightest from my year onto his books. Including me, of course. Well, especially me. I was a bit naïve, I suppose. I guess we all were. After a couple of lucky breaks – the few telly jobs I did – the agency went nowhere very fast. That's how I came to be doing' extra'work … and he got me the modelling job too. Desperation on all sides. When it collapsed around his ears he went back to Oxford, which is where he comes from, to do some directing at the Playhouse. And we … split up.'

'I see. You left him? Or he left you?'

'Hard to say exactly. But I think it was more he leaving me than the other way round.'

'And your parents knew nothing about this?'

'Not really. They met him a couple of times. I was still using the flat we're going to as a postal address – and when the thing with Jeremy folded I went back there for a bit. Till things got really bad last year – I mean money-wise – and I moved back to Newchurch. Did I ever tell you the name of the farm, by the way? It's called Mockbeggar. At that particular moment I thought it kind of appropriate.' Oliver gave a sympathetic grunt of a laugh. 'Anyway,' Orlando stopped outside a house that was not all that different from the ones in Oxford Road, if a little shabbier, 'here we are.'

Once they were inside and up the stairs it became clear that Orlando was keen to waste no time there. He bent and picked up his post from the mat, found the envelope that had come from the college and, like Oliver an hour earlier, slit it open with his forefinger. A frowning perusal, then the frown broke into a smile. 'Snap,' he said. 'Pass. Grade B.'

'Champagne later,' said Oliver.

They collected a couple of bags of belongings from Orlando's room. (*His room*, Oliver thought, looking quickly round it, storing the memory. *His bed*.) Some items were to be stored at Oliver's flat, a few would travel with them to Spain. Oliver saw few signs of Orlando about the place. Pictures, CDs and books had probably already gone down to Mockbeggar, Oliver guessed, or else were packed in the bags they were about to take to Kilburn. Orlando seemed pleased when they were outside again and the door was shut behind them.

Back at Oxford Road, Orlando suggested, half jokingly, that Oliver should call Donald, tell him they were going to Seville and, did Donald want anything delivered while they were down there? Oliver's answer was brusque. 'We're not going to touch that man with a barge pole. I've been incredibly lucky – we have – so far. Much luckier even than I used to think. Don't let's push it, or we'll both end in gaol, and it won't be a cosy little double cell together.' He told Orlando what David had told him about the painting going missing from the gallery in Madeira.

In the afternoon, their last in London, they visited the Caravaggio exhibition at the National Gallery, pointedly going nowhere near the rooms dedicated to early Flemish and German work, but wallowing in the feast of colour and sensation provided by the assembled works of the Italian painter. 'I've told you about Jeremy today,' said Orlando as they walked round, competing to find the artist's depictions of his own handsome face in the luminous canvases. ' Now tell me about Adi. Who left who and why. And how you met.' He didn't say this particularly quietly, but in a candid, businesslike tone: it clearly intrigued some of the other visitors to the exhibition who were peering into paintings nearby.

Oliver gave him the short version. 'We met at a concert at the Festival Hall. Actually a series of three concerts. We'd both booked single season tickets for all three and happened to have adjacent seats. At the first one we just talked, and went to the bar together in the interval. The second time we went on to a club together and then – well, you can guess how the evening ended.'

'You're such a bloody romantic, Oli…'

'You not, I suppose? The ending was about as prosaic as could be. He had a few affairs in the end. I wasn't supposed to mind, although I did. But when I started to play the field a bit, that did for him. We split, and in this case it was definitely him leaving me. Quite amicable, but final. I bought him out of the flat. He went back to Germany nine months ago, with someone he'd met. We haven't contacted each other since.'

'Is that what'll happen to us, do you suppose?' Orlando asked. 'Is that the way it always goes?'

'Is that the way you want it to happen?'

'Of course not.'

'It doesn't always have to be like that. With some people I know, it isn't. But I can't prove it to you by looking at myself. All I can say is … I want you all to myself for keeps. If that isn't asking too much of both of us.'

'Perhaps we should take it one day at a time then,' suggested Orlando, sounding entirely serious, 'like reforming alkies.'

They watched the late evening news, glasses of the champagne that Oliver had promised in hand. There were some lengthy items: reaction in Rome to the news of John-Paul II's death, with footage of crowds of pilgrims descending on the city; there were the changing arrangements for the Prince of Wales's wedding; the postponement, also on account of the Pope's death, of the the forthcoming election campaign; then the announcement that MG Rover, flagship of British car-making, had finally rolled over and would be put into administration. Other items were dealt with briefly in the remaining few minutes, but then Oliver and Orly both sat up, rigid with alarm, and sending miniature shock waves rippling across the sparkling surface of their celebratory champagne. 'The painting of the Nativity by the medieval German master, Lucas Cranach, reported missing from the National gallery's collection in February, has been discovered safe and in good condition in Germany. It was one of a number of stolen paintings, having an estimated total value of eight million pounds, seized in a police raid on a private house near Munich this morning.'

They looked at each other in shocked silence for a moment. Then, sounding a bit unsure of himself, Orlando said, 'Munich's nowhere near Cologne, though.'

'It's near enough,' said Oliver.

TEN

The news of the discovery of the missing Lucas Cranach kept them awake and talking into the small hours. They tried to focus on the fact that, even if Oliver were implicated in this business, his role was only a peripheral one, and on the thought that the police, if they did want to investigate him, were unlikely to make a priority of this, were unlikely to start yet. But this was only speculation, whistling in the dark. It was equally possible that Oliver's name was already on a' wanted'list at ports and airports and that attempting to leave the country today would be to walk straight into a trap. There was no way of knowing which guess was the right one – short of phoning the police to ask.

This was not Oliver's only anxiety. He had the gravest doubts about the reliability of the job offer – and the flat offer – that had so casually been tossed their way, like bones to hungry dogs. And beneath this lay the deepest cause for worry of all: Orlando himself and their new and untested relationship. Oliver was unsure whether it was he who was taking a young, naïve and unsuspecting young man into the unknown, towards potential disappointment and disaster, or whether it was the other way around. He went uneasily to sleep.

*

Their flight left Heathrow in the late afternoon. There was no police cordon around the terminal. (Of course

204

there wasn't: it was the fact that they even looked for one that betrayed the extent of their fear.) At check-in Oliver felt his breath catching, coming in shallow draughts, and, looking at Orlando, saw beads of sweat prominent on his forehead and upper lip. A trained observer would know at once that they had something to hide. Wouldn't they?

'Did you pack all your luggage yourselves? Leave anything unattended at any time? Did anybody ask you to...?' 'No.' 'Boarding at sixteen forty-five. Have a good flight today.'

Orly had said it was Oliver's turn to have the window seat, which Oliver accepted. There was a downside to this arrangement. Orlando was endlessly clambering and nuzzling his way across him in order to see the things he would miss by sitting upright in his own seat. 'Do you see? St-Malo: the citadel, the docks – and the Bay of Mont St-Michel.' If you were going to be clambered over and nuzzled by someone on a plane it was nice that that someone was Orlando, but they were only just crossing the French coast and there were still over two hours to go. But then Orlando pulled his perennial pretty-boy trick with the male cabin crew and secured a second gin and tonic before the in-flight meal, and a double ration of wine when the meal came, and Oliver forgave him. One of the stewards looked closely at Orlando and said, 'Aren't you the guy in the Post Office ad?' And Orlando said, 'You're the first person who's ever recognised me. Can I have your autograph?'

Towards the end of the wine, suspended at thirty-six

thousand feet above the earth and its cares, a state of equilibrium seemed to have been reached. They were equidistant from the failures and complications of their lives in England and from the trials and uncertainties that awaited them in Seville. Fears were offset by hopes, their separate pasts in balance with their joint future. It was a brief, charmed moment. Orlando put his left arm around the back of Oliver's neck. It made Oliver feel awkward for a second. Despite his openness about the fact that he was gay, he had a residual feeling that you weren't supposed to do this sort of thing on aeroplanes. But then he relaxed. If the cabin crew wanted to tell them it wasn't permitted, let them. Trying to imagine this mind-boggling scene made Oliver giggle, and he then had to explain, sotto voce, to Orlando what he was laughing at. Meanwhile, though the western sky was still light blue with a pale apricot horizon stripe, night had fallen like a dark gauze across the ground below, and they saw the lights of towns and villages of Spain: jewels strewn in clusters upon the velvety black.

Landing, they had to make a detour to avoid a thunderstorm. The pilot announced that they could expect a normal landing: which had the opposite of the intended reassuring effect. They sank through clouds that towered like cathedrals, at first silvered by the moon above, then glowing pink and mauve within, their vaults and arches bright with diffused lightning flashes. For the second time Oliver found himself wishing he wasn't so near the window. But Orlando was crawling over him to get a better view, heedless of commands to fasten seatbelts, excited by the panorama of the storm. 'It's like we're in that painting by Blake, you know, the Fall of Lucifer,' he said. A sudden flash just then lit up his face.

'Don't,' said Oliver, and shut his eyes.

They bumped down through the energy-packed, ballooning clouds as if falling down stairs, but then emerged into calm. The city of Seville appeared: a lighted cart-wheel which performed a slow half-turn in the tilting port-hole then slid away behind. A minute later they landed smoothly on the tarmac of their new life.

Warmth hit them as they stepped out of the plane: Seville's daytime April temperature had scarcely dropped with the onset of the dark. The thunderstorm had not visited the city, though it still grumbled and sparked among the mountains away to the north. The smells were of kerosene, vegetation, orange blossom.

An airport coach took them into town, past tantalising floodlit glimpses of a city that Oliver did not yet know, and whose geography it was not easy to guess at during their arrival through alternating broad and narrow streets. The great minaret, the Giralda, appeared often and at unexpected points of the compass, seeming to float above the roofs and silhouetted palm tops of the suburbs. Near it rose the crenellated mass of the cathedral, monster size, while at the ends of streets strange Moorish buildings appeared then disappeared like apparitions in the Arabian Nights.

Orlando had done his research with the Rough Guide,

had phoned ahead and booked a *hostal* for their first night. Although by émigré standards they were travelling light, they had a big wheeled suitcase each and backpacks: they hadn't wanted to spend their first evening roaming the streets, trying to find accommodation door to door. The address Orlando had found them was not far from the Puerta de Jerez, where the coach deposited them, though even a ten-minute walk with luggage is very different from a ten-minute walk without any. But Orlando had again booked them somewhere close to the cathedral, and Oliver found time, as they trundled their belongings past its towering Gothic front and filigree roof line, to register the beauties of the lamp-lit streets, take in the vibrancy of the life that was lived here, and feel a cautious delight in the unfamiliar sounds and smells of – dared he think this? – his new home.

They were shown into an airy, white-walled room in their *hostal* in Calle Gamazo. There was a large double bed – the young man who showed them the room had not allowed himself even the flicker of an eyelid – and then an old bay window in the Moorish style, which the Spanish call a *mirador*, and which, thanks to its overhanging, wrought-iron-framed construction, offered views directly down into the street as well as outward and across, and then nosily sideways towards the neighbouring houses.

Orlando threw himself down on the bed, Oliver followed him, and they rolled and cuddled for a minute, then lay apart, staring up at the scalloped ceiling as though they expected to read their futures in it. Orlando suggested they go out and catch a few drinks and a *tapa* or two.

'Go easy on the drinks,' Oliver said. 'Big day tomorrow.' But he was as eager as Orlando was to get a feel for the town.

They didn't need to go far. At one end of the next street reared up the inescapable cathedral, the size of a small city state; at the other end the river ran, a trough of reflected lights. In between lay half a dozen small bars. They visited three: one a cave of blue patterned tiles and twinkling lights; one bare as a convent cell, with vast amphorae in a dark space at the back that gave the visitor an appropriate sense of awe; at the third a vast crowd of students milled energetically on the pavement, nursing ultra-cheap drinks and turning beer crates into impromptu, ever-shifting, arrangements of seats and tables, then erupting spontaneously from time to time into rowdy song. In the smartest of the three bars they ordered a *ración* of bull's tail. Oliver felt a bit queasy when Orly told him that they were barely a hundred metres from the bull ring, but managed to forget his reservations when the flavour of the meat, falling off the bone among the vegetables and wine-dark gravy, hit his palate. Eventually they stood on the river front, leaning over the balustrade. There were stars overhead, floodlit white buildings along the opposite bank, streetlamps and palm trees, the traffic crossing the San Telmo bridge, all reflected in the polished mirror of the river below. Oliver finally set his doubts and fears aside. 'I like it here,' he said.

'I should hope you bloody do,' said Orlando.

*

They could have set out in shorts the next morning, the weather was so comfortable; but they were not tourists, and the working population was not wearing anything so frivolous. They compromised and dressed in short-sleeved shirts with their interview ties. It was the first time they had seen each other wearing anything so formal. Out in the streets swifts screamed exhilaratingly as they sliced the blue sky overhead; the air was full of the warm scents of orange blossom and horse dung; bright flowers cascaded from lemon-and-white-painted balconies; a few lazy insects buzzed. They had breakfast standing at the counter of a corner café that was as busy at this hour as Piccadilly at its best. They ordered what the locals were having: glasses of milky coffee, finger-burningly hot, and crisp *tostados* on which they trickled shining green olive oil from graceful glass decanters with long snouts. Then they had a thirty-minute walk to make through a web of white-walled streets, lined with glaucous-leaved orange trees, neat as pom-poms, and starry with blossom, drenching the hot air with scent.

Their destination was a heavy-looking stone building on the no-nonsense corner of a busy shopping street. They climbed wide stairs and entered a small dark office where a small dark woman sat behind a reception desk. Orlando said, in what he hoped was the correct register for the occasion, *'Tenemos hora con el Señor Guttierez*

López.' He gave their names.

The young woman did not look overjoyed to see them. Oliver thought she reacted to their names with a flinch. 'I'm sorry,' she said in English. 'Señor Guttierez López can not see you.'

'But we have an appointment,' Orlando switched to English too. 'We've just arrived from England.'

'Do you mean he can't see us now,' Oliver spoke for the first time, 'or that he can't see us at all?'

'He can't see you at all.'

'There must be a mistake,' said Orlando. 'We start work here on Monday.'

'I think that can not be possible,' said the woman. 'He has no more vacancies at present.'

'I spoke to him on the phone...' Orlando began, dropping back into measured Spanish as if that might put everything right.

'Listen,' Oliver cut in, 'is he in his office at present?'

The woman looked alarmed, her brown eyes growing wide. 'You can't go in.'

'Don't worry,' said Oliver. 'We won't do that. We'll just wait here, if you don't mind, till he comes out.' He looked around the dull brown room. There were two uncomfortable-looking chairs. He plonked himself down in one of them. 'All day if necessary.' He patted the other chair and looked meaningfully at Orlando. Orlando looked helplessly at the woman and then sat on the second chair. Oliver and the woman stared at each other for a full half minute. At the end of that time the woman picked up a phone, pressed a couple of buttons, and said something into the mouthpiece that Oliver could not catch. She put the phone down.

A few more seconds passed. Then a door opened and in came a little rotund man with a politely small moustache. 'Mr Kidd, Mr Watson,' he addressed them at once. They both stood up. Señor Guttierez López did not offer to shake their hands. Nor did he offer a smile. 'There has been a misunderstanding. I have been looking for two new teachers. I specified a young couple. Over the telephone with one of you – I don't know which – I heard your names as Orlando and Olivia. I spoke yesterday, by chance, to our mutual friend Felipe Suarez, who told me it is not Olivia but Oliver – a man. A man who is already in his thirties.'

'We've come all the way from England,' Oliver said in a steely voice. 'At your invitation. You've let us waste our money and our time.'

'And my time also,' said the other, now positively scowling at Oliver. 'I have had to go to some trouble at short notice to find another, suitable couple I could engage. I'm sorry you have had a wasted journey. I telephoned you – one of you – yesterday in the morning, and again in the afternoon. There was no answer. I suppose you had already left. Now, I am sorry but there is no more I can do for you. If you are still looking for work in September feel free to contact me again. Thank you for your interest.' Abruptly he turned and disappeared back through the door.

Orlando and Oliver looked at each other. For the moment no words would come. There were a few words that Oliver would want to say to Orlando, but not till they were outside. Shaken, they turned towards the door.

A noise like a sneeze made Oliver look back. 'Listen.' The receptionist was holding a slip of paper out to them. 'My brother works for another school. Maybe he can help you. You go to this place.' She pointed to an address she'd written on the paper. 'This evening. Nine o'clock. I call him. I tell him meet you there.' Seeing distrust in both their faces she tried to put them at their ease. 'The address is a bar.'

*

'You should have checked the situation properly at the beginning,' Oliver began, as soon as they were on their way downstairs, both ashen-faced. 'I thought at the time it was all too casual.'

'Then you should have picked up the phone and checked for yourself,' said Orlando. He sounded close to tears. 'At least I made the call in the first place. You didn't.' They were out of the building now and back in the sunshine.

'That's because it was your idea. You wanted to come here, because of a vague suggestion from a man we met in a bar, instead of applying for a job in the proper way.

Against my better judgement I went along.' He tried to make his voice sound gentle: the disappointed lover rather than the angry friend. Reducing Orlando to tears in the street would make nothing any better.

But Orly wasn't ready to dissolve just yet. 'What about you meeting a bloke in a bar back in England and running stuff through customs for him? Bet you didn't take up references.'

'Orly…'

'Oliver… Oh fuck it. Look, I'm sorry. You're right. OK?'

'I'm sorry too … my darling.' It was the first time Oliver had ever called him that, and it was to his own eyes that tears unexpectedly sprang. 'But it's my fault too. I should have taken charge of the thing myself. Not left it all to you.' It was not yet eleven o'clock in the morning, but Oliver didn't protest when Orlando suggested they should sit down outside the first bar that presented itself and have a beer.

The day was lost, the day had won; they surrendered themselves to it. They wandered the streets and byways, the Alameda de Hércules, the Calle Jesús del Gran Poder; they viewed the remains of Roman walls and the Basilica de la Macarena. They saw the inside of the Casablanca bar; flopped down on stools in the courtyard outside the Casa Roman, where they were served by a handsome waiter whose flies were kept decently closed only with the aid of a giant safety-pin; they ate oranges bought from a pavement stall.

'Don't you notice,' Orlando said, 'each place has its own special colour?'

'Here being?'

'Lemon? The zest, brilliant yellow, the pith shining white. Then a darker yellow too: the colour of rich egg yolks,' he switched into a Mummerset accent, 'laid by the best free range hens.'

'The thing now is,' Oliver said, 'what do we decide to do next? Take the first plane home? Go along to this bar tonight – which will probably turn out to be a wild goose chase? Or cut our losses and have a holiday here before going back?'

'Go to this bar this evening of course,' said Orlando. 'We can't just go back. At least I can't. And I don't think I can afford just to have a holiday. My father would do his nut. Got to stay on and try to get some sort of a job.'

Oliver saw the point about Orlando's father. He had not forgotten his recent conversation with his brother. 'OK,' he said. 'We'll do that. But we're not penniless yet. There's quite a bit of my redundancy money still left.'

'Yes, but not enough to for you to live on for ever.' Orlando sounded shocked. 'And I'm not supposed to be living off you, remember. That's not how it was meant to be.'

Oliver didn't need to be reminded about the limits of his reserves, even if he was reassured by Orly's attitude to a source of money that was not strictly speaking his. Oliver's funds had been dwindling as his weeks of unemployment had multiplied to months, and the cost of the training course had made further inroads. In any case, most of the redundancy money was set aside in a special account and couldn't be accessed simply by pushing a piece of plastic into a hole in a white and yellow Sevillian wall. He'd been buoyed by his payments from Donald: fourteen hundred pounds in all. They had made him feel briefly rich. But where was that money now? Hans's rent cheques would be a plus, but they would do little more than cover the mortgage and the odd repair.

They passed an attractive little *pension* as they walked along the Triana riverfront, with bright flowers outside and an offer, chalked on a board, of rooms at half the price they were paying at their *hostal*. 'We could bear that in mind if we have to penny-pinch in a few days'time,' Oliver said.

They spent the hottest part of the afternoon by the river, stretched full-length under the palm trees near the Torre del Oro, and looking up at its Moorish battlements through the waving-finger fronds. Just yards away boats plied up and down the Guadalquivir, and a procession of local life passed by. The population seemed extraordinarily young to Oliver, its chief occupation flirting with the opposite sex. Somehow that gave Oliver a feeling of deep melancholy, whose shade was nevertheless picked out with bright gleams of hope. The sun sparkled between the silhouetted, slowly moving palm-frond fingers, and Orlando, tickling Oliver's navel with a finger, leaned over him and, laughing, told him he'd been asleep.

*

They decided to take their CVs with them to the evening meeting, just in case, but not their certificates as well. But they got them out and showed them off to each other all the same. Orlando's diploma from drama school in Birmingham. Oliver's degree certificate from Nottingham. 'A first – you never said,' Orlando reproved him, though he sounded more than impressed. Orlando's HGV licence... 'HGV licence?' Oliver queried. 'What did you bring that for? I didn't know you had one anyway.'

'My father made me get it a couple of years ago. So I could drive the farm lorry if and when.'

'And did you?'

'Sometimes it came in handy. Taking sheep to Ashford when there was no-one else available.'

'To Ashford? No, you needn't tell me. I've worked it out.'

'Anyway, he always said you never knew when it would come in useful.'

Oliver looked around them, at their whitewashed

hostal bedroom, at the silky yellow counterpane they sprawled on, through the *mirador* to the narrow street outside. 'You never know, I suppose.'

Orlando would have hit the bars again at six, but Oliver, mindful of Bernd's warning, managed to keep him otherwise engaged till nearly seven. Then he gave in. They made a slow and steady crawl along the *paseos,* and through the streets, between then and nine o'clock. A beer at the Casa Moreno on Mesón del Moro, then through to Morales, the time-warped bar they'd been to the previous night, with its Arabian Nights amphorae in the background gloom. A copita of cold pale manzanilla seemed more the thing in this reverent atmosphere than beer. A bit of a backtrack then to the Casablanca bar in Zaragoza street, then north through zigzag alleys to la Antigua Bodegita on the Plaza del Salvador, near the old red-walled church. There was still time to watch the world go by, sitting out in the broad square. They had a *tapa* or two, but planned to eat properly later, once their meeting – if it ever took place – was over. Then it was just round two street corners to the Casa Antonio Los Caracoles (Antonio the Snails) for a glass or two of *tinto*, after which, finally, and almost punctually at nine o'clock, they found their way out onto Calle Imagen and to the address where their meeting was – perhaps – to take place.

It was a more workaday bar than the others. Orlando said, 'He won't come,' deadpan and suddenly despondent, as they entered. 'And how will we recognise him if he does?' But he was wrong on both counts.

Moments after they had accustomed themselves to the relative darkness – for daylight was still just clinging on in the streets outside – they saw the receptionist they had met that morning arriving through another door with a man. He looked as much like her brother as you could reasonably expect, even if he was twice her size. Oliver, who had just reached the counter, offered everyone a drink.

Away from her place of work the receptionist was a different person. Oliver's memory had preserved her in tones of sepia and black; there had been something guarded in her manner and voice. Now she appeared a lively thirty-something Spanish *macha*, in an outfit where old gold and cherry red complemented the black. Her dark hair, worn high, bore highlights of chestnut. Her name was Concepción. 'That was not just, this morning,' she said, accepting a Coca-cola, 'and what he said was so not correct.' Was her English idiom more up to date than his own, Oliver wondered, or had the words simply come out in the wrong order? 'Two young people came to see him yesterday – very young – but boy and girl, what he wanted. He gave the jobs to them. I think that after that he call Felipe to contact you, not before. But he was so too late. This morning I felt myself...' She shook her head, failing to find an English adjective equal to the task of expressing how she had felt. She introduced her brother Toni, but he only smiled a quick acknowledgement of Oliver, being already deeply absorbed in conversation with Orlando in Spanish. He was a few years younger than his sister, Oliver noticed, with thick black curls and big eyes.

219

'You are very assertive man,' Concepción went on with Oliver. 'I notice. You deal with Eduardo in the right way.'

'It wasn't the right enough way to get us jobs,' Oliver said, trying to make a joke of it but sounding bitter all the same.

'Forget him,' said Concepción. 'You are in Seville. There is only one way to be. Happy!' To Oliver's astonishment she laughed aloud, almost with a scream, like someone overcome at being the surprise winner of a game show. Toni now half turned towards them. They were still all standing at the bar, the men with beers on the counter near them. *'Gracias, señor.'* He raised his glass to Oliver, and then went on in Spanish which, to his surprise, Oliver found himself understanding without difficulty. Perhaps it was the drink. 'And welcome to the greatest of all beautiful cities. When the devil wishes to really tempt a person this is where he sends them. It's absolutely true. My cousin – but no, you will be bored. Your friend...' he placed an arm around Orlando's shoulder and beamed at him for a second '...he is a very handsome man. He will be... No, listen, my boss, he is coming here to see you at ten. He will...'

'Your boss is coming here? To meet us? At ten? Tonight?' A delighted nod was the answer to each question, while Oliver's sense of horror grew in geometrical progression with each one. They were not dressed for an interview and were in no state for one after the quantity they had drunk. Nervously Oliver fingered the folded, creased CV in the back pocket of his denims.

'He looks forward to meeting you. I told him how you are very experienced teachers and just what he is looking for.'

'I don't think…' Oliver's Spanish was not up to going on. 'Orly, can you explain to him – we're not expecting an interview. Can it be rescheduled? Does he have a phone?' He watched as Orly put all this to Toni.

But Toni didn't see that there was any problem at all. It wouldn't be like an interview at all, he said, more like a friendly meeting between fellow professionals. He called to the barman and, before Oliver could stop him, ordered a fresh round of drinks.

Within the next few minutes it became clear to Oliver, even in his fuzzy state, that Concepción was as interested in him as her brother was in Orlando, as she engaged him in ever more searching conversation, asking him whether he had a house in England or a flat, and what kind it was and where, while it was as much as Oliver could do to stop himself from physically removing Toni's hand from the various parts of Orly that it kept alighting on like an opportunistic fly. It was actually a relief when someone else arrived, came up to them, and was introduced by his first name, Salvador: Toni's boss and the head of the next-door language school.

Salvador shook hands with a beaming smile. Oliver couldn't help making the comparison between him and the glowering Eduardo of this morning's encounter. Salvador was large, sleek and silver-haired, with expressive eyes. Like a seal, Oliver thought. He indicated that they should sit at a table, and then chose one that was quite large – as it needed to be to accommodate Salvador, Orlando, Oliver, and Toni and Concepción as well. If this was a job interview, Oliver thought, it was the strangest one in his experience.

'Thank you for seeing us,' Oliver began quickly, not daring to let Orlando speak first in case he came out with something inappropriate; he hadn't had a chance to check how drunk his lover was. 'I'm afraid we weren't expecting an interview this evening, and we haven't come dressed for one, or even prepared.'

Salvador, carefully dressed in suit and tie, now removed the tie and unbuttoned his shirt collar, with all the ritual of a priest disrobing after Mass. 'No problem. Maybe you will feel better now.' He explained that he had a sizeable business teaching languages to secretaries and office staff. Teachers came and went, he said; he was always needing new people; he could use the two of them starting next week. Concepción nodded encouragingly at Oliver.

'We have our TVs,' said Orlando brightly, 'but not the tificates and things to sport them.' He was naturally unaware that in Oliver's private realm he had been forbidden to speak. He fumbled in his jeans, having to half stand in the process. He was not looking his best, Oliver thought with a sinking heart. Oliver reached in his own back pocket and handed over his crumpled life history, at the same time as Orlando lurchingly delivered his.

Salvador looked the papers through, quite carefully, still beaming. It wasn't until he turned them over as if he hoped there might be something further on the back, and found there wasn't, that his smile began to fade. 'You certainly have a lot of experience,' he said, 'and I congratulate you on the breadth of your respective achievements. It's only that you don't appear to have much experience when it comes to teaching English.' He aimed a look in Toni's direction which was perhaps a gentle reproof. Toni shifted on his chair and looked at his beer glass as if he'd only just spotted it.

'You only get experience by getting experience,' said Orlando. Salvador ignored this, while Oliver privately gave thanks that he'd navigated that particular reef of consonants without mishap.

'The other thing is,' Salvador went on musingly, 'that while you, Oliver, have an exceptionally impressive first degree, our friend Orlando has not.'

'It's the equivalent,' Orlando said. 'A diploma from a drama school. Because I went to drama school insteadiversity. It's unusual to do both in Britain. So it amounts to a shame.'

'I'm afraid the Spanish authorities would not see it like that,' said Salvador, generously replying to what Orlando had meant to say rather than to what he actually had.

Oliver came hastily to Orlando's aid. 'The training college in London thought it was good enough. They accepted him, like me, on a post-graduate course.'

'Absolutely,' Orlando came back. 'They said my qualifications were appropriate.'

'They may well be appropriate in London,' said Salvador. He was one of those professional users of English who take pride in speaking it with greater fluency and exactness than most native speakers. 'And I've no reason to doubt your capability, but unfortunately I am not allowed to employ any foreign nationals who have not got a university first degree. This was an agreement reached many years ago between our government and the unions to protect the livelihoods of Spanish teachers of foreign languages, of whom there are a great many. I might wish it was otherwise – and you certainly must do – but I'm afraid there is nothing I can do.'

Orlando stood up. He was very red in the face. 'OK, Oli, that's it. Let's get out of here.'

'Sit down,' Oliver told him, then turned quickly back to Salvador without waiting to see if Orly had obeyed or not. 'I'm sorry. I must apologise. As I said, we weren't in interview mode so late in the evening and it came as a bit of a surprise…'

'Oli, I'm going *now*,' he heard Orlando say. He either hadn't sat down or had quickly got to his feet again.

Oliver protested, 'Orlando, wait! There's still things

could be discussed. One job would be better than none.'

'Well, to be honest, Oliver,' said Salvador, leaning forward, now looking rather pained, 'there is the question – in your case too – of lack of experience. And I do normally employ people rather younger than yourself. I was thinking of making an exception in this case, but...'

'Oh come on,' called Orlando, 'I told you, let's get out.' He was having difficulty keeping his footing in the confined area between the table and his chair. He moved into more open waters and tacked towards the door. It was Oliver's first experience of Orlando angry. He gave up.

'Well, thank you for seeing us anyway,' he said to Salvador, trying to smile urbanely but in fact producing a fearsome leer, then he too got up and, rather unsteadily, made his way after Orlando.

He caught up with him in the street outside, which was now softly lamp-lit. Plucking at his sleeve to stop him marching on, he said, 'There was no need for that. We could have swung one job out of him if you hadn't lost it.'

Orlando pivoted towards him. 'One job! We didn't come here for one job!'

'We'd have pooled the money, you pillock, and something would have come along for you sooner or later.'

'Then it will for both of us.'

Someone caught up with them just then and placed an arm around both their shoulders. Toni. '*Lo siento*. I'm sorry. I didn't know.' He spoke rapidly, while Oliver felt his nervously exploring hand touch the back of his neck, run down his spine and momentarily pat his bottom. 'Salvador is very correct about everything. He has to be. His school is a quality one. But there are other schools here, many in fact, where the rules are not so strictly applied. I can't give you any contact names, I'm sorry, but you could try the *paginas amarillas* and ring round a few tomorrow. Then you've got all next week to get something sorted. The week after that's the *Feria* and everything closes down. Sorry, but I must get back to the others.' He turned rapidly and disappeared. Oliver found that the intimate attentions that had so annoyed him when they were bestowed uniquely on Orlando had not upset him so much when equally divided between them. He decided, rather belatedly, that Toni was both handsome and rather nice.

'We'd better get you something to eat,' he said, practically.

Orlando said, 'What I need's a fucking drink.'

Oliver decided the remark was better ignored than contradicted. He also chose a nearby pizza restaurant, although that wasn't exactly *tipico*, but he was thinking in terms of a mop-up operation rather than a gastronomic treat.

They did sober up to some extent over a pizza and a bottle of wine, consumed at a very leisurely rate. (Oliver made sure of that by keeping the bottle on his side of the table.) Orlando was struggling inside himself with an oncoming fit of the sulks. 'It's all very well for you,' he said. 'You're a graduate. The world's your oyster.'

'Don't exaggerate…'

'I know you're blaming me…'

'I'm not,' said Oliver, trying not to smile.

'I can feel you are. How was I to know they only employed graduates here? They might have warned us at the college…'

'Have you finished? Finished eating, I mean. We get the bill, walk home. OK? Enjoy the night air. Start putting things right in the morning?'

Orlando nodded, then grinned. The sulks had gone as miraculously as hiccups.

They followed the main street slightly downhill, through the Plaza de la Encarnación and its hive of buses, guessing that they would eventually find themselves at the river, and could get back to their *hostal* from there. It was a more sensible option than trying to retrace their steps through the back streets in the dark. The city centre showed no sign of closing up. Shops in the street of the Reyes Católicos were brightly lit, if not necessarily all open, and a parade of people still thronged the pavements. Street lamps shimmered through the dark foliage of the orange trees, their diffused rays making the leaves gleam against the night. The traffic was still heavy and the noise of car horns, heels on flagstones, greetings hurled across streets, music spilling out of bars, was as intense as it had been at midday.

They stopped for one or two beers. They were quite sober now. In one of the cafés a white-haired man in a heavy coat broke spontaneously into *cante jondo*, without rising from the table where he sat and drank with friends, and somebody produced a guitar and unselfconsciously fell in with him in an improvised, at times elaborate, accompaniment. Everybody listened attentively; they knew the rules: when to clap, when to shout an interpolation, when to drum the floor. Orlando and Oliver just listened. After a few minutes the performance stopped as suddenly as it had begun. Oliver glanced at his watch. It was three o'clock.

And then they were on the river bank, among beds of tall aromatic shrubs, under a canopy of palms. 'I'm sorry I was such a prick earlier,' Orlando said.

'It doesn't matter,' said Oliver, slowly undoing Orlando's belt and studs, easing down the waistband of his jeans. 'I love you just the same.'

ELEVEN

They had a lot of sex that weekend. They talked about it too, opening up about their previous experiences in the way that serious lovers will usually do at some point – the occasion being a rite of passage on the new journey on which they've found themselves.

'There was this boy at school,' confessed Orlando. I… I suppose I fell for him. He liked me too, but I don't think it was quite the same. Christopher. He's married now anyway. I saw them both last time I went hunting.' He paused. They both thought, Easter, less than three weeks ago; how long a time that seemed. 'We did the usual things together.'

'Usual things?' Oliver queried.

'I mean like catching frogs and climbing trees. Pony riding. Though that might not sound so usual to you.'

'Except the pony riding, it does.'

'But we also took to sleeping together. From the age of eight. If we slept over at each other's houses we insisted on it. Naked.'

'Jesus, you started young.'

'Just harmless fun, you understand,' Orlando clarified. 'It was all perfectly innocent. Unless the fact that I enjoyed it means it wasn't. When we were eleven we stopped. Became a bit too aware I suppose.'

'The Garden of Eden.'

'Pardon?'

'And they discovered how naked they were.'

'I suppose. There was just one time though, when we'd have both been seventeen. We found ourselves standing next to each other, having a piss, at the loo in the local pub. And we saw we were both excited. We looked at each other and the next thing – well, you can guess. We thought someone would come in and we'd have to stop. But nobody did. It only took about a minute – the novelty I suppose – then we went back to join the others and finished our pints. We never mentioned it and it never happened again. Mind you, I can never take a leak in that particular pub without remembering.'

'And was that the first time you'd ever done anything with a bloke?' Oliver asked.

'Oh no,' Orlando answered lightly. 'There were other kids at school before that. From when I was fifteen. But just businesslike wanks you understand.'

'You do surprise me,' said Oliver, feeling decidedly unsettled. The solid floor on which he stood was shifting again. But it was always like that with new relationships, he knew. You built them around the limited knowledge you had of each other at the beginning, the way a mouse would build its nest among the standing corn stalks. But the corn stalks were never still: they shivered in the wind; they grew.

Oliver told Orly his own, slightly less precocious, story. He had kept his hands to himself till he was eighteen. Then, within a few days of arriving at university it had happened. A boy at a freshers'party – called Jim. They had seen the future in each other's eyes, at least as far as that evening was concerned, right at the beginning of the evening across the (yes, really) crowded room. And, despite spending only a small part of the evening in each other's company, they had left together and headed back to Jim's room. There, Jim had taken Oliver to bed and fucked him and, a little time afterwards, Oliver had returned the compliment – with a little help from the marginally more experienced Jim. Jim had worn a condom but had been quite happy to let Oliver enter him without one. Oliver's lack of experience was only too apparent, his enthusiasm notwithstanding. Jim had had no difficulty in believing him when he said he'd never done anything like it before.

'Did it last?' Orlando asked.

'For a couple of weeks.' Oliver was achingly conscious that Orlando and he had only made it as far as four. 'We sort of thought we'd fallen in love, but we'd only just arrived at university and we quickly found there were a hell of a lot of other fish in the sea. I was soon buying my own condoms, if you see what I mean.'

'In bulk I would imagine,' said Orlando, deadpan. 'And girls?'

This wasn't a question Oliver liked too much,

especially when it was put to him by a younger man whom he was still trying to impress. But he made a clean breast of it. 'I've never had one. Never wanted. Never tried.'

'Oh wow,' said Orlando, but then added, 'I guess you were too much in demand at the other end of the ballroom.'

'Whereas you've had hundreds, I imagine,' said Oliver, trying not to sound as if the answer would matter to him.

'Actually, no,' Orlando said. 'Just two. And only once in each case.' There was silence for a second, and then they both began to laugh.

'You little fox,' said Oliver. 'Marmalade cat, no way. You're a fucking little fox cub all along. You've had me believing you're a fully paid-up bisexual boy – and highly experienced at that – and all on the basis of just two pokes...'

'That's about the size of it.' Orlando admitted.

'...When you're actually as gay as I am.' Oliver had been quietly caressing his lover's penis through his denims for the last ten minutes. Now he undid the studs in a pretence of fury and set to work on it in earnest, while Orlando did the same with Oliver's.

*

They didn't spend the whole weekend making love.

Friday was a busy day, even if, after the late and drunken evening before, it had begun rather late. At breakfast in their neighbourhood café all heads were swivelled towards a large television screen and they swivelled theirs too, to discover that the focus of attention was not a football match or even a bullfight, but the solemn funeral of Pope John-Paul II in Rome. In view of the sudden death of their own hopes for jobs and a flat, it seemed grimly appropriate. 'At least we're luckier here with the weather,' Orlando pointed out. Beyond the plate-glass window the sun was smiling on Seville's streets, while on the television the skies of Rome seemed uncertain and overcast, and the robed cardinals struggled to save each other from being partially unfrocked by a mischievous, unruly wind.

They went to the tourist information office and were allowed to hunt through the *paginas amarillas* for phone numbers of language schools, which they carefully copied out. They found time to telephone a few before the weekend finally drew the shutters, and were feeling more cheerful once they found themselves invited to go and meet a few people with possible jobs to offer in the week ahead.

Then, with nothing further to be done before Monday, they became tourists by default. Orlando, who had been here before, was Oliver's guide. He showed him the cavernous cathedral, and Oliver was suitably awed. Huge paintings hung on the stone walls: dark canvasses depicting soulful-eyed saints; and of Christ, ivory-white and bleeding, against a background black as death. Side chapels lay back behind elaborate iron grilles. Tier upon tier of lit candles rose up in corners, impregnating the darkness with their seeds of light. There was the gargantuan tomb of Christopher Columbus and the equally colossal gold screen, the *retablo*, that towered sixty feet behind the high altar and measured forty feet across, its front carved out, in rows and columns, into New Testament scenes, and statues of the saints. 'It's like the biggest chocolate bar you ever saw,' said Orlando disrespectfully. 'All in gold foil, and the squares show through when you press it with your fingers.' The shock of sunshine that greeted them when they emerged was, oddly enough, the highlight of the whole experience.

Nearby were the Moorish palaces of the Alcázar, rambling and intertwined with their lush gardens. Orlando led Oliver among citrus-planted courtyards, under sculpted ceilings, through groves of pomegranate trees, in sunlit air that was scented with jasmine, myrtle and box. They entered the Barrio Santa Cruz. through a vaulted tunnel where an old house had been built over a crooked lane. The tour of this warren of alleyways then became something of a bar crawl. Orlando said this was a necessary and serious piece of research: in future they would know the right places to come. The Casa Roman, with smoke-dark hams dangling among the beams. The Bodega Aviles, with its bottles of marmalade-tasting orange wine and its original mahogany bar counter, so worn away by the centuries that it had almost ceased to exist. The Bar Modesto, which Orlando remembered as quite small, now expanded and occupying half the premises along a small street.

Orlando didn't phone his father that weekend. He said he would wait until he had some good news to relate. Wouldn't his father be worried, Oliver asked, if he didn't hear anything at all? Orlando hadn't even let his family know that he'd arrived in Spain. But he was absolutely certain now that there would be good news in a day or two; there was no point worrying people unnecessarily. What if there wasn't any good news in a day or two, Oliver wanted to ask, what then? But he held his tongue. They would find out' what then'all too soon. And he didn't ring any friends or family back home either. Unless one counted Hans as a friend. Hans had moved into Oliver's Kilburn flat on Saturday. Oliver phoned him on Sunday to check that everything was all right, and Hans answered cheerfully that all was, 'just very fine'. He'd collected the keys from a neighbour as had been arranged, and had set up a standing order for the payment of his rent. Oliver thought that was just very fine too, even if most of the income would go straight out again by way of the standing order that paid his mortgage.

Monday arrived with the prospect of two interviews. One was in the Macarena district, about two miles away from their *hostal*; the other was near the coach station in the Prado de San Sebastián, which was nearly as far again in the opposite direction. But as the weather continued warm and bright, they set off with hopes to match.

Orlando had done the talking on the telephone, using

his Spanish to charm receptionists into giving him direct access to heads of schools. He thought the person he had spoken to at the Macarena school had sounded most encouraging. But arriving, climbing dark stairs, approaching a reception desk, Oliver thought with foreboding that this would only be a replay of the previous week. They were shown into a comfortable office. The head of school was friendly but frank. It was very useful, he told them, to have a face to face meeting, but when it came to actual jobs, well no, there wouldn't be any vacancies to be expected until September. The walk to their second interview, even though broken by a lunch stop, seemed extremely long. 'My back's beginning to hurt,' Oliver announced. Orlando wasn't over-sympathetic. 'Blisters on the feet, me.'

That evening they found a cheaper place to eat at than the bars and bodegas they had been frequenting up till then. It was at the far end of smart Calle Sierpes, though appropriately a little distance back from it, since it was a long way from being smart itself: a studenty place that did small hamburgers for small prices – you watched the meat being nonchalantly flipped around on the grill – as well as red wine that was as dark as ink, and whose spectacularly low price told you all you needed to know about the quality of tomorrow's hangover.

The days began to blur. An interview in the suburb of Nervión, near the football stadium. Again Oliver was found to be too old, and Orlando's qualifications insufficient, although they had been pronounced acceptable over the phone. They walked back along the highway taken by the airport coaches, which overtook them at regular intervals in a fine haze of exhaust fumes and dust. And an interview across the river in Triana delivered yet another rebuff; they more or less expected that by now. Walking back from it they passed the pretty *pension* with flowers outside that had caught their attention the week before. Still the board propped up beside the doorway advertised rooms at half the price they were paying in Calle Gamazo. Oliver looked at Orlando. 'What do you reckon?'

Orlando nodded. Neither of them needed to spell out the obvious: that their money was haemorrhaging away on living expenses and nothing was coming in. Oliver rang the bell beside the *cancela*, the wrought-iron grille that is the entrance to Sevillian courtyard houses. Through it they could see a clean-swept tiled hallway with one or two tall green plants in pots. Beyond, it opened into an inner patio. Orlando looked back at Oliver. 'It couldn't be all that bad,' he said.

And it's only going to be for a few nights, Oliver thought. If no job materialised before the weekend they would be heading home. He would go public with this thought at some later date – at a time of his own choosing.

A white-haired, matronly woman appeared on the other side of the *cancela*. She asked what they wanted and they told her. She had considerably fewer teeth than she might have done at one time, but she smiled agreeably enough while she told them she had a double room available, with balcony and shower, at the price advertised on the board. They asked her to hold it for them for an hour while they checked out of Calle Gamazo and fetched their things. They would spend some time, later that evening, wondering which of them had been the more culpable in neglecting that most obvious of precautions: inspect the room first. Orlando, because he spoke the language better? Or Oliver, because he was supposed to be the more grownup?

It was a long hot walk, weighed down with luggage, from Calle Gamazo. Down past the bull ring to the river and along the Paseo de Cristóbal Colón. Across the double span of the San Telmo Bridge, then back along the riverfront on the Triana side. Oliver was in pain with his back by the end of the journey. He didn't mention this, neither did he enquire after Orlando's blisters. For when they did arrive at their new home, discovery followed unpleasant discovery in such quick succession that neither of them had time to formulate any comments to each other at all, and they had only stunned silence to offer the old woman, who now presented them with their key.

The balcony they had been promised turned out to be a mere section of the gallery that ran along the inner wall of the patio at first floor level, and off which the bedrooms – closed by solid wood doors – all led, like prison cells. The patio was filled with daylight, it was true, but that daylight came filtered through blue-tinted corrugated plastic sheets, which had been further darkened by an accumulation of pigeon feathers and dung. The bedroom received no natural light at all.

When the door was shut it was an unventilated box containing two iron bedsteads of the kind to be seen in old pictures of hospitals or boarding schools. The bedroom roof was also corrugated: it looked to Oliver like asbestos sheeting. 'We can't stay here,' Orlando said. His voice was low and rasping in his throat.

Oliver lay down – almost collapsed, on one of the beds. 'I can't go anywhere else,' he said. 'Not now. Not with luggage. My back's done in.'

'We'll get a taxi.'

'Oh yeah? We've so much money to spend on taxis. And anyway, go where?'

Orlando was silent, sitting wretchedly on the other iron bed. The silence went on for ever. The words *You go if you want* kept rising to Oliver's lips but he bit them back. He didn't know what he'd do if the kid said yes. Orlando might have been biting back hard words too, but in the end it was he who spoke first. 'I'll never leave you here, you know.'

'Thank you.' Oliver's answer came in a whisper, but then he went on more firmly, 'We'll stick it for one night. Tomorrow we'll find somewhere better. I promise.' But he didn't know how the promise was to be fulfilled.

'Where's the fucking shower, I'd like to know,' said Orlando.

'I think you'll find it's a communal one, at the end of

the gallery, next to the loo.'

'Oh Jesus Christ,' Orlando said. 'I'm not even going to unpack. I'll give your back a rub and then let's go out and get a bloody drink.' Oliver had to agree. But they had to ring the bell at the *cancela* to summon the old woman with the keys to let them out.

They made further discoveries. Oliver's mobile phone could not get a signal anywhere inside their *pension* – which they had already started to refer to as their prison. Most of their fellow inmates were migrant workers, the unemployed, or simply dossers. 'When you come to think of it,' Oliver said, 'we're all in roughly the same position, them and us.' Though they had come across someone in a slightly worse case than themselves on their travels round the city. He was about Oliver's age and, they thought, German: they had guessed at his nationality from his accent when he had been trying to cadge cigarettes in the Morales bar. His ragged hair fell on his shoulders and he carried all his possessions in a satchel on his back. They had seen him several times, haunting the river bank mostly, whiling away the hours of sunshine lying under a date palm with lizards for company and a bottle of something nameless by his side. Once they glimpsed him disappearing into an abandoned workmen's hut under the Triana Bridge with a couple of other grubby, ragged men. 'Wonder how long before we join them,' Orlando said. Oliver didn't try to reply. Orlando's enthusiasm, which had flown before them like a bright banner during their first optimistic days in Seville, was on the wane now – the banner at half mast.

How did this' third world'operate here in Seville? Begging? A little light dealing in marijuana? Oliver didn't intend to wait and find out. 'Listen,' he said, over a drink in the Bar Morales, 'we need to make a decision. I say we give Seville until the weekend to deliver something in the way of a job. And if it doesn't, we get the plane home. What do you reckon?'

He was afraid that Orlando would dig his heels in and want to stay till all their money was gone and they really were reduced to the condition of beggars, and so he was relieved when Orly slowly nodded his head and said, 'I guess you're right. Next week's the *Feria* here and all the schools'll be shut. Everything that doesn't close rockets in price, and you need to be a millionaire to afford a room for the night. I know that.'

'I'm glad you're with me,' Oliver said. 'But the next thing is – where do we go if we do go back?' He looked down at the table and his wineglass for a second. 'I mean, if you still want to live with me, that is.'

Orlando looked at him sternly. 'Of course I do. You know that.'

Oliver found himself smiling, and discovered that it hurt. 'We can't very easily go back to Oxford Road, now Hans is renting it.'

'There's always Kentish Town, I suppose,' Orlando said diffidently. 'My old room's been snapped up, but there'd always be a floor for us – until we got something better sorted.'

The fact of having made a decision of some kind, even a negative one, did make them feel slightly better, and their situation began to appear less dire after a cheap greasy snack and a few drinks. But things didn't go on appearing better drink by drink: the law of diminishing returns from alcohol saw to that. They were subdued and depressed when they eventually crawled into their single beds in the stuffy darkness of their new home. Neither of them had the heart to suggest sharing.

'Did you hear rats in the night?' Orlando asked Oliver in the morning. Oliver nodded. He had heard something, and hoped it wasn't rats, but Orlando's diagnosis, coming from a farm boy as it did, confirmed his gloomy suspicion. He shuddered involuntarily.

They were on their way by bus to Carmona, thirty kilometres away, for one more interview. They drove past Seville airport and saw a British aircraft rise gracefully from the runway. They exchanged glances but had no need to say anything.

The result of the interview was a foregone conclusion; there was no element of surprise any more. On the way downstairs they looked at each other's dishevelled clothes. They did look more like tramps now than teachers. Even Orlando's beauty was clouded over with grime and disenchantment. Thanks to his blistered soles he was walking with a limp.

They bought bread and chorizo for an impromptu

picnic, which they ate by the city wall, where the town comes to a sudden stop at the Puerta de Córdoba, and the countryside appears wonderfully framed by the Moorish archway as if viewed through a giant keyhole. 'It looks so white,' Orlando said, referring to the landscape before and below them. The old Cordoba road, no longer in use except by farm carts, dropped steeply away from the gate before continuing across the wide plain.

'I see what you mean,' Oliver said. 'It looks like the end of summer, not the beginning. Everything's so parched and dry.' Dark cypresses and stands of green-brown holm oak punctured the vast panorama here and there, but for the most part the grazing land had the shimmering, silvered-over appearance that goes with prolonged lack of rainfall.

Back in Seville, they agreed to spend one more night at the *pension.* They thought they could just about face that if they were going home at the weekend. They also felt unable to summon the energy to spend the evening *hostal*-hunting and trundling luggage yet again. In the morning they would phone the airport, or find a travel agent's, and sort out tickets for the plane. 'And another thing,' Oliver said, wrinkling his nose. 'We must get to a launderette.'

'There's a *corrida* tomorrow evening,' Orlando announced. 'I don't suppose…'

'No I would not,' said Oliver.

'It's not like you imagine,' Orlando tried. 'I went once

before. Right here. At the Maestranza.' He jerked his thumb towards it: Seville's historic bull ring, standing just across the road from the river bank where they were strolling among the flower beds and palms. 'You think, crowds baying for blood and all that stuff. But it isn't. The atmosphere's just incredible, it has to be experienced to be believed, but it's an atmosphere of great respect – almost religious respect – given equally to the matador and the bull…'

'Oh come on,' said Oliver. 'That's bullshit… I mean, you know…' They both giggled in spite of themselves.

'It is true, though,' Orlando persisted. 'Yes, it is usually the bull who gets killed, but not always. Sometimes it's the matador.'

'Oh, really. And the victorious bull is reprieved to live to a ripe old age, showered with honours? I doubt it.'

'You're happy enough to eat the tail when it's served as a ración,' Orlando said reasonably. 'You're just squeamish about the dying bit. Like you are with farming.'

They had been round this particular course several times since they had known each other. Fox hunting, farming, eating meat – which Oliver of course did – and round and round again. Oliver knew Orlando might go on all evening if he didn't do something to change the subject. He took his mobile out of his pocket. 'I haven't checked for messages today,' he said.

There was just one message. It was from David, saying

he needed to talk to Oliver about something that' might be rather important'.

Oliver stopped still where he was, and Orlando came to a halt beside him, standing silently while Oliver called David back. In twenty years of knowing him, Oliver could not remember David ever phoning with such a cryptic message. It made him anxious.

David answered at once. 'No news from you; how's the job going?' he began as soon as Oliver had given his name.

'No good news actually,' said Oliver. 'I'll explain in a minute. But there is no job. At least, not the one we went for. And no other job yet. If nothing gives before the weekend we're coming back.'

'Shit,' said David, with uncharacteristic emphasis. 'Look. That may not be a good idea. Coming back, I mean. That's what I wanted to warn you about.'

Oliver felt his stomach clench. 'Warn me?'

'There's two things I thought you ought to know, and *pdq*. About that missing painting that turned up in Munich. Well, the police have arrested two men in London in connection with it. It said on the news they're still looking for others. The other thing – meanwhile – is that Donald has disappeared.'

'Jesus.' ('What's wrong?' Orlando wanted to know.)

'There may be no connection. The guys in the pub

haven't made one – at least not yet – but they're joking quite freely about him doing one dodgy haulage job too many. He used to be in the haulage business before he retired…'

'Yes I know all that,' Oliver said impatiently. 'But are you saying it's not safe for me to come back to England?'

'I don't know if I'm saying that. I can't possibly know if it's safe or not. All I'm saying is that I wanted you to know everything that I knew – do you understand me? – so that you can take it into consideration if you do decide to come back.'

'We pretty well had decided…'

'Look.' David tried to be more reassuring. 'Things blow over. Even for real criminals. Police don't keep on looking for them for years.'

'Years?!'

'Well, months then. Look, I wasn't expecting you'd be coming back for a few months at least, anyway. You said' we'just now. I take it that means you haven't lost the Marmalade Kid.'

'Not yet, at least.'

'Well, that's one good thing, I suppose.'

'The one. The only.' (Aside to Orlando, 'Talking about you.')

They talked a minute more, and David finished by promising that he'd keep Oliver up to date with any further developments, no matter how insignificant they might appear. Though he added that, for Oliver's sake, he couldn't afford to appear too interested in news of Donald. At least nobody at the Rose and Crown had asked after David's friend from London who had met Donald in the pub twice. If they could remain un-reminded of Oliver's existence, so much the better.

Orlando was impatient to know what David had had to warn Oliver about, even if he could more or less imagine. Soberly, Oliver spelled it out.

'It means we can't go back,' Orlando said, his face inscrutable for once.

'It means I can't.'

'It means we can't. No Cat without Oliver. No Oliver without the Cat.'

'Thank you for that,' said Oliver.

The sun was setting, turning the sky apricot and making the Guadalquivir run gold. Skeins of egrets flew in orderly formation overhead, their white feathers briefly rosy in the sun. Then the light faded and night laid its seal on the town. Oliver and Orlando walked till late up and down the river bank, trying to think what they could do. Their previous best option, to return to unemployment and a floor in Kentish Town, not even very attractive before, was now fraught with the possibility of Oliver's being arrested on arrival at

Heathrow. Other than that? They could journey from Spanish town to Spanish town until someone, somewhere, provided them with work. Or they could, expensively, travel to another country where Orlando's lack of a university degree might not prove such an obstacle. Stay where they were and they would find themselves joining the dossers by the river.

'The thing is,' Oliver said, 'I'm totally in the dark about what the police – or the Customs and Excise – know, and what they can do. I had nothing to do with that area of the Home Office. Can they find out where I am by tracing calls from my mobile, for instance? Get the number of my bank account and see where the withdrawals are being made? That means I have to think very carefully about making any withdrawals at all, or at least be very careful where I do it.'

'Maybe they have powers to freeze the account completely,' said Orlando. 'Starve you into giving yourself up.'

'Jesus Christ,' said Oliver. And then, 'I'm sorry about this, Kid.'

*

Lying awake, alone in bed, Oliver thought that even if he ended up in prison it could hardly be worse than the claustrophobic box of a room he now found himself in. Except for one thing. If he went to prison he couldn't take Orly with him. Three times Orlando had said he wouldn't leave Oliver alone in this mess. But he probably would if things went on getting worse. Young people did that, and if Orlando did, well, Oliver would hardly blame him. But he was sure of one thing. He would not be the one to abandon Orlando. As he was thinking this he heard a faint sound coming from the other bed. He couldn't be sure but he thought Orlando might be crying. 'Are you awake?' Oliver asked quietly, but there was no answer. However, the noise stopped. Oliver slid out of his bed and crossed to Orlando's. He climbed in behind him and kissed the nape of his neck. Then he moulded his body against Orlando's naked back and reached round to caress him in the place where he knew the comfort would be appreciated most.

*

'There are other countries, of course,' Orlando said. 'Like we said last night.' He already looked brighter this morning, sitting in the laundrette in shorts and T-shirt. His other clothes, with Oliver's, were going round and round in one of the rickety washing machines that lined one wall. Oliver thought suddenly of Madeira, and the pleasant surprise it had been to find himself there back in February; then of wanting to take Orly there and share it with him. Probably that was why his next words were, 'We're not exactly a million miles from the Portuguese border.'

'That would do,' said Orlando. They had already quit the *pension*. The laundrette was a stop-off on the way back to the *hostal* in Calle Gamazo, which Oliver had phoned in order to check they had a room available. Oliver would find the money for that. To hell with all their penny pinching. Oliver didn't want to hear Orly crying himself to sleep again as long as he lived. Today he wanted to be able to spoil him rotten, to wrap him in cotton wool and keep him in a trouser pocket, safe from all harm. He'd even take him to the bullfight if that was what he wanted.

'Or even another town in Spain,' Orlando said. 'There are other ways to earn a crust than by teaching. We could head out to Córdoba perhaps. Or Málaga again.'

'Málaga,' said Oliver, struck by a thought. 'We never got back in touch with Felipe to tell him the story of his precious job.'

'Point,' said Orlando. 'We can call him up today. Should have thought of that before. He helped us once, so who knows? Maybe he can again.'

'You are being a little Pollyanna this morning,' said Oliver. He smiled. 'Though it's better than last night's tear-stained lost boy. But to say Felipe helped us… Dragged us out to Spain on a wild-goose chase, that's all he did for us.'

'Beg your pardon, sir. He did happen to get you out of the country just when the net was closing in on Donald. Don't forget that.'

'Point taken,' Oliver said. There was a great commotion beside them as the machine with their clothes in went into spin mode – it sounded more like take-off mode – and started to millimetre its way across the floor.

'Give me your phone,' said Orly. 'I'll try and raise him now.' Oliver fished in his shorts for his mobile and handed it to him. Then they both took the few steps to the door and out into the sunshine, with Oliver casting one or two anxious backward glances towards the throbbing, racketing machine.

Orlando got through at once, to his and Oliver's surprise. He reminded Felipe who he was and related the story of the great job disaster. Felipe made a sucking sound through his teeth and then said a few words of commiseration which even Oliver, straining his ears a few inches away from Orlando's, managed to hear.

'The thing is,' Orlando explained, 'we're in a bit of a mess, and we're phoning just in case you knew of anyone else with a couple of jobs going.' No, Felipe did not, but if their searches took them as far as Córdoba they were welcome to stay with him. It was an offer that, given the hundred miles' distance between the two cities, could probably be made without much fear of its being taken up. As for jobs, Felipe added, as if having a second thought, if they could give him a contact number, he would let them know if any new ideas came into his head. But that was the most he could do. 'Unless of course,' he threw in, 'one of you has an HGV licence.'

'As a matter of fact I have,' Orlando said.

TWELVE

They took their leave of Seville on Sunday afternoon,
just as the city was gearing up for the week-long *Feria*:
its annual firework display of dance and drinking,
costume and high spirits in the sun. They felt there was
something perverse in this: they were experiencing a
wonderful sense of release as they said good-bye to one
of Europe's most seductive cities, a place that most
people harbour the ambition to visit, not to escape from;
and especially at this time of twenty-four seven partying.

The baggage they carried into the Santa Justa station
was no less heavy than when they had trailed it from
hostal to *pension* along the streets, yet they felt a
lightness, knowing that this time they were going on to
something definite: they would have cash in their hands
as early as tomorrow evening.

What Felipe had told them on Friday was this. The
lorry driver and' second man'that his company
employed were on holiday for the next two weeks. The
replacement pair engaged to cover for them had, at the
last minute, let them down. Had Orlando phoned an hour
earlier or an hour later they would probably have been
out of luck. But as it turned out... They would be paid
day by day, according to some complicated scale based
on time and distance – Orlando didn't take in or worry
too much about the details – and there would be work
most days: delivering and unloading the furniture,
mostly office tables and chairs, that Felipe's company

made. The first trip would be early on Monday morning. Felipe would meet them himself at Córdoba station on Sunday evening and give them somewhere to sleep for the night.

In the end they had gone to the *corrida* after all. Oliver was not only anxious to spoil Orly after all he'd been through, and ready to give in to him over anything he might want, but he was so overjoyed by the unexpected offer of work – even work unloading lorries – that his scruples about witnessing the death-throes of six *bravos toros* – who were going to die anyway, whether beneath his gaze or not – seemed rather beside the point.

They had had seats quite well back, which meant the cool shade under the arcade. They were lucky: on the far side of the ring the sun blazed mercilessly on the tiered spectators. They had sat through the six nearly identical ballets, each with its own unhurried sequence of acts: first the entry of the mounted, grey-and-white-costumed picadors with their butchers'hats, and the bull's effortful attempts to toss or gore the thickly padded horses, then the bandoleros with their debilitating darts, and finally the pas de deux between bull and matador, the loneliest of moments, as each – literally – faced his death. Sun and shadow, long silences and eruptions of noise – shouts from an expert crowd, *'la musica, la musica,'* fanfares and Moorish-sounding bugle calls. Death suddenly, and silence then, and cheering – the bull dragged off in chains by a harnessed team of plumed horse, the matador receiving his award.

It wasn't exactly the same each time. One bull refused

to fight and had to be led out again, decoyed by docile bullocks – exotic, beautiful animals with long horns and yak-like coats. One matador was briefly upstaged by a teenager who vaulted the crush barrier into the ring, made passes at the bull, his denim jacket for a cape – enveloped in its folds he'd smuggled in his sword. Good-humouredly the matador gave way, gave him his moment in the sun, before the attendants arrived to seize him and march him out, and then Oliver was starkly reminded of his own unique entrance onto a ballet stage, to arrest Othello years ago.

Life, death; death, life. They followed each other like the cycle of some well-oiled machine whose routines were as old as time. The atmosphere electric and intense, the emotion of the crowd swelling and erupting at pre-ordained times, while the yellow sea of sunlight that had filled the arena retreated little by little in the face of the advancing crescent of shadow: a shadow which moved like an eclipse across the sand and the banks of faces on the other side. The advancing crescent's edge was indented like teeth – these were the shadows of hoardings on the building's encircling roof – and so, by the end of the two-hour spectacle, when the sun's hold was finally dislodged from the arena, it was as if this were done by a huge, curved, inexorably closing jaw. Orlando had watched with riveted attention but had not joined in the vocal displays of enthusiasm of their Spanish neighbours. He was not stupid enough to ask Oliver if he had enjoyed the experience as they clumped their way out and down the crowding stairs, he had simply said a careful thank you to him for agreeing to come. And Oliver had not quite been able to say that, despite himself, he had been impressed by the experience and, in some way that he wouldn't care to go far into, deeply moved.

Then Orlando had at last got round to phoning his family, borrowing Oliver's mobile. Oliver tried not to listen, but inevitably did get most of it. Orlando told his father that he was starting work on Monday, though in Córdoba, not Seville, and no he hadn't got a place to stay yet. He could give his father Oliver's phone number in case he needed to contact him. Oliver? He was the friend he had come to Spain with. What? Yes, he was going to work in Córdoba too. 'It wasn't exactly an easy conversation,' Orly said as he returned the phone.

'They never are,' said Oliver.

Oliver had wondered whether to phone his sister or not. But before he could decide, he had got a phone call himself. It was from Bernd in Germany. He didn't even know that Bernd had his mobile number.

'What are you doing?' Bernd began in a slightly hectoring tone. 'And where are you? I have a very confusing phone call from Hans. He says the police have called on him, looking for you. At first they thought he was you, and he had to show his passport to prove he was not – though I guess his accent helped. Is this about that picture frame?'

Oliver apologised to Bernd for not getting in touch. 'You know how it is. You tell yourself you'll contact friends when there's good news … but then the news gets worse and worse and so you don't.' He gave Bernd an update.

Bernd tutted and whistled. 'I am sorry, my friend. You do not have a good time. You know, if ever you need my help…'

'I think I'd better call Hans,' Oliver said. 'Find out how much the police know. You don't suppose they've bugged the line, do you? Bugged? You know. Tapped… Oh, what is it in German?' But Bernd got the idea anyway.

Oliver had then phoned Hans. They were able to assuage each other's anxieties a little, but only a little. 'Thank God you are OK,' was Hans's reaction to Oliver's call, which was a positive start at least.

'I'm sorry,' Oliver began. Were all his phone calls going to begin with those words from now on? He explained his side of the story as briefly as he could, putting as good a gloss on his own actions as he could manage. It would be good practice for when he eventually did have to face the police. He learned that the police did not know very much yet. The name Oliver Watson had been given to the German police by a man arrested in Cologne for handling stolen goods, and handed on to their counterparts in Britain. They were routinely checking out all the Oliver Watsons on the British electoral rolls. Their interest was mildly aroused by the fact that Oliver had disappeared to Seville without leaving an address. Fortunately, at that time Hans had not had Oliver's mobile number, so had not been able to divulge it when the police asked. On the other hand, he had been obliged to give them his sister's phone number ('Oh shit,' Oliver said) and then the police had asked to see Hans'rental agreement – from which they had copied down his bank details. ('Fucking hell.') The conversation with Hans ended amicably. At least Hans hadn't said he was going to quit, or withhold the rent or anything; indeed he seemed to have enlisted himself in the ranks of Oliver's friends: something which Oliver was quite happy about. He had never needed friends quite as much as now. They had agreed that for the time being they would communicate, if they needed to, via Bernd.

At least, Oliver thought, as they queued for tickets in the vast booking hall, the decision of whether or not to phone his sister had been made for him. He would wait for her to ring him first. There was still half an hour before their train left. They killed it sitting over a cold San Miguel at a bar with a view back over the city. There were the same sights that had welcomed them eleven days ago: the Moorish minaret, the Giralda, wearing its Catholic crown of belfry and gilded weather vane on top; the Gothic-tracery roof line of the cathedral sprawling beyond, and in the middle ground the lively mosaic of orange roof tiles, palm trees, church domes and convent towers, glowing in the afternoon sun. Eleven days ago that vista had beckoned them with opportunity and promise. Now it merely mocked their failure to conquer or even make any impression on the town.

'El Ultimo Suspiro del Moro,' said Orlando, and Oliver understood quite well what he meant – even though they were in the wrong town.' The Moor's Last Sigh'was a mountain pass on the road south from Granada – the last place from which you could turn back and see the city before it disappeared behind the hills, and it was there that Boabdil, the last Moorish king of Granada, had turned back and wept as he rode away from his lost kingdom long ago.

'And you know what Boabdil's mother said to him?' Oliver asked.

'Yes, actually. You needn't test me.' There was a trace of irritation in Orly's answer, which Oliver made a mental note to be careful of in future. 'She said,' Thou dost well to weep like a woman for what thou couldst not defend like a man.'Some mother!'

Oliver remembered that Orlando had lost his own mother less than a year ago, and thought perhaps he'd steered the conversation in an unfortunate direction. Still, it was Orlando who had brought up Boabdil's situation and compared it, if only by implication, to theirs. In losing a kingdom, Boabdil had lost more than they would ever, together or separately, attain. And yet, unlike achievements, which can be great or small, a sense of loss and a sense of failure are not susceptible to gradation but carry about them a whiff of the absolute.

The line to Córdoba followed the Guadalquivir upstream all the way; the river's meanders were marked at first by swerving lines of eucalyptus trees across the plain where cotton and tobacco grew; then later, as the hills on either side drew closer in, river and railway ran together beneath towers of rock where ruined Moorish castles perched and ravens circled. Then the landscape opened out again and the train slid them to a stop at Córdoba station in the late afternoon glare.

The stocky figure of Felipe was immediately visible on the platform, rather to Oliver's surprise: the years had left him with a less trusting attitude to people and their promises than his younger friend's. Felipe greeted them with unfeigned pleasure, but could not conceal a look of dismay as his eye fell upon their substantial luggage. Oliver saw this and quickly said, 'Don't worry. We can leave these at the station. We're not planning to stay for a month.'

Felipe grinned his relief. 'No need for that, but perhaps we could leave the big stuff at the factory – in one of the offices I mean. More space. It's only two minutes from here. You see, I live with my parents right now and…'

'Yes, we understand,' said Orlando.

'I'm divorced,' Felipe felt compelled to explain. 'Since last year. I have a daughter,' he added, as if to excuse the embarrassing fact that at the age of about thirty he was still in the parental nest.

'Sure, whatever,' Orlando said, which Oliver didn't think altogether appropriate in the context. Perhaps Orly's mind was somewhere else. But he was relieved to find that Felipe had a car parked outside, and that they wouldn't have to traipse to the factory on foot.

Felipe's company operated from a small industrial estate near the station. The place was Sunday-afternoon shut, and Felipe used a key to get them through the gate into the compound. Buildings were ranged all around, but the thing that caught their attention was the chunky yellow-painted Series P Scania parked up beside the loading bay. 'Big, isn't it?' Oliver said and looked at Orly, only to discover that he'd said quite the wrong thing. Orlando's face had gone a pale grey colour and he looked as miserable as Oliver had ever seen him.

'Can I have a practice with it this afternoon?' Orly mumbled, and had to repeat himself to be understood.

'Unfortunately I don't have the keys.' Felipe was letting them in to the main office block with a big bunch of other keys, then de-arming the burglar alarm. 'The logistics manager couldn't be here this afternoon. But don't worry. I've arranged for him to meet you this evening with all the information you need for tomorrow, maps and everything.' They parked their luggage next to Felipe's assistant's desk, and then were on their way again. As they drove out of the compound Orlando cast a Boabdil-like glance back at the lorry he would have to get to grips with in the morning.

Barely a minute later they had drawn up beside a white-painted apartment block, still on the edge of town, and a minute after that were upstairs and inside a very small flat, being introduced to Felipe's parents, who spoke not one word of English. Oliver's Spanish deserted him entirely, and it was left to the still subdued and anxious Orly to do the best he could. If the flat was small for three, for five it was a traffic jam. They all had a tiny coffee, standing in, overflowing, the kitchen. Yes, they said, the living room floor would be fine for them both to sleep on, and smiled gratefully, though the space between the sofa and the TV set would not have done for two adults who were not already very intimate. 'Perhaps we'll go out for a walk,' Oliver heard Orlando say to his hosts. It did seem to be the only option.

'Listen,' Felipe told them, 'Meet me at eight downtown. I'll be with Francisco – logistics, the man with the maps. At La Mezquita – it's a bar, you can't miss it – on the corner by the mosque.' He seemed quite happy they'd decided to go out.

'Are you sure you're OK?' Oliver asked Orly, as they wandered down the broad street towards the centre of town. Orlando was morose and silent, which worried Oliver. 'I mean, about this lorry-driving business. We can always duck out if you…'

Orlando turned on him furiously. 'I'm OK. I tell you I'm OK. I'm not ducking out of anything.'

'Sorry,' said Oliver. 'I only asked.' They walked on in silence for a bit. Then Oliver said, 'Tell me, when did you come here before?' This seemed an innocuous way to get back on speaking terms, and Oliver was relieved to find that it worked. Their previous lives were still only partially explored territories, hinterlands that they both still took pleasure in mapping.

'It was when I came to Andalucía with you-know-who. We stayed at a small place near the Plaza del Potro, I think. You?'

Oliver laughed. 'I came here with Adi about three years ago. We stayed in a small place near the Plaza del Potro too. It might have been the same one. I'll show you when we get there.'

They dropped into a bar on the edge of the old quarter. 'First today,' said Orlando, sipping his golden beer. He obviously didn't count the one at the station in Seville. Oliver wondered if he ought to be worried by that. He determined to keep an eye on Orlando's intake during the evening ahead.

Oliver's phone jabbered in his pocket. He shot Orly a meaningful glance. 'My sister.' But it was his brother.

'What the fuck have you been doing?' Lawrence didn't wait for an answer. 'Jenny's had the police calling round. She's most distressed. Nobody knows where you are or what you're up to. Now you're obviously up to the neck in something illegal. How do you think that makes us feel?'

'Look, Lawrence. How do you think you're making me feel? If Jenny was upset, why didn't she phone me? Why did she get you involved? It's nothing to do with you…'

'Oli, I'm just trying to…'

'I haven't done anything illegal. I hope Jenny told

them that. I don't like your bloody attitude. You can tell Jenny I said that. Don't phone again unless you've got something constructive to say. Thank you.' He cut his brother off.

'Christ, man,' said Orly, visibly startled. 'Talk about defence being the best form of attack.'

'I think you mean the other way round.' But Oliver had also surprised himself. He'd been wanting to let Orly know he was concerned for him, that he knew of his anxieties about the next morning, but Orly hadn't let him and, anyway, he wasn't sure if he'd have been able to do it without seeming to patronise him. Now that tension had been released in his vitriolic outburst against his brother. 'Oh fuck,' he said. 'Why did I do that?' As if he didn't know. He grimaced. 'Just when I need all the friends I can get.'

They made a walking tour of the centre, a voyage of re-acquaintance. They saw the flower-bedecked Juderia, the old Jewish quarter, where each apartment tried to outdo its neighbours with balconies that overflowed with flaming geraniums and starbursts of aloes. They skirted the enormous Mezquita. Its precinct wall reminded Oliver bizarrely of the old railway carriage works at Ashford; the look of those weed-grown walls was indelibly imprinted on his memory: after all, they formed the background to his first study of Orlando, when he had tried to memorise his physiognomy, sitting across the aisle from him on the Marsh Link train. They did not go inside. They had both seen round the Mezquita before. They promised themselves they'd revisit it tomorrow – if they got back safely. They left unspoken the thought that it would be a kind of thanksgiving for their return. People still did things like that, Oliver realised, even when they'd stopped believing in God.

They walked by the river, watched its currents eddying among the foundations of old Roman water wheels, which were crumbling now and sprouting with fig trees. On an inaccessible beach below them a party of feral cats lazed in the last of the sun. How had they got there, they wondered? Were they kittens that had been tied in sacks and thrown to drown, and had then made Houdini-like escapes? And what did they find to live on? Did they swim? Swifts and swallows whizzed between the old brick piers, almost wetting their wings among the whirlpools and white-water rapids, and the evening sun lit the whole scene in a slanting blaze.

It wasn't difficult to find the Mezquita bar. They went in on the stroke of eight. Inside, as promised, was Felipe. For the second time Oliver was impressed and surprised. He had certain preconceptions about Spanish ideas of punctuality as well as about human nature in general, but Felipe seemed determined to give the lie to them. On the other hand, he did look as if he'd had a few drinks already. With him was a man whom he introduced as the logistics manager Francisco, a rotund fellow with a laconic manner, who looked as if his Sunday had consisted of a long late lunch and a very recently ended siesta. He did not seem fazed by the prospect of entrusting his Scania to two unknown Englishmen. The lorry had been loaded on Friday afternoon, he told them. Tomorrow's trip wouldn't be too strenuous, although there would be an early start. Delivery of school desks and chairs to a town called Linares. Oliver and Orlando looked at Francisco blankly. He beamed back. 'No problem. Here's the map.' It had been considerately marked up: the delivery address was highlighted, so too were the council rubbish dump and a filling station on the outskirts of Córdoba where the company had an account, as well as motorway service areas and other truck stops. 'You get the keys from the night guard. He'll give you the manifest too. Check it against the cargo, sign it, give him one copy, keep the other two.' The briefing went on, over a couple of beers, and then Francisco left them. 'You understand,' he said, shrugging his shoulders: 'the wife.'

'A very demanding woman,' Felipe explained when the door had closed behind Francisco. 'You know, it's good to see you both.' He smiled. 'When I first met you, you weren't sure if you would be coming here together. But now you are here. I think that is good. Maybe, if I knew what I know now when I got married...' (Here it comes, thought Oliver, I was right all along.) 'You see, I've always preferred to do it with men.' He took out a cigarette and lit it. 'Mind? – I thought, if I get married that will cure it. You know, even fifteen years ago Spanish boys were still taught to think like that. Of course marriage was no cure. Now I just take the opportunities I can.' He shrugged, his smile a little nervous now. 'Meeting you has been ... how to say? It gives me a feeling I can be myself.' Oliver thought glumly that he could see where this was leading, and tried to catch Orlando's eye, but his eye would not be caught.

Felipe took them round several more bars, despite Oliver's protesting noises about an early morning start. And even Oliver's protests were only half-hearted. They needed to eat something after all, and a sequence of tapas with the drinks seemed to be the only way of achieving that. At one point Oliver had to excuse himself to visit the loo, and a few minutes after his return Felipe did likewise, leaving Oliver alone with Orlando, who took the opportunity to lean across the table and inform him, gravely, 'When you were away, he asked me if we were into threesomes.'

'Well we're not,' Oliver said firmly. 'What did you say?'

'What did I say?' Orlando came back with a vehemence that startled Oliver. 'What does it matter what I said – or what I ever say – when it's you who always makes the decisions. Unilateral Oli. We don't, you say. How do you know we don't? We've never discussed it. You never consult me. On anything.'

'Orlando…'

'We don't do this, we don't do that… It's always you who decides.'

'Orly, please don't do this to me.' Oliver's voice betrayed his hurt and surprise. 'Do you … want to have a threesome with Felipe?' He sighed and looked away.

'Or a twosome maybe.'

'No, of course not. I don't want either of those things.'

'OK. So is that what you said to him?' Oliver tried to sound reasonable.

'I said we'd never done a threesome yet. That we'd never discussed it.'

'Christ almighty, Orly. That's just great. You leave our bedroom door wide open – for me to get up and shut.'

'It's not a big deal.' Orlando had his sulky voice now: Oliver had only heard it once before, when they had been turned down the second time for a job in Seville. 'I'll tell him to forget it. It's just I don't like being shoved around all the time: told what to do and what to think.'

'Listen, Orly, it's…' He almost said 'for your own good' but stopped himself just in time. 'Look, I never did threesomes with Adi – because I'd had a few before and I didn't think they'd be good for a long-term relationship. It's just age and experience, that's all.'

But Orlando bridled just the same. 'If you really want to know, I've had a few threesomes myself. I'm not so green as you think I am. And I didn't think they were such great shakes either.'

'So why,' Oliver asked, 'are we arguing over something that neither of us actually wants to do? What's brought this on? This sudden … vitriol.' But he knew really. The poor kid was scared stiff about the next morning. Anyway, Orly was spared having to answer, because Felipe came back at that moment and grinned even more broadly at them both.

Orlando did what he'd said he would. On the walk back he took Felipe aside, out of Oliver's earshot, and told him politely but firmly that he would not be invited to join them for the night. 'It wouldn't have done anyway,' said Oliver as they got ready to bed down on the cramped floor space. 'I mean just look at it.'

'Well actually,' said Orlando, 'that wasn't exactly what he was planning. He was going to take us out to a comfortable hotel.'

'So that was it.' Oliver was suddenly angry. 'You really did consider it. You'd have slept with him – had us both sleep with him – in return for a comfy bed and a few mod cons.'

'A lot of women get married for less,' Orlando countered.

Oliver exploded. 'Do you want to marry Felipe?!' And then immediately, 'Look, forget I said that. We shouldn't be arguing tonight.' It was already past one, and they would have to be up at six. They lay side by side in tense silence, their bodies rigid but touching because there was no space to do otherwise. Oliver was cross with himself. It was his fault, not Orlando's, that they couldn't go back to England. He hadn't done very well by the kid. He'd brought him away from that awful *pension* in Triana, it was true, but after only two nights in a decent *hostal* again they had ended up here on a hard, cramped floor, unable to move without tumbling religious knick-knacks. He had been too ready to take Orly's truck-driver bravado at face value and had more or less forced him into taking on a job that clearly terrified him. And then he'd chewed his ear off for merely toying with an offer, albeit a compromising one, of a better billet for the night. He reached out for Orlando's hand but couldn't find it. He stroked his bare chest instead. 'I'm sorry I spoke to you the way I did.' No response. 'Tomorrow we'll have some cash. We can find somewhere else to stay. At least for tomorrow night. Things'll get better. I promise.' He was rewarded by an extraordinarily well-aimed grab at his balls, and a quiet, *fooled-you-there* kind of laugh.

*

Barely were they asleep, it seemed, when Orlando's travelling alarm clock was bleeping its fragile wake-up call. They got up quietly to avoid waking the house, and carried out minimal ablutions. They discovered that Felipe's parents had left a Thermos of coffee for them to find in the kitchen, and were disproportionately touched by the gesture. 'Yeah,' said Orlando, yawning. 'Got to remember, people who collect crap religious ornaments are also the ones who do things like this.'

Oliver was impressed with Orlando. Considering the amounts he drank, he was remarkably disciplined about early morning starts – unlike every other actor Oliver had met. He put it down to his upbringing at

Mockbeggar Farm.

Perhaps because the light of day is so strong in southern Spain, the pre-dawn dark seems even more intense there than further north. They felt the darkness in the street outside as something primordial: a throwback to the time before God said *Let there be Light.* But after a minute's walking the arc lights of the industrial estate appeared around a corner and they found their way to the factory easily enough. The night guard answered their call at the entry-phone and opened the gate. Keys were handed over and documents signed. Oliver did most of the talking. He could see sweat beading out on Orlando's upper lip and didn't need to ask him how he was feeling. They walked out to the lorry, opened up the back and checked the cargo of tubular metal and plastic tables and chairs against the manifest. Orlando walked around the vehicle and gave a professional-looking kick to each of its many tyres. So far, so good, Oliver thought bravely.

Oliver could have done with a leg-up, getting into his seat: the scramble up was so steep, the cab door so high. It was almost a surprise to see Orlando clambering in from the other side when he finally hauled himself in. They seemed a long way apart: a third, uncomfortable looking seat came between them, perched astride the broad bulkhead that was the engine housing. 'I've never driven anything as big as this before,' Orlando confided as he shut the door. 'Bit scary.'

'No way,' said Oliver. 'You'll get the hang of it.' He wanted to hug him.

Usually, when you buy or even hire a car, there is someone to lean over you and show you how to find reverse gear and where the light switches are. But, with the night guard returned to his cabin, Orlando and Oliver were on their own. There were whole panels of light switches, power-assisted braking; Oliver thought it was like the cockpit of a jumbo jet – not that he'd ever sat in one of those either.

The radio boomed out at them, as soon as Orlando turned the key, at a truly health-endangering level of decibels, and they spent some time trying to locate the switch to turn it off. They spent a few more minutes experimenting with other switches and gadgets, and then at last Orly slipped the clutch and gingerly edged across the yard and out through the gate into the road. There was no traffic. This was just as well but even so, after half a minute of slow and uncertain progress in low gear, Oliver felt that he would have to say something. 'Shouldn't we be on the right?'

'Jesus Christ!' Orlando swung across to the other side with a panic-stricken wrench at the wheel that had them mounting the pavement when they got there. 'Why didn't you tell me?'

'Darling, I just did. Do you want to stop a second? Relax for a moment?'

'It's OK,' said Orlando, without seeming to move his lips. 'We'll make it.'

A roundabout was upon them at once but, to Oliver's

surprise, Orlando negotiated it impeccably, seeming to have recovered quickly from his loss of nerve. 'You're sure you're OK?' Oliver repeated, as Orly experimented with a higher gear. There was self-interest as well as concern for the kid in his question: Oliver would be spending most of the next two weeks in the front seat of this vehicle, his safety in Orlando's hands.

'I'll be all right. Getting it sorted now. It's just that – to be honest – the trucks I drove for my father were much smaller than this. And I only ever did it a couple of times.'

'Yeah, well,' said Oliver, peering at the road ahead, at the map in his hands, and at the side-face, almost in silhouette, of the boy whom it was his self-appointed task to protect. 'Next right and then left.'

They drove through the industrial outskirts of the city and then, passing the university, were accelerating on the main road east. Unaccountably Oliver thought of his graduation day. Traffic was beginning to build up and the sky ahead of them grew light, bringing far-off mountains into focus, at first hazy, then sharply defined. Then flaming wedges of sun prised the distant crags apart and Orlando switched off the batteries of lights. Half an hour later they halted for a breakfast of coffee and *tostados* at one off the truck stops that had been marked for them on the map. At last Orlando permitted himself to smile at Oliver. 'Got it sussed,' he said.

Other truck drivers greeted them with nods or a gruff *buenos dias* but then their faces would succumb to looks of puzzlement, as if the fair-skinned strangers didn't quite fit the part they were playing. Back on the road, and finding themselves nearly halfway to where they were going, Orlando pulled off his shirt as if to inhabit his role more fully – the method actor? – and a few minutes later Oliver did the same. The road had been an easy one, following the Guadalquivir upstream along the northern edge of the plain. Only towards the end of the eighty-mile journey did they find themselves climbing the olive-studded foothills of the Sierra Morena.

It was still only mid-morning when they arrived in Linares and worked their way round to their delivery address, a school on the outskirts. There was a caretaker to help them unload the cargo and stack it in the school hall. Then they reloaded with the old furniture which – this was part of today's job – was to go to the dump. Stripped to the waist as they were, they attracted the interest of most of the girls in the playground: Orlando especially – his complexion and hair colour rarities in that part of the world. When they drove off at last, youthful female waves and smiles receded in the driving mirrors.

The dump was on the other side of town. Oliver asked Orlando to drive through the centre. 'My chance to try to get some cash out of a machine while we're here. Assuming I've not been frozen. But if the police are tracking me, they're going to have a job finding me in Linares.' So they drove into the small, un-touristy town. It didn't look the sort of place where anyone would go looking for a foreigner with any expectation of success.

Oliver called out when he saw a street with a Banco de Andalucía in it, and jumped down as soon as Orly had pulled up. He typed four hundred euros into the ATM and stood back as if defying it to refuse him. Rather to his surprise it did not, and Oliver collected his cash with a sense of triumph that the honking of car horns – by a little snarl-up of drivers who were annoyed with Orly for blocking their way with his lorry – did nothing to diminish.

An hour later they had thrown the discarded furniture onto the municipal dump and were on the road back to Córdoba, feeling in no particular hurry. They stopped for some lunch between Bailén and Andújar, and then left the lorry by the roadside while they went a little way among the olive trees, lay down beneath the shade of one particularly large one and, albeit rather uncomfortably, made love. There was no point, they had reckoned, in bringing the lorry back to base before the end of siesta time if they wanted to get paid.

They returned the lorry, its diesel tank duly replenished – 'For God's sake don't spoil everything by putting petrol in,' Orlando had warned Oliver through the cab window – and collected their cash. Orlando seemed a different animal from the one that had set out so fearfully that morning: Oliver could imagine his tail wagging. Felipe was at his desk in his office. 'We're going to look for a room for ourselves tonight,' Oliver told him, 'now we've got some money. It was kind of you and your parents, but we don't want to be in the way.'

Felipe took this on the chin, smiled courteously and said they would easily find somewhere at a reasonable price. It didn't seem that he was going to mention threesomes again. 'No doubt we'll run into each other in one of the bars downtown later,' he said. 'Though for the moment...' He gestured towards the piles of paper on his desk to indicate how busy he was.

They moved into a small hotel near the Plaza del Potro. It was the one where they had both coincidentally stayed on previous visits, an almost inevitable choice. It had a beautiful central patio, open to the sky, with spacious rooms arranged around it. They booked a double with a bath rather than a shower. That was the luxury they looked forward to most: neither of them had seen a bath tub since they left England. Oliver sat on the side and watched the naked Orlando climb in, but then changed his mind, stripped off, and joined him in the water.

Oliver felt as contented that evening as he could remember being. Thoughts of police investigations, of an angry brother and sister, of the mysteriously disappeared Donald, faded into insignificance: worries no more troublesome than gnats. His joy in Orlando's transformation from the frightened child of early this morning into this evening's triumphant trucker, laughing again and radiant with life, was complete. They had dinner in a restaurant, as if they'd received a month's salary rather than a single day's wage for driving a lorry. Briefly they ran into Felipe and a couple of his friends in a bar, but there was no awkwardness in their encounter, and they finished the evening, just the two of them, on the patio of their hotel with a bottle of wine, sitting, rather surreally it seemed to them, in leather armchairs under a canopy of stars.

*

In the morning they took a bus out from the city centre to the factory. There was the business of checks and signatures and Orlando's talismanic kicks to all the tyres, then they were back on the road. Today they took the motorway south towards the coast; their destination was Nerja, a short distance east of Málaga. Their route had them skirting Montilla, and then the faded beauty, Antequera, fifty miles further south. They climbed into the Sierra de las Cabras. 'Seven hundred and eighty metres at the pass, the Puerto de las Pedrizas,' Oliver read from the map. 'That's – er – two and a half thousand feet.'

'You'll make me giddy,' Orlando said. 'I prefer it in metres.' But he sounded confident enough, negotiating their winding passage through the mountains, and Oliver was pleased for him. Ahead, where the valley of the Guadalmedina met the sea, the city of Málaga sprawled along the coast.

'Remember Málaga!' A mere month ago. A lifetime away. They bypassed the town centre, the cathedral was just a distant tower glimpsed from the suburbs, but then, leaving the town by the coast road, they passed a sign to El Palo. 'The fish restaurant.' 'The walk along the beach.' The knock of the waves, Oliver remembered.

The sound of Orly's jeans, scritch-scritch as he walked. The chaos of his own thoughts. This was a strange revisitation – like watching a powerful film on fast forward. A walk along a beach that had lasted an hour and a half, and transformed their lives. A distance covered by a lorry in two minutes, just a couple of blocks inland.

Friendly mini-mountains, tree-studded, climbed away on their left. The Osborne bull stood in proud silhouette on a rocky spur. On their right the open sea. Another half an hour and they were in the narrow streets of Nerja, heading down to their destination, a restaurant on the Calle Puerta del Mar. Orlando looked at his watch as they drew up. 'Eleven, dead on,' he announced, pleased with himself. 'Time for a beer?'

The proprietor, or manager, came out of the front door and directed them to a delivery area round at the back. 'There's two blokes who'll help you unload,' he told them. 'But you might want a beer first. Come into the bar when you've parked up.'

'What did I tell you?' Orlando said.

'OK, but let's go easy,' Oliver warned. 'Got to get us back.' He wished he could find a way of saying things like this to Orly without sounding like a parent.

They knew that Nerja was a haven for British ex-pats of a certain age, while the Germans tended to hang out at Torrox, a few miles back along the coast. They were not surprised, then, when they entered the sun-filled bar, its

French windows open onto a sea-view terrace, to find it peopled, at this hour of the morning, with grey-haired English-speaking men, one or two with their womenfolk. What Oliver was quite unprepared for – and Orlando completely unaware of – was that one of them, who bore an uncanny likeness to Michael Foot, was the recently disappeared Donald Faircross, lately of the Beckley Rose and Crown.

THIRTEEN

Oliver's immediate thought was to turn round and slip out before Donald could spot him, but Orlando, ordering *dos cervezas por favor* insouciantly, and rather more loudly than necessary, had attracted the attention of the ex-pats. Donald's head twisted round, his eyes met Oliver's, and they both froze for a second, Donald in astonishment, Oliver in horror. Orlando, still oblivious, went on chatting about nothing to the barmaid in Spanish. Then Donald got up and walked towards them, hand outstretched. Blinking his eyes behind thick glasses, nodding his head, 'What brings you here?' he asked, as genial as ever Oliver remembered him.

Oliver took his hand rather limply; though his handshake was normally a firm one: something on which he prided himself. He turned to Orlando, who was now registering mild surprise. 'Orlando, I'd like you to meet…'

'Michael. Michael Davidson,' Donald cut in, smiling. 'Better that way for everybody. Hallo Orlando. Pleased to meet you.' He turned back to Oliver. 'But what a surprise.' He looked them both up and down, jerking his head about as though that aided his powers of observation. 'You don't look like you're on holiday to me. Not looking for work by any chance?'

'Actually we are working,' said Orlando, unusually tartly for him, Oliver thought. Oliver explained that they were in the middle of delivering some furniture. Once they'd had their beer they had to go off and unload a truck.

'The yellow one that pulled up at the front ten minutes ago? Big beast, that one. Mind you, you couldn't lose it easily, painted that colour.' Clearly Donald – Michael – still kept his eyes open to the street. 'But you'll want some lunch after that I guess. Not too busy to have lunch with me, are you? Say, in ... in an hour? Hour and a half?' He looked back to where the other ex-pats were sitting, ignoring the conversation at the bar. 'But not here, I think. Let's say the Pata Negra at half-past twelve. Next block, just round the corner.' He drew a map with his hands on the bar in front of him. 'I might have a proposal. You might be interested. You might not be.' He grinned unexpectedly wide. 'But let's have lunch anyway. Now I'll let you finish your beers in peace.' He turned and shuffled away back to his friends.

'Who the hell...?' Orlando began. Oliver told him.

*

'Of course we don't have to have lunch with him,' Oliver said, when the last chairs and tables had been deposited in the hotel's function room. 'We can just cut and drive out of town if you want.' He meant that was what he wanted. But Orlando's curiosity had been whetted, and besides, he was not someone who too willingly said no to a free lunch. Reluctantly Oliver accepted Orly's decision that they should go along.

What was the appropriate behaviour, Oliver wondered, when you found yourself sitting down to lunch with someone you'd expected, even hoped, never to see again? With someone you were more than ever convinced was a crook, and who, because of your association with him, was the cause of your not being able to return to your home country? Oliver had no answer to this and so he sat down with Orlando at Donald's table in the Pata Negra as if nothing were amiss, and with a pleased-to-be-here smile. He would leave it to their host to bring up the difficult subjects in his own time.

'Gazpacho, some chorizo with a salad, an omelette – how does that sound?' Michael invited, relieving them of the burdensome responsibility of choosing from an à la carte menu at someone else's expense. They both said that sounded good. Would they have beer or wine? Oliver got his answer in first. They'd stick with a small beer each if that was all right. They had a long drive to make afterwards. He wasn't brave enough to look at Orlando as he said this.

'So you're driving lorries,' Michael said, at the same time beckoning a waiter over. 'Well, any port in a storm, I reckon And down here you're in as good a place to do it as any.' He broke off to give their order in rapid Spanish, which surprised his guests somewhat. 'Taxi driving from Málaga airport, for instance. Be surprised how many Brits won't trust themselves with a local driver. Problem of lingo. Your Spanish must be pretty good though.' He peered searchingly into both their faces in turn. 'Doing a language course, weren't you?'

'Not exactly,' Oliver said. 'Teaching English as a foreign language.'

Michael shrugged. 'Can't help you there. Don't move in such exalted circles' self. But if you were on the lookout for driving work... Or, how can I put it, advanced driving – which might be more remunerative...'

'Donald,' Oliver broke in, 'I mean Michael – are you quite sure you're safe down here? Aren't people going to come looking for you?'

There was a hiatus as three beers arrived. Donald took a careful sip from his. 'And if they do? They'll be barking up the wrong tree. Looking for the wrong man. Nothing I've ever made money from has been illegal. Nothing.' His lips closed with a smacking sound.

To his surprise Oliver felt himself smiling. 'How can you say that? When you've had to up sticks, move out here, and change your name – all on the same day the Lucas Cranach was discovered in Munich.' This made Orlando look round a bit anxiously, but no-one was listening to them. Oliver went on. 'The police are even looking for me.' That sounded like a boast and caused Orlando to snicker. 'Or do you mean that it's Michael, the new you, who hasn't broken the law yet?' Oliver wondered as he said this whether passing yourself off under an assumed name might not be against the law too. Perhaps it depended what lengths you took it to.

Cheques, passports…?

'Neither of us has broken the law,' Michael said smoothly. 'One carries out clients'commissions, my friend. One takes them at their word. Ah… Here is the gazpacho.' He turned to Orlando. 'You may expect an old ex-pat who's come to roost down here to eat nothing but English breakfasts and fish and chips. You'd be wrong. My little woman's Spanish. She'd have joined us for lunch, only she's gone up to Frigiliana with a friend. We've had a place out here for years. The other side of Málaga. Still have it, but it's rented out now. A prudent step while things blow over.' He looked back at Oliver and blinked at him and jerked his head reassuringly. 'Which they will. Which they will, Oliver. You'll see.'

'And you live here in Nerja now?' Orlando asked.

'On the edge of town.' He searched in an inside pocket, pulled out his wallet, and extracted from it a card which he gave to Orlando. 'Looks like the pair of you work as a team.' He gave a chuckle, pleased with himself for coining this euphemism. 'That could be very useful. Lorry driving… If your present tour of duty comes to an end, and if you're still interested, I'm sure there'd be projects we could handle together. Even quite lucrative.' He turned his attention to his soup.

*

They discussed the offer once they were alone together and on the road again. They had parted from Michael on friendly terms and said they would get back in touch. In

Oliver's case the polite formula had been no more than that. But Orlando seemed to have other ideas. 'Might be a good move,' he said, 'for when this stint with Felipe comes to an end.'

'You have to be joking,' Oliver answered. 'You may not be in trouble because of that man yet but I certainly am. Up to my neck.'

'So? That can't be undone by steering clear of him now. And if you're in trouble already you may as well be hung for a sheep as a lamb. And we've, like, so many other offers of work coming in.'

'The logic's all on your side, I know,' said Oliver wearily. 'But my gut feeling remains. We should run a mile from Donald. Sorry – Michael. You go and work for him if you want, but count me out.'

'Well, let's see how we both feel in a couple of weeks, shall we?' Orlando was learning how to deal with his Oliver in *that's-out-of-the-question* mode. 'Anyway, talking of being hung for a sheep, how would you like to have a go at driving this baby for a bit?' He chuckled.

'Now you are joking.' They were embarked on the steady climb towards the Puerto de las Pedrizas – which Oliver translated as the Pass of the Partridges, though Orly said that wasn't quite right. Orlando was managing the climb expertly, Oliver realised: carefully judging his speeds in relation to other vehicles, occasionally overtaking, sometimes being overtaken himself. His had been a steep learning curve since he had hesitantly nudged the vehicle out of the factory yard the previous morning. Now he said,

'This thing's a doddle. Handles easy as anything.' They had ridden to the summit now, and the wide sunlit plains of the Genil and Guadalquivir were opening out in front of them like the promised land.

'You weren't saying that yesterday morning,' Oliver said. 'But I'm glad you've got it sorted. I'm proud of you.' He leaned across the engine bulkhead and tousled Orly's hair. He wondered if you could do more intimate things with someone while that someone was driving a lorry. He wondered if other pairs of truck drivers ever did, before wresting his mind back to the subject under discussion. 'Though I'm not up for having a go myself. Unqualified and uninsured. What if I pranged it?' They let the matter rest.

Back at base in Córdoba they were again paid in cash, making anew the old discovery that cash in the hand does wonders for the morale. They ate and drank well that evening. Over the next few days they had shorter, easier runs to do. They went to Baena. They went to Carmona, on the road back to Seville, where they'd had a job interview in unhappier times two weeks ago. In the evenings they relaxed in the warm embrace of their new home town, Córdoba, lazing by the river, and getting to know the wines of Montilla. They went to Osuna, once the capital of a historic dukedom, now asleep and faded, alone in the vastness of the plain. And then, on the way back from there, Oliver surprised both Orlando and himself by saying, 'You know, I wouldn't mind having a turn at the wheel. Road's straight enough. And flat.' There was hardly any traffic on it either, which had emboldened him. 'Just for a few minutes, between places to stop.'

Orlando pulled off to the side, they got out and changed places, then Orly talked Oliver through the controls, though he knew them pretty well already by sight, now that he'd spent several days watching his lover handle them. The unexpected thing was the sudden doubling of his range of vision by the two enormous mirrors: two rear-facing bat's ears of information. Oliver found himself with the ability of Janus, to see in both directions at once. After taking a couple of deep breaths he pulled slowly out onto the empty highway. For each gear change Orly called out encouragingly, 'Go, go, go,' and Oliver found himself accelerating through sixty, then eighty kilometres an hour, in charge of something ten times bigger than he'd ever driven before in his life. Once his pulse had steadied he found he was enjoying it.

'Say when you want to stop,' Orlando said after they'd gone a few miles.

'No, I'm fine.' Oliver drove for more than twenty kilometres. Then he looked round at Orly who had gone rather quiet. To Oliver's consternation, he appeared to be fast asleep. He called his name loudly and Orlando awoke.

'Don't scare me like that!' Orly spluttered as he came to.

'You scared me. Falling asleep!'

'Shows I trust you – darling.' It was the first time Orlando had called him that, though Oliver had been using the endearment to Orly now for weeks. Oliver felt a warmth that penetrated to his bones: it was like the feeling he got coming out from an air-conditioned building into the sun.

'We're almost at Écija. Can we find a lay-by and you take over? I don't think I want to drive through the centre of the town.'

'Sure,' said Orlando. He consulted the map. But before he could pinpoint a stopping place the town was upon them. Oliver drove into the traffic with heart in mouth, but there was nothing to be done except plough on, and a few minutes later they were in open country again on the other side. Then Oliver did stop, skidding in loose stones at the side of the road and raising a massive plume of white dust. He felt his legs buckle under him as he got out of the cab and had to clutch at the foot of the door to steady himself. 'I think I've lost weight,' he told Orly.

'Now you know how I felt a few days ago,' Orly said.

That evening they read in El Pais about a bad accident in the centre of Madrid. A lorry had ploughed into a police road-block and someone had been killed. The driver of the lorry was a foreigner, unlicensed and uninsured. Oliver and Orlando looked at each other, both their faces rather pale. 'I was a bit lucky today, I guess,' Oliver said eventually. 'Quit while I'm ahead, don't you reckon?'

Orlando nodded slowly. 'Pity in a way though,' he said. 'I could have got used to having you do half the work.'

The following day was going to be a bit of a treat, they thought. They had a run to Granada to make, but with no need to be back before the following afternoon. Their boss Francisco had told them in his laid-back way that they could stay the night in Granada if they wanted. It would be OK for them to park up the lorry overnight on the industrial estate where their delivery was to be made, so long as they told someone what was going on. They debated whether they should find a *hostal* to stay in when they got there, or spend an uncomfortable night on the seats of the lorry: the cab was not fitted out as a sleeper. Forking out for rooms in two different cities on the same night did strike them as a bit extravagant for people in their situation but on the other hand... They decided not to decide until they got there.

Their delivery address lay a little way outside the city centre on the northern side, so they didn't have to navigate through the town. Orlando did all the driving. Oliver earned his keep instead when it came to the unloading, but when that was done they declared a private holiday and took a bus into town.

The afternoon sun was painting the outer walls of the Alhambra their hallmark red as they gazed up at them from the Albaicin. The Moors'palace seemed to sprout from its rocky spur as if it had grown from seed, like the cypresses around it, rather than being built by man. The River Darro ran swift in its sunless gulley a hundred feet below. And as a backdrop to the whole, the Sierra Nevada reared up towards the summit of snow-capped Mulhacén and led your gaze into the blue.

These days you could visit the Alhambra till late evening, enjoying the building lit for night. Peering down through latticed windows, you saw the afternoon's scene reversed. The town was laid out way below, pin-pricked with a thousand lights, and sending up to you from time to time the bark of a dog or motor-bike, a waft of guitar or song, and sometimes with uncanny clarity a snatch of conversation or a laugh.

Afterwards they ambled back down the steep Cuesta de Gomérez and hit the bars. Granada was the place, they both remembered, where tapas still came free with the drinks. The more you drank the better you got fed. And the better you kept the cold out. It was easy to forget, arriving in the warmth of a late spring afternoon, that at two thousand feet sundown brought with it a vicious chill. It was a degree of cold that, after weeks in balmy Córdoba and Seville, they had almost forgotten could exist. They had no early start to make, so a little overindulgence in alcohol in the sensible pursuit of food and warmth could be forgiven, they told themselves. They'd done nothing about finding a *hostal*. They could sleep in the lorry as they had almost planned.

The ringing of Oliver's phone in his pocket startled him. He was standing with Orlando, propping up the bar of the Castañeda. It was after midnight. Nobody had phoned him since he had given his brother an earful last weekend, and he was planning to wait till the next one before getting back in touch with Bernd. But this caller turned out to be Felipe. He was full of apology for ringing so late, but something urgent had come up. There had been a machine breakdown at the factory. It was a – Felipe didn't know the word in English and Oliver didn't recognise it in Spanish. He handed the phone to Orlando. Who listened carefully to what Felipe was saying, nodding his head. Then he told Felipe to wait, and turned back to Oliver. 'He wants us to do an extra job while we're down here. One of the biggest lathes in the shop has gone down and they won't be able to start up in the morning. But there's one down on the coast that he wants us to collect and bring back. Can we? It's extra money.'

Oliver nodded vaguely. 'Suppose so.'

'It's a bit of an early start. We need to get to Almuñécar for seven o'clock.'

'Jesus Christ, Orly. It's nearly one. We've both been drinking.'

'They're offering double money. It's an emergency for them.'

'OK,' Oliver said. 'It's you who's got to do the driving. If you think you can, I'll go along with it. But if you decide no, I'm behind you too.'

'Up to me,' said Orlando. He made a big-eyed face and a pantomime of a gulp. Then he spoke back into the phone and said yes. Details and instructions came flooding back. Orly gestured to Oliver to get paper and pencil and Oliver asked urgently for them across the bar.

They took a taxi back to where the lorry was parked. They set Oliver's phone-alarm for five o'clock. Upright in their seats, and fully clothed, they dozed intermittently. When the alarm went off they found themselves stiff and headachy, but there was nothing for it except to get going, only getting out of the cab first to piss, on opposite sides of the their lorry but still comfortingly in earshot of each other. Coffee, washing and bowel movements would have to wait till they came to the truck stop which was marked on their map, a little way south of Granada.

All of which went to plan. Spanish cities never sleep, but it was still vastly easier to navigate the centre of Granada at that hour than it would have been in the daytime. They studied their map as they finished their coffee at the truck stop, among the tiny number of other drivers who were dotted around the barn-like cafeteria. Their road would climb to the pass of the Moor's last sigh, *el Puerto del Suspiro del Moro*, at eight hundred and sixty metres. 'Two and a half thousand if you want it in feet,' Oliver volunteered. Then there would be a long steady descent to the coast at Motril, and a final run westward along the coast to their destination. When Oliver did the conversion it worked out at sixty miles. They looked at their watches. Gone half-past five.

'There is another way,' Orlando said. 'I did it once on a bus.' He drew his finger down the map, showing where the old road to the coast branched away at the Suspiro, running direct to Almuñécar through Otivar and Jete. 'We'd save ten miles at least.'

'We'd also be climbing mountains,' Oliver objected. 'Look. It goes right across the Sierra del Chaparral. Where's the pass, now? Here. Twelve hundred metres. That's nearly as high as Ben Nevis. And look at that lot on the way down.' He was pointing to the hairpin bends. In fact that stretch of road looked more like part-unravelled intestine.

'I know about those,' said Orlando combatively. 'I've been there, I've seen it. If a fucking bus service can get across in one piece, then so can we.'

Orlando was still under some remnant influence of alcohol from the evening before, Oliver realised. But he'd driven them safely out of Granada, and his driving skills had improved exponentially over the past few days. Oliver also calculated that he would be sobering up minute by minute as they went along. The testing ground lay half an hour ahead at least. 'Well, if you're sure,' he said. 'It's your decision. But it'll still be night nearly all the way.'

'Headlights,' said Orlando. 'Our lorry is equipped with headlights for just such situations.' Oliver didn't like him in this mood but he knew him well enough by now: he would be sweet and reasonable again in an hour or so, as the remaining alcohol was neutralised by his system. In the meantime he had to sit back and let him get on with it.

They were soon at the Suspiro. It was about as unromantic a place as could be imagined, with a filling station and concrete flyovers. Difficult to imagine the defeated Boabdil here on horseback with a baggage train. Still, Oliver did twist round in his seat to see the famous last view of Granada, the Alhambra, picturesquely floating above the city in a shimmer of floodlighting – a piece of technology that Boabdil could never even have imagined. Oliver wondered if Orly might have had second thoughts about his decision, and would stay on the main road to Motril. But he clearly hadn't. He indicated right almost unnecessarily early, as if steeling himself to do what he'd made up his mind to, and then turned up the slip road where the exit was signed to Almuñécar and Otivar.

For some ten miles the road slid gently downwards and then when it did start to climb again it was such a gentle ascent that Oliver decided Orlando had indeed made the right decision and that it was he, Oliver, who had been silly, making a fuss about nothing. They passed the sweeping headlights of an occasional car or lorry coming the other way. Then a couple of miles of steeper gradient and two rather sudden hairpin bends brought them – surprisingly soon – to the pass. There would probably be a fantastic view in daylight, Oliver said, and Orlando reminded him he'd be able to see it in just a couple of hours' time on their journey back.

A sudden flash from out of the darkness: it seemed both distant and near at the same time, suspended in a sky that appeared to reach down as well as up. It came

again. 'A lighthouse beam,' said Orlando. There was
surprise and almost laughter in his voice.

He's OK now, Oliver thought, relieved. He said, 'We
must be nearly at the coast.'

'Not that near,' said Orly. 'It's thirty kilometres by
road including bends. Though less as the vulture flies.'

'A lighthouse seen from a mountain,' mused Oliver.
'Things you don't...'

The descent was suddenly steep and took them by
surprise. The first hairpin was upon them at once, a left-
hander. A bend so sharp and sheer that you couldn't see
any more road ahead until you were nearly round it.
They heard stones at the road-edge crunching, some
flying noisily up at the underside of the lorry, as the back
of the vehicle hauled itself round. They pitched
downward towards the next one. 'Slow,' Oliver shouted,
but they seemed to take this one even more precipitately.
The headlights'beam slashed a bright arc through
vegetation so thick it might have been jungle. 'She's
running away,' came gasped from Orly in the darkness.

'Use the gears.'

'Declutch and I lose her.' The next left-hander, and the
headlights swept their beam out into empty space. No
north or south any more, no east or west. Somehow –
another awful crackle and skid of stones – Orlando
dragged the lorry round. 'I can't...' he began. And then
he interrupted himself with a single word that filled
Oliver with the worst terror he had known. Not so much

a word as a scream. The scream was, 'Jump.' Oliver had never heard a man scream before. He hadn't been entirely certain that they could.

*

Darkness. Utter dark. Alone. Cold. Silence, terrible and close. Those sensations, in that order. A smell. A mix of smells. Foliage, like a box hedge, or maybe pine, and with it diesel fuel. Oliver was lying, or sprawling, on his back among leafy branches or thick undergrowth. He didn't remember how he'd got here – wherever here might be. Had he in fact jumped when Orly told him to? He'd pressed the release button of his seat belt, he remembered that. I want to go to sleep, he thought, and heard himself give a cry, a pathetic whimper like an abandoned dog's. He heard the cry repeated; it became a word. 'Orlando.' He wanted to do everything at once: check that he was on the ground, not in a tree; check that he had no broken limbs; find… 'Orlando.' He was shouting it, again and again. He was standing, uninjured so far as he could tell, upon the ground.

There ought to be a lorry blazing like a torch among the trees, he thought, but there wasn't. Just the silence, empty of Orlando, and that sinister smell of diesel on the air. 'Orlando.'

It wasn't so dark once you were used to it. An ice-cold moon looked down at him through branches of tall pines. He was only a couple of yards inside the belt of trees, on terrain that sloped up almost vertically from the road. Three downward stumbles brought him onto level tarmac. The road was entirely blocked by the back of their lorry. It was not on fire, not even smoking, and its lights were out. The cab was buried among the broken trees. Oliver made towards it, willing himself not to cry. He was on' his'side of the vehicle. The cab door was open, impossibly agape, flung forward, hinges smashed. He climbed up and looked inside. It took a while to make sense of what he saw in the jagged shards of moonlight. Where the engine block had been, between their two seats, was now the splintered trunk of a tree. The lorry had impaled itself upon it. Oliver hardly knew how to look beyond it but he had to. The driver's door was gone, but the driver's seat was intact. Leafy branches filled the aperture where the windscreen once had been. An airbag hung slowly deflating like a landed parachute. The steering wheel was more or less in place. Oliver realised the significance of that. Orlando, whether alive or dead, had not died in here. He checked quickly behind the seats, salvaged the two backpacks they had brought with them, then climbed back out. He would have to walk round the back of the truck to see if Orlando – if Orlando's body – was lying on the other side. He felt sick. His brain was in overdrive, running all his thoughts at once: about his own sister and brother, oddly enough; about Orlando's father and what he, Oliver, would have to tell him; about the extraordinary way the lorry had hit the tree dead-centre, shunting the engine through the back of the cab yet leaving both seats intact – almost as if Orlando had planned it that way. 'Orlando…'

'Oli?' They met, coming together from their opposite

sides, at the back of the lorry, where its tailgate almost overhung the drop on the inside of the bend. There was a hug and, from Orlando, a sudden storm of tears. His head was very wet, Oliver's hands discovered, and it was not all the result of crying. His hair was sticky, and the moon showed dark lava-flows on temple, cheek and neck. 'You're bleeding.' He tried to feel a wound, dreading the discovery of a gash or hole beneath his curls, but there didn't seem to be anything as terrible as that.

'It's nothing bad,' Orlando said. 'Come on. We've got to get away.'

'What do you mean?' Oliver couldn't take this in. The discovery that Orly was alive, walking and talking, and with only superficial injuries had turned the worst moment of his life into the best. 'I love you, kid,' he said.

Orlando was clutching at his elbows, violently shaking him. 'Must get out of here.' He seemed out of control.

'No. Wait. Someone'll come. There'll be help.'

Orlando was clearly in shock. Hot weak tea with sugar. Only there wasn't any. Wouldn't be any for miles. For hours. There were water bottles in the backpack. Perhaps Oliver was in shock too.

But Orlando manhandled him, roughly, turning him round, forcing him to walk with him, down the steep descent towards the next hairpin. 'Don't do this,' Oliver protested. 'We need to stay calm. Sit down. You'll bleed worse.' When Orlando's head knocked against his own, Oliver could feel the blood spill onto himself. 'Your face is a sheet of blood. You look terrible.'

'Just a graze. Head wounds always bleed like that.' They had come to an uneasy stop in the middle of the road, Orlando still gripping Oliver tightly by the wrists.

'Let me hold a hanky to it…'

'We can't stay here. They'll test me. Breath test. Way over.'

'Yes but…'

'And you're on the run from the police already.'

'In England, Orly, not here…'

'That'd soon change if we wait for the police to find us. I'll go to prison. So will you.' Orlando felt wet all over. He was weeping again, bleeding copiously as well. Perhaps he'd wet himself at some point. They were scuffling, almost fighting, in the road, fifty yards down from where the lorry blocked it. Oliver had the geography of the accident in his head now. They'd failed to take a right-hand bend, the lorry had crossed the road and embedded itself in the trees to the left of the road where the ground rose steeply. On the other side the land dropped sheer away. Had it been a left-hander that they'd come to grief on… 'Come on!' Orlando's voice was half shout, half sob.

'Where?' Oliver came fiercely back. 'Where are you

saying we should go to? Walk through the night to… To where? We're in the middle of nowhere, stuck on a mountainside as high as the Cairngorms.' He realised as he spoke that the lighthouse beam they had seen from the pass had disappeared from view during their brief, precipitate descent.

'We'll get down to the coast. Hide out there. Michael will help us.'

'Michael?'

'Donald. Michael. Whatever his name is.'

The accident's affected his brain, Oliver thought. That injury to the head. Changed his personality. I'm alone up here with a person I don't know any more. He began to feel panic again, as he struggled, grappling wrists with Orlando; the two backpacks which he had somehow threaded onto one arm were like buffers between them.

'OK, OK.' Oliver finally surrendered. 'Let go of me. We'll walk for a bit. Talk things through. Decide what to do.' Orlando released him. Oliver took his handkerchief out of his pocket. 'Give me your head.' Side by side they walked on down towards the next bend, whose contours showed dully in the moonlight. Thank God for the moon at least, Oliver thought. He pressed the handkerchief, which was hardly antiseptic, to the side of Orly's head.

At some point I've got to turn him round, Oliver thought. Get back to the lorry. Deal with this like adults, in the proper way. He wondered how this was to be done. Physically he was no match for Orlando: he couldn't wrestle him into an arm-lock and march him up a mountain road. And yet persuasion didn't look much likelier of success.

Above them came the sudden blast of a horn. A vehicle had come upon their lorry and was unable to pass. They heard the slam of a car or truck door and muffled shouts. Orlando hissed in Oliver's ear, 'Run.' Then he grabbed him again and with a sudden access of strength – more than Oliver had imagined Orlando possessed – pulled and dragged him at a jog-trot down the road and round the angle of the next hairpin. Oliver was still trying to keep his balled-up hanky in contact with Orly's blood-matted hair. His protests came now as whispers. He realised this was because he didn't want the people reconnoitring round the lorry to hear them. Because in the end he was on Orlando's side in this, not theirs. And he realised he had lost the argument with Orlando, and Orlando had won. They slowed to a walk again.

Another minute and they could see headlights approaching from below, twisting up the corkscrew bends and sometimes disappearing altogether among the trees and crags. Oliver had one more try. 'We'll flag them down.' *El ultimo suspiro*.

'Like hell we will. When they get near, hide in the trees.' Orlando, pressed against him, felt not only wet all over now but cold. He needs all kind of help, Oliver thought, and there's none that I can give.

It was two or three minutes before the climbing vehicle

turned onto the stretch of road that they were standing on, and just as it did, Orlando grabbed fiercely at Oliver and dragged him behind a jutting spur of rock. The headlights, which belonged to a small pick-up truck, went climbing past, and the red tail-lights followed them out of sight around the higher bend. One more hairpin and that pick-up too would come to a halt against the immoveable obstacle of the Scania they'd left there.

'You're in a bad way,' Oliver said as they resumed their progress down the mountain. He could fight no longer, nor protest, and Orlando no longer had to hold him or drag him. Instead they walked side by side like two friends, Oliver still clamping a handkerchief to Orly's head, and with his other hand clasping his cold fingers to give him warmth. It was too late to do anything else except go along with him. If he loved him. And he did love him. That was the only thing that Oliver now held certain. And stay with him was the only thing he knew to do

FOURTEEN

They stood on the sharp bend in the road where it
nudges round the four thousand foot peak of Jaloche,
and the view runs ten miles down the Rio Verde to the
sea. It had taken them an hour to get this far. They had
followed the hairpins down, and then another set of
bends had led them up again, hugging the mountain
ridge to the left. To their right the slope tumbled away to
the stream bed a thousand or more feet below. But ahead
of them the lighthouse was back in view, its ten-mile
distance a vertiginous plunge. It still flashed its simple
message, though dawn was crowding into the sky and
lighting up the sea away to the south east. Tendrils of
habitation were visible along the coast: the fringes of
Almuñécar and Motril, half hidden by outcrops of rock.
The silvers, greys and blacks of moon and shadow were
dissolving second by second into browns and greens
near at hand; below, the distant sea began to come blue.
Orlando, whose mood had swung wildly during the last
hour, was just this minute fiercely practical. 'Nerja's
over there.' He pointed south west. 'Only about fifteen
kilometres.'

'In a straight line maybe. But look at that.' Oliver was
being practical too. The view in that direction was
blocked by another mountain ridge, rising not much
higher than the place where they stood, but still a
thousand odd feet of climb up from the bed of the Rio
Verde that lay in between. 'You seem dead set on
getting to Nerja. Michael isn't the Wizard of Oz, you

know. He's not going to be able to magic everything all right.'

'So what idea do you have that's so brilliant then? Tell me a better place to head for and I'm with you all the way.'

Oliver didn't have a better idea. 'So tell me your route plan.'

'We won't be able to carry on by road in daylight. We'd get picked up.' They had already had to jump off the roadway several times and hide behind thorn bushes or lie prostrate on the bare slope to avoid being skewered by passing headlights. Several vehicles had come climbing past. Two had been police cars coming up from the coast; one had been an ambulance, and that had only deepened Oliver's sense of shame and guilt. Nothing, of course, had been coming the other way.

'We just have to go over the top,' Orlando said. 'It's not the dark side of the moon.' Though he sounded anything but confident as he said this. 'I think it's a nature reserve or something. People hike here. There'll be trails. Way-marks.'

'We've got one bottle of water each and no map,' said Oliver. But he had nothing else to say. *Let's go on by road. We'll give ourselves up.* It was too late for those now. He'd made his choice earlier: to go along with Orlando, running away from the crash scene – it had been that or risk losing him altogether. There were no more options.

They followed the road another hundred metres round its corner of rock. Oliver had the sense that they might tumble off and fall all the way to the far-off sea. The lighthouse that had so dominated the night earlier was now faded to an irrelevant flicker at the edge of the blue water. A trickle of gold was seeping along the horizon. It beaded up in the centre, brighter than any number of lighthouses, and then the sun broke free. Oliver looked at his watch. It was just gone half past seven.

A path led down from the road. It was so insubstantial it might have been made by animal rather than human feet. But because it led – or at least set off – along a bearing towards where they guessed Nerja must be, hidden behind the long ridge, they followed it. Down to the river, or stream, over rock and through scrub made up of broom and prickly pear. The path meandered and corkscrewed. It took longer to get to the bottom than had seemed possible, looking from above. And this is only going down, Oliver thought, as the sea view slipped away and vanished, leaving their portion of sky hemmed in by peaks and crags on every side. There was still the other side of the defile to go up once they'd made it to the valley floor. 'Have you done anything like this before?' he asked Orlando, who had been brought up in a part of England as flat as a billiard table.

'On holidays. Lake District. Once in the Pyrenees.'

Oliver, who had once walked the Pennine Way but had never been near the Pyrenees except in an aeroplane, felt a faint lessening of his sense of desperation. But it was very faint. On the opposite slope, which seemed to aspire more and more to the condition of a wall as they neared it, were patches of tree cover – small umbrella pines and occasional chestnut – which would help to conceal them from the road they had left: from the eyes, perhaps the binoculars, of the Guardia Civil. But the trees would also make it harder for them to maintain their heading, at least until the sun had climbed back into their bit of sky.

In the daylight Oliver was able to examine Orly's head wound better. The bleeding had stopped, though the congealed flow had made a horrible mess of his hair. But Orlando had been right: the wound was only superficial. Oliver dabbed at it again with his hanky and a little water from one of the bottles, but it was a token gesture only, rendered ineffective because of Orlando's matted hair. Orly's denim jacket, his T-shirt and jeans were dark with dry blood. Oliver had guessed that Orly had wet himself earlier; he wasn't going to ask; but if so, at least that had dried up too. Oliver turned his attention to Orly's cheek, and scrubbed at it with the handkerchief. It was the one part of him that he could make more presentable with the equipment at his disposal. 'You look like Raskolnikov in Crime and Punishment,' he said. Then he risked a joke at his lover's expense. 'You've bled down the whole hillside. They could track you with bloodhounds. What do you think of that, Mister Fox-Hunting Man?'

Orlando took this in good part. 'When we get to the river we can wade along it and throw them off the scent.'

A minute later they were at the river, the Rio Verde, a

mere trickle over stones, though there was telltale evidence all around – flotsam high in nearby bushes – that it could become a torrent at times. 'Did you ever read Laurie Lee?' Oliver asked. 'He spent a winter at Almuñécar during the Spanish Civil War. He was sent up into these mountains to deliver a message to a farmer about a consignment of hand grenades. He came to a river – maybe this one – that was so deep in flood that the farmer carried him across on the back of a swimming horse.'

'We won't have to cope with that, I hope,' Orlando said. 'There hasn't been any rain down here for months.' One second he was standing tall, talking and being practical, the next he was grey-faced, his eyes glazed, and clutching at Oliver. 'Help me stand,' he said quietly.

Oliver didn't. He helped him instead to lie down on the ground rather than simply falling to it. He looked around. Tall broom bushes near at hand hid their position from the road. He was thankful for that. He loosened Orly's trousers, because he vaguely remembered that was what you were supposed to do, then he lay down beside him.

'What are you doing?' Orlando whispered.

'It's OK. You fainted. Get a bit of water down you. Then rest a bit.' Oliver helped him raise his head enough to take a gulp from the bottle, then let him lie back. A moment later Orlando had gone to sleep. Oliver surveyed him anxiously, half sitting up next to him. He wondered how much blood Orly had lost. Was he still in shock? Or suffering something more serious? If so, there was nothing Oliver could do about it out here. A number of useful things had survived in the two backpacks, but Oliver's phone was not among them. He wondered how they could even have thought of climbing a mountainside with Orly in a state like this.

At some point Oliver must have fallen asleep too, because suddenly he was looking up at Orly who was sitting up beside him, and squinting in bright sunshine. Orly looked as if he had been crying again. Oliver blinked at his watch. It was after ten o'clock. Crickets chirped like phones.

'I've fucked up big this time,' said Orlando. 'I panicked. I've done the wrong thing at every turn.'

'Don't think like that…'

'Drank too much. Crashed the lorry. Panicked and ran away. What a little shit you must think me.'

Oliver sat up. 'Far from it.' He studied the mess that his lover's face had now become, and was conscious of the disintegration of his poise, and the puncturing of his self-esteem. He said, 'On the contrary, Marmalade Cat, bedraggled one, I've never loved you more.' Strangely enough, it was true.

Orlando stood up without saying anything, but reached down a hand to pull Oliver to his feet too.

Oliver said, 'Can you walk OK?' He was very unsure about Orly's physical state. But Orlando nodded. 'Then shall we have a go at this bit of a hill?'

They crossed the Rio Verde without getting their feet wet, hopping from boulder to boulder. Then they followed a track, a goat track perhaps, that led promisingly upward among the scrub. It was the first of many. Some petered out, others came to abrupt stops at slides of un-climbable scree. They retraced their steps time and again. It was a couple of hours before they had regained the height of the road they had left on the other side of the defile. They could see it quite often, when the trees and scrub were sparse around them. It was a couple of miles away now, a fragile ribbon wrapped around the side of a mountain. Then at last they began to rise above it, climbing slowly in the same direction as the sun, which had caught them up while they slept and looked like overtaking them on their westward journey if they didn't make better headway soon.

Once or twice they saw flocks of goats which peered at them from unexpected heights, then vanished again on secure, invisible roads of their own. At one moment Orlando pointed into the sky. Two fawn-feathered griffon vultures were sailing overhead. 'Search party's out,' he said, and Oliver was pleased for him, that he was at least trying to make jokes again.

They tried not to think about the top. How near to it they were, how far. It was futile to guess, as the upward slope unrolled before them like an endless carpet, studded with boulders, clumps of pampas grass and small pines. From time to time they went on hands and knees. Oliver was past thinking: wasn't this all a bit dangerous, with nothing but trainers on their feet and no mobile phone? Catching his breath sometimes with the effort, as he heard Orlando beside him also do from time to time, he simply climbed.

Then, almost imperceptibly, the slope began to flatten out. They didn't mention this to each other, dared hardly to think it to themselves, in case another towering wall of rock should appear over the edge of the view. But they were not wrong. The sky came down to them, the land ceased to rise, and they stood on the summit of another world. By luck rather than design they had reached the top of the ridge a long way from its highest points. One of those was a sizeable peak that blocked the view of the sea when they looked due south. Instead, the Mediterranean appeared in two sweeping segments, one on each side of the ridge peak, brilliant in the sun. It still looked deceptively near, but no more so than it had done when they first saw it from the road. Looking back to where they had come from, they could no longer see that road, though the peak of Jaloche was still monumentally in view. But behind it now rose the Sierra Nevada, tier upon tier, with the white crown of Mulhacén just visible thirty miles away. Lower down the valley of the Rio Verde they could make out the ochre and white colours of a village, which Orlando decided must be Otivar. But when they looked ahead of them, in their south-westerly direction of travel, they saw no gentle descent to Nerja, but another ridge that rose beyond the nearest valley floor, another one beyond that, and then tall mountains once again. 'Jesus Christ,' said Oliver.

'Cheer up,' said Orlando, to Oliver's surprise. 'I reckon this is the highest point. Look straight. Forget the mountains. Those next two ridges aren't quite so high as this. Once we're over them Nerja can't be far. I reckon we've come a quarter of the way.'

'It's one o'clock already, Orly.' He didn't need to add that their water bottles were nearly empty now, although they had been as careful with their contents as they could.

'Let's stay high for a bit,' Orlando said. 'Follow the ridge west, till we see a nice valley to walk down towards the sea. Find a farm and ask for a glass of water.'

Oliver looked uncertainly at him. Was he joking? Or delirious? But apparently he'd meant what he said, for he led off westward along the undulating crest of the ridge, while small surprised birds flew twittering from the sparse thorn bushes at their approach. 'At least we're not being followed,' Orlando said.

'No baying hounds snapping at our heels,' said Oliver and instantly regretted it. Any reference to fox hunting could be relied upon to elicit a polemic on the subject from Orlando, and if Oliver had felt secure in the belief that Orly would be too out of breath to deliver one now, he had reckoned without the fact that they were no longer climbing steeply, but walking on easy gradients, now up, now down.

'I suppose you think,' Orlando said, 'that I imagine

foxes enjoy the chase. Well,' course I don't. Foxes don't enjoy things. Well, not in the way we do. Sunshine, I suppose they enjoy that, and sex too. But sangría's lost on them.' Oliver smiled to himself. Perhaps Orly was still his old self after all. 'You'd perceive things differently,' Orlando went on, 'if you lived on slugs and beetles, and crunched up live mice. And slept in a hole in the earth. They don't go all gooey at the sight of fox cubs, you know.'

'I suppose they do remind people of dogs and cats,' Oliver admitted.

'Early man had worked with dogs for thousands of years, d'you know, before anyone thought of giving them a basket. People really don't understand that. I didn't always. When I was a kid I used to catch yellow-neck mice in the yard – in a box trap so they were unharmed. I made big cages for them, all nicely furnished with twigs and branches and nest boxes. Fed them every day. Fruit, grain – muesli they liked – and salad leaves. They had names. They had children. But the children had to be let go. Then they had to take their chances among the dogs and cats, and the Little Nipper traps my father set. It took me a long time to understand that. There's two different worlds for animals in our minds. One's a luxury one – keeping pets, being anthropomorphic – is that the right word? – being sentimental. But the other one's the real nitty-gritty one: you have to kill the rats and rabbits and foxes, or at least some of them, or they'll eat everything you have and you'll starve. You can't make an exception for foxes just because kids think they're pretty.'

'I see all that,' said Oliver, who was watching an aeroplane trail grow across the sky, heading north from the African coast. 'I know they've got to be controlled. It's just the thought of people enjoying it that revolts me.'

'Oh come down from your bloody pulpit, Oli. Have you never shot a pigeon with an air gun? Never caught tiddlers in a stream?'

'No, actually,' said Oliver, a bit po-faced.

Orlando looked at him closely. 'Never pursued young men simply because you wanted to have sex with them?'

'That's different,' said Oliver. 'I never wanted to kill them.'

'I never said you did. Anyway, unless you're a total vegan, and the kind of person who tries to avoid treading on ants by accident, you don't have a leg to stand on. Every time we eat meat we're killing for our pleasure. We could live on lentils and rice if we wanted to. And as for foxes dying in pain, all animals die in pain. They get ripped to bits by other animals, or they get injured and diseased, in which case they die of starvation...' He hesitated before the next word, because it was a bit close to the bone right now. 'And thirst. You'd probably want to take them all to the vet and have them painlessly put down.'

Oliver had to admit that he probably would. And the

thought struck him that, despite the miserable plight they were in, on the run from the police in two countries, with no destination in sight, and their water stocks nearly gone, he could not imagine a better situation to be in than this – with Orlando, his own Orlando, alone together, even if gently arguing, scrambling along what might have been the ridgepole of the world, with mountains, sparkling sea and sun-swept sky for background, breathing clean snow-scented air. Perhaps, he thought, those hunted foxes did in some way enjoy the chase – though obviously not the capture – after all. 'Hmm,' he said, a new picture of Orlando suddenly forming in his mind, 'I suppose you wear green Wellingtons and all.'

'' Course,' said Orlando. 'What would you rather have me in – little shiny red ones?'

At last they left the heights and clambered southward down the slope. There was another trickle of a stream to cross at the bottom; another, though marginally less daunting, ridge to climb. Orlando had been right to keep going west along their ridge path. They had gone beyond the line of the second ridge they'd earlier earmarked as their next big challenge. Now they only had to face the one they'd thought of as the third. Even so, that would be the equivalent of tackling two Munros in a single day. Assuming they made it.

The sun was past its zenith now, but it baked them as they descended into the valley. The stream at the bottom was a bitter disappointment. They saw themselves drinking deep from its clean cold current and replenishing their by now quite empty bottles, but it was not to be. The drought had put paid to running water here. A few stagnant puddles lurked, and they tried to lap at them like dogs, but the water tasted foul. There was no depth to sink a bottle in and fill it, even if they'd wanted the muddy stuff. There was nothing for it but to press on, waterless, up the second climb of the day. But it was good, at least, to feel the cooler breeze a couple of hours later when after another painful upward scramble, they reached high ground again. This time the valley that lay spread out ahead of them had a different, tamer look. Fields lay below: groves of citrus and almonds, broad expanses of red soil dotted with olive trees. They followed a slightly broader track downhill, and found themselves walking more and more often in the shade of trees. The sea was only intermittently in sight now, a blue blink between the pines. They were hungry, and each could hear the rumblings of the other's insides. As for thirsty... They sipped from time to time at their bottles as a kind of reflex only; the gesture was as empty as the containers were themselves.

'Pigs,' Orlando said suddenly, and stopped and pointed. Oliver felt a prick of fear. For some reason he had thought *bulls*: perhaps he'd been unconsciously expecting them. But pigs they were, a rather primitive and shaggy kind, rooting around under the trees. 'There must be a farm,' Orlando said reasonably. 'They'll give us water.'

They peered around hopefully as they continued their descent, but no sign of human habitation appeared. But then, quite unexpectedly, there was a road. Not a tarmac-ed one, it was all rough stones, but it had been made for vehicles at least. It wound its way up the valley into the hills behind. Its bottom end obviously met the road along the coast. They followed it down. The sea was now completely out of sight. Curious how near it had seemed at dawn when they were many miles from it, yet now that they were getting close, they had the sense of being far inland.

Oliver saw the house first. It was a low, stone-built, colourless building, half hidden by a ring of trees. Chickens and geese could be seen strolling about in front of it, then as they came up to it a filthy yellow dog hurtled towards them from nowhere, maniacally barking. Oliver was alarmed by this but Orlando took it in his stride; he crouched down, facing the oncoming animal and it stopped in its tracks. Orlando spoke to it in Spanish and a second later another voice could be heard, calling the dog off. It ran back towards the door of the house, in front of which – they had not noticed this before – an old woman was sitting, camouflaged by the branching shade of an old tree, and dressed in a winter-weight assortment of scarves and skirts and shawls. She was busily engaged, it seemed, in the process of knitting yet another one. They made their way towards her slowly, afraid that their dishevelled, and in Orlando's case blood-spattered, appearance would alarm her. Orlando hailed her. 'Ola.' She replied in a mutter of Andaluz-accented Spanish that Oliver couldn't manage to decipher.

Orlando turned to Oliver with an expression of incredulity on his face. 'She wants to know if we've come to buy saffron.'

Oliver almost laughed. 'Do we look like people who've come to buy saffron?'

Orlando, maintaining his sang-froid, told the woman that their most urgent need was for water. If she would be kind enough to oblige them in this matter they might consider making a purchase of saffron afterwards.

Slowly the old woman got to her feet. She held out her hands for their empty water bottles and then disappeared into the dark interior with them. A minute later she returned, with the bottles filled to the top. The two men barely spared the time for the briefest thank you before guzzling the new supply with desperate urgency. The woman eyed the once again empty bottles and then looked up at them quizzically, peering out of dark eyes that were as hard and bright as conkers. 'You have walked a long way. *Claro.* Where have you come from?'

'We're hiking,' Orlando told her. 'From Otivar to Nerja.' That was approximately true, but they could see the old woman was not sure whether to believe them. 'Are we on the right way?'

'More or less,' she answered. 'But look now, you're injured.' She glanced, more suspiciously now, from one to the other. 'What country are you from?'

'England,' Oliver said. He might have lied, said Germany or France, but there didn't seem much point.

'You have no tent with you and no provisions. Hikers. *Tsss.* I know who you are. You are from the *camión* that crashed last night in the mountains. It was on the radio. The police are looking for you. If you go on the coast road to Nerja they will easily find you. But you can not stay here either. My son will be back in a few minutes.' She looked anxiously towards the winding track and down the hill. 'You have somewhere safe to reach in Nerja?' They nodded. 'That is good. But you must set off again now or you will not reach Nerja before dark.' It was already past six o'clock. 'Wait here. I will fill your water bottles again. Give you bread to take, at least.' For a second time she held out her hands for the empty bottles and disappeared inside.

She returned with more than she'd promised. A loaf of bread, the water, and a couple of chorizo sausages each, which she gave to them with a furtive air, as if the trees were even now stuck with her son's eyes. She also had a pencil, and a crumpled brown paper bag, on which, leaning over her chair and using one of its arms to press on, she drew a map. 'Follow the track down the hill,' she told them, 'but not all the way to the road. You'll see the new motorway being built beneath the track ahead of you. Turn right as soon as you see the bridge. Here. There's a path…' She sketched it roughly. 'It takes you round the base of Mount Romero and brings you out above the Nerja caves. After that you must decide for yourselves. At least you can see where you are.'

They thanked the woman profusely, or at least Orlando did. Then they did offer to buy some saffron. The woman went back in and, very quickly, returned with a tiny sachet. It was extraordinarily expensive. 'Now you must go,' she said. 'My son…'

Reiterating their thanks they turned and went, following the twisting lane down the valley. The yellow dog, a tail-wagging friend now, came with them to begin with, but then they heard its owner call it back and it obeyed. A moment later they had to scuttle off the track and into the trees, when the sound of an approaching car heralded the return of the old woman's son. As soon as it had passed they decided this was the time to polish off the bread and chorizo. They wolfed it all in about a minute, which resulted, in Orlando's case, in a bout of violent hiccups.

It was an easy walk – four kilometres downhill – compared with what they'd had to tackle earlier, even if they were footsore now, and achingly tired. They leaped for cover once or twice more as vehicles came past. As they wound lower the way led them through groves of orange and lemon where hoopoes flew on lolloping wings among the trees, and once they heard the comforting, homely sound of a cuckoo.

The white scar of the motorway construction site at last appeared in front of them, and they branched right, on what they hoped was the path the old woman had marked for them. It was at that moment that Oliver's own reaction to his gulped chorizo manifested itself. His stomach seized in a sudden spasm and he was obliged urgently to drop his trousers and squat beside the path while Orlando politely looked the other way. There was nothing to clean up with except a fistful of grass. It was so rough that Oliver thought it might have hybridised with cactus.

Time measured itself on two contradictory scales. Their own progress was slow and laboured. But the sun, which usually travels slowly, almost imperceptibly, across the sky, was today racing along its great arc towards its setting position beyond the mountains. They had lost sight of it for a time during their descent of the valley. But now, skirting the southern edge of the Romero peak, they were trailing after it again. Once more their path took them over rough and inhospitable mountainside terrain. Once more they were in sight of the sea; once more they could trace the paths of aeroplanes, like needles pulling white woollen threads from out of nowhere above the African coast. For a full twenty minutes each vapour trail would grow across the sky, before the mountain peaks inland hid it from view.

They sang fragments of songs. They played I-spy. Anything to get them through this last long leg of the journey. To Oliver's surprise, Orlando volunteered one of his audition speeches: Mercutio's Queen Mab speech from Romeo and Juliet.

> *She comes in shape no bigger than an agate-stone...*
>
> *Her chariot is an empty hazel-nut,*
>
> *Made by the joiner squirrel or old grub,*
>
> *Time out o'mind the fairies' coachmakers....*

True I talk of dreams,

Which are the children of an idle brain,

Begot of nothing but vain fantasy;

Which is as thin of substance as the air,

And more inconstant than the wind, who woos

Even now the frozen bosom of the north,

And, being anger'd, puffs away from thence,

Turning his face to the dew-dropping south.

He did it well, Oliver thought: striding along, and framed against the most spectacular backdrop that the speech could ever have been delivered in front of. Oliver wondered once again how Orlando had allowed his acting career to fizzle out. Then, turning his own face towards the dew-dropping south, he saw that Nerja was coming into view around the flank of the mountain, just a couple of miles away and a little way below. The lights were coming on down there. Oliver's watch said nearly nine.

It was still just light enough to see the path and not to stumble and fall among the loose stones, but it soon would not be. The last flaming banners of the departed sun flew beyond the darkening sea, and the black saw blade of Africa's mountains cut upwards through the distant horizon. Almost directly below them now, and only half a mile away, was another area of light. It was a vehicle park, where people the size of ants were swarming into matchbox buses. 'That'll be the caves,' said Orlando. 'The famous Cuevas de Nerja.'

'Reckon we could hijack a tourist coach?' Oliver said. 'Ride off like Queen Mab?'

'Dunno. We might be able to get aboard one. Let's go down and see.'

'Watch where you're putting your feet now. It's almost pitch dark.' Ten minutes later they were homing in on the car-park lights but quite unable to see their immediate surroundings. They held onto each other as they stumbled forward and down. The last of the tourist buses had gone by the time they reached the car park. But even as they arrived under the floodlights, like a pair of moths lured out of the dark mountains, headlights came bouncing towards them up the road. For a moment they froze, ready to take flight again into the dark hillside, but within seconds the lights had metamorphosed unthreateningly, not into the police car that they feared, but into a taxi. They walked towards it. Orlando leaned in at the window and asked if the driver was free. He apparently said yes, because then Orlando was opening the door and motioning to Oliver to get in.

'There's always a few stragglers left behind at the end of the day,' Orlando translated the driver's Spanish. 'He says it's usually worth driving out here on the off chance.'

Oliver wasn't listening. He was busy winding down the window as a matter of urgency. Both of them now smelled foul, what with Orly's blood and both their sweat – and Oliver now realised that his earlier dysenteric discharge had not entirely avoided the back of his shirt. He didn't want to be ordered out of the taxi on grounds of hygiene. He thought it lucky that the interior light was dim. The taxi driver might have recognised them if the radio bulletins had included any sort of description. Orly's red hair would be a perfect giveaway. Still, would the driver have turned them in and risked losing his fare?

Orlando cut in on his thoughts. 'I thought I had Michael's address in my wallet...'

'Oh, for fuck's sake...' Oliver's spirits crashed. Now that they were almost there. Couldn't the boy ever get anything right? Was he incompetent in every department except bed? Then he pulled himself together. 'I think ... perhaps ... I can remember it.' And he did. A bit haltingly, but he did it. Even including the post code.

'Jesus,' said Orlando. 'How did you manage that?'

'Home Office statistician for you,' Oliver said. 'I told you before.' Orlando was not the only one who was being prone to mood swings that day.

They had hardly expected to find themselves arriving by taxi. It was just as well, though, because they would have been hard put to find Michael's house otherwise; it was in a new and upmarket villa development on a low hillside on the west side of town. But now they were there. They paid the taxi man and were alone.

'Smart place,' said Orlando, and Oliver pulled the bell by the gate. You couldn't enter the walled garden without being interviewed over an intercom, which then unlocked the grille. The voice on the intercom was female, Spanish. Presumably Michael's wife. She asked who they were. Oliver gave his name, then Orlando explained that Michael had offered to help them find work if they needed it. Yes, Oliver thought, but not at ten o'clock at night, not stinking and in a state like this. He was more than surprised when the woman's voice, sounding almost pleased at their arrival, said, *'Si si. Los dos camionistas. Adelante!'*

Though the woman did look taken aback when she actually saw them, and presumably smelt them, standing filthy and dishevelled in her entrance hall. But she seemed determined to make the best of it and give them a welcome. 'I'm Carmen,' she introduced herself, gamely holding out a hand. She was a small, fiftyish woman, still handsome, with thick black hair and those luminous Spanish-chestnut eyes; though hers did not have the hard quality of the eyes of the peasant woman they had met in the afternoon. 'My husband is not here to welcome you himself. He is away on business tonight. He will be back tomorrow.'

She had been alone in the house, yet had opened her door to two male strangers at ten o'clock in the evening, and taken them in. Oliver felt himself on the verge of weeping with gratitude. 'Do you know about the lorry that crashed, up on the old Granada road?' he asked her. 'That was us.'

'I heard something on the radio but didn't pay much attention. Anyway, crash or no crash, you seem to need help. Quite immediate things. A bed for the night. A shower. Use of the washing machine.' Glory be to God for practical people. 'Michael will be back tomorrow evening. He will know how to advise you for the longer term.' It was almost as though they had been expected.

The house they found themselves in would have seemed comfortable under normal conditions. But to people in the state that Oliver and Orlando had been reduced to, it seemed luxurious, palatial even. Something out of a fairytale. There were Moroccan carpets on the marble floors, and upholstered white settees which, for the present at least, they forbore from sitting on. The pictures on the wall might have been rather poor quality reproductions of famous canvasses – the Hay Wain was prominent among them – but Oliver found reassurance even in that. In view of other circumstances about which he was far from happy, he was glad not to find the walls hung with genuine Monets and Van Goghs. Above all, the place was clean: wonderfully, gloriously clean.

Carmen showed them a bedroom with two single beds, and a bathroom with a shower cabinet, and left them to it. They took a shower together – the first time they had done this – and exhausted though they were, and though the shower was more practical necessity than pleasure, they did not neglect to enjoy the experience of soaping each other down. But Oliver was businesslike enough to make a point of re-examining Orly's head wound. He got it clean enough, but was unable to apply a plaster: there remained the problem of the matted hair. Indeed, Orlando's hair also represented a problem of another kind. Not many lorry drivers in this part of Spain sported locks of quite such colour: even in touristy Nerja they would attract attention. But that was something to be dealt with in the morning.

Twenty minutes later, with towels wrapped around their waists, they were sitting perched at the breakfast bar in a kitchen so new-looking that the term' state of the art'would not have over-described it. They were eating omelettes that Carmen had cooked. They felt light-headed and almost numb, partly from physical fatigue, but partly from a sense of disbelief about everything that had happened to them this day, from the way it had begun, with their lorry careering off a mountain road south of Granada, to the way it was ending, here and now, in a degree of comfort and safety beyond their most optimistic dreams.

From the adjoining utility room came the comforting glugging and chuntering sounds of the washing machine as it strove to return an acceptable degree of cleanliness to the only sets of clothes that they now possessed.

FIFTEEN

They didn't wake till midday. Woke amid clean sheets and duvet, then came downstairs to drink fresh coffee, and ingest an extraordinarily sticky but delicious Spanish cake of a kind they'd never encountered before... Just what was required for their blood sugar levels. Oliver went into the town on his own and bought a green baseball cap. Then he borrowed a pair of scissors from Carmen, and one of Michael's razors, and did what he had to do, though it almost broke his heart. Orlando's glorious locks went into a bin liner. They made him altogether too identifiable; and dye – without a very public visit to a hairdresser's salon – was not a viable option. With his head shaved, and a sticking plaster attached halfway up the crown on one side, Orlando wore a somewhat startled look, as well he might, though once the baseball cap was in place he did look more like his old self. A phrase came into Oliver's mind from somewhere: God tempers the wind to the shorn lamb. He wished fervently that it might be true.

They didn't go out again, but sat in the sunshine in the walled garden, with its oleanders, its bougainvillea and its lawn of springy, spiky, blue-green grass. They felt like spoiled convalescents, as Carmen brought them at different times tea, coffee and beer. They could hardly believe their good fortune in finding such hospitality here, but neither could they bring themselves to mention it to each other, as if it might melt away, fairytale-fashion, if they did. Carmen went out twice on errands of her own, while a woman called Conchita went to and fro within the villa, doing ironing and other household chores. Conchita showed no curiosity about the sudden new visitors. Perhaps she was used to unlikely, not to say shady, characters turning up at the villa out of the blue. Perhaps lack of imagination had been the quality that landed her the job.

Michael arrived at eight o'clock. Oliver had to make an effort to stop thinking of him as Donald, though his physical resemblance to Michael Foot did help somewhat. His wife had clearly put him in the picture over the phone, since he was quite unsurprised to see them. 'Been in the wars,' he commented in a neutral tone as he peered searchingly at the new-look Orlando. 'The tonsure's a sensible idea, I think. They gave your names and descriptions on local radio this morning.'

'They're seriously looking for us then,' Oliver said glumly.

'At the moment yes. Yesterday and today. Probably for two more days. But not longer. You'll need to keep your heads down for a day or two, but you won't have to worry too much after that. So long as you don't get yourselves into trouble with the Guardia for some other reason.'

'The British police are looking for me too, remember,' Oliver said.

'So you keep saying,' Michael said dryly.

'What I meant was, will the two searches link up, do

you think?'

'Unless there's a European Arrest Warrant out for you already, I don't expect anyone's going to make the connection. You've made the local news down here, but not the national. A lorry crashes in the mountains, the drivers run off because they'd been drinking perhaps, but there's no link with criminal activity.' He frowned and blinked, then peered closely at Oliver. 'At least I suppose there isn't. The lorry wasn't carrying anything that wasn't kosher, was it?'

'Not that we knew of,' said Orlando. The three of them were still sitting out in the garden, while the sun began to make going-down signals above the mountains to the west. Carmen could be heard, busy in the kitchen.

'They'd have found it by now if they had, I think.'

Oliver was suddenly stabbed at by a new anxiety. 'My mobile phone. I lost that at the crash site. Do you know if they've found that? It'd give them access to all my contacts, including…'

Michael cut him off. 'Including a certain Donald Faircross who recently disappeared from East Sussex, leaving no contact address or number. But not to me. Though I hear what you're saying. Mobiles are dangerous from that point of view. I have nothing to do with them. But there was no mention of finding a phone on the news. Perhaps you've got away with that for now.'

'For now,' Oliver said, feeling a tug of nausea. At

some point he would have to steel himself to ring his mobile number.

Michael smiled at him, for the first time this evening. 'Take things one day at a time. That's the way to live out here. We'll keep listening to the news. See if anything develops. Meanwhile,' he turned towards Orlando, 'keep your cap on for a week or two when you go out.' He returned his attention to Oliver. 'Córdoba might be another matter, though.'

'Most of our belongings are in Córdoba,' Oliver said, and discovered that, just then, he missed them terribly. A favourite jacket. A few very precious CDs that he'd packed against the day when he would once again have equipment to play them on. He'd imagined playing them to Orly, drawing him into the beautiful dreams that were opera, showing his lover what they meant to him, sharing those special feelings with him and bringing him closer.

'There's times when you have to let go of the past,' Michael said rather curtly. Which was all very well, Oliver thought, if he was thinking of his own situation, but Michael had at least had all this to come out to when Sussex had become too dangerous: villa and garden; someone to iron his shirts.

'Jesus Christ,' said Orlando. 'It'll be the second time we've had to leave everything behind in three weeks. Six changes of address in that time.' He too was thinking about the few carefully chosen treasures that he'd brought to Spain with him and which he would now probably never see again.

'I think you lads might feel better about things if I found you a beer,' said Michael. He got up and went towards the house to get some.

*

They stayed with Michael and Carmen for two more days. Carmen insisted they spend their time resting and recovering from their ordeal. Only Oliver ventured out once to call his mobile from a phone box. The mobile appeared to be dead, which was reassuring. Michael was generally out during the day, doing whatever wheeler-dealing he indulged in these days, presumably setting up his moveable headquarters in whichever bar he happened to be. In the evenings Carmen cooked dinner for all of them.

'How do you manage without an office?' Oliver asked Michael during the course of their second evening meal together. He had noticed the absence of any room or even corner in the villa that was dedicated to business. 'No computer, no mobile phone.'

'Face to face dealings whenever possible,' Michael said. 'And letters when necessary. Just as people always used to. These days the police are into your emails, your computer files, mobile-phone calls and bank accounts at the drop of a hat.' Oliver was not cheered to be reminded of that. 'But they don't take so much notice of the humble post. Not like in the days of Good Queen Bess.'

'Sounds reasonable,' said Orlando, who had never

owned a computer or mobile phone either. 'You're not always waiting for something to be discovered, like we are, with Oliver's mobile somewhere on a mountainside waiting for a dog to nose it out of the undergrowth any day now.'

'Can we just shut up about this?' said Oliver brusquely. 'As Michael said, let's just take it one day at a time.' He thought, we're talking as if we're a bunch of crooks already, all in something together. It wasn't a thought that pleased him.

'Oh you men,' Carmen intervened. '*Los hombres! Negocios, negocios!* Always business, business, business.' She pushed a dish of spinach and chick-peas towards Oliver.

*

After two days had passed without any further mention of them on the airwaves, Oliver and Orlando found enough confidence to go out together to shops and bars and beach. They bought a couple of changes of clothes, a pair of shorts each, and swimming trunks – as well as mundane things like toothbrushes and paste. They had enough cash, thanks to their payments from Felipe's firm in Cordoba and the fact that they hadn't settled their bill for the *hostal* there before setting out on their last journey to Granada. They felt bad about that, but then they felt bad about a lot of things. But, one day at a time, they told each other.

Then Michael announced that he had found them

somewhere a bit more permanent to live and a source of income that would enable them to afford it. 'After all,' he said, 'the one place no-one will expect to find you is behind the wheel of a lorry.'

Oliver looked at Orlando, who looked back at him with a look of abject dread. Michael picked this up. 'When you come off your horse you get back on again, soon as possible. Farmer's lad like you should know. And it won't be big lorries this time. Little ones. Not much bigger than vans. You'll do all right.'

'It's not just that,' Oliver said. 'We're in big trouble right now. If there's anything that's not legit...'

Michael held up a hand. 'I give you my word. There won't be. If you have any suspicion, even the slightest doubt... You just stop. Check everything. Everything you carry. Look under the bonnet if you like. Go to Málaga airport. Look at the taxi drivers there. British ones. See the same faces month after month, year after year. They don't disappear, you know. Don't all get carted off to prison.'

Oliver looked at Orlando, but his face was giving nothing away. 'OK,' he said heavily. 'We'll see.'

Michael had found them a roomy apartment in a block of holiday lets. Surrounded by foreign tourists, they would blend in easily, and attract less notice than in a more Spanish environment. Their flat was owned by an associate of Michael's who used it in the winter and rented it out for the summer. They didn't need to know his name, nor he theirs. They would hand over the rent weekly to Michael.

It was near the town centre, just one block back from the sea. There were two bedrooms and a big living area with a well equipped kitchen in one corner. There were carpets and comfortable furnishings, pictures on the walls, shelves of books, and a TV. There was a sound system as well. Too bad they had no CDs to play on it. There was a south-facing balcony and below it a communal swimming-pool. For two people who needed to pick themselves up off the floor it was not a bad place to begin.

Oliver and Orlando wanted to treat their hosts to dinner before they finally left them, but by this time cash was running out. Payment by plastic, or withdrawals from a cash machine anywhere near Nerja would pinpoint them exactly, if anyone was on their trace. But Michael handed Oliver notes from his own wallet, telling them to think of it as an advance on their first day's wage, and then accepted their invitation for himself and his wife. Oliver took them to the Pata Negra, where they feasted on garlic prawns and partridge stew, with two or three bottles of Rioja to help it down.

'But who actually manages you?' Orlando asked Michael out of the blue, late on in the evening, when his tongue was rather looser with drinking than Oliver would have wished.

Michael didn't seem offended, but laughed. 'What do you mean?' he said.

'Everyone has a boss,' Orlando said. 'Even the Pope reports to God.'

'Well,' Michael said, 'I'm not sure you'd really want to know that. You work for me. You know that much. Probably best you don't know more than that. I know who I work for. But I don't know who employs him. Safer that way. By the same token, my manager, if you want to call him that, knows nothing about you. Fair dos?' He gave Orlando one of his most penetrating looks, which had the effect of silencing him for at least half a minute.

'Oh business, business,' said Carmen. '*Siempre los negocios*. How you men do talk.'

'And drink,' Oliver said, with a warning nod towards Orly. 'Remember we've work to do in the morning.' But then he relented, and topped Orly's glass up anyway.

*

The first job that Michael got for them involved driving an unthreatening small truck that didn't even require HGV papers. They picked it up from a builder's yard just where the main road entered town from the west and a mule grazed nearby in a paddock. As Michael had instructed them to, they gave their names as Pete and Andy to the wiry Spanish man who came out to meet them, and he handed over the keys without fuss. Their job was to pick up some furniture from Air Cargo at Málaga airport and deliver it to a British ex-pat household a little way further down the coast. It was an easy day's work, their destination Mijas: one of the smaller Pueblos Blancos, perched among hills at the back of Fuengirola, with a grand view down to the Med. There were a few twists and turns on the way up, and Oliver watched Orlando for signs of panic as he negotiated the bends. But there were none, though Orly did do that bit of the drive with his lips rather firmly pressed together. And then everything else went as planned. The address was easy to find, the furniture not heavy, and they were home by four o'clock. Oliver took the wheel for the whole of the return journey. Why not? If they were pulled over for any reason, he told Orlando, they'd had it anyway, whoever was in the driving seat. One day at a time. They did inspect the goods, though. Looked under the bonnet as well. Felt a bit foolish, finding nothing whatever that could give grounds for suspicion. Not even a set of dominoes.

Other one-off deliveries followed. They went to flashy Marbella and tacky Torremolinos, to Coín on the edge of the Serranía de Ronda, up into the hills to Vélez Málaga, and further west to Estepona. Cargoes included crates of soft drinks, a consignment of potatoes in sacks and, one morning early, a load of fish in polystyrene boxes, which they picked up from floodlit Málaga docks. All their cargoes seemed squeaky clean. Only in fairy stories were gold rings concealed in fish. The days passed and they saw and heard nothing to suggest that the local police were still interested in them. They began to relax.

They shopped in the fish market for pearly pink prawns and slate dark mussels, from which Orlando would concoct the freshest tasting paellas ever. Sometimes they had early starts and early finishes; sometimes the working days were very short, and then they would spend time swimming, and sunning themselves on the beach.

They had bad consciences about the crashed lorry, but there was nothing they could do about that now. The unpaid *hostal* bill in Córdoba was another matter. They sent cash, folded inside a sheet of paper, with a note quoting room number and dates, but no names. Not very hopefully they added a request for their luggage to be kept safely until they were able to come and collect it. They learned that Carmen was going to visit someone in Madrid. They gave her the letter, so she could drop it into a post box there when she arrived.

Earning cash in the black economy, spending what you earned, living from day to day. Maybe this was what Oliver had been looking for when he'd decided – in Madeira, months ago – to get out of England. He hadn't dared to dream that he might have someone like Orlando to share the experience with. On the other hand, neither had he envisaged being on the run from the police, wondering each day when the knock would come at the door. But this must be the way all the petty criminals who lived holed-up on the Costa del Sol felt. People he'd occasionally, shamefully, envied, yet who were unable to enjoy it fully because they were all of them waiting for that knock. Now Oliver, and Orlando, had joined them. It must have been like this in the Garden of Eden: knowing that any day now – probably in the cool of the evening – God would come asking for his apples back.

*

Other residents in their block regarded them with polite curiosity. 'You lads here on holiday or what?' one leather-faced Irishman addressed them, in the nearest bar, on about their third evening.

'Sort of,' Orlando answered, thinking that a vague form of honesty would be the best policy. 'But we've got a bit of a holiday job – through a friend.'

'That's what I wondered. I seen you up and out at some God-forsaken hour in the morning, then driving past in a truck half an hour later.'

That reminded them both that even holidaymakers had eyes and ears. Orlando thought it prudent to remain inseparable from his baseball cap whenever they were outside the apartment, though, after the first couple of days, and when the sticking-plaster had become redundant, Oliver ceased to shave his lover's head. Even so, its return to glory would lie many weeks ahead.

Their jobs were arranged at very short notice. They never knew what they would be doing the next day: whether it would be a short trip or a long one; or a day for spending lazily on the beach. Instructions came via the bar that was situated conveniently next to the entrance of their apartment block. The barmaid would look up when they went in and tell them there was a note for them, or there had been a phone-call. Sometimes

Michael would be sitting there in person, sometimes it would be the man who kept the lorries in the builder's yard on the edge of town, next to the paddock with the mule. Or the note would instruct them to meet Michael in another bar. It was during their second week that the note behind the bar invited them to dine with Michael and Carmen at their villa.

'Got something a bit more interesting for you tomorrow,' Michael said, once the three of them were sitting at the table in the garden, with its view of the bay in the declining sun. Carmen was, as usual, creatively out of sight in the kitchen. 'It's a full day. You get a night away, in a hotel, if you want one. Expenses paid. Algeciras tomorrow morning to pick up a package, then up to Valdepeñas to deliver it in the afternoon.'

'Valdepeñas?' said Orlando. 'Wine country. It's halfway to Madrid.'

'Money's good,' said Michael unemphatically. 'As for the route…'

'We'd have to go through Córdoba…'

'There are several good ways of getting there from Algeciras.' Michael's tone remained even; his face was a mask of blandness. 'You wouldn't have to go near Córdoba. I'll show you on the map. It won't be a lorry this time, just a car. Of course if you'd rather…'

'I think we'd need to discuss it,' Oliver said. 'I mean Orlando and I.' The word *package* had made his stomach churn. With Algeciras as their first destination –

the principal ferry port for North Africa across Gibraltar Strait – it was the drugs connection, rather than the stolen arts market, that seemed impossible to ignore. It was at that point that Michael told them, as if he'd just remembered a minor detail, what the money was. Orlando gave a low whistle. It was a sum out of all proportion to the lorry-driving wages they'd been getting from Michael, or Felipe for that matter, up to now. And even those had been generous when you took into account the fact that there were no deductions. Orlando and Oliver looked at each other, read in each other's eyes a terrible, shaming truth. That every man had his price. Everyone in the world, even your wonderful lover, could be bought if the price was right. The gaols of the world were full of men who knew that. This was the moment for Oliver to take charge of the situation. Just say no. Easy. Time to stop playing up to Orlando's absurd notion of who he was. But it was Orlando who spoke. 'We're up for it,' he said, then looked away, unable any longer to meet Oliver's eyes.

They went indoors to look at the map. As Michael unfolded it in the living room, a letter fell out onto the floor. Oliver picked it up. It was stamped and ready for posting. Oliver couldn't help reading the name and address. *Mark Deakin, Calle San Esteban 15, Apartmento 4 iz, Estepona*. He handed the letter to Michael, who took it without fluster or haste. 'Thank you,' he said. 'I'd wondered where that was.' He put it on top of the television, out of their way. Then he spread the map. 'Now, see here.'

They would collect a hire car from Málaga railway station, having first travelled there by bus. They would use Oliver's passport and driving licence. This would have alarmed Oliver, if his feelings had not now gone way beyond alarm. He went through the motions anyway. Wouldn't the car-hire attendant remember his name from the news reports? Michael brushed this aside. The crash was weeks ago now. Other shocks and names and scandals had come and gone in the meantime. 'You go to the desk alone. The attendant sees the names of a dozen British tourists every day. He's not going to clock a name like Watson. You could show him a passport in the name of Sherlock Holmes and it wouldn't ring a bell. Then you pick up Orlando as you drive out of the car park.' Oliver wasn't reassured.

It was an early start next morning. They did not attract attention in the bus going to Málaga, with its mix of ex-pats (Germans predominating at that hour), locals on their way to work, and a sprinkling of energetic tourists. They reconnoitred the spot where Orlando would wait for Oliver to pick him up when he had the car, and split. Oliver did the necessary at the car-hire desk, expecting at any moment to be stopped in his tracks by a hand descending firmly on his shoulder. But that was a feeling he was used to now, and a few minutes later he was opening the door of their new transport and letting Orlando in.

They changed places on the outskirts of town. Orlando would to drive to Algeciras, then Oliver would do the first part of the long drive inland to Valdepeñas. They would change over again when and wherever they stopped for lunch. They knew the first part of the route well: the coastal motorway that had taken them to Marbella and Mijas. But then, beyond Fuengirola the sunlit coastline turned a corner, revealing the uncompromising outline of the Rock of Gibraltar twenty miles away across the bay, towering out of the sea like a dark sail. Beyond lay the Rif Mountains of Morocco, not as small now as they had appeared from the mountains behind Nerja. From somewhere on that mysterious Other Side a package of something nameless, something awful, was already making its way towards them by boat. This thought crossed both their minds but they chose not to mention it. They had both trained themselves to defer anxious feelings about what might befall at their destination until they were almost upon it.

The Rock grew huge ahead, then slid away to their left, to reveal the port of Algeciras sprawling before them on the other side of its bay, basking at the water's edge like a lizard in the morning sun. They followed road signs to the ferry port. 'It ought to be easy,' Orlando said, 'to find a ferry port. Straight along the shore, you'd think. But it always turns out to be a labyrinth. Same every-bloody-where.'

But then, when they least expected it, the ferry terminal appeared in front of them, through a slalom of queuing lorries. The Tangier ferry had just docked and cars and foot-passengers were filing off. 'How's that for timing,' said Orlando.

'Don't be flip,' said Oliver soberly. 'Just don't.'

They were to pull up just behind the taxi rank, as if lost and looking for directions. When they were approached by two Moroccan men – as it was hoped they would be if all went to plan – they had a nonsense question to ask, in English. 'Is this the right road for Brihuega?' It was to be the map drill they had used in the cafeteria at Málaga station all over again: no tourist would be asking directions from here to an obscure mountain village north of Madrid. They stopped the car as directed. Immediately a taxi hooted them; its driver shouted something. Orlando stepped out of the car and did a lost tourist mime – hands waving, then clapped to his head, idiot smile – while simultaneously, and to Oliver's surprise, two men came hurrying up on the passenger side. The window was already down. Oliver asked his stupid question about Brihuega. The two young men were not bad looking, Oliver found time to notice. 'We have the box,' one of them said.

Oliver saw the box. It was almost the last thing he'd been expecting: the kind of tin box a workman carries, the kind that opens out into a double rack of trays for different tools. The man spoke again. 'You do us a favour please?' He was fairish-skinned, with wavy brown hair and hazel eyes. 'You go to Marbella on your way? You take us please?'

'I don't know.' Oliver felt the first stirrings of fear. 'Not part of the deal.'

Orlando, still outside the car on his side, now called across the roof, 'We don't know you.'

'Help us.'

'And you don't know us either.' Suddenly Orlando was in charge. 'No guns? No tricks?' There were shakes of heads. 'Get in. One in front, one behind. Stay that side. Oli, come out my side. Now in the back behind me. Quick.' Oliver found himself obeying without protest. The two Moroccans were in the car within a second, Oliver sliding over the gear lever and out, in again through the rear door quick as a rabbit, and Orlando back behind the wheel. Two taxi drivers were out of their vehicles and running towards them. 'Any trouble and we push you out,' Orlando said, engaging the gears and accelerating away with a great crescendo of engine noise. Hearing those words coming from Orlando's mouth, Oliver felt the breath knocked out of him with astonishment. One of the taxi drivers caught the rear of the car a blow with the flat of his hand.

There were road signs everywhere, pointing to every conceivable destination. Oliver found just enough breath to be useful. 'Marbella right-hand lane,' he called. A second later, 'Marbella left,' as Orlando wove his way through the maze of the ferry terminal approaches. At least Marbella was well signposted, Oliver thought, and gave thanks that their passengers had not asked to be taken somewhere more difficult – like Brihuega.

'Sorry we fright you,' the Moroccan sitting next to Oliver said when it was clear they were not being pursued. He was the fairer-skinned one, the only one who had spoken till now. He looked a couple of years older than his companion. 'We need get to Marbella, but

I think someone at the customs control recognise us. We need move quickly. Get away, see?'

Oliver turned to him. 'What are you? You're not terrorists, are you?' 'No way,' said the other, with a serious shake of his head. 'We're couriers, same than you. Call me Alain. My friend's Mohammed.'

Couriers, like them. They were all in this together. Crazy this might be, but it gave Oliver a moment's feeling of relief. 'Oliver and Orlando,' he said, and shook hands. Orlando was negotiating one more lane change in the approach to the motorway.

'Moroccan people don'like terrorism. Protest against.'

'Yes, I remember,' said Oliver.

'Oh, but also you remember the bombs in Madrid. Of course. That was Moroccans. But crazy Moroccans, see?' He tapped his head twice, in the most international gesture of all. 'Most of us not like that. Not – *fanatiques* – how do you say? We don'want take over the world. Don'want take Spain back from Spanish. You should live and let live other ones.'

'I agree,' said Oliver. 'You Muslims?'

'Ye-es. Of course. Moroccans are Muslim, like French and Spanish are Catholic. But I don'face Mecca six times a day or go mosque on Friday. If God is counting how many people in mosque every Friday – you know? – he wasting his time, when so much bad happening in the world.'

'You're right,' Oliver said. 'It would look a bit as though God wasn't too good at prioritising. Mind you, if he wanted to do a count-up of how many people went to church in England, it wouldn't take up that much of his time.' He heard himself talking in this way, calmly discussing God with a Moroccan drug smuggler, and could hardly believe it, given the situation they were all in.

Alain seemed to get the joke, for he gave a quiet chuckle. Then he said, 'You two. Are you – you know – are you gays men?'

'Yes we are,' said Orlando from the seat in front. Suddenly free from the complications of the port area and with a straightforward approach to the motorway now ahead of him, he was back in the conversation.

'It's crazy,' Alain went on. 'In Morocco women – girls – are difficult, so young men take boys because they have to. In England you can have every woman you want, but still you wanna be gay guys.'

'I wouldn't say you could have any woman in England you wanted,' Oliver cautioned. 'Even these days. You'd still have to be a bit careful how you went about things.'

Mohammed gave vent to a loud guffaw. Oliver had guessed from his silence up to that point that he knew little if any English. But now he turned round towards the back seat and, jabbing a finger in the direction of his friend, said in that language, 'He's big liar. He's big gay man too. Gay like me, like you.' He giggled, and the

345

severe line of Alain's mouth softened to a sheepish grin.

'OK, OK,' Alain said, and half-raised his two hands in a gesture of surrender.

They talked of all kinds of things as they made their way along the *autopista* to Marbella. Including the Iraq war. Though, to Oliver's surprise, the opinions expressed were temperate and considered. Even Orlando's. What was not discussed was the tin box that lay at Alain's feet. The Moroccans'journey to Marbella was dealt with by Alain in a few short sentences. 'Marbella? You know. Opportunity. Two jobs out of one ferry crossing? Why not?'

Orlando drove them down to the sea front, once they had left the motorway and had entered Marbella itself. The Moroccans insisted that that was as far as they needed to be taken: they would make their own way from there. They took their leave with grins and thank-yous, and left them with the box.

'You were very decisive back there at the docks,' Oliver commented as they drove off again. 'One in the back, one in the front – push you out if you try anything. How did you come up with that all of a sudden?'

'Yeah,' Orlando answered. 'I saw it done in a police series on the telly. Can't remember which one. Thought I'd give it a try. See if it worked for real.' Sometimes, Oliver thought, there could be advantages in having a boyfriend who'd been an actor.

They drove on, round Málaga airport. Then headed

inland, across the Partridge Pass and through the olive-studded hills towards Granada. They had lunch at a café outside the town of Loja, perched dramatically above the River Genil where it cuts through the great Sierra. The tool kit came into the café with them. Orlando had been for opening it up, as soon as they had stopped the car, and having a look inside; there was no lock on the box after all; but Oliver stopped him. 'You really do not want to know. Believe me. This time more than ever. Change your name from Orlando to Pandora if you open it. And if you do you're a dead man anyway. I'll chuck you out of the car myself and leave you for the vultures.' To Oliver's surprise, Orlando allowed himself to be overruled.

Beyond Granada their route took them briefly back into familiar territory, near to Bailén and Linares, where they had made deliveries for Felipe a month ago. Oliver, who was in the driving seat now, made a detour into the centre of Linares, the last place where he had dared to visit a cash machine. He repeated the experiment at the same hole in the wall. Cash was still available, he discovered, and was pleasantly surprised. He was clearly not important enough to have his assets frozen.

They crossed out of Andalucía through the Pass of Despeñaperros. The sinister sounding place name reflected its history. *Throw the dogs down*. The dogs had been the Moors, following their defeat at the battle of Navas de Tolosa in 1212 – the ancestors, possibly, of Alain and Mohammed. The crags on both sides of the road were dark and bristling with pine trees, but at this time of year the effect was lightened by splashes of yellow broom. Then it was downhill towards the vast plain of La Mancha, with Valdepeñas only thirty miles ahead.

They reached their destination in the late afternoon. It was a suburban villa on the outskirts of town, in a landscape of green vineyards. A middle-aged man took delivery at the front gate without any ceremony at all. No invitation to come in for wine or coffee, no small talk. Perhaps it was better that way. They felt wonderfully free as they drove away again; it was the feeling Oliver remembered from walks through airport arrival halls earlier in the year: Funchal, Gatwick. The feeling of having got away with it again.

Back through the Despeñaperros Pass, south into Andalucía again. They stopped at Jaén to spend the evening and night. 'Think big this time,' Oliver said. So they chose to stay at the Castillo de Santa Catalina, high on a spur of rock above the town. They dined amongst suits of armour in the vaulted hall, then walked in the warm air with the lights of the city below, the feras and stresses of the day they'd lived through draining slowly out of them.

In bed later, Orlando said, 'Pity our Moorish friends couldn't stay. We could have had one each.' Oliver hoped he was joking.

SIXTEEN

When they had been paid Oliver and Orlando had more cash about them than they felt comfortable with. They decided that they would send some of their surplus cash back to their banks in England, stuffing high denomination euro notes into envelopes with covering letters. They posted these from a remote village and hoped for the best. The rest of their money they had to carry around with them: there were no safes in their apartment block. They crammed the back pockets of their jeans and shorts, then sewed them up tightly with strong thread. In other garments they created inside pockets out of patches, which they cut from a tea towel. They had to unpick them every time the clothes went into the wash. It was laborious, but the best they could do.

After Algeciras they went back to doing short runs in small vans. With a massive sense of relief. Oliver made the discovery that an earlier fantasy of his was realisable after all: that it *was* possible, if the engine block were not too enormous, to give blow-jobs or hand-jobs to lorry drivers as they drove along, and that the drivers – at least when they were Orlando – appreciated this very much.

But then Michael offered them two more trips to collect things from Algeciras docks. They tried to argue each other out of accepting both jobs, but quite uselessly, skirting the real issues. Neither of them could bring himself to utter the words that needed uttering, the words that would have brought them to their senses. Words like *crazy*, words like *money*, words like *drugs*. They read newspaper reports of an international drug-trafficking ring being rounded up on the Costa del Sol, of arrests in Marbella and Estepona, and assets seized. They brought these reports to Michael but he brushed them away. Those people had nothing to do with him, or with them. They had nothing to worry about at all, he said. Of course they did worry, worried till they were almost sick, but in the end the money won.

They collected cars for these trips from the airport, a different rental company each time. The first package was a carrier bag which they couldn't help but see inside. It contained parts of a car engine, pistons, valves and so on, reposing on a large wad of greasy rag that was pungent with diesel oil. It was a smell they knew only too well: since the lorry crash it had haunted their dreams. They were not tempted to investigate the rag. The second time it was a small brass box which was locked. Both packages were handed to them by stern-faced Spanish men, neither of whom asked for lifts to anywhere, or wanted to cause any kind of scene, but simply disappeared again into the crowds around the port.

*

Two young men had come to stay in their apartment block. They didn't realise they were in the same building initially. They spotted them first playing Frisbee on the beach. They were clad in shorts (one pair each) and a T-shirt (just one between them). They looked about Orlando's age or a bit younger. The bare-chested one was small and slender, but just avoided being skinny. He had long brown frizzy hair which was scraped back and bunched in a long thick ponytail. His eyes were dark and lively: mischievous, Oliver thought. The other was taller, angular, with short pale ginger hair and a sharp nose. His eyes were friendly and pale blue. Oliver, self-appointed guardian of Orly's virtue, judged him the less threatening of the two as the days passed and they saw them again, first in their downstairs bar, then in the entrance hall of their block. By now they were exchanging smiles and nods.

They met properly next time they coincided at the bar next to the apartment block entrance, and started to chat, sitting on stools around the curve of the bar counter. The taller one was Jimmy, his smaller friend was Dave. They both lived in Bradford, though Dave came originally from Hull. One of the first things they imparted – as though it were a matter of urgency that the other two should know this – was that they both had girlfriends but had decided to come away on holiday together without them. They had clearly decided at the outset that Orlando and Oliver were a gay pair and needed to get this formality out of the way in order to avoid misunderstandings later. Dave was a cook in a vegetarian restaurant in Bradford: it was a profit-share venture and the kitchen and waiting staff were also the owners. Jimmy was one half of a window-cleaning business that more or less ran itself when he wasn't there. They had met at university, which they had left less than a year ago, and stayed friends since.

Orlando and Oliver were more sparing of their
biographies. They had fancied a change from Britain,
they said, had got qualifications to teach, and had come
down here to look for work. But none had materialised
and so they too were having a bit of a holiday, which
they were paying for by doing odd jobs for a friend.
What sort of jobs? Oliver selected the least interesting
ones. Delivering to sea-food restaurants; helping ex-pats
install their furniture. As for the friend, he was someone
who lived some way the other side of Málaga. Oliver
hoped that neither Michael nor the lorry man would
walk into the bar as he was saying this. Then the subject
was changed, to Oliver's relief, by Jimmy saying to
Orlando, 'Don't I know you from somewhere? On TV?'
And Orlando explained about the Post Office ad, which
had them both smiling and saying oh yes of course. Then
Dave pleased Orlando by saying that he also
remembered him from Monarch of the Glen, without any
prompting.

Each pair bought a round, then left the bar separately
before they found themselves caught up in each other's
company for the whole of the evening. 'Girlfriends or no
girlfriends,' said Orlando as soon as he was alone with
Oliver, 'I bet you those two screw each other. Bet you a
thousand euros.'

Their paths kept crossing, and the periods they spent
together grew longer as the days passed. They played
football together if they met up on the beach, wearing
almost nothing, and with the goal posts made out of their

discarded clothes. Oliver wondered how many such goal posts had ever had thousand euro notes stitched into them. Though perhaps in this particular location it wasn't such a rare occurrence. Orlando wasn't that good at football. Less good than Oliver in fact, and that surprised him. He remembered a moment's fantasy he'd entertained during the first days he'd known Orly: of the two of them playing together for a team called Real Ale Madrid. Well, here it was happening. And if Orlando was a less than brilliant player, well, dressed as he was, he did look lovely while he was doing it. Which was nice for Oliver. He was only afraid that, if the other two actually did sleep together, they would decide that Orlando was rather lovely too.

Evening beers together progressed, as the days passed, from two a night to three or four, and then they sometimes went in search of tapas together. They visited each other's apartments. Orlando cooked bull's tail. He bought one whole, frozen, like the straight, tapering branch of a tree, and the butcher sawed it into manageable logs on a circular saw at the back of the shop. Orly stewed it very slowly for hours with onions and carrots in red wine. The two visitors were generous with their appreciation, especially the chef, Dave. He might work in a vegetarian restaurant but, they had already discovered, he pretty frequently waived his own rules. 'I do shoot rabbits for the pot,' he told them. 'There's a group of us with cross-bows.' Oliver could see Orlando's ears prick up at that. He hoped that he wasn't going to warm to Dave too much. As a vegetarian he had seemed rather less of a threat.

They went to a club. Oliver and Orlando hadn't gone looking for one before, but Jimmy and Dave knew about this one. It wasn't a gay place, though gay-friendly. They stayed late and got pleasantly drunk but when the two Bradfordians – whom Oliver had taken to calling Bradford and Bingley – latched onto a group of Spanish girls, Oliver and Orlando left them to it.

Orlando made it his business to ferret out the address of a gay club and invite the two young men to try it out with Oliver and himself. They would have to wait a couple of days before they could do this, though. Orlando discovered the place, closed, on a Monday. And the notice on the door made it clear that it opened Wednesdays to Sundays only.

Before that, though, the barmaid in the local bar handed Oliver a note asking them to meet Michael at the Pata Negra for lunch the next day, the day scheduled for the visit to the gay bar. Oliver showed the note to Orly. Both knew what it meant. 'The last ones worked out OK,' Orlando said.

'Don't you think,' Oliver said to him, 'it's time to quit? While we're ahead. In the money. Not in clink.'

'I know,' said Orlando. 'Scary.' But a look on his face told Oliver that their thoughts were the same. Their last two jobs had been small, banal, legit. They'd actually missed the danger, missed the risk. Oliver found it hard to believe it of himself, but it was true. You were terrified when you set out on one of those jobs – abject with fear. But the high you got when you'd come through and made it safely home! And then, a few days later, amazingly, you wanted more. This must be how fighter pilots felt. This was what got them through. Oliver said,

'We'll see what the money is. Then decide.'

Michael began with the money for once. Five thousand euros each plus expenses. Expenses and half of the fee to be paid in advance, the balance on their return. Orlando and Oliver looked at each other, then looked away. 'So long as it doesn't involve bungee jumping,' Oliver said.

'Only driving,' said Michael blandly. 'But it is short notice. You go tomorrow. It's a tanker.' He caught sight of a look of alarm on Orly's face. 'Don't worry. It's not petrol or haz-chem. Only wine.'

'Expensive wine,' said Oliver archly.

'Now you know better than to talk like that,' Michael said, with a quick smile that was switched off almost as soon as it was on. 'I haven't told you where you're going with it yet.' He set it all out. They would be away for four nights, possibly five. They were to travel to Valdepeñas by bus and there pick up a tanker full of red wine. They would drive it to an address in the south of France, near Carcassonne. After delivery at dawn on Saturday they would have the morning free while the tanker was pumped out. The wine was going to be bottled in France and then sold on. They would pick up the tanker again at midday and drive it back the way they had come, empty.

'The French bottling Spanish wine?' Orlando queried. 'There must be a few people who're unhappy about that.'

'A few feathers have been ruffled,' Michael said. 'There's a group called the Crav in the south of France – rural vigilantes, let's call them – who've got a bit of a down on wine imports. There could conceivably be a bit of argy-bargy if you were unlucky enough to run into them, but you wouldn't be in any real danger. Actually, having drivers from a neutral country would probably help to keep things calm, if it did get a little bit interesting.' Michael looked at each of them in turn, blinking once or twice as he changed focus. 'That's why I thought of you.'

'What about the border?' Oliver wanted to know. 'We're wanted by the police in two countries.'

'No problem,' Michael said. 'Remember France and Spain signed up to the Schengen agreement – unlike Britain. No frontier checks of any kind. The old border posts are unmanned. And in France you're not wanted by anyone. Nothing could be simpler.'

'Not wanted yet,' Orlando said under his breath.

*

Oliver urged Orlando to postpone the club visit until the following week, when they would be back from their trip, but Orlando didn't want to listen. He'd been hyperactive these last few days, excited, almost high. Oliver thought this had something to do with his new-found friends but guessed his mood was further heightened by anticipation of the forthcoming trip to France, of the money, and of the possible danger that went with it. And today there was yet another new bee buzzing in his bonnet. Back in Britain a young man called Otis Ferry was up in court. He was a devotee of fox hunting – his career as well as his passion – and had broken into the House of Commons, with others, and brought proceedings to a highly public stop during the anti-ban protests of the previous November. Otis Ferry was something of a hero of Orlando's, and he was following the case with more than just dispassionate interest. Even Oliver had to agree that Ferry was at least cute and charming. But then that went for Dave too.

They compromised about the club. They would go for a short time, but then make their excuses – pleading that they needed an early night before their start in the morning. They told Jimmy and Dave they were taking someone's furniture to France – it sounded less interesting than a tanker of wine, which would have attracted questions as a magnet attracts iron filings – and they wouldn't be around again until after the weekend.

After all that, the club wasn't up to much. It was a small basement bar, rather grubby, with a few token revolving coloured lights. As far as Orlando and Oliver could tell, they were the only gay people there – unless they counted Jimmy and Dave, and they were still not sure about that. Nevertheless, when it was time to go, Oliver found himself unable to dislodge Orlando, who clung limpet-like to his never-quite-emptying glass of sangría – not one of his usual drinks – and to an interminable conversation with Jimmy and Dave about … pigeon racing. Oliver tried gamely to drag him away, but without success, until finally, to his own surprise, he lost his temper and marched out of the bar by himself in a huff.

He was no sooner up the steps and in the cool of the street than he regretted his exit and his petulance. It had been unwise to leave Orlando drinking heavily in the company of two young men, one of whom he clearly fancied and who, whether gay himself or not, almost certainly fancied Orlando in return. But Oliver was not in the mood to accept the loss of face that would have been his reward for going back in. He clumped through the dark streets to the apartment, moodily swigged a couple of glasses of wine, standing stripped to his shorts on the balcony, then, with Orlando still not back, he kicked those off and went to bed.

Orlando got back at four. At least he had arrived. And at least he was alone. But he was hardly sober. 'Just come to bed,' Oliver told him. 'Get some sleep. Big day tomorrow.' Big day today. They would be getting up in three hours'time.

But Orlando wasn't in that sort of mood. 'Why did you leave us?' he wanted to know, standing in shorts and T-shirt, swaying slightly, beside the bed. 'Right party-poop, you.'

'Orly. Because…'

'You've no sense of fun. No idea how to enjoy usself. At least those guys know how to enjoy usself. Holidays. Picking up babes. Smoke dope. Generally hang, hang out. Do toot.'

'For Christ's sake, Orly.' Oliver sat up in bed, wide awake now and cross. 'You've never talked like this before. Sober or drunk. What's got into you? Get fucking undressed and come to bed. Anyway, what's toot when it's at home?'

'Charlie. Cocaine. Every-fucking-body knows that.'

'Well I didn't. And neither did you before today.'

'And what do we do while other people are having fun? Fuck nothing.'

'Orly, stop it.' Oliver leaned out of the bed and grabbed his wrist, pulled him to a sitting position on the bed beside him. 'We have great times. Don't forget it. Travel. Adventures. A flat by the sea in the sun. And we love each other. Isn't that better than all the other things? We've got each other. Isn't that enough?' Oliver found himself on the verge of tears. He said, more softly, 'It's enough for me. Isn't it enough for you?' To his relief he saw Orlando nodding his head slightly, though he was afraid he might have wrung this acquiescence out of him by dishonest means: by words and tone of voice, the way a hectoring parent gets the reluctant agreement of a child. Nevertheless he went on in the same mode. 'You don't really want to do those things, do you? Cruising in bars? Drugs? Threesomes with Felipe? With Bradford and Bingley?'

Rather mechanically, Orlando was shaking his head to signal that, no, he didn't. He too was tired, and probably beyond arguing further, wanting a quiet end to the night. Oliver stroked him gently as Orlando softly unfurled across him like a collapsing inflatable toy. 'Aren't you happy with me, my darling?' He could feel tears working their way down his cheeks. But no answer came back from Orlando. He was asleep. Oliver undressed him with much effort – he was a dead weight – and with a heavy heart. Then he stowed the naked body into bed alongside him. Experimentally he tweaked his cock once or twice, but there was no response of any sort.

Oliver lay awake and miserable. Orlando was probably right. In vino veritas. He did need the stimulus of other company, younger company, people his own age. Anybody would. Orlando had spent two months without so much as speaking to anyone of his own age group. It was all very well for Oliver, having the Kid as his decorative trophy, having the Marmalade Cat to keep him entertained. But perhaps Orlando was not an animal bred for captivity. As time went on – if time were to be allowed them – Orlando would want to make new friends. He'd need to, Oliver understood. Then, given a bit more time, he'd want to screw around. That idea, that until now had only occasionally glanced in through the back windows of his mind, now stood immoveable in his conscious thought for the first time, and weighed there like a stone. It weighed in his stomach too, making him feel sick. Orlando was still only a kid, while Oliver, since he'd met him, could never forget for a second that he was thirty-eight. And even though he was still youthful, and horny and athletic in bed, and even though he had a remarkable big cock for someone of his size – well, Orlando was used to all that now, and had done everything with that cock, short of sado-masochistic things they both drew the line at, that it was possible to do.

He was quite sure Orlando had not had sex with Dave or Jimmy this evening. After years of living with Adi he would have recognised the signs. In the state he was in this evening, Orlando would have been either unable to perform – Oliver already knew that about him – or else, in the unlikely event that he had, then he'd have been incapable of the dissimulation required to cover it up. He certainly hadn't showered, but neither were there any of those telltale signs like unfamiliar scents or spattered clothes. It was possible that he'd done cocaine with them, had let himself be persuaded into hoovering up a line. Oliver wasn't so good at recognising the signs of that. Well, he decided, he wouldn't task him with that in the morning. It would only make things worse. He'd just make bloody sure to keep the kid out of any such situation again. Orly as piss-artist and wannabe alcoholic he could handle. Orly as coke-fiend on top of that would be a bit too much.

It was a good job they were going away. Even on an errand that looked the most danger-prone that they'd undertaken up to now. How dared Orlando say that Jimmy and Dave led more exciting lives! Their adventures with girls in bars, or with drugs in bathrooms, were nothing compared to what Orlando and he had done together. The highs they got – to say nothing of the money. The other things just didn't measure up. And yet, all this adventure, all this risk, living with heart in mouth from day to day. Would it always be like this? Would it have to be? Was this the only way he could compete, to keep Orlando his? It would get a bit wearing in time. When – if – the months turned into years. He didn't want always to be on the road with Orly, always on the run. He wanted to keep him safe, and wrapped in cotton wool. He cuddled around the collapsed and snoring boy as he indulged the thought.

Over-protective now. That was what he was being. It seemed he couldn't win. He thought of Joe Orton and Kenneth Halliwell. How Halliwell had kept Orton all to himself in their early days together: claustrophobically going off to bed together as soon as it got dark, to save on light and heat; not seeing friends. How disastrously that had ended. Would Orlando, mad with frustration, one day beat Oliver's brains out with a hammer in the middle of the night? Then he remembered that it had been the older Halliwell and not his youthful protégé who had killed his lover in jealous rage. After Orton had become famous and Halliwell had not. That muddled the parallel. Oliver was still trying to untangle this when he fell asleep.

*

The morning began almost immediately, with the

alarm clock nightmarishly bleeping. The atmosphere of the row they'd had a few hours ago hung around them, and clung, like the stench of stale vomit. They both had hangovers, Orlando a major one, and Oliver had to feed him aspirins and Alka-seltzers while he staggered around, bumping into his clothes. Who said they didn't do drugs? Fortunately they'd thrown spare clothes into their backpacks the evening before. They found that, in providing for four or five days away they had in fact packed everything they owned. All that was left of theirs in the apartment was the contents of the fridge, the fruit in the bowl on the table, and one or two kitchen utensils that weren't provided and that Orly had insisted they bought. Even now the backpacks were by no means bulging.

Oliver said quietly, 'You're sure, Orly? Sure you want this? It's not too late to call it off. Use your hangover as an excuse? Say you were still pissed?'

'I'm not still pissed,' Orlando told him sharply. 'Sobered right up. But you... You want to chicken out now?'

'Chicken? No way. Just trying to be sensible for once.' But Orly had called him cool once, months ago. He couldn't let himself lose that. That Orly should call him chicken now... 'Come on,' he said. 'If you're OK to drive in a few hours'time, let's go.'

They caught the early bus into Málaga as the sun came up, then found the coach to Granada. Another coach, then to Jaen and yet one more for the last leg, through the Despeñaperros Pass, which brought them to vineyard-hemmed Valdepeñas in the middle of the afternoon. The atmosphere between the two of them improved as the day went on and their hangovers wore off. They didn't mention the events of the night before but talked practically about the task in hand, and the details of their journey – probably the most sensible way to deal with the mini-crisis. They travelled through sunlit mountains and heat-hazy plains, with vast cloudless Spanish skies above, and that helped too.

The winery was just a few minutes'walk from the *estación de autobuses*: part of a small industrial estate, and next to a hypermarket. A long concrete shed formed one side of the complex and silvery tankers were parked alongside it. Through large openings in the walls could be seen the tops of stainless steel vats. But the guard at the gate directed them to an office closer at hand, in a smaller building.

A thin wiry man with greying hair greeted them, went briskly through the paperwork and gave them cash for fuel. 'Listen,' he told them, 'I'm supposed to check your paperwork too: things like licences. Especially after what happened in Madrid last month. But I'm a busy man and sometimes I forget. So make sure you drive carefully, OK, and don't go looking for trouble with the police.' They assured him they would not. He unlocked a drawer in his desk and fished out a bunch of keys. 'Ignition. Cab doors. Fuel tank. (Diesel. Don't go putting fucking petrol in.) And these two are for the outlet valves. Hand the lot over to the guy who takes delivery.

He'll give them back after.' He smiled. 'It's quite lucky for us that you've come our way. One or two deliveries have run into a bit of trouble with the Crav. Heard of them?' They nodded. 'Rural activists, to put it politely. Quite a force in that part of France. They see themselves as successors of the resistance fighters back in World War Two. Hiding out among the hills and so on. On the other hand you could just think of them as bandits.' He stopped, and smiled again.

'How likely are we to be stopped, do you think?' Oliver asked. Orlando's better Spanish enabled him to put a supplementary. 'Are they violent? Are we going to find ourselves at knife-point?'

'Being stopped is a remote possibility. Very remote. But you'll be arriving there in the dark. Hard to spot. If you are stopped they won't give you a hard time – since you're English. That's why you're so useful to us. That's why you're being paid so well. But you're not being paid to do heroics. Understand? If you did get into any bother – you won't, but if it happened – you'd hand over the keys and do as you were told. Or scarper, if doing what you were told did not appeal. OK?'

They both nodded glumly. The man's attempts to be reassuring had had the opposite effect. Oliver thought about the money they had sewn into their clothes. There was no such thing as a real place of safety. For the first time in his life he wondered how you went about opening a numbered account in Switzerland.

The man, who was called Pablo, walked them out of

the office and across the yard, with their library of maps and dockets. The sun beat down fiercely. Pablo gave them a brief demonstration of the controls. 'Driven a tanker before?' They shook their heads. 'She may not look all that big, but liquids weigh heavy. Never forget what a weight you've got behind you. Think ahead or end up dead.'

'Muchas gracias,' said Oliver. A few minutes later they were on the motorway, heading north towards Madrid. There was no air-conditioning and they drove with windows down, with the hot summer smells of the Castilian countryside blowing in at them. They both sat bare-chested and be-shorted in the macho way that their occupation seemed to call for, even if they were both a little paler than the norm for that part of the world.

'I don't like the sound of this *no heroics* stuff,' said Orlando, who was driving the first leg. 'Nor the *scarper if things get heavy*. What if we got split up?'

'Plan A,' said Oliver authoritatively. He'd just spent a few minutes thinking rather hard about this. 'We get back to Nerja under our own steam. No hanging about in Madrid, Valdepeñas or anywhere else.'

'And if something were to – oh I don't know, but anyway – supposing that wasn't an option – for any reason. What…?'

Oliver didn't press him on the *for any reason*. 'We'd push on into France. Plan B. Make for Toulouse, let's say. And in the last resort, Paris. Rendezvous at the

British Council. We are supposed to be English teachers after all. They wouldn't see anything strange in that.' The British Council had been talked of, when they had been on their training course, as a potential source of employment. 'And if – for any reason – we couldn't get there in a hurry, we'd phone in and make contact like that.'

'Blimey,' said Orlando. 'You have thought it all out.'

'Civil Service discipline,' said Oliver.

'Don't suppose you've got the phone number?'

'There are limits even to that.' It seemed they were friends again.

A couple of hours later they were on the Madrid ring-motorway, and an hour or so after swinging eastward out of that they stopped, before it got dark, at a town called Medinaceli – because they liked the name. Orlando thought he remembered that the Rough Guide said it was worth a visit. But the old town was perched on a high outcrop that they didn't feel like hiking up to, and you couldn't go sightseeing round medieval streets in a wine tanker. So they left that for the return journey and settled for parking up in the station yard at the bottom, then checking into a handy *hostal*. They got some supper at a nearby café, then sleep-deprivation kicked in and they staggered up to bed.

As they were undressing, Orlando came out with it. 'I was bang out of order last night. I really was. I'm sorry. And I am happy with you. Totally happy. In case you were wondering.' It was more than Oliver had dared to expect. They made love then, forgetting their tiredness, with the special kind of intensity that is reserved to people who are making up after a row. Wild cat, not for domestication? Come off it, Oliver thought. Orlando was nothing if not a tame boy. He was Oliver's and he needed Oliver more than he needed anything. The crossing into France held no terrors for Oliver as he grasped Orlando in a post-coital squeeze. Everything he could possibly want was here.

*

They made a fuel stop early on, next day. Although the tank had been full when they set out, this lorry was evidently a thirsty one. As Pablo had said, the load was heavier than you thought. Oliver jumped down to do the filling, guiding Orlando as he inched the tanker towards the pump. The filler cap, which Oliver opened with the key, was attached to the lip of the inlet pipe by a sturdy chain to prevent its getting lost or forgotten. But Oliver noticed something else. From an attachment on the inside of the cap a nylon thread like fishing line ran down inside the pipe, presumably disappearing into the tank itself. Oliver had never seen such a thing before, but then he hadn't had much experience of lorries. He tried not to jump to any conclusions. He would try to forget it. He certainly wouldn't mention it to Orly.

Before he had finished, Orlando appeared at his side with a copy of the Daily Mail, which he had bought at the kiosk. 'Guess what. Otis Ferry's got off.' He waved the paper under Oliver's nose. 'Conditional eighteen months'discharge. Has to pay costs, of course. Still, great news.'

'Hmm,' said Oliver. His feelings on the subject were not so straightforward as Orlando's, but he would keep them to himself.

Castile gave place to Aragón, and in the afternoon Aragón made way for Catalunya. Distant mountains showed to the north. They were not going to try any short cuts across the Pyrenees. Mountain by-ways had lost all appeal for Orlando. So they followed the main traffic route past Barcelona and round the eastern end of the mountains where they fell away to the sea. They passed a turn-off to Sitges, a place they had both been to before. Orlando thought it might make a pleasant night-stop on their homeward journey. Oliver was fine with that. If Orlando wanted a night out in the gay bars there, he'd go along. Let him get it out of his system, and with luck it might put the pleasures of the company of Messrs Bradford and Bingley into perspective.

They crossed into France at the Pass of le Perthus. The abandoned customs posts, disused only for a few short years, looked as ancient and useless as anything you might find in a museum: surgical implements of the Middle Ages perhaps, or racks and thumbscrews. The relief they felt at having navigated this far without mishap was tempered by the knowledge that they had entered a country where Spanish wine was not very welcome. But though their lorry carried Spanish number plates, at least it was a plain silver colour, without livery or logo. Oliver, who was driving, took one hand from

the wheel and inserted it comfortingly into the cleft
between Orlando's thighs.

*

They stopped to eat at a Relais-Routier outside
Narbonne. They allowed themselves a couple of glasses
of wine each. With only forty miles left to go they felt
they were as good as there. 'French wine, you notice,'
said Orlando, pouring from the carafe.

Oliver said, 'French wine, you suppose.'

They drove the last leg in the dark, with Orlando at the
wheel and Oliver holding up the map in the dim light.
They found the turn-off from the *autoroute* just before
Carcassonne, but almost immediately had a nasty
surprise. Police cars and fire engines half-blocked the
road where a level crossing was. The place swarmed
with men in uniform. They were waved through by a
gendarme. The police had other things to do than pull a
Spanish truck driver over just now. Beside the railway
line a signal box was ablaze. Firemen played hoses on it,
lit by the flames like demons in the darkness. They
drove on and the scene, mysterious as a Hieronymus
Bosch painting, disappeared behind them into the night.
They crossed the Canal du Midi, then climbed through
small bedtime villages until they reached the town of
Éringues. They parked in the main square as per their
instructions. Two other lorries were parked there, their
cab windows dark and curtained, their drivers
presumably already asleep.

They got out and reconnoitred. The single bar in the square was already shut. Just as well. The less attention they drew to themselves and their cargo the better. The square was not an ornamental one, but the sort of place that hosted a weekly market, and was given over for the rest of the time to the parking of cars and lorries, and the playing of games of *pétanque* in the dust. The road ran straight through the square and on each corner a narrow alley led off it between the low stone houses. They were not tempted to explore further, but got back into their cab and settled down for the night, after locking themselves in. Pushing their seats as far into the reclining position as they would go, and still wearing the clothes they'd travelled in, they prepared themselves for sleep. It wouldn't be very comfortable, but it wouldn't be the first time they'd done it, and they could be sure of a better billet tomorrow – and a shower or bath.

'Here we are with all our worldly goods about us,' said Orlando, 'and all our money in our clothes. Like people from another century. Proper wayfarers we are.' Wayfarers. It was not a word that Oliver would have come up with in a hurry. Yet it was wonderfully apt. It was one of those things about Orlando, a sudden choice of words that got you under the ribcage. Those moments when the beauty of him hurt.

*

Suddenly it was daylight and there was a commotion outside. Voices shouting. Then an odd noise that Oliver had never heard before in real life. But he knew at once what it had to be: a rifle firing round after round. Now there were men at both doors of the cab. Both the doors swung open, levered by fierce crowbars, the locks smashed. *'Les clefs, les clefs.'* Someone was in a hurry for the keys.

'OK.' Orlando's voice. 'Cool it. You can have them.'

'No heroics, Orly,' Oliver called out, but the warning was superfluous: there weren't going to be any. With the keys in their hands the men – four, five of them? – lost all in the two drivers. Shocked and still barely awake, Oliver and Orlando tumbled out of the cab together on the off-side. A small pick-up truck was parked across the front of the lorry, blocking its escape. But the pick-up was empty. All the action was round the back of the tanker. Diesel could be seen draining from the shot-up fuel tank, but their attention was quickly drawn to the fountain gush of red wine that was just then unleashed as their attackers found the keys and opened the valves. Although it was only six o'clock and the sun barely risen, a small crowd was gathering in the square, and in the houses all around windows were clattering open and curtains being twitched. The men wasted not another second. Rushing back past Oliver and Orlando, of whom they still took no notice, they jumped into their pick-up, started the engine and seconds later were racing out of the square. Oliver just had time to notice that the pick-up had no number plates. 'Still feeling sympathetic to the plight of French farmers?' he said, surprised at himself for being able to make anything even approaching a joke.

Orlando didn't have time to answer. A car came racing

into the square from the other end. The passenger window was down and a video camera was pointing out of it. The car stopped abruptly and someone leaped out of a rear door with a microphone like a small dog on a stick. The camera panned rapidly back and forth across the scene before focusing on the jet of ruby liquid still gushing almost horizontally out of the back of the tanker and rapidly turning the square into a shallow red lake. The sun just now began to shine into the square through one of the little alleyways and lit the scene as spectacularly as if it had all been arranged on purpose. 'Shit,' said Orlando, 'we're going to be on French TV.'

'Until now the only country where we're not wanted by the police,' Oliver began to say.

'Jesus Christ, no,' Orlando shouted, bending down beside the ruptured fuel tank. It had almost emptied now, but Orly's attention had been caught by something else. Two of the bullet holes were neat and round, but in their excitement the gunmen had fired off far more rounds than were strictly necessary to do the job, and several bullet holes had combined to form a long gash in the side of the tank. And caught in the rip was something that appeared to be made of silver paper, pushed against the jagged edge by the outpouring diesel and itself slightly torn. Visible in the tear was something white.

'Drugs in the fucking fuel tank,' Orly said hoarsely.

'We knew, we knew,' Oliver's voice was almost a whisper. 'It's what we always knew. We've got to get out.' He put his hand on Orly's arm. One of them was shaking. Perhaps they both were.

'We'll have to split,' Orlando said. 'Your plan B. No
going back to Spain.' They were back at the cab, fishing
out their two backpacks, trying to be quick and efficient,
but not showing signs of panic to the camera twenty
yards away. Was it on them at that moment? They dared
not look.

'Your cap,' Oliver said. Orly swiped it off the top of
the dash. 'You leave the square that way.' He pointed
towards one of the two alleys. 'I'll go the other.'

'The TV crew…'

'I'll handle them. Walk, don't run. Carcassonne. Train
to Toulouse. Meet there this evening. Station.'

'And if not…?'

'Like we said. Paris.   British Council. Find it
somehow. Find you.'

'Love you,' Orlando said.

'And you. Set on.' Oliver slapped Orlando on the back
and turned away from him. He found himself walking
calmly towards the television crew. Like those birds that
bravely run towards an intruding dog or sheep to distract
attention from their offspring to give them time to
escape. The man with the mike turned to him at once.
'Talk to you in a second,' Oliver said to him in English,
addressing the TV audiences of the world. Then, 'Got to
have a fag.' He sauntered away slowly as if he were

going to do just that, longing to look back to see if the camera was following him, to see if Orly had got safely away, but knowing everything would be over if he did. He reckoned it would be half a minute at most before someone discovered the cocaine. Amazingly no feet pursued him. Behind him he heard an eye witness begin to give his story to the camera, staking his claim to his five minutes of fame. *'J'étais juste là...'*

It was only seconds before Oliver reached the corner of the square where the other alleyway led off. He would be out of sight once he had turned the corner into it. He prayed that it would actually lead somewhere, and wasn't just a dead end. He turned into the alley. He could hardly believe his luck. It led between houses, gardens and sheds, opening at the bottom onto another little road. Beyond that, a sunlit green sea of vines. His saunter gave way to the fastest sprint he could remember running. A minute later he was across the lane and plunging in among the vines. He ran on, more slowly now, stooping to avoid being seen, and stumbling from time to time on clods of soil or stones. Before another minute had passed he heard the distant wail of police sirens behind him, approaching the no longer sleepy little town of Éringues.

SEVENTEEN

The vines were just coming into leaf. Their topmost tendrils waved level with Oliver's chin. Half crouching, and with head and shoulders bent, he was able to progress at a slow jogging pace, occasionally pausing to peer above the surrounding vine tops to check for pursuers, like a hare in a hayfield. After a time it became clear that the vineyard was a very extensive one and that his path, which was dictated by the lines of planting and the rows'supporting wires, was taking him more and more steeply downhill, towards the south. Arriving last night they had crossed the railway line – where the signal box had been on fire – and then two big waterways, all within a minute of leaving the motorway. Presumably all these lines of communication ran in parallel along the floor of the valley below.

Oliver's jog-trot slowed to a crouching walk: a gait he maintained, with increasing discomfort, for a further twenty minutes. By this time the hum of the motorway was audible – though the traffic was still invisible, hidden by a line of plane trees in the valley bottom. No other heads appeared above the surface of the waving green sea around him; the nearest farmsteads were over a mile away. He grew bolder, and walked upright at a leisurely pace. But that leisurely pace belied the feverish activity of his brain, which was running at full speed as he tried to work out what to do next.

The first decision was forced on him quickly, as he

reached the line of plane trees and saw the ground unexpectedly fall away at his feet, to reveal the Canal du Midi lying below in a shallow cutting, fringed with bright yellow iris flowers. The rows of vines continued in exactly the same alignment on the far side of it, as if they chose to ignore the rude cut that the canal made across their orderly progress. No bridge was in sight in either direction, though the distance you could see was not that great: Oliver had arrived at the canal on the inside of a bend. He left the safety of the vines behind him and scrambled down through bushes and thyme-scented grass onto the towing path below.

Oliver didn't even consider the idea of swimming across. Shoes and shorts and backpack ruled that out. Even if he got safely across, everything would be sopping wet, including the wads of banknotes in his pockets. His choice lay simply between right – west – or left. As the town of Carcassonne lay just a few miles to the west, with Toulouse, his that day's destination, some sixty miles beyond, he turned right, along the towpath, without hesitation.

Voices carry well across water, especially when their owners have loud ones, and so it was a snatch of conversation a few minutes later, rather than the put-put of the engine, that alerted him to the approach of a boat rounding the bend behind him. The conversation was in English. To Oliver, in his situation, it seemed surreal. A woman was saying, in a cut-glass Home-counties accent, 'I have heard it said that the cassoulet is superior in Carcassonne.'

'As I remember, it is,' replied a second diamantine female voice.

'Then we must make a point of sampling it while we're there. A *dégustation*.'

A third woman's voice chimed in. A little lower, plummier. 'But not at lunchtime, don't you think? A little heavy for midday.'

Oliver turned round. The boat was now well in sight, about a hundred yards behind him and steadily gaining ground. It was a large and heavy affair. Oliver decided it was an old barge that had been converted, and in the process reduced to half its original length. It was still pretty big: some ten metres long and with about twice the beam of a British narrow-boat. Three silver heads could be seen across the top of it, clustered near the wheel at the stern. To arrive in Carcassonne by boat, at midday, under the protection of a party of genteel English ladies struck Oliver as about the most desirable thing that could possibly happen next. Summoning his voice to the most refined enunciation it was capable of without descending into parody, he called out, 'If you're going to Carcassonne, you couldn't possibly take me with you, could you?'

The on-board conversation ceased. The three silver heads bobbed towards each other and then turned in his direction. Two of the women were sitting down on the roof or top deck of the boat, the third head was a little lower and behind: it belonged to the helmswoman, who was presumably standing on a lower level in the stern.

The woman nearest to Oliver called back simply, 'Who are you?' Her hair was swept back at the sides of her head. Her face was narrow, lined, adorned with silver-framed glasses. She looked like someone who stood no nonsense.

Oliver didn't need to raise his voice: the placid water acted as a perfect soundboard. He said, 'Oliver Watson, formerly of the Home Office, currently looking for work as a teacher of English.' He waited to see how this would go down.

'We'll take you if you can jump,' said the woman at the wheel. She was softer and rounder of face than the first one who had spoken. 'It's a bit weedy by the bank. Don't want to foul the propeller.'

'Let him on by the bows,' the first woman said. And so it was done. Two seconds later the front of the boat was nosing in among the irises, while the stern was kept safely out in midstream. Then, at the precise moment that the boat made contact with the bank, Oliver jumped aboard.

Try not to look too grateful, too relieved, he told himself as he clambered up the half dozen steps from the well-deck onto the roof and made his way towards his rescuers. They must continue to think they were simply giving a lift to a gentleman, not aiding and abetting an internationally wanted criminal in his getaway from the forces of the law. Calmly the third of the women, the one who hadn't yet spoken to him, offered him coffee and a croissant, which he accepted, and then she slid off her perch and disappeared below to go and get them. The other woman on the deck motioned to Oliver to sit there too, which he did, after checking he wasn't blocking the view of the helmswoman, whose head was just a foot or two from his bare knees. They introduced themselves. The three women were all academics, with positions – Oliver guessed senior ones – at different universities in England. Their respective disciplines were geology, economics and French. They had been taking summer holidays together for nearly thirty years, although not every year, and not always all three of them together. Two had husbands whom – as Dave and Jimmy with their girlfriends – they had left at home.

Oliver resigned himself to telling his tale. He tried to keep as close to the truth as he reasonably could. He had little experience of lying. Adult life had been reasonably kind to him until recently and so he had had little need to. He was afraid he might be rather bad at it, and resolved that his first steps should be modest ones, reckoning that it was surely safer to tell a little lie well than a big one badly. He said that he had recently qualified in TEFL, because he had earlier lost his job in the Home Office shake-up, and that he was spending his summer combining a ramble around Europe with a search for work opportunities in the autumn. They asked if he had had any offers yet. No, he said, not so far.

'If I may say so,' said the woman nearest him, the one with the scraped-back hair, and whose name was Eleanor, 'your present costume might count against you when it comes to interviews – even in EFL.'

Oliver had on light beige shorts, trainers without socks and a blue T-shirt. He'd worn them overnight and for the whole of the previous day. 'I do keep a smarter set of clothes in my backpack,' he answered, managing a half smile.

They were passing the burnt-out signal box by the time the third woman, Susan, returned with his coffee and croissant. It was pointed out to him. 'The work of the Crav,' Eleanor said. 'We read about it in the paper. Back towards Narbonne they brought the whole line to a stop.'

Oliver feigned surprise, saying nothing about having seen the blaze and the busy firemen at the spot less than twelve hours ago. He had reason enough for concern, though. He was depending on the railway to get him to Toulouse this evening. Even if the three women were going that far it would take them a couple of days. Anxiously he scanned the railway line. No trains had come past in the ten minutes since he'd come aboard the barge.

Oliver scanned everything anxiously, though he tried not to let it show. The towing path, for Orlando; the nearby vineyards and fields for signs of police. Once or twice a lone figure or a couple came in sight, and then Oliver experienced a frisson of fear, which only subsided when the figures had fallen unthreateningly astern. Then his heart did start to pound when he saw a dark blue gendarme car parked across a bridge directly ahead of them, its two occupants standing nearby and looking casually around. Oliver opened his backpack and half buried his head in it, muttering something about a handkerchief. When he re-surfaced, the bridge was behind them: they had passed unchallenged beneath it.

With a sense of guilt, and a feeling that this was profoundly perverse, Oliver began to enjoy the morning in this unexpected but strangely pleasant company, watching nature sliding past at a relaxing three or four miles an hour. Nobody except his three ladies had been on the water as early as seven o'clock, the time he had met them, but as the hours passed more pleasure boats were untied and joining them on the waterway. A couple of trains puttered past, a hundred yards away, and Oliver was relieved to see them. Oliver took a turn at the wheel, at first over-steering madly, to the merriment of his companions, but then settling to a steadier course down the centre of the canal, pulling a little way over to the right once or twice when another boat came past from the other direction. Moorhens crossed jerkily in front of them and twice water voles chugged across, low in the water but holding their noses clear, their silver-line wakes stretching back all the way from one bank to the other.

Eventually the town of Carcassonne appeared from behind the hillside, intermittently visible through the line of plane trees that still bordered the canal. But it took longer actually to get there, as the canal's course took them on a horseshoe-shaped detour to the north. With its hilltop profile of battlements and cone-topped turrets the city evoked the Middle Ages, part in shadow, part gilded by the morning sun. 'We ought to see guards patrolling the battlements,' Oliver suggested to Eleanor as they drew closer. And then, almost unbelievably, that was exactly what they did see. 'Some mock-medieval pageant, no doubt,' was the unfazed response of the professor of French. It was better, Oliver thought, than a modern gendarme.

They wound their way into the city beneath the wall of the old town, and moored conveniently near the station, which was just across a bridge. Oliver's escorts invited him to lunch with them, but he declined. They parted company on the towing path, and as he shook their hands Oliver thanked them for picking him up. Their three intelligent but smiling faces, their smart grey hair, and their practical outfits of shirts and three-quarter-length trousers remained etched in his memory like a photograph as he turned to leave them in that peaceful sunlit place. Just how grateful he was to them they would not know until they saw that evening's TV news.

Across the bridge and into the cool interior of the station. Oliver looked carefully around for policemen, and then at the departures board. A local train bound for Castelnaudary and Toulouse would be leaving in half an hour. He was in no mood for hanging about and being a tourist in Carcassonne. He bought a ticket to Toulouse – a return, so that his intentions would not appear too transparent to anyone who might come checking – and then waited on the platform, in some agitation, for the train to arrive.

When it finally pulled in, and then out again with Oliver but not too many other people on board, he did feel marginally safer, though every time it slowed down for some wayside halt among the vines – Pexiora, le Ségala – fear would grip him until he'd scanned the platform, assured himself that no uniformed persons were standing about on it, and the train was securely on the move again. Only now did he have time to think consciously about what had happened to Orlando. He had scanned station platforms for him before now – Ham Street, Ashford – and today had more than half hoped they might find each other catching the same train at Carcassonne. Still, they'd agreed Toulouse, and this evening; no particular form of transport had been mentioned, and Oliver had hardly anticipated doing a part of the journey by barge. Either Orlando would be with him in Toulouse this evening or he'd be in police custody – which would certainly be on the local TV news – and Oliver would have to decide what to do then. Either way it promised to be a long afternoon's wait.

Toulouse station was reassuringly big, crowded and anonymous. Oliver's first action was to dive into a small tourist shop that opened off the booking hall and, just as he had done for Orlando a month ago, buy a baseball cap, and jam it hard down on his head. It was a white one: there was no other choice.

Toulouse: city of sunshine and glowing red brick, of *bon-bons à la violette*, and rib-sticking cassoulets. Oliver was in no mood to enjoy it. He sat the afternoon out on park benches and outside cafés, in the shade rather than the sunshine, keener to see who was around him than to be seen himself. He was surprised to see four members of the French Foreign Legion strolling through a square, but he told himself there was no way they would be looking for him. More worrying were the policemen he saw at a distance from time to time, in twos and threes. But of course they would be there in the normal course of events. Provided he kept his distance from them all would be well. He managed to keep away from the station itself until four o'clock, but then it drew him like a magnet, and he made a thorough exploration of all parts of it – even the underground arcades and subways full of luggage lockers. After that he retreated to a bar opposite the main entrance: it was on the other side of a bridge over the Canal du Midi, but it still commanded a clear view of the people going in and out, from a safe enough distance.

Three hours in a bar could pass in a flash in the right company. But if you were waiting for that company to arrive, chain-drinking small slow beers, it was the most excruciating tedium. There was a television on inside the bar, and Oliver kept half an eye quietly on its Saturday afternoon football games, patiently awaiting also the early evening news – if that should come on before Orly arrived. It did. And if Oliver had wanted publicity for himself he could not have been more pleased. Although the first item was about the referendum on the EU constitution that the French people were going to the polls to decide the following day, the second item was that morning's excitement in Éringues. The footage of a tanker-full of wine splashing as if from a fire hose into the square of a provincial town, lit a glorious jewel red by the dawn sun, was a gift to the medium. And then there was he, almost at once, his hair sleep-dishevelled, saying in English that he wanted a cigarette – there was a subtitle in French in case anyone didn't get the gist – and would be back in a minute. There were no shots of Orlando, with or without Oliver. Film of them retrieving their backpacks from the lorry, and of Orlando putting on his baseball cap as they hastily parted would have been a gift to the authorities, but it seemed that the camera had missed that little scene, captivated by the drama at the rear of the vehicle.

Oliver tried to be invisible, skulking low in his seat behind the window-corner table, his cap pulled down almost over his eyes but not quite. If he kept one eye glued to the television screen, then the other one was glancing constantly out through the window at the station entrance. Meanwhile his virtual self appeared again and again on the screen, while his words and appearance were picked over ad nauseam by the other occupants of the café. The report stressed the dual nature of the event: the attack by the Crav on a consignment of Spanish wine, and the subsequent discovery of a haul of cocaine with an estimated street value of a quarter of a million euros concealed in the fuel tank. It was thought there was no connection between the two things. Though none of the perpetrators of the wine sabotage had been apprehended, it was obvious they would not have shot bullets into the fuel tank if they had known what was hidden there. The Spanish police were giving their full co-operation and the keeper of the lorry, the manager of a winery in Valdpeñas, was helping them with their enquiries. The identity, even the nationality, of the man – believed to be one of the two drivers – who wanted a cigarette remained a mystery. Of the other driver nothing had been seen at all. There wasn't even a description. There was some speculation that one or both of them were members of the Crav.

From time to time Oliver peered cautiously out from under the peak of his cap to see if anyone in the bar was making any connection between the missing man on the television and the stranger, solitary at his corner table. Nobody did. Not even when – daringly – he summoned the waiter to his table for a fresh glass of beer. But, as the evening bulletins followed one another, the clip in which he featured was repeated so many times that he felt like a stage actor taking endless, unwelcome curtain calls.

There was still no sign of Orlando. Oliver would have to move from where he was before it got too dark to see the people coming and going at the station. Then there would be a decision to be made: to take a train to Paris overnight, or to sit this awful evening out till the bitter end and, if Orlando still hadn't materialised, go on to the capital in the morning. Outside, the brick-built city was turning flame and pink as the sun sank lower in the sky. Oliver made his decision just as dusk fell. Next door to the café was a small hotel. He went in and enquired in tentative French about a room for the night. Yes, they could let him have one. He paid cash in advance, saying he had an early start in the morning. *'Anglais?'* they asked him.

'Nein. Deutsch,' he said with an uncomfortable laugh. He went quickly back to the station and did another

thorough tour of the platforms, subways, restaurants and waiting rooms. Then he sat in the station bar, over another long slow beer, until numbers had thinned so much as to make him conspicuous. He went outside and hung about, standing or pacing up and down, for an hour or so in a patch of shadow where a streetlamp was missing. At last, some time after midnight, cold, stiff and miserable, he gave up and walked back across the canal to his hotel. What could have happened to Orlando? The police hadn't caught him, if the news reports were to be believed. He'd had plenty of time to get here by bus or train, even if he'd had to walk the first ten miles. To say that he had money in his pockets was not so much an understatement as a joke: he had more cash on him than he'd carried before in the whole of his life.

Alone in his single bed – a novel situation after the last companionable months – Oliver found his distress only increased. Was Orlando similarly tucked up safe in bed somewhere? Or sleeping rough? Or what? Oliver barely dozed through the short summer night. At seven he got up and handed back his key to the night porter. *'Auf viedersehen,'* he said, and then marched out, his baseball cap once more pulled down firmly at the front.

There were several policemen at the station when he arrived there, but they didn't seem to be in search mode – at least that's what he hoped – as he bought his ticket (single this time) to Paris and boarded the next express. Before the train came in he'd had a last look around the station for Orly. Though not very hopefully.

His train took him across the river Lot at medieval

Cahors with its fairytale bridge of towers and pinnacles, then the Dordogne at Martell, and then wound its way beneath picturesque hilltop villages and along wooded riversides. It was a journey he would have liked to share with Orlando. And he found room among his anxieties for the thought (a new discovery this) that he would have no heart to enjoy anything by himself any more: that without Orlando by his side nothing would ever come to mean very much.

He arrived at the Gare d'Austerlitz in the early afternoon. *Le Tout Paris* was engaged in the business of voting for or against the European Constitution, and the streets were more than usually full. There was no point attempting to rendezvous with Orlando today. He remembered somehow that the British Council was situated in the Rue Constantine, and he decided to find it. He found a street plan and saw that the Rue Constantine was near the Invalides, some six underground stops away. In normal circumstances he would have liked nothing better than to walk there along the banks of the Seine but the urgency of his search went against that, and so he went underground and bought his ticket for the RER.

The British Council was housed in a handsome stone building, opposite the wide open space that led to the gilded dome of the Invalides. There was no Orly kicking stones in the street outside, but he had hardly expected that. At least he knew now where to come tomorrow morning.

Oliver walked on a little, and soon found himself on

the left bank of the Seine, with the chestnut trees of the Tuilleries opposite and the Île de la Cité and Notre Dame parting the waters a little way to the east. He had once stayed in a cheap and characterful hotel on the Île de la Cité when a backpacking student, and he decided to make his way there now to see if he could get a bed for a couple of nights. It would be like paying a visit to an old friend, with all the consolations that implied. But as for real friends, he knew no-one in Paris.

The hotel was one of a row of sixteenth-century brick houses in the Place Dauphine: a flask-shaped square with plane trees dotted around its open centre and with an exit towards the river at the narrow end, by the Pont Neuf and the statue of Henri IV. The staircase still wound up like honeysuckle inside the entrance hall, where backpackers still milled around. A small room was available, at a remarkably cheap rate for the area – hence the milling backpackers – and Oliver took it. There might be fleas, but no matter: he had somewhere to sleep. Once he'd shut the door, he tested the bed by lying on it full length.

*

He woke in discomfort and in the dark, wondering where he was, how he had got wherever this was, and why he was fully clothed, even to the extent of trainers, tightly laced and painfully constricting the blood flow to his feet. Groping around, he found a light switch and could look at his watch. It was four thirty a.m. He had slept for twelve hours.

He got up, emptied his bladder and drank two glasses of water. He changed his shirt and reinstated the baseball cap which had fallen off his head at some point during the night. He was ravenously hungry. He went downstairs and let himself out, prudently leaving behind the backpack which he had been seen carrying on the TV news. If the Place Dauphine was beautiful in the daytime, it was magical by night: silent and empty, save for ghosts. Streetlamps filtered through the leafy branches of the plane trees; the shuttered houses slept, cosy and secure.

Oliver made his way across the Pont St-Michel, where the floodlit domes and towers of Paris glittered in reflection in the black water below. In the Place St-Michel one or two people were about – on what business Oliver did not speculate – lurking along in front of the barred cafés and shops. He smelled bread cooking and followed his nose to a *boulangerie*. It wasn't open but a light was on. Oliver banged on the glass door. To his surprise, a figure appeared from the back of the shop: a young man in T-shirt and shorts. Presumably the night shift in a bakery was hot work. The man stopped when he saw Oliver. Oliver reached into a pocket and held up a one-euro coin. He smiled encouragingly. The young man came forward and opened the door.

'Croissant?' Oliver said diffidently. *'J'ai grand faim.'* He thought that was probably what you said. He held out his coin. The other grinned, took the money and came back with two steaming golden crescents. 'The till is locked. I can't give you change. Come back for it later.'

'It doesn't matter. Thank you. *Tu es très gentil.*'
Oliver heard the door lock behind him as he turned away
to wolf down his first solid food in two days.

It began to grow light. For an hour or so Oliver
wandered by the Seine, his wanderings punctuated by
periods of sitting by the riverside, preoccupied with
guesses about what would happen in the course of this
new day. By six o'clock it was broad daylight: blue sky,
and the sun beginning to pry its way between the
buildings of the Île de St-Louis, and more people were
about in the streets. These had the look of being on
legitimate business. They were people on early shifts
walking to work, or on their way to open cafés and
market stalls. There was a small army of bakers'delivery
boys, like the one who had sold Oliver his croissants, all
in shorts and with very white thighs and calves. At last
Oliver found a café opening up: someone was cranking
open the security grille, then setting tables out on the
pavement. Oliver went in.

He was pleased – though in normal times he wouldn't
have been – to find that the café had a television high on
the wall, and the television was on. He'd seen no news
the previous day and was desperate to know the latest
developments in his own story, if there were any. He
ordered a coffee, then sat glued to the screen.

The early morning news was taken up almost entirely
with the results of yesterday's referendum. The people of
France had said no to the proposed European
constitution. The results were analysed and commented
on at great length, with pundits and politicians of every

stripe being wheeled on to have their say. Other items were relegated to very small time-slots indeed. But just as Oliver was beginning to think that the events in Éringues had slipped out of the news altogether, there was the footage of the tanker, spraying its liquid cargo out across the cobbles of the village square, and himself saying, yet one more time, that he needed to go and get a cigarette. But there were no developments. No activists from the Crav had been picked up, and there was no news about the identities or whereabouts of the two drivers. The manager of the winery in Valdepeñas still denied any involvement in drug trafficking, but had admitted having employed illegal immigrants as drivers on occasions in the past. The drivers on this occasion were not illegal immigrants, apparently, but European Union citizens. They had been sent to him by an Englishman he'd met in a bar. He didn't remember the names of any of them. Which was a plus, Oliver thought, even though he remembered that they had introduced themselves to him as Andy and Pete. That was the end of the item. Oliver wondered at what time the British Council opened its doors. From beneath the peak of his cap he ordered another croissant.

At eight he made his way to the Rue Constantine. The British Council was not just open but bustling. Students milled in the entrance hall, staff at the reception desk were giving directions, answering Monday morning queries. It reminded him of the training centre in Piccadilly, except that most people were speaking French. Oliver hung back until the crowd had thinned and the reception desk was relatively quiet. Then he approached the person who looked the friendliest, a young woman with jet black hair in a bob and a pleasant, intelligent looking face. *'Parlez-vous anglais?'* he asked.

'Yes of course,' the woman responded. 'What can I do for you?'

'I arranged to meet someone here today,' Oliver said. 'Only we forgot to arrange a particular time. Will you be here all day? At the desk I mean.'

'Till twelve o'clock only,' the woman said.

'Then I will come back again at twelve,' Oliver said. 'The person I arranged to meet is called Orlando Kidd. It's vital that we don't miss each other.'

'And you arranged to meet him here?' The woman's face wore a doubtful frown.

'We're both English teachers,' Oliver explained. 'We're travelling Europe looking for work.'

The other's features rearranged themselves into a smile. Clearly Oliver's explanation was satisfactory. 'So if he comes in you'd like me to tell him you'll be back at twelve? Or…'

'No. I mean yes. Tell him I'll be back at twelve. That'll be best.' Oliver thought he'd never before been so grateful to anyone for catching on so quickly. It brought a tightening to his throat. Then he remembered he'd had the same feeling when the baker's boy had opened the door to him and let him have a croissant. He remembered the kind women who'd stopped their barge and taken him aboard…

'Are you all right?' The woman was looking at him with puzzlement – or concern.

'Yes, sure. I'm fine.'

'Are you … quite sure?'

'Yes.'

'Because…'

'No, it's OK.' Oliver brushed at his face with the back of his hand. 'I'll come back at twelve. I'd be so grateful if… My name's Oliver Watson.' Oliver began to turn towards the door but then, remembering that he was in France, turned back and held out his hand to the young woman. She took it and said,

'I'm Nicole. I'll give your message, Oliver, I promise. I can see that it's important. See you at twelve.'

'*Á plus tard,*' Oliver said, the long unused French expression coming to him unbidden, like an unexpected gift.

Oliver returned to his hotel. There were some sunglasses in his backpack, which he had not been wearing during his impromptu television appearance. He put them on and went out again. He found a Prisunic in a street just off Place St-Michel and bought underwear and socks, a cheap pair of chinos and a couple of short-sleeved shirts. By the time he had taken this load back to his hotel room and changed into it, it was getting on for twelve. He set off again along the quays of the Seine towards the British Council.

Nicole was still at the desk. Her expression was friendly, but it was not the look of someone who has good news to impart. 'I'm sorry, Oliver, but your friend hasn't been in. And he hasn't telephoned either. I told the switchboard to expect a call from a Mr Kidd and to pass the call to me if it came. But it did not.'

'Thank you,' Oliver said. From the bottom of his heart. He had forgotten to plan for a phone call.

'But I have something to tell you.' Nicole leaned towards him and spoke more softly. 'Please don't be frightened. I have told nobody and I will tell nobody. But, you see, I know who you are.'

Oliver just gaped at her.

'I have seen you on television. So has everyone in France. Probably everyone in Europe. Luckily for you, people in Paris are not very observant. They walk in the streets and travel in the Metro, but they live all the time inside their own heads.'

'It's the same in London,' said Oliver.

'So I don't think you have to worry too much, now you are more – how do you say? – déguisé.'

'Disguised. Thank you … for trusting me. I mean, for not turning me in.'

'Turning you in. That's a new phrasal verb for me. I must remember. But seriously, if you are in trouble, I mean, if you would like to talk, I finish in two minutes. We could go for a coffee. But only if you would like. I have already instructed the afternoon staff to look out for your friend.' Her eyes were light brown, and joined in her smile.

'A coffee would be nice,' said Oliver. He smiled too, for only the second time that day. 'I mean, that would be just great.'

They had their *cafés crèmes* outside a gleaming brasserie, all glass and brass, beside the Seine, with Notre Dame pinnacling over the willows and chestnut trees across the water. Oliver told Nicole his story. Though not all of it, of course.

'But you had no idea what was in the fuel tank?' Nicole asked.

'No,' Oliver said. 'And yet, we only had to think of the sum of money we were being paid, and so, of course, yes. If you can understand that.'

'Yes, I understand. In my family my brother is gay. My parents don't know that – and yet they do know, at the same time. You are gay too, I think.'

'Yes,' said Oliver, and felt himself blushing slightly. Perhaps it was on account of the youth and attractiveness – and the simple niceness – of his companion.

'And Orlando?' she queried gently.

'Yes.'

'Well, that is good, at least. It would be … I mean, if he wasn't… I'm sorry, I don't know the right adjective.'

'Nor do I,' said Oliver. 'But you're right, of course. It would be.'

Nicole had trained as an English teacher but had never practised as one. What she really did was paint. It was because of her artist's discipline of constant observation that she had recognised Oliver from the television when he came to the reception desk, baseball cap or not. She lived with her boyfriend in the Quartier Latin. He worked in an art gallery in the Rue de Seine. It was as well that one of them had a proper job.

They talked for nearly an hour. When Nicole got up to go, it was with an invitation to dinner for the following evening. Orlando was to come too, if he had materialised by then.

EIGHTEEN

Oliver returned to the British Council twice more that day. There had been no sight or sound of Orlando. The next day he called four more times: twice by phone, twice on foot. Oliver thought that without this evening to think about, the walls of his mind would give way before a tidal wave of despair. But thanks to his contact with Nicole, and the strength that gave him, he managed to resist the swirling, raging, battering thought that Orlando wasn't going to come. Resolutely he told himself: tomorrow he will come; tomorrow there will be news.

Nicole's flat was in the Rue Racine, no more than twenty minutes'walk from Oliver's hotel. It was housed in the kind of nineteenth century building the Parisians call an *immeuble*, and whose floors are put to different uses. An antique shop was on the ground floor, a firm of solicitors – *huissiers de justice* – above, then came the cosy home that Nicole shared with her partner Jean-Marc. Stairs went on up after that to three more floors, but Oliver had no need to follow them.

It was bizarre, given his predicament, to find himself guest of honour at a dinner party. But, in the eyes of his hosts and the other guests, he was a celebrity: the mysterious man from the news reports who had appeared in their midst, coming clandestinely to the Rue Racine; and they the chosen few, the only people in Paris who knew who he was. Nicole had told Jean-Marc and their other guests about Oliver, with his permission, and swearing them to secrecy, so that for the first time in days he was able to sit down to a meal without either sunglasses or a baseball cap on his head.

Jean-Marc was a very handsome young man, about six feet tall, whose eyes somehow lit up the room every time he smiled. The other two guests were Nicole's brother André, and his boyfriend Jérome. At nineteen and twenty respectively they struck Oliver almost indecently young to be a couple. Nicole's brother was tall and very slim, yet he managed, in a way that is lost to men past the age of about twenty, to look quite muscular at the same time. (Oliver would have claimed Orlando, at twenty-four, as the exception.) He had a longish face, from which earnest, smouldering eyes peered out from under a thatch of black hair. When he spoke he was serious and polite. Jérome was shorter and of a thicker build – a bit like Oliver himself in fact – with fair hair, blue eyes and a ready smile. Oliver found himself immediately at ease with him. He felt that if Jérome ever had problems getting on with somebody it would be the other person's fault, not his. Jérome worked for Jean-Marc in the gallery in Rue de Seine.

André and Jérome lived a few streets away, they told Oliver, in a small flat high up under one of Paris's mansard roofs. If you craned out of the window, they said, you could just about see the top of the Eiffel Tower. Oliver would have to come and visit them there.

The meal was eaten around a plain wooden table in the kitchen, Nicole and Jean-Marc leaping up from time to time to rescue things from immolation on the nearby stove. They had a warm salad with gésiers and croutons nestling among feathery endive leaves, followed by a chicken, simply roasted in butter and lemon, then another salad and varieties of cheese. To finish there was a clafoutis that Nicole had made herself and that even Oliver managed to find room for.

Nicole said it was a pity Oliver couldn't fill in his time by doing a bit of English teaching at the British Council, since he was technically qualified. But even if work was available it wouldn't be possible for someone in Oliver's position to do it. The British Council would need a tax code and bank account details: any work Oliver did now would have to be paid in cash, and with few questions asked.

Oliver said nothing about the money sewn into the linings of his clothes. But even that would not last for ever, and he knew he would soon have to start supplementing it.

'We have a busy few days at the gallery,' Jean-Marc said at this point. 'Hanging a new exhibition for a *vernissage* on Friday night. We maybe could use an extra pair of hands – casual rates of pay, all cash. Would that be – uh – at all interesting?' He smiled a little anxiously, thinking perhaps Oliver might feel the offer inappropriate, the task demeaning.

But Oliver said yes, he'd very much like to do that. Taking courage, Jean-Marc asked him if he'd like to stay on for the *vernissage*, the private view, helping to serve drinks and hand round canapés. To this Oliver had to say no. He'd surely be recognised, unless Jean-Marc was happy with the idea of a waiter handing round the bubbly in sunglasses and baseball cap. They all laughed, and Jean-Marc said, yes of course: Oliver's contribution would remain limited to the picture-hanging and other necessary jobs on Thursday and Friday, which were not too much in the customers'eyes. They shook hands on it, Jean-Marc adding, 'Something to tide you over for a bit – until Orlando arrives.'

*

…As if a merchant were looking for rare pearls, and now he has found one pearl of great price, and has sold all that he had and bought it. He cherished it and it grew in his heart, until it grew as great as all the world. One day he went to the place where he kept it, out of all sight save his own, and found it gone.

Oliver awoke crying, wracked with convulsive sobs, his face a wash of tears. The words that had come to him in his waking half-dream – the first verse from Saint Matthew, the second and third from his own unconscious – told him, this morning, what he had been refusing even to consider for the past four days. The truth of his situation. That he had lost Orlando.

For four days Oliver had dealt with Orlando's absence as a problem that needed to be worked on and solved. Overnight, everything seemed changed. Oliver hadn't dragged Orlando's face and form before his imagination's eye, nor his voice into his inward ear since they had split up on Saturday. But today he was everywhere with him. While still in bed, the scent of Orlando's sun-warmed skin found its way into his nostrils; he felt the warm pressure of his body against his own: chest against chest, leg against leg, those vanished curls tousled in his face. And when he got up and went out into the Paris day it was the same. The sound of him would hammer in his head: a noisy ghost. His voice, uttering a sudden phrase or half-heard sentence, would startle him so that he would turn round in the street and expect to find him by his side; his disappointment every time came with a hard metallic edge and taste, like a spoon accidentally bitten on while eating. Then he would hear, clearly – and unmistakeably Orlando, this – the little grunting, quacking, farmyard sounds he made when he was being fondled or fucked. And, rounding a street corner, time and again, there he would be, sometimes in summer clothes, sometimes incongruously in his long winter coat, but always bare-headed (no baseball cap for him now) and with his full head of sunset hair. Seeing Oliver his face would burst into a smile. Oliver would each time startle, and open his mouth to call out, astonished, but no cry emerged, and the vision would vanish as quickly as it came.

Memories of Orlando swarmed around him like bees around a hive. Orlando's weak jokes, precious to Oliver as winter sun-gleams. Orlando at the Nerja apartment,' forgetting'to get dressed after his post-work shower, and cooking dinner provocatively in the buff. His pair of tom-cat balls and springing cock. Orlando doing Mercutio's Queen Mab speech magically, high on a hillside against the backdrop of the Mediterranean and

distant Africa, sunset-splashed. Orlando who, unlike
Oliver, would eat cold lamb for pleasure, even the hard
fat. He said he could probably eat tallow candles too,
were he offered them: as a child he had actually eaten a
beeswax one in the local church where his mother had
used to do the flowers. Orlando, young and needy,
vulnerable and sometimes inept, and needing all the care
and protection that Oliver – and only Oliver – could
give.

For some reason Italian adjectives, like opera titles,
went racing through his mind in pursuit of Orly's
fugitive essence. *Orlando furioso* – during their rare,
upsetting, rows. *Orlando giocoso*, high on vino tinto and
three last – *las penultimas* –beers. *Orlando amoroso*
(most of the time, thank heaven). *Orlando dolente*,
failing to get job after job in Seville. *Orlando lacrimoso*,
lost on a mountainside after writing off a lorry and
nearly killing the pair of them, and needing all the
comfort Oliver had power to give. *Orlando il Magnifico.*
Sempre. Perhaps the English adjectives just weren't
strong enough.

Oliver had failed him. Nobody in the whole of Oliver's
life had loved him as Orlando did. And in return, nobody
had been to Orlando what Oliver was: lover, protector,
stalwart, friend and guide. Till Oliver had let him down
– let him go, just like that. 'You go that way, I'll go
this.' Whose stupid idea was it to separate in Éringues?
They could have stayed together: run through the
vineyards, travelled by barge and train; they'd be
together now in Paris – or Madrid – or Mexico; it didn't

matter where. It only mattered with whom.

Where was Orlando now? He couldn't be in police custody: that would have been on the news. Yet he had plenty of money on him, so he should have made it to Paris by this time. Unless he'd been robbed of his money. Beaten up. Left to die. Deliberately killed. Oliver's breath caught in his throat. When Orly had needed him most, fighting for his life and terrified, he hadn't been there. And if now dead, then his body – where?

Or he had been kidnapped by the Crav. Demands for ransom would be forthcoming. But to whom would they be made? Maybe he had joined the Crav of his own accord. He had told Oliver that he had some sympathy with their point of view. He had strong opinions about farming in general, and also had what Oliver considered a self-destructive tendency to align himself with lost causes: fox-hunting, bull-fighting, vanishing ways of rural life. But if Orlando had wanted to join those outlaws, then that meant he had done it in preference to rejoining him. And this brought Oliver to the most terrifying possibility of all: that, for all his protestations of undying love, Orlando had seized his chance to do what he hadn't felt able to do before – constrained perhaps by timidity, or weakness, or a simple desire not to hurt his lover's feelings: had seized his chance to finish with Oliver for good; Orlando had quite simply left him.

*

It was a simple task in principle. One hundred and fifteen pictures from the gallery's previous exhibition had to be unhooked from their mountings on the walls and taken down to the basement, while eighty-three new ones had to be brought up and hung in their place. But both jobs needed to be carried out simultaneously because of the limitations of space. Both sets of pictures were to go in a particular sequence. Numbers, pictures and titles needed constant cross-referencing and checking. It required a muscle power and energy, a good deal of care and finesse in handling the exhibits – especially on the bend in the basement stairs – and mental concentration as well. The pictures going downstairs were oil paintings, Paris cityscapes mostly. They were bright in colour and buoyant in mood, and Oliver was not at all surprised to see that more than half of them had on them the bright red stickers that meant, *Sold.* Coming up were rare photographs from the nineteenth century, sepia and grey, and broodingly atmospheric. Some were streetscapes, or country scenes with labourers at work in the fields. Others were studio portraits, mostly of women in, for their time, quite daring states of near-undress. Just one featured a young man stripped to the waist, and Oliver was jolted into remembering his studio session with Berndt.

Working with Oliver all the time was Jérome, relaxed and smiling, and treating Oliver like an old friend – as if they'd always known each other. Jérome's company and conversation was hardly enough to put troubled thoughts of Orlando out of Oliver's mind, but in the circumstances it was as good as anything he could have wished. It was also extremely good for his French.

At midday they broke for a lunch of baguettes with *rillettes* and *cornichons* at a café. 'If you want to stay on in Paris a bit longer but without forking out for a hotel,' Jérome said, a bit carefully, 'you can always stay at ours.' He glanced up at Oliver with a wary sidelong look, but when he received no immediate brush-off from him the look metamorphosed into a grin.

*

Small but cosy was Oliver's first impression of his new home. And high. The mansard roof gave a characterful slope to the outside walls, and the windowslooked onto the top half of Notre Dame, chunks of the Louvre and the Grand Palais and, on the other side, as promised, the summit of the Eiffel Tower.

Jérome asked him ingenuously, and so early on that it made Oliver smile, where he thought he might go to next, 'that is, if Orlando doesn't turn up within a couple of weeks.'

Oliver found himself giving an answer, which he hadn't known before, thinking it through as he spoke. 'I'm not going to be in too much of a hurry to cross the Channel. Stay in the Schengen countries, I should think. Maybe go to Germany. My ex-boyfriend came from there. Adi. Short for Adrian. He lives near Hanover. Though I don't think I shall be dropping in on him. I've got another friend, in Cologne.' Bernd. Friend of last resort. He could go there. Phone him first. 'Problem is,

I've lost my mobile with all my numbers. Normally I'm good at remembering numbers, but I don't remember his. Double zero four nine, then two two one... But that's only the codes for Germany and Cologne.'

'We could get it easily enough from international enquiries,' Jérome said. 'But no hurry with that. You've only just arrived. You want a glass of wine?' He got up and went into the kitchen to look for some.

'You do cocaine?' André asked him suddenly.

'No, never,' Oliver said.

'Neither have we. Only I thought everybody in England did. And especially with you being a trafficker and all. Just asking.'

Oliver blinked in surprise. 'I never really saw myself as a trafficker, you know,' he said, just as Jérome was returning with a bottle and three glasses. 'I think Orlando tried the stuff once, in Spain, though he didn't let on to me.' Orlando in Spain. Perhaps he was there now. Back in Nerja with his two little friends. Bradford and Bingley. For the moment Oliver couldn't remember their real names. The thought made him wince. Orlando with two other men, out of his head on coke... But what double standards here! Oliver himself was now enjoying a bottle of wine with two personable boys whose sexual orientations, unlike Bradford's and Bingley's, were in no doubt. What would Orly think of that?

'You'll find him again,' Jérome was saying gently, as if he'd been keeping in step with Oliver's wandering thoughts. 'You'll get him back.' Jérome grew on him day by day.

'Your parents know you're gay?' André asked. His questions popped out like rabbits from his own thought processes rather than arising smoothly from the line of conversation. It made Oliver smile.

'They did. But they're both dead now. They had no trouble with it though. At least they said they didn't.'

'And Orlando's?'

'His mother's dead. She didn't know, he said. His father still doesn't. At least that's what Orlando thinks.' Oliver looked at André and Jérome in turn. 'And yours?'

The younger two looked at each other. Jérome spoke. 'Not yet. It's easy for them to imagine we're just two friends who share a flat, at our age. We haven't tried to disillusion them. Guess we'll have to some time. It won't look quite the same, two men sharing a flat together and neither with a girlfriend when we're thirty.'

'How long have you been together?' Oliver asked.

'Six months,' Jérome answered. 'Think we'll make it?'

It was longer than he'd had with Orly. 'With a bit of luck,' he said.

*

The picture hanging was finished early. That was often the way with tasks that seemed endless. In the fog of action you didn't see the end approaching, then suddenly they were done. But there was something else that Oliver didn't see. An elderly couple in the street outside who peered through the window. He didn't see them but they saw him. He didn't see them exchange looks, didn't hear the woman say, in French, something like – 'Isn't that him?' Or the man's answering nod, that indicated that it certainly was. Nicole had said the Parisians were an unobservant lot, but of course that couldn't be true of them all. The couple walked rather urgently away.

Oliver stayed on at the gallery, chatting and drinking espressos with Jean-Marc and Jérome. One could easily fall for Jérome, Oliver thought. Fortunately he was not in any state to do anything stupid. He didn't want to go to bed with anyone, or feel strongly about anyone, who wasn't Orlando. He couldn't imagine right now that – supposing Orlando was gone for ever – he ever would. And Jérome was far too young, and had a nice boyfriend of his own age, even if he did have a pleasing, and unusual, access to Oliver's wavelength. He tuned into it just then.

'You don't have to go to Cologne, *tu sais*. You can stay with us for as long as you want. Weeks. Months. Forever, if it suits you.'

'It's a tempting offer, Jérome.' Oliver could surely find teaching work that was paid cash in hand somewhere in this city of millions. The sofa hadn't been very comfortable, but the companionship of his hosts – Jérome especially – more than made up for that. 'You know, I'd like that very much. I'll certainly stay the weekend but after that… The police will catch up with me one day. It won't go well for you and André if I'm at your place when they do.'

Jérome gave him one of his sunniest smiles. 'Sometimes you think he's dead. I know you think that. You try to hide it from us, but I can see it anyway. He's not dead though. I promise.'

Oliver laughed his surprise. 'You can see that too?'

'No. Only I hope it for you so much. For both of you. That it must be true.'

'You're quite something, you are,' Oliver said. Maybe he could afford to stay on in Paris for just one more week.

*

In the end André was the waiter at the *vernissage*, while Oliver and Jérome stayed at the flat and prepared dinner, to be ready when he returned. Quite the little family we're becoming, Oliver thought, peeling potatoes, while Jérome chopped onions and diced pork.

André returned with news. Two plain-clothes policemen had walked into the *vernissage*, flashed identity cards and told Jean-Marc they were looking for a young Englishman, possibly named Watson – though that might simply be an alias – in connection with stolen works of art, and also trafficking drugs. They asked Jean-Marc to keep a look-out and to let them know if he had any suspicions about anyone who came into the gallery. Keeping his composure, and with a straight face, Jean-Marc had said he would.

This was enough to give Oliver – and Jérome – quite a jolt. But there were some things to take comfort from. The police weren't certain about his name. This meant they had not conclusively identified him as either the courier in the case of the stolen Lucas Cranach, or as the mystery man in Éringues who so badly wanted a cigarette. But what pleased Oliver even more was the fact that the police had described him as young.

The pork stew was eaten in a serious atmosphere, with discussion about what Oliver should do next, and when, running in a loop. Later, the flat striking them all as a bit claustrophobic this early summer night, they went for a beer in Place St-Michel. They had just ordered when André whispered hurriedly, *'Vite, on file.'* As they turned towards the door, Oliver saw two men arriving at the bar, dressed as if for a colder time of year, one of them talking on a mobile phone.

'Where?' Oliver asked as soon as they were outside.

'Taxi rank.' André jerked his head towards the other side of the square. The place was thronged, mercifully, and they dodged their way towards the line of waiting cabs. Jérome opened the door of the front one. There was a dog asleep on the seat next to the driver, so they all piled into the back. There was no reason why the two men in the bar should have been police. Overcoats, a mobile phone... But they were all seriously rattled now.

Decisions were taken precipitately, the three of them talking at once. Round the block. Time to leave Paris now. Cologne. Gare du Nord. Pick up backpack and belongings. André ran up the stairs for them while Oliver and Jérome in the taxi did a second tour of the block. 'Did you get his things from the bathroom?' Jérome was anxious on Oliver's behalf. 'Of course,' André said, breathless with running up six flights of stairs. Then it was back to the Place St-Michel, across the lamp-jewelled bridges of the Île de la Cité and up the long straight Sebastopol Boulevard, left into Magenta... It was impossible to know, in the heavy traffic and the dark, if they were being followed or not. The Gare du Nord loomed ahead of them. Oliver paid the driver. They tumbled out.

The departures board listed a cornucopia of destinations: Calais, Amsterdam, Hamburg, Copenhagen... The overnight train to Berlin, with a stop scheduled for Cologne would leave in twenty minutes. André went to the window with some of Oliver's cash and bought him a ticket. Jérome kept Oliver company for those last few minutes, lurking in the shadows by a wall. The minutes lengthened. 'Even at this time of night there's always a queue,' Jérome said calmly, with his hallmark smile. André came trotting back, ticket and change in hand. Goodbyes were said which turned into hugs and kisses. The one with Jérome was unexpectedly highly charged. Perhaps Oliver should not have been surprised. For both of them it was hard to let go. But let go they had to, and Oliver turned away and sauntered casually, though with heart in mouth, along the platform and climbed aboard the long and very solid-looking train.

A few platforms distant stood the sleek and even longer Eurostars, milk-grey liveried, with their yellow blaze and navy trim. A couple of policemen were standing near them, watching the passengers embarking. They surely couldn't be looking for Oliver. Or could they? He couldn't guess how important the search for him might be: what level of priority it had been accorded. Were there lookouts for him posted at every port and airport around Europe?

Nobody came on board the train to arrest him. At least he didn't think they did. It was hard to monitor, or even see, all the doors of a train comprising some fourteen coaches. He felt marginally safer when the train at last pulled out. It left two minutes late, and what long minutes those had been.

In principle he would have to spend the night sitting bolt upright in his seat but mercifully the train was not full. A lot of people got out at the first stop, which was Compiègne, and then Oliver was able to curl up, although not very comfortably, on a row of empty seats.

He awoke in terror, with a hand shaking his shoulder. But it was only the ticket controller. Where were they now? he wanted to know. About fifty kilometres beyond Charleroi, the inspector said. And was that in Belgium, Oliver asked, or were they still in France? *'En Belgique.'* As far as he knew he wasn't wanted for any crimes committed there. He stayed awake for a couple of hours, peering out at the black, blank night, trying to read the names of the dimly lit stations they rushed through, and hearing only the hum, swish and rattle of the hurtling train. It was not until they had pulled into, and then pulled out again from, the big station at Aachen, and he knew beyond a shadow of a doubt that he was now on German soil, that he permitted himself to fall back to sleep.

It was dawn, then day, and the train was slowing down for Cologne – he adjusted his mind to the German spelling, Köln – where he was decanted onto the platform of the Hauptbahnhof at just after six o'clock. Leaving the station he saw policemen everywhere. Perhaps that was normal here. Reassuringly, they took not the slightest notice of him. Getting his bearings was easy. The twin spires of the cathedral reared up almost opposite the station approach. He only had to get round to the other side of it and he would find himself in the Altstadt where he was confident he could quickly find Bernd's flat.

He looked at his watch. It had hardly moved since he got off the train. He killed some time over a coffee in an early-opening workmen's bar. Then, when at last it came round to seven o'clock – which was still early on a Saturday morning to go calling on friends – he made his way through the streets of the Altstadt to where Bernd lived. The sight of that front door, recessed between two shop fronts, was surprisingly familiar and comforting. He rang the entrance buzzer. There was no reply at first, which in view of the early hour did not disconcert him.

He waited for a minute and buzzed again. This time he heard a window open above him, and he looked up towards the sound at the same moment as a head craned out. But the head didn't belong to Bernd, familiar though it was. Oliver found himself staring in astonishment into the eyes of Adi, who had been his lover for six out of the last seven years.

NINETEEN

'Have you really taken up smoking?' Adi's asking this question so immediately on regaining the power of speech was typical of him. His surprise at seeing Oliver standing on the pavement below him was not quite as great as Oliver's at seeing him. Adi at least knew of the connection between Oliver and Bernd already, while Oliver had not imagined coming face to face with his old partner at the window of Bernd's apartment in his wildest dreams.

The three of them sat perched on stools in Bernd's kitchen: Oliver fully dressed, Adi in a dressing gown that Oliver didn't recognise, and Bernd, who had been in the shower when Oliver rang the bell, draped in a towel that Oliver remembered only too well. And that question, coming from Adi, with his handsome, almost ascetic face, the eyes coal-dark but kindly, carried Oliver immediately back into a past in which the two of them had known each other, with their strengths and faults, their beauties and failings, better than anybody else on the planet. Adi, wanting to know very precisely some detail or other that Oliver thought mundane or irrelevant, as he tried to make exact sense of some new situation, making it quite firm and certain in his mind, as if erecting scaffolding before constructing his own opinion, formulating a reaction to it. 'Have you really taken up smoking?'

'No, of course not. It was the first thing that came into

my head. I'd never been on TV before. All I could think of was that I needed an excuse to get off it again as quickly as I could.'

Seeing Oliver below him in the street, Adi had withdrawn from the window and padded down the stairs at once. On the doorstep it hadn't been necessary for Oliver to say anything to indicate his need. In half a second Adi had looked him over to make sure he wasn't injured, looked around them, and then bundled him indoors. After a moment's hesitation they had embraced for a second and then Adi had led the way upstairs. Bernd emerged from the shower just as they entered the flat, and he treated Oliver to his own look of astonishment, followed immediately by a smile, a kiss and a hug, in which the only awkwardness lay in the fact that Bernd's towel nearly fell off him, and he wasn't sure whether decorum obliged him to keep it fastened round him or not. In the end he let it fall to the ground, but wrapped it around himself again unhurriedly once the embrace was finished. Now he began to make coffee, while Adi checked the window again, just to make sure that Oliver had not been followed.

Oliver pondered on the extraordinary fact of Bernd and Adi's being here together today. Germany's population was eighty million and Adi lived in Hanover, two hundred miles away. Soon Oliver would have to ask how this statistically improbable conjunction had come about. But as it was he who had turned up unannounced on Bernd's doorstep and not the other way round, it was only reasonable that they should expect to hear his story first.

The day after they had seen Oliver's famous appearance on TV, a picture of him, alongside one of the gushing wine tanker, had appeared in all the German papers. But the story had immediately faded, driven out of the international news by the referendum results in France and Holland. They knew nothing more, and now they had to be filled in.

It took some time. Oliver's audience kept interrupting him with questions and – especially in Adi's case – their own thoughts about what might have happened to Orlando. Adi was still as Oliver remembered him: clear-sighted, clear-thinking, but expressing himself with a bluntness that verged on insensitivity. He had no hesitation in saying that he expected Orlando had rejoined the two boys – Jimmy and Dave, Oliver now remembered – at Nerja. If Oliver wanted to get him back he would need to go down there, once things had cooled off, and find him. Oliver noticed the ghost of a frown hovering over Bernd's face as Adi said this, even though he did his best to hide it.

Bernd moved to the fridge and brought out chunks of *wurst* of different kinds, and pots of jam, while Adi started carving into massive loaves of crusty bread whose textures were enlivened by a mass of whole grains and bright gleaming seeds. There was no doubting where he was. Back, and at home, in Germany. Or perhaps Germany had come back home to him.

'You haven't asked me how I came to be here,' Adi

said, pouring coffee. Despite the dressing gown, quite a lot of him – almost as much as of the towel-wrapped Bernd – was on show as he moved around. He still looked good, Oliver decided.

'I was waiting for you to tell me,' Oliver said. 'Kind of agog to know, actually.' He turned and smiled interrogatively at Bernd. Presumably it was Bernd's story too.

'I saw the pictures of you,' Adi began. 'You know. British Workman. One of them was on the cover of a gay magazine I caught sight of in a bar. It gave me a shock, you can imagine. I looked inside and there were all the others. They were pretty amazing. I mean by that, that you looked amazingly good. I wanted to point you out to all the people in the bar, to all those strangers, and make some sort of claim – to knowing you, to having been your partner for so long – but of course it was not possible. Then I thought I must get in touch with you. I phoned to Oxford Road. It made me nervous I must admit. I wasn't too surprised when a German guy answered. I guessed you'd acquired a bit of a taste for us.' Adi smiled. It was a soft, gentle, self-deprecating smile that Adi himself was unaware of, but which Oliver knew only too well and, because Adi knew nothing about it, had learned to love. 'But then I was surprised. Hans told me who he was, and that you'd gone off to Spain with this kid Orlando, had got into trouble with the police, and a few weeks later vanished off the face of the earth. But he gave me Bernd's number, and said he might know how to track you down.'

Oliver looked at Bernd, half-expecting him to take up the story at that point. But he saw that he was gazing intently at Adi, taking pleasure from hearing the story from Adi's lips, and there was no mistaking now what that look meant.

'That was three weeks ago,' Adi continued. Then, with the precision of all people in his situation, 'Three weeks and three days. Of course I had no idea it was Bernd who had taken the photos. That came out in the course of the phone-call.' Adi delivered this straight, almost deadpan.

At that point Bernd did come in. 'Quite by chance I had to be in Hanover a few days later. I suggested we met up for a drink.' He laughed unselfconsciously. 'Well, you know...'

'Has he had his pictures taken yet?' Oliver asked.

'Yes,' Adi answered. 'That was back here one weekend after. Show you later.'

After the traumas of being looked for, and perhaps recognised, by the police in Paris, Oliver found himself reluctant to venture outside Bernd's apartment, where he felt protected as much by the welcome his hosts had given him as by the walls and locks and windows. That first day Oliver slept a lot, in Bernd and Adi's bed, while the bed's regular occupants went out to do the weekend shopping – and took the opportunity, Oliver supposed, to talk about him. He telephoned Paris, calling Nicole's flat and also Jérome and André's, but they were all out, presumably doing their own shopping for the weekend. He left Bernd's phone number, though not his name, at both addresses and left it at that; he didn't want to hunt them all down on their mobiles. He didn't expect any news of Orlando: the British Council would be shut until Monday, and if Orlando had let a week go by without contacting the place he was hardly likely to try and do so over the weekend, if he ever did.

His calls were returned during the afternoon. Nicole was relieved that he was safe and had not been followed to Cologne. There was no sign, she said, that the police had connected him either with herself and Jean-Marc, or with her brother and Jérome. She was pretty sure that their phone lines were not under surveillance. There was a certain sound you heard, she said – at least some friends had told her this – that indicated when the spooks at the Hôtel de Ville were listening in: a sort of hissing; and she had heard nothing of the kind. She would miss him, she said, and she hoped they would meet again when things were *plus calmes*.

Jérome phoned a little later. He and André took turns to talk to him; Oliver could almost see them good-humouredly grabbing the phone from each other. They too were quite sure that their phone line had not been tapped: there was a sound you knew to look out for – some of their friends had experienced it – like a series of clicks.

In the evening, with a mixture of bashfulness and pride, Adi showed Oliver the photos that Bernd had taken of him. Naked in many of them, he looked pretty

good, and Oliver had no reason not to tell him so. At the
end of the evening a bed was made up for Oliver on the
sofa in the living area. Oliver had neither expected nor
wished for any other arrangement. The hunted fox, he
was grateful to have somewhere safe to lay his head, to
be with friends.

*

Oliver decided not to shave on Sunday morning. He
hadn't done so on Saturday either. A beard would not be
much of a disguise, but it would be something, along
with the sunglasses and a cap of some sort – though the
baseball cap he'd been wearing when he was spotted in
Paris would have to be exchanged for something else.
He came close to deciding that he wouldn't set foot out
of doors until the beard had grown quite long – say to
Father Christmas length – but the other two talked him
round. He wasn't wanted by the German police and, if
he'd been seen in Paris there was no reason why they
should expect to find him in Köln. So he was persuaded
to come out for a stroll along the tree-lined embankment
of the Rhine, and to sit outside a café in the Alter Markt
and enjoy a beer. Jammed down on his head was a
woolly ski hat that belonged to Bernd. 'Remember,' said
Adi, looking at his hunched and nervous looking
companion, and suddenly laughing, *'Du bist nicht der
Elefanten-Mensch.'*

*

Adi got up at the crack of dawn on Monday to take the
train back to Hanover and his work. Trustingly he was

leaving Oliver alone with Bernd, which Oliver thought was good of him. But it was clear that what went for Oliver held good for Bernd too: Bernd's love for Adi, and Oliver's for Orlando were like magnetic fields, or whatever it was that kept the planets in their own orbits and prevented them crashing into each other in flames.

Oliver thought about Adi and Bernd. They'd spoken on the phone, they'd met over a drink. You couldn't ask them what had really happened. You couldn't ask people how they had fallen in love. You could more easily ask a couple what they did in bed. At least that question could be answered, even if in practice it probably wouldn't be. But the other how or why could not. It was like the fiendishly clever movement of an old chiming clock. This lever clicked on that one, engaged a cog, an arm was raised – there weren't even names for all the parts, so numerous, so complicated and so delicate were they – until finally the system was sprung, the chime rang clear, and two people who had been separate were suddenly one. It had the inevitability of a duet in Mozart. The analogies broke down only when you came to realise that in the case of love, nobody, unlike the clockmaker or composer, knew why, knew how.

It had been like that with himself and Orlando. But with them, unlike with Bernd and Adi, it had never settled down into a routine. (Oliver thought the word' routine'in a positive sense just then.) Each new day had brought with it some new emergency, ostensibly from an external source: a lorry crash, a failure to get a job, a brush with crime or with police. Yet was it really from outside? It wasn't Orly's doing: his life had seen nothing quite like that before. It wasn't Oliver's doing either: It seemed to be some new thing: a streak of energy, bad energy, bad luck perhaps, that their coming together had brought into being with that magic chiming of the clock. If they got back together again – and Oliver was aware how big an *if* it was – they would have to do better. Oliver didn't know the how of that either, but he made it now his main resolve.

*

Bernd and Adi phoned or texted each other two or three times a day, like teenagers. Oliver spoke on the phone every day to Nicole, or else to Jérome and André, and received the same information each time: that there was no news of Orly. Oliver expected nothing else by now, but the routine of the phone calls had taken on a momentum of its own. Struggling with his French and the far from perfect English of Jérome and André, Oliver found himself exchanging thoughts and news with a little group of people who had somehow become his newest best friends. It had been a funny way to build up such a network, he thought.

In the middle of the week Bernd announced that he had a project for Oliver. Oliver hoped it wouldn't be nude modelling. He wasn't sure that, even with the magnetic fields of their respective loves to shield them from each other, they would be able to resist the temptation presented by that. As it was, he had noticed that the brief chaste hug they had given each other before going to their separate beds on Monday night had extended on Tuesday night by several seconds. Oliver had done a quick mental calculation. At least, on Friday Adi would be back.

But it wasn't nude modelling. A man Bernd knew slightly was in need of English lessons, in a hurry. Private classes. Five hours a day for three days. The man was going to join an American company and needed a brush-up. Oliver said yes, though after a brief hesitation and the voicing of a few doubts. Wouldn't he be recognised? His voice…

Bernd hardly thought so. Nearly two weeks had passed since his TV appearance, and the world had moved on. Oliver had had his hair trimmed, he had the ground plan of a beard carefully shaped around chin and mouth. Someone attending classes with a professional English teacher, especially one who had been recommended by a friend, would not be expecting a wanted criminal to walk into the room.

The classes began next day. They were at the client's flat in the Hohenzollernring. Oliver went along with some apprehension. He had never taught before, except within the protective context of his training course. He had no books or materials to take with him, and was armed only with a block of A4 paper and a pen. But his fears soon melted away. His student, Lothar, was about thirty, smartly dressed and good looking. Full of energy, and with an optimistic outlook on everything in life, he had excellent English already and wanted mainly to talk, about everything under the sun, and be corrected as he did so. Oliver found the sessions gave him a great sense of satisfaction; he was more than able to fulfil his brief. For the last ten days he had been the needy dependent of everyone he had met, from the ladies on the barge to Nicole and Bernd. For once he could be useful to someone else.

Oliver began to wonder whether Adi, for all his lack of tact, had been right when he said that if Oliver wanted to get Orlando back he would have to return to Nerja and confront him face to face. He began to think about trying to contact Michael. Surely the police would have got to him by now. A phone call to his villa – even if he could remember the number – would simply result in the more speedy apprehension of Oliver himself. Perhaps he should simply turn up unannounced. Take a plane. With luck he wouldn't be asked to show a passport. He would discuss it with Bernd and Adi at the weekend.

But when the weekend came Adi had a new piece of cold logic to apply, like steel, to Oliver's unhealed wound. 'I've been thinking,' he said, over a Friday evening drink in the bustling beer hall of the Gaffel Haus, 'and I'm wondering if you've been thinking the same thing. Orlando hasn't come. You haven't gone to Spain. Are these things telling you – the second one coming only from your unconscious, I admit – that it might be time to let him go?'

'Adi, I don't think…' Oliver began. Bernd said nothing, but a frown had appeared on his face while Adi was speaking.

'Think about the Marschallin in *Der Rosenkavalier*,

how she surrenders Octavian. Maybe that is how these things are meant to end. When the age difference is so great. Otherwise… Remember Oscar Wilde – we saw the film, remember, with Jude Law. The hold that Bosie had over him. How it ruined him. In the end cost him his life.'

'*Halt's Maul*, Adi, would you just shut up?' Bernd sounded almost angry. 'Maybe you would behave like Octavian; maybe when you were younger you did. Don't make the mistake of thinking that Orlando must be exactly like you. Orlando whom you've never met. Remember that I have.'

'All right,' said Adi. 'I'm very sorry, both of you. But I only said what I think. And the reason why is not that I want to hurt Oliver. It's precisely that I don't want Oliver to be hurt – by Orlando or anyone else. In case it isn't clear to Oliver or you, I'll say it: I care about Oliver very much. I don't want his emotions played with, I don't want to see him tortured in this way, by someone who – I think – does not deserve anyone half so good.' He was almost in tears.

'Adi, you've said enough,' Bernd told him. 'Oliver, sorry.'

'You don't have to apologise for me,' Adi flared up. 'He knows me well enough.'

'It's OK,' Oliver said. 'I know what Adi meant. Adi, I think you're wrong, but I haven't taken offence. Now can you catch the waiter's eye and get us another drink?'

As Adi looked away, Oliver and Bernd exchanged glances, though neither could be quite sure what the other's said.

*

'No two relationships are the same,' Bernd said later that weekend. 'Probably Orlando does still want to be with Oliver. He may have simply got his wires crossed about the arrangements to meet up.' It was nice of Bernd to say this, nicer still if he really thought it. But Oliver's doubts about Orlando were growing. Had he managed to get his wires crossed about all the plans? About Toulouse, about Paris, about the British Council? He was finding this harder to believe. Adi's words had struck home. As so often in the past, Oliver had disagreed strongly with him at the time, but had later come round to thinking that perhaps he was really right.

He couldn't help contrast his situation with Adi's. Oliver, lonely without Orlando, pining and fearful, unable to discover if Orlando was even alive and if he were, whether Oliver was loved or not. While Adi was blooming. He looked better than Oliver had ever seen him. He had a new self-confidence, even contentment. Almost for the first time since Oliver had first met him Adi seemed able to relax. He'd at last found someone who was absolutely right.

Perhaps it was time to move on. However many the misunderstandings it would not have been beyond Orlando, as a last resort, to have contacted Hans at Oxford Road. Even if he didn't have the number, he could have found it somehow. Or could he? He hadn't passed that test with regard to the British Council.

Oliver tried to imagine what the future might hold, were Orlando to reappear, were they to pick up the threads and go on from where they had left off. He tried to look ten or twenty years ahead – at an Orlando whose physical beauty had already lost its bloom, at a middle-aged, paunchy and ruddy-faced Orlando, who had long ago drunk his way through Oliver's redundancy payout, and had still not made much of a success at anything he'd turned his hand to. Was that vision of the future something he desired so much that he would sacrifice the whole of his happiness for it? How long did you go on saying' one day at a time'and hoping against hope for something that, in the end, might not deliver very much? Oliver argued these points with himself over the next couple of days. And as he did so he felt the power that Orlando held over him beginning to wane. Nothing new was coming into his life to replace it, but for the first time he was able to imagine that one day something could. His lessons with Lothar were coming to an end. He was sleeping on the sofas of long-suffering friends – Jérome, André, Bernd, Adi – and had no future in view, other than Orlando, who was becoming a less reliable prospect every day. He could not go on like this. He would have to pull himself together. Start life again. He had nothing to keep him here. Or anywhere.

*

Oliver's last lesson with Lothar had just finished. There would be no-one back at the flat. Adi had gone back to Hanover. Bernd was out on a shoot; he would be home later for a meal which it was not yet time for Oliver to cook. Oliver turned in at the door of a bar. Almost at random, though not quite. He'd been in here once or twice over the past ten days. There was a juke box in the corner offering a menu of nostalgic hits, many of them British; many of them he knew.

He wasn't able to listen to serious music these days. The music he loved, any so-called 'classical' music would have knocked him sideways. Even to imagine himself listening to the great trio in *Der Rosenkavalier* – so lightly tossed into the argument by Adi – was upsetting. Nor could he have borne Beethoven's *An die ferne Geliebte*, let alone *Die Winterreise*. Even a sentimental Victorian ballad like Tom Bowling would have been too much. Golden pop oldies, though, he could just about sit through, sipping a beer, in the early evening.

Or so he had thought. Until now.

There was something in the air that night... *Fernando...*

Oliver's ears pricked up at that small coincidence of two syllables. He sat rigid in front of his beer glass, taking in every word of the song, every note of its accompaniment, as if he had never heard them before.

I'd have done the same again... Fernando...

He felt as if the song had been written especially for him, and for this moment, and that its meaning had been hidden from him before today, unable to reveal its power as if he had been under some spell – a spell that decreed this moment and no other was the one in which he would be enlightened. The one syllable of difference was a mere detail. It really cut no ice.

Orlando… Fernando… Orlando… Orlando.

The potency of music, cheap or otherwise. The power it had to hurt. The power it had to reproach you for your lack of faith. The power it had to change you.

*

'You've been crying,' Bernd said to him when he came home a couple of hours later, to find Oliver busy preparing supper in the kitchen. He had not been chopping onions. 'Plus, you're a little bit drunk, I think.'

'I have to get him back,' Oliver said. He was surprised that Bernd could tell he had been crying. He had got himself back under control over an hour ago, and had even washed his face, checking himself in the bathroom mirror as carefully as any Hollywood heroine. 'It's no use hiding out here in Köln, waiting for him to find his way here somehow – or turn up in Paris after all this time. And I'm not going to get over him. Though I have to admit that just during the last twenty-four hours I was beginning to think that I could – that Adi was right.'

'I'm very happy to hear it,' Bernd said. 'I didn't want to think you might abandon hope, and try to get over him. I couldn't say anything before, though. I wanted you to do whatever made you happy, no matter what I might think.' He paused for a moment. 'If it's chilli oil you're looking for, it's on the second shelf.'

As they cooked and then ate supper they did their best to come up with constructive plans. 'There must be other people in the world who know him,' Bernd said reasonably. 'Apart from those two types in Spain. He must have friends in England. A family certainly.'

'There was a house in London, which he shared with friends. In Kentish Town. I don't know the phone number. Though I suppose I'd find it if I actually went.' Oliver made an effort. 'Twenty-seven A. Can't get the street name. It'll come back, given time. He wasn't that close to the people there. I'm not sure he had many friends.' Or am I just making that up, Oliver thought, because I want it to be true?

'What about his family, then?'

'His father and brother live in Kent itself. On a farm near a village called Newchurch.'

'Then contact them.'

'You're joking! Orly's father would skin me alive.'

'Not over the phone he couldn't. Couldn't fire a shotgun down the line. He might shout at you, or refuse to tell you where his son is, or put the phone down. But what have you got to lose? If he became abusive you'd just hang up on him yourself.'

Oliver immediately felt ashamed. Why should one

adult feel afraid of what another adult might say to him over a phone line? 'Of course,' he said.

'Do you know the number?' Bernd persisted.

'No I don't. If I did, I might have thought to phone it before now. I know the name of the farm. It's called Mockbeggar. Orlando found the name ironic, but it was an irony he seemed to enjoy. He was – is – like that. Has a bit of a masochistic streak. Though not in a physical way,' Oliver added hastily, seeing a questioning look hover upon Bernd's face. 'And not when it comes to sex.' When it came to sex, Oliver thought, Orlando was reassuringly ordinary, comfortingly normal – within the parameters of being gay, of course.

'Then let's look at the *Internationale Telefonauskunft* as soon as we've finished eating.' They did. Bernd dialled a number, pressed a button, waited a bit, and a minute later was writing down the phone number of Mockbeggar Farm.

It was ten o'clock. Nine o'clock in England. Even in the height of summer farmers should be home and indoors by now. There was no point delaying things. Bernd withdrew to the kitchen, leaving Oliver by the phone. Even so, in this apartment without doors, he could hear everything if he chose to listen. Oliver took a deep breath and tapped out the number. The phone was picked up almost at once. 'Kidd,' he heard. The voice was deeper than Orlando's, but it carried the same trace of a Kentish burr.

Oliver tried to keep his breathing steady and his voice under control. 'Am I speaking to the father of Orlando Kidd?'

There was a silence – to Oliver it seemed a very long one – then the voice said, 'And who are you?'

'My name's Oliver Watson. Am I speaking to Orlando's father?'

'My God,' said the man.

'I don't know if Orlando is alive or dead,' Oliver blurted. He felt his hands and legs – though not his voice, thank God – beginning to shake. 'Do you know?'

Another pause. Then, 'Oh, he's alive all right.'

'And where is he?' Oliver asked urgently. 'Is he with you?'

'No,' said the other. Did Oliver detect a hint of sadness in that firm no? 'No no. He's still abroad. One of the Canary Islands.'

'Which?' Oliver was desperate to know, even as he was astonished at the news. Orlando in the Canaries? What on earth had taken him there? He wanted to put the phone down then and there, rush to the airport… He saw himself traipsing desperately from island to island, in absurd fast-forward mode, asking in Spanish at hotels, nightclubs, on farms…

'Card was from… No, not Canaries exactly. From… Funchal. That's, er…'

'Madeira,' said Oliver. 'And you have an address? A number?'

'Look, Mr Watson.' Orly's father, if it was he, seemed to be having a change of heart. 'I've told you more than I really wanted to. I wasn't exactly expecting to hear from you. And I don't welcome the thought of you getting back together with my son.' So it was the father. 'You're both adults, I know, so I can hardly stop you. But I'm not minded to hand you his contact details, that's all.'

'But would you give him mine?' Oliver almost begged. 'At least let him know I...'

'I think this conversation's gone as far as it should,' said the elder Kidd. 'Goodbye Mr...'

'Wait,' said Oliver. 'If I came to see you ... to talk to you in person ... would you at least let me...?'

'Where are you phoning from?'

Oliver had got beyond caution. 'Germany. Cologne.' At the very least, Orlando's father might let that slip to his son, if only by accident.

'You're a wanted man over here, I suppose you realise that. I think you'd find it unlikely they'd let you in and then let you go on your way.'

'But if I did make it... If I did get through...'

There was a pause, maybe even a sigh at the other end. 'I suppose if you made it that far I might not actually set the dogs on you.'

'I'm used to being hunted,' Oliver said. 'With dogs and without. But thank you anyway.' Oliver wasn't sure what he was thanking Orlando's father for. He put the phone down.

Orlando was alive, not dead. Resurrected for the second time since he'd known him. Once thrown clear, to survive a lorry crash; now returned to him from the grave again. The Cat of nine lives. The other possibility that Oliver had dwelt on so much recently, that Orlando no longer loved him, became reduced to something of little importance. Orlando was alive, alive-oh, and nothing else mattered in the world.

TWENTY

'You don't know anyone in Köln who arranges false passports, do you?' Oliver asked.

'No I do not,' said Bernd. He laughed, though it was rather a strained laugh: the conversation they were having had little of the light-hearted about it. 'Whatever kind of circles do you think I move in?'

They had left the apartment together, shortly after the end of Oliver's phone conversation with Orlando's father, in animated if friendly disagreement about what Oliver should do next, and were continuing their summit meeting over a beer in the neutral, noisy territory of the Gaffel Haus. Bernd had at first expressed admiration for Oliver and his courage in tackling Kidd senior. But that had turned to appalled incredulity when Oliver had told him what he intended doing. 'You can not go to England. Absolute not. You would walk into exactly the dangers that you have been running away from for months. Arrest. Imprisonment. If you went to prison you could not be with Orly again for years.'

Oliver knew this. He also knew what Bernd was too kind to spell out, but must also have been thinking. That Orlando would be unlikely to wait for him for years, unlikely still to want him when he came out. And that if Orly already, even now, didn't want him, then his grand gesture, his ultimate gamble – that he could get into the UK and then persuade the father to put him back in touch with the son – would all go to waste, and his life to ruin.

'Why don't you let me phone the father back?' Bernd suggested. 'Let me try to persuade him to see reason and give Orlando's address to me even if he won't give it to you.'

Oliver thought this was wonderful of Bernd: brave and quixotic in the best German tradition. He also knew that it could never work. He could imagine the reaction of an Englishman of Orly's father's age and background to being phoned by a totally unknown German, and then asked in very directly worded English for his son's current address. 'It's kind,' Oliver said, 'and I love you for it very much, Bernd, but it hasn't a snowflake's chance in hell. *Es gibt nicht die Spur einer Chance.*'

Bernd had to agree. But he had not given up all hope of persuading Oliver not to put his head in the lion's mouth of the British authorities. 'Then just go straight to Funchal. You won't need a passport at all if you're lucky. They won't be on the lookout for you in Portuguese territory, just as they aren't here and weren't in Belgium. Orlando made it there safely, that's clear, and if he could, then so can you.'

'Well, yeah…'

'How big a place is Funchal anyway? I've never been there, but I've been to the Canaries. The towns there aren't very big. And they weren't full of redheads either. I don't expect Funchal's much different.'

'You're right. Of course you're right. But supposing Orlando was simply passing through? He might have got a job on a cruise ship. Sent a postcard when they docked. Next stop might be Tenerife, the Azores, Tobago…'

'Ja, aber…'

'The other thing is,' Oliver went on, ignoring the yes, but, 'I think I ought to be doing things by the book for once. Putting things straight – especially with Orlando's father – for the sake of the future, if you like. If there's going to be a future.'

Bernd caught at one of Oliver's hands across the table top and looked him hard in the eyes. 'For Orlando and you there will be a future. I do hope it. But there won't be a future if you end up in prison. No young man will wait that long. Even a saint would not.' He paused, let go of Oliver's hand, swallowed a mouthful of beer. 'I think we need to get Adi in on this discussion.' He pulled his phone from his pocket and tapped the number that gave him instant access to the phone in Adi's pocket.

'Adi…' Bernd brought his partner quickly up to date, though, conscious that he was in a public – if unheeding – place, he was a little careful with his words. Oliver became' *unser gemeinsamer Freund'*– our mutual friend, England' *seine Heimat,*'and so on. 'He's having a crisis of conscience,' Bernd finished up. 'Wants to run the gauntlet of the authorities for the sake of putting things right between himself and the world – and our mutual friend's father in particular.'

'That sounds typical,' Adi said. 'He has a kind of masochistic streak buried in him somewhere. Sometimes it rises to the surface and gets out. Look, put me on to him.' Bernd surrendered his phone to Oliver.

'Listen Oli,' Adi said. 'Don't do this. Go to Madeira, go anywhere, stay with us in Köln, but don't try and tough it out with Immigration in England. You're being like Oscar Wilde – waiting in that hotel…'

'The Cadogan,' Oliver supplied.

'Waiting for the police to come, when he could have got to France and saved himself. Offering himself up as a sacrifice … for…' (he went into English) '..for bloody Bosie. And much good it did him.'

Oliver repeated the arguments he had already used with Bernd. The phone passed back and forth between them. At last Bernd and Oliver realised they had lost: Oliver's mind was made up. Then first Adi, and next Bernd, offered to lend Oliver their own passports to travel on – which would have been an immense risk to themselves were Oliver to take either offer up. But he did not. Even a cursory inspection of Adi's or Bernd's passport would show that Oliver looked nothing like either of them.

*

Oliver caught a plane to Stansted the next day. He and Bernd had woken up to the news, on the radio, that Michael Jackson had walked free from the court in California where he had been tried on child abuse charges. That outcome struck them, along with the rest of the world, as little short of miraculous, and it gave them new hope that Oliver might walk unscathed through the British passport and customs controls when he arrived.

He phoned nobody in England to say he was coming, not even Hans. But he did phone Nicole in Paris to give her his mixed bag of news. 'That Orlando is alive is wonderful enough,' she answered him. 'Wherever you go, whatever happens to you, just hold on to that.'

Passport controllers did look at you more closely in these post nine-eleven days. Dark glasses and a ten days' growth of beard were powerless against them when they held your clean-shaven photograph in their hands. Oliver would just have to trust his luck and hope to be waved through by some official who wasn't actually thinking about him. As Michael – Donald – had once reminded him, Oliver Watson was a common enough name.

He was used to being nervous at airports. That had been a part of his life for half a year. But this morning check-in and embarkation went without a hitch. Only when he took his seat in the plane did Oliver feel a stab at his heart. Since meeting Orlando, Oliver hadn't been on a flight without him. But today there was no Marmalade Cat to sprawl across his lap and point out landmarks on the ground. The jowly businessman who sat next to him was hardly a substitute. So, once they were airborne, Oliver had a go himself. It was a clear day. He made a guess at Brussels – big city, big airport – then Dover docks, which were fairly unmistakeable, and the estuary of the Thames. Peering past Dover, into the indistinct blue-grey where Kent faded into cloud, he imagined Mockbeggar Farm just down there: his destination of tomorrow, if he ever got that far.

His backpack was full. He had bought a few clothes and shoes in Germany, and had actually ditched the old backpack and bought a new one, choosing its colour carefully: an unchallenging mid-blue. But it was still hand baggage. He hoped he would pass for a returning visitor: someone who would attract little attention; someone who had only gone to Cologne for a long weekend. It had worked before.

He queued at passport control. Looking ahead he could see that the checks were quite perfunctory. The queue moved encouragingly quickly. Then he saw someone, a man in a light grey suit, pass behind the officers at the desks and glance briefly down the queue before he disappeared. For some reason Oliver thought the face looked familiar. It was a round, cherubic face, furnished with a pair of alert blue eyes: the man it belonged to looked about the same age as Oliver was himself.

The queue continued to move fast. Just before Oliver reached the desk the man in the suit appeared again. Again he scanned the queue casually – a professional reflex, Oliver supposed – but this time his searching eyes met Oliver's. Oliver held his gaze dully for half a second before looking unhurriedly away. He was becoming a good actor. His experiences this year had given him as good a training in playing nonchalant as Orlando's drama school could ever have. In Oliver's peripheral vision the man disengaged his own gaze and walked away.

Oliver was anxious now when he came to offer his passport for inspection and felt himself sweating slightly. Were immigration officers trained, like dogs, to smell fear? But this one waved him through. He felt his chest expand and then contract. The familiar, involuntary, sigh of relief.

'Mr Watson? Would you mind stepping this way please?' It was the man who had looked at him a few seconds earlier, now suddenly re-materialised at Oliver's side. Did Oliver remember him? If so, from where? The man guided him courteously out of the moving crowd, towards a doorway in the far wall. He was tall, solidly built. He did not clap a hand on Oliver's shoulder, nor even touch him. Oliver thought back to the time when he'd walked out onto a stage to arrest Othello, as an extra in the ballet. 'Put your hands near, but not on, his shoulders. Dancers don't like to be touched,' the régisseur had told him. Was he being gently arrested now?

The door led into a corridor from which side doors opened off. Oliver's escort showed him through one of them. 'Have a seat.' They were in a small, plain room, furnished with one bare table and four tubular steel chairs. An interrogation room, Oliver realised grimly. He had been interrogated by a sniffer dog in just such a room in Madeira.

It was when the man took a seat at the table, opposite

him, that Oliver remembered. They had been to school together. For a foolish half second Oliver thought that was going to make everything all right. The man's name was…

'Jim Mahoney. We were at school together, as it happens.' He said this politely but without a smile. From his pocket he produced a card. Oliver read: *HMRC, James Mahoney, Deputy Director of Customs, Anglia Region.*

'HMRC?' Oliver queried.

'Her Majesty's Revenue and Customs. We – by that I mean Her Majesty's Customs and Excise – merged with the Inland Revenue back in April this year. You might not have known about that, as I think (correct me if I'm wrong) you were out of the country at that time.' This time he did permit himself to smile: an open, white-toothed Irish smile – and then it all came cascading back.

He would have been about three years below him, Oliver thought. He had not known him well. Except for one incident he might not have remembered him at all. But he had been in detention once when Oliver had been a prefect, in his last year. Oliver had been taking the detention. The boy – Jim – had made a fuss about wanting to go to the loo throughout the whole forty-minute period. Oliver hadn't let him go; had thought the kid was acting up. But in the end the boy, who must have been fourteen, had actually wet himself, and suffered the noisy derision of his peers when a flustered Oliver had finally let him leave the room. It was not a promising background to this present meeting.

'You're a wanted man, Mr Watson.'

'You can call me Oliver. You used to.' You probably called me Fidget too, behind my back, Oliver thought.

'Thank you. And by all means call me Jim.' Again that baby-faced Irish smile. Still the curly hair, even if it had darkened from blond to mouse, and was pin-pricked here and there with silver – though that could be seen only if you looked very closely. Oliver did. 'Of course, you're not surprised to find that we stopped you. Wanted for questioning in connection with the theft and illegal export of a Lucas Cranach painting back in February. More recently, a possible involvement in drug-trafficking between Spain and France last month.' He stopped. He and Oliver looked at each other for a moment in silence. Then Jim Mahoney went on. 'I don't know which has been the bigger surprise. To find you trying to get back into Britain when you must have known you wouldn't make it even as far as the baggage reclaim. Or to find you mixed up in a criminal network in the first place. I seem to remember you as a rather religious young man when you were sixteen or seventeen.'

'People change,' said Oliver, stony-faced. He was conscious suddenly that he needed to pee. He hadn't gone since leaving Bernd's flat. 'Are you going to arrest me?' he asked.

'Probably,' said Jim.

'Probably?' Oliver queried carefully. 'Why not certainly, when you know who I am and seem to have a clear idea of what you think I've done?'

'Shall we leave that on one side for a moment?' said Jim smoothly. 'Do you want to smoke? You can if you want to.'

'I don't smoke,' said Oliver. 'I never have.'

'That's what I remember from school. But I thought you must have taken it up since. There you were on all our TV screens just a few weeks ago, telling the world you needed a cigarette.'

'It was just something that came into my head. I didn't particularly want to stay and be interviewed just then. Perhaps that was foolish of me. But I wasn't thinking too clearly at that moment. You see, I'd just seconds before discovered what was in the fuel tank. Before that I'd had no idea.'

'Interesting,' said Jim. He rubbed his chin with the knuckle of his forefinger. It was a gesture that Oliver immediately remembered. 'Sometimes it's the most interesting things that come out by accident. Tell me – what made you get involved in this business? Criminality.'

'I don't know about criminality,' Oliver said. 'I took on some courier work because I needed money. I'd lost my job.'

'Lots of people lose their jobs. And everybody needs

money. We don't all turn to crime in order to get it.'

'You keep saying crime, criminality. I would dispute that. I haven't knowingly broken any law.'

'You're welcome to argue that in court, of course. But you'd be up against some pretty tough arguments the other way. However, that's all for another time.' Jim smiled. 'But, you know, Oliver, we're both civil servants, so we both know about redundancy payouts in the public sector. A Home Office statistician. You must have been making … well, you know that more exactly than I do. So tell me, since – I'm pretty convinced – you didn't do it for the money, then why?'

Oliver continued to stare at him stony-faced, but he said nothing.

'All right then, let me tell you what I think. You thought you'd have a little game with the law. A little fun, at the law's expense. The law is an ass, you may have said to yourself, so I'll pull its tail. Smuggling's just a game, you thought.' Baccy for the parson, brandy for the squire.'Just an innocent pastime. Nobody gets hurt. A picture goes missing from a gallery – a picture that hardly anyone's heard of – and nobody really minds. The insurance'll pay. Then drugs. Nobody gets hurt by drugs. Although when I was at school I do seem to remember one prefect in particular being dead against them. But as you say, people change.

'So we agree, don't we: these days, nobody gets hurt. Certainly not the growers enslaved by poverty, in some of the poorest countries in the world, their lives and their children's lives in hock to the barons. And not the kids in the West whose lives are being blighted by the ready availability of drugs on the street. Prices are tumbling. Supplies have never been more assured. Thanks, in a small part, to you.'

Oliver felt his forearms shaking. He pressed them hard down on the table. 'I wasn't a drug runner. I knew nothing about that part of the business at all.'

'So you say.'

'I knew nothing about cocaine coming across the Gibraltar Straits. Everybody knows it's a route for hashish, obviously…'

'Come on, Oliver. The routes are many and various, whatever drug may be involved. You can't possibly claim total ignorance, unless you've spent the last ten years in a hermit's cell. But never mind. Let's try another tack. Perhaps you really didn't try to take your little revenge on the State for giving you the chop. Perhaps you didn't think through the consequences of your actions. Perhaps you really weren't as bright as we all thought you were at school, and as the Home Office obviously thought you were until recently. So what other reason could there be? Was it perhaps a jump at the chance of a little adventure in middle life? Or maybe, just maybe, you were doing it because you wanted to impress someone. Someone younger than you perhaps, to whom you wanted to give some reason to look up to you; to give them something they could admire you for.

Just maybe. Perhaps I am digressing. Another point. Perhaps *the* other point. Tell me: what brought you back here to British shores so urgently today, when you'd been assiduously avoiding your home country for so long?'

Oliver thought for a moment before replying. There seemed no way to avoid at least a partial disclosure of his reason for returning. No point in concealing it. 'I was trying – I am trying – to find someone. Someone I lost touch with in Spain. I thought they might be back here in the UK.'

Jim's eyebrows rose in an expression of mock surprise. 'You must have wanted their company very much to have taken such a risk. He, or she, must be a very special person. Now I wonder whether this person might have been the same person you left the country with at the beginning of April. I mean, of course, Mr Orlando Kidd.'

'Jim,' said Oliver, leaning forward across the table, 'I believe I'm right in thinking I don't have to answer questions without a lawyer present. Isn't that true?'

'If, or when, I arrest you, that's the time you'll be wanting a lawyer. And you shall have one of course – one of your own choosing. But for now we're simply having a civilised chat, aren't we? At least that's what I thought. So no, of course you don't have to answer. But as to whether or not it's Mr Kidd you're looking for, well I think I'll take your answer as a yes.'

Oliver wanted desperately to ask him how much he knew about Orlando. Was he too wanted for questioning by the British authorities? Did he stand in as much danger as Oliver did? It crossed his mind that Orlando's father might have tipped off the immigration services. He hoped not. Though it was more than a hope. He had formed an impression of Orlando's father's character during their brief exchange on the telephone. It was of a man who would not do a thing like that.

Plenty of people could, in all innocence, have supplied the information that he and Orlando had left for Spain together. His sister, his brother, Hans, the training college… He refused to ask, fearful of a trap. 'Look, Jim,' he said, 'while we're being civilised – is there a loo somewhere here I could use? I badly need to pee.'

Did the ghost of a smirk flit across Jim Mahoney's face just then? Oliver would have found it hard to blame him if it had.

'Well, let's see. That raises a bit of a problem. If I arrest you all appropriate facilities will be provided. But then of course, the time for civilised chats would be at an end. Of course you're free now to leave the room and head towards the public toilets in the baggage hall, but then I'll be forced to arrest you if you do.' He paused to let this sink in. 'So you see, it's a bit awkward, isn't it?'

'Look,' Oliver said, unable now to keep the anger out of his voice, 'why don't you go ahead and arrest me now if you're going to do it at some point anyway? What's the point of playing cat and mouse with me like this?'

Oliver thought he could see one possible point, but he tried to put it out of his mind.

'If I arrest you,' said Jim calmly, 'there's a very high chance – no, I would say almost a certainty – that you'll be put away for a considerable time. And I'm not talking about months. It would be years, Oliver. Years and years. A very long time to have to wait for Orlando. And an even longer time for Orlando to have to wait for you. At the age of twenty-four the years ahead look a good deal longer than they do to the likes of you and me.'

'For fuck's sake, what do you want from me?' Oliver was nearly shouting. 'And I really do need to piss.'

'Funnily enough, I'm more than ready to believe you there. But I hope you've noticed I've been very forbearing in not asking questions about Mr Kidd. I could, for instance, have asked you if he was with you in the cab of the wine tanker that so spectacularly hit the headlines in the south of France last month. And if the answer to that question turned out to be yes, then he would find a lot of interest taken in his whereabouts all of a sudden by other people besides you. But at the moment there is no reason why he should be wanted for questioning by anyone – at least in Britain. Which puts him in a happily different position from yours – at least for now. I could also have asked you where exactly you think he might be now, and how and where you were planning to look for him. But I've been very good to you, you see, and not put any of those questions.'

'What,' Oliver began very deliberately, 'do I have to

do in order to be let go?'

'Ah, now you're asking. Well, Oliver, I've begun to think we might come to some sort of an arrangement. An informal one, based on the mutual trust and respect that exists between us. A sort of gentlemen's agreement.

'Please,' said Oliver, 'just tell me.'

'Perhaps I'd let you go and find your Orlando – and perhaps I'd agree not to ask those unasked questions about him – if you would then agree to leave this country again as soon as possible, say within a month. We could say it was as though you hadn't really arrived here this afternoon. It would be a period of truce between us – quite a generous period of time, don't you think? I'd agree not to have you hunted down within that time, and nobody would follow you when you left the country again or try to trace you wherever you went to live.'

'Surely you don't have that power.' Oliver's voice was weak.

'Look at me, Oliver,' said Jim, 'and think about it. Nobody knows you're here except me. Nobody has to. It will be as if you never came. The man on the desk didn't know who you were. Your passport wasn't stamped. All that I have offered I have power to deliver.' His voice modulated into a less triumphal key. 'What I don't have the power to promise is that the French and Spanish authorities will leave you in peace. I can't promise that. However I can talk with them, and probably persuade.

We're lucky at least that there isn't a European Arrest Warrant out for you yet. If there was there'd be no hope. As it is, there's a good chance they'll do what I ask. We all find ourselves owed the odd favour in this international cooperation business, as I'm sure you can imagine. So, provided you didn't actually stray back into their territories, I think you would probably be able to breathe reasonably easily.'

Oliver was appalled. It showed on his face. Jim went on. 'Don't worry. There are plenty of places in the world where you haven't done any damage as yet. Italy and Portugal come to mind as two of the nearer ones. Oh, and Belgium. You wouldn't actually have to go as far as Buenos Aires or Tibet.'

'I don't know what to…'

Jim leaned forward over the table towards him. Oliver was conscious of the physical bulk of him: he occupied about twice as much space as he had done aged fourteen. 'I think you've been made a wonderful offer, Oliver. You didn't really want to come back to Britain today, did you? You were afraid you'd be arrested. Well, that would remain the case. Nothing would have changed. But now you'd have the bonus of some time to find Orlando and put your affairs in order before you leave again. What outcome could possibly be better? Be honest with yourself. When you took your plane this morning you feared the worst. You weren't expecting anything half as positive as this.'

That was true. 'I suppose,' Oliver said slowly, 'it's an

offer I'm hardly in a position to refuse.' He would just have to hope that Orlando would see the matter in the same light – if he got as far as finding him. 'Now, please, do you think I could…?'

Jim Mahoney looked pained. 'Yes, OK, but I'm afraid it's not quite as simple as that. Before I let you go I would have to ask you just one more thing.'

'And what would that thing be?' Oliver still wasn't there.

'Oh come on, Oliver. You surely know. You must have watched enough spy movies and police series to know what I'm going to ask you now. You must also know that you're no more than a pawn in this business. A very small, small potato. Do you really think Her Majesty wants the expense of detaining you at her pleasure for several years? It's not you we're after. You're supremely unimportant to us; you must realise that. So you must also know what we're really looking to you to give us.' He paused and stared coldly across the table into Oliver's eyes. 'I want to know where your instructions came from. Who paid you? Who put you up to all this – to borrow an expression you just used yourself – this playing cat and mouse with the law. Name him, or her, please, Oliver. Do it now and my offer stands.'

Michael – Donald – and his kind wife Carmen, who had taken them in at Nerja when they had arrived dirty, injured and distressed. Michael who had found them a flat, got them jobs, set them on their feet… 'I'm sorry,' said Oliver, 'I can't do that. You see, I never knew her name.'

Joe leaned back again. A small sigh of exasperation escaped his lips. 'Give me a break, Oliver. You can do better than that.' A thought appeared to strike him. 'Or on the other hand, maybe you can't. Maybe lying doesn't come easy to you even now. Maybe that's something I should give you credit for.'

'I told you…'

Jim pushed back his chair and slowly stood up. He must be well over six foot, Oliver thought. One metre eighty-five or nearly. 'One more time. Please, Oliver. The name.'

'I'm sorry, I just don't…'

Jim nodded towards a door in the side wall a few feet away. It was not the one they had come in by. 'I'm here today on an official inspection and audit. It's a busy day for me. There's a lot of paperwork still waiting for me on the other side of that door, and I think I'd better go through there now and get back to it. And while I'm doing that I'll let you stay here a little longer and see if you can remember what I think you'll manage to if you just concentrate a little harder. In fact, you can have as long as you need.' He walked towards the door, but turned back to look at Oliver when he reached it. 'I'll be in here on my own. You just come and tap on the door here,' he tapped on it himself as if to show how it was done, 'as soon as you've decided what you want to happen next.' He gave a little smile as he said this, then he opened the door and walked through it, closing it neatly behind him.

Oliver's bladder tweaked at his nerves. He looked around the room. He hadn't really taken it in before; his eyes had been focused entirely on Jim. His detention room was grey-walled and windowless, unless you counted the line of glass blocks that ran along one wall just below the ceiling. They were like the glass squares that let light into pedestrian subways and that you could safely drive a bus over. The two grey doors, the table and the chairs. Had the room been less Spartan the tiny CCTV cameras in the corners might not have appeared quite so prominent.

He really means me to wet myself, Oliver thought. It's in revenge for that time at school. And I wasn't trying to make that happen. I never wanted to see him humiliated in front of his classmates.

Oliver thought about the options that presented themselves to him now. He could not betray Michael – Donald – like that. Such a thing was not in his book. If he stayed here it was only a matter of time before he pissed himself. And what then? Knock on the door and say, OK, you've won, arrest me now? At that rate he might as well save both his dignity and his denims and knock on the door now. Arrest me now.

He didn't have to wet his trousers. He could unzip and urinate in a corner of the room against the wall. Or in the middle of the floor, since the cameras were going to catch him at it wherever he was. He could jump up on the table and do it brazenly, impudently, from a height, to indicate to whoever was watching the CCTV monitors exactly what he thought of them.

He realised that he could do none of those things. The same options had been available to young Jim Mahoney all those years ago, but he hadn't been able to summon the nerve to put any of them into practice either.

So, he must go and get himself arrested, and do it now. But then what? After his well-earned comfort break the real interrogation would start. They'd get to Donald somehow. With tricks and traps. They probably knew his name already. He'd be able to do no good for him.

Ouch! He'd nearly lost control. Concentrate!

He and Donald would both end up in jail. He would never see Orlando again. His principled stand would go for nothing. His life would be at an end. He stood up, hesitated for a second, then walked to the door and knocked.

'Donald was the first name I knew him by,' Oliver said. 'Later he called himself Michael. Michael Davidson. When I last saw him he was living in Nerja. At the Villa Burriana, Avenida del…'

'Yes, yes,' said Jim Mahoney. He had risen from the desk he was sitting at when Oliver entered the room and had turned towards him, but without walking in his direction or inviting Oliver to approach or take a seat. They faced each other standing, a couple of metres apart. 'Yes, we know that.'

'You knew already?' Oliver had suspected it. Nevertheless he still felt utterly sick.

Jim Mahoney nodded slowly. 'Yes. And I'm afraid your generous reflex, your desire to protect him – though I notice that it lasted somewhat less than three minutes – came too late. Michael Davidson, alias Donald Faircross, died last night.'

'Died? How?'

'Of a bullet. A drive-by shooting. An occupational hazard for the criminal fraternity on the Costa del Sol, as you probably already know.'

'But who…?'

'Someone with an axe to grind. Turf wars down there. It'll be in all the papers. You'll be able to read it for yourself once we've let you go. Assuming we're still able to do that, of course…'

'His wife. Carmen. What about her?'

'She died too, I'm afraid. Sorry to be the bearer of such news. But it was mercifully quick, if that's any comfort to you at all. These people know what they're doing. No struggling or unpleasantness.'

'Dear God,' said Oliver faintly. He was shaking his head. Then he found that he was crying. 'Please,' – it was almost a whimper – 'please let me go and piss.'

'Your change of heart just now gives me hope,' Jim said quietly. 'Hope for you too. Perhaps you will be getting out of here after all. Even if not in time to make it to the bathroom. You see, what I really want to know is – now that Donald, or Michael, is no longer around to tell us – who it is, or was, who was controlling him.'

'Fuck you, Jim Mahoney, and may you rot in hell!' Oliver's words were distorted by an explosion of rage and tears. 'I don't know that. How do you expect me to know? I've done everything you asked. You've tricked me, humiliated me, made me betray my own integrity by betraying a good friend – who now you tell me is dead. So all for nothing. Now – just – let me go. At the very least let me…'

'One minute more, Oliver,' Jim said calmly, raising a hand in a just-wait gesture. 'Try to remember something. Anything. A name. An address maybe. Anything at all that you may have overheard, or possibly saw.'

It came suddenly to Oliver. The envelope that had dropped out of the folds of the map. Michael saying: *Face to face dealings whenever possible. Letters when necessary, just like in the old days.* 'Michael Deakin,' he heard himself say. 'Estepona. Calle San Esteban – number fifteen, I think. Apartment… Apartment number four, on the … on the left.'

'Thank you,' said Jim Mahoney. He smiled at Oliver. Almost beamed at him. 'Thank you,' he said again. He sounded as though he really meant it.

Oliver scrambled across the baggage hall to the gents. He unzipped himself frantically. Hearing, and gazing down at the urgent splashing waterspout, he reckoned he had had only seconds to spare. It was no victory at all though. Jim Mahoney, a mere ghost from his schooldays, had managed to strip him of his integrity and self-respect, the only things, except Orlando and a tiny handful of friends, that he had prized. Yet it was worse than that, Oliver thought, shaking himself and stowing away, zipping back up. No ghost or shadow had done this to him. In pursuit of a vision, a mere glimpse of a red-headed young man on a train, he had brought this destruction upon himself.

TWENTY-ONE

It was in the newspapers, just as Jim had said. Though not splashed across the front pages. Oliver had to search for the small paragraph tucked away inside. Donald Faircross, also calling himself Michael Davidson, and his wife Carmen, had been gunned down from a passing car as they walked towards their own car after dining in a Nerja restaurant, the Pata Negra. Oliver stared at the words as he sat in the London train. He felt quite numb. He felt as if it were he that had died.

Oliver was let into his flat in Oxford Road by a young woman. He was not surprised. The surprise had been Hans's when Oliver had phoned him from the airport to ask if he could spend the night – on the living-room put-u-up if the second bedroom wasn't free. Hans had told him he was most welcome, that the second bedroom was free, and that he would find that Hans now had a girlfriend, who lived at Oxford Road with him.

Oliver took to Jodi at once. At least part of him did. The part of him that still skated on the functioning, busy surface of life: the part of him that wasn't dead. Jodi was a Muslim. She had converted to Islam when she'd had a relationship with a Tunisian a few years previously. It had created a major storm in her Catholic family at the time, but she wasn't going to convert back again in a hurry just because she'd changed her man: a no-nonsense attitude that appealed to Oliver just now. Hans was fine with that: he had no particular religion himself.

And his English had improved remarkably.

Hans had heard nothing from Orlando. Oliver hadn't expected him to; he had asked routinely. He gave Hans a heavily edited account of what had happened at the airport. He didn't tell him that he'd sold his soul. 'Do you want to keep the flat on?' he asked Hans. 'I mean indefinitely.'

'Actually yes,' Hans said. 'I didn't know... I mean, not hearing from you for so long, I didn't know what you intended. But...'

'I don't suppose you'd be interested in buying the place?'

Hans and Jodi looked at each other. 'Could we have a day or two to sleep it over?' Hans asked. 'It could be a possibility.'

Oliver had been' sleeping things over'on the Stansted Express. To dispose of his assets in England seemed to be the only safe course of action, given that he was effectively to be banished from British soil like a medieval courtier who had fallen from grace. Sell the flat, transfer his bank balance abroad. He had little else. A few crates of books and the opera CDs he'd hoped one day to share with Orly. He'd hoped. Did that hope still exist? Oliver wasn't sure. He didn't know whether Orlando had still wanted him even when he was alive: he gravely doubted that he'd want him now that he was dead.

*

To love that well which thou must leave ere long. A Victorian flat in a tree-lined road in North-West London. The Kilburn High Road with its multi-ethnic bustle, its market stalls and traffic, its rows of small shops, in one of which he bought a mobile phone the following morning. How small a claim those mundane things and places had staked to his heart during all the years he'd lived here. But how dear they seemed to him now. He was glad he did not have to tear himself away from a view in the Lake District, a mansion in the Sussex Weald – or a farm in Kent.

Once he had retrieved his phone book from what was now Hans's studio, and entered all its contents into his new mobile, he got on his way. Hans had urged him to phone ahead to say that he was coming. But having already done that, from Germany two days before, Oliver didn't think that a second approach by phone would improve his chances of a welcome at Mockbeggar.

He took a train to Sevenoaks, and then he hired a car. Public transport did not deliver you to farm gates, and he didn't want to arrive in a taxi: he needed to be able to leave at a moment of his own choosing.

It was motorway nearly all the way, M25, M20, hugging the edge of the North Downs, which sparkled green with the freshness of early summer. In places haymaking had already started. He left the motorway just after Ashford, from then on following thread-thin roads across the Marsh, stopping from time to time to consult the map. His last drive had been across the

Pyrenees. The Romney Marsh presented a less daunting face. It was as flat an expanse as any sea, though the lanes were bordered with elder-flowering hedgerows and the skyline was broken by rows of trees. Church towers showed across great distances. Farms too, and their vast, hangar-like metal barns, every mile or so, gave the impression of a panorama of aerodromes. But this was redeemed by the landscape's peppering of pretty houses, mostly of pink brick. They had roof-tiles of different colour reds all mixed together, dark and bright, chocolate, cherry and orange, like – Oliver thought – the hairs on Orlando's head. He remembered now with shame how, when he was trying to fall out of love with Orlando, just days ago, he had conjured a vision of him at forty: fat, unlovely and red of face. How had he dared to? How had he bloody dared? When Orlando was forty he, Oliver, would be in his mid-fifties. How beautiful in Orlando's eyes could he expect to be then? How lucky beyond belief he would consider himself if Orlando was still a part of him then.

He stopped for lunch at a white weather-boarded pub, a littler short of the village of Newchurch. He would need to ask precise directions for the last mile or two. Besides, you did not endear yourself to people by turning up just as they were sitting down to eat.

A half pint of Harvey's and a cheese sandwich. Oliver had almost forgotten such things. The bar was dark, beamed, garlanded with hops. A wide open hearth would have hosted a blaze on winter nights. But today the sun blazed outside, in the bluest of skies. Other people's conversations came to Oliver with extraordinary clarity. He had been surrounded by Spanish, French and German for so long, unconsciously straining his ears to make sense of what people said, that now those ears were at a heightened pitch of receptiveness. Hearing his own language around him again, it was as if he had turned up the volume of the radio in order to listen to a clavichord recital, and then had his eardrums hammered when that was followed by an overture by Wagner.

A woman was talking to an older man at the bar. 'They're different round here. They're not the common one, which is *rana temporana*, but the marsh frog, which is *rana something-else*. That's why they make that noise.'

'We had an injured one in the garden once,' said the man. 'One of its back legs was hanging at the back by a flap of skin. I cut it off with scissors. Put the little fellow by the pond. We thought he'd die in a day or two. But blow me, old Tom was still alive, swimming round in circles, when the kids went off to university. Lived for bloody years.'

'Tough as old boots,' said the woman.

To love that well which thou must leave ere long. 'Excuse me,' Oliver butted in. 'Does anyone know the way to Mockbeggar Farm?'

'Simon Kidd's place? You're looking for Simon Kidd?' Everyone knew the way. They marked it on his map, drew diagrams on a napkin. He thanked them.

Then he finished his sandwich and beer and drove on his way.

The name, Mockbeggar, was on the gate, which was a no-nonsense iron one, set in a brick wall that separated the farmyard from the road. Oliver had already driven past the house, which had its own front gate, a white wooden one between two low-cut hedges. The house was as beautiful as any he had passed in the neighbourhood: of old pink brick and with a roof of brown and red tiles; longer than it was high, it looked as English as a loaf of crusty bread. Oliver had time to notice its cottagey window panes and homely white front door as he slowed the car, but he didn't try to call there. It was a working day and he thought it would be more businesslike to make himself known at the farm. He stopped, got out and worked the iron gate open, wondering a little anxiously about dogs. Though he was cheered by another notice on the gate, hand-written, that said: *Kittens available to good homes*. He closed the gate behind him, ready to leap back over if necessary. Orly had told him how friendly the dogs were. However, he wouldn't have thought to give the dogs the same information about Oliver. A couple of them came to investigate him, but he was relieved to see that they had wagging tails and didn't bark.

The yard was surrounded by a jumble of barns and other buildings. Some were old brick and tile structures, one was modern, metal and massive, the kind of aircraft hangar affair he'd seen all across the Marsh. Another one had a line of stable doors, for horses to lean their heads over. Oliver couldn't see if there were any horses at home today or not.

From one of the nearer doorways a man appeared. There was no doubting who he was. A couple of years older than Orlando, he had the same red-hot-ember shock of hair, the same blazing blue eyes, though not Orlando's too-good-to-be-true looks. Still, many a man was decently handsome – as Oliver himself was – and yet still did not have Orlando's looks. But the big surprise was this. Orlando, Oliver had thought, was tall enough at around five eleven, and had nice farmer's-boy muscles. But his brother was about six foot five, and muscled like a fighting bull. To Oliver's surprise he smiled when he saw his visitor. 'So you made it then. We didn't think you would.'

'How did you know who I am?' Oliver remained wary.

'Saw you on the telly,' said Orlando's brother.

'I see,' said Oliver. 'It looks like the whole world did.' Oliver's five seconds of worldwide fame: the non-smoker informing the human race that he wanted a cigarette, before disappearing like a smoke ring himself. Now he held out his hand, caution mixed with hope, like a child offering a lump of sugar to a horse. 'Oliver Watson.'

'Martin Kidd.' They shook. 'Dad's haying right now, a couple of fields away,' Martin said. 'Reckon it's him you've come to speak to.'

'I suppose it is,' said Oliver, hearing a tinge of regret

in his own voice. He couldn't expect that introduction to go as smoothly as this one. Somehow he had always pictured Orlando's brother as older than himself, like his own brother Lawrence. And of course he wasn't. Oliver still had ten years'seniority, which was something he had never thought about. But neither had he imagined that he'd be quite so big. 'Listen,' he said, 'can I talk to you first? I mean before I see your father. I'd like to know… You must all hate me very much.'

Martin's fair face was very reddened by sun and wind. That was clearly its permanent state. All the same it darkened now with a deep blush: a phenomenon that Oliver was only too familiar with on the face of his little brother. 'Hate you? I don't know. It's difficult…'

'I understand if you do. I'm here because I want to find your brother. If you, or your father, would let me have a phone number I'd get out of your lives for good. I imagine you'd want that.'

'Talk to my father,' Martin mumbled, and looked down at the ground.

'Yes, I will. But when? Where? I don't know the etiquette of farms. Should I come back later when he's finished work?'

Martin hesitated before replying, but whatever answer he might have made was redundant before he could utter it. Round the corner strode another ox-sized man, this one in his late fifties – a fact Oliver knew because Orlando had told him – and with sandy hair that was only just beginning to fade towards white. Stand one on top of the other, Oliver caught himself thinking, and they'd be twelve foot ten, or just under four metres high.

Simon Kidd stopped still when he saw Oliver. He might have recognised him from the television or he might not, but he clearly had no doubt as to who he was. Then he resumed his walk and came up to them. He did not hold out his hand to Oliver, though he looked at him hard for a moment before turning and addressing his son. 'Bolt's sheared and I've used all my spares. Can you go and sort it? Now?'

'Yup,' answered Martin, and abruptly turned and went. Orlando's father turned his whole body towards Oliver. For a second Oliver thought he was going to floor him with a punch.

Perhaps he had wanted to but had controlled the urge. 'So,' he said instead, 'they let you in.'

Oliver had to tilt his head back in order to look the huge man in the eye. 'On certain conditions, yes.' The feelings of sickness and black despair rose up inside him as it always did now when he thought about those conditions. Not that they were ever very far below the surface.

'What the fuck did you think you were doing, Mister Watson?' Simon Kidd's voice was quiet. His anger showed in his eyes and in the tension visible throughout his grandly-constructed frame. 'Not that it's my business or that I should care – if someone I've never met is stupid enough to run off to the Costa del Sol and get mixed up with a gang of criminals. Except that – Christ Almighty – you decided to take my son with you. Who, unfortunately, is very easily led, as I know to my cost. And so I have to make it my business. And to make you my business. It gives me no pleasure to be dealing with you. To being eyeball to eyeball at last. Satisfy my curiosity maybe, but no pleasure at all.'

'I'm not a crook,' Oliver said, and was surprised at the firmness of both his voice and his conviction as he said it. 'I've made some mistakes in life, and I've done a few stupid things. Getting to know your son was not one of them.'

'You'll appreciate that I don't see it quite that way myself. You lure him away to Spain on the pretext of some tin-pot job, then get him mixed up with criminals and abandon him when things get sticky. Like some little …weasel. A little rat.' He grimaced involuntarily as if he had just bitten into something disgusting, and his head shook. 'You look to me, Mister Watson, no better than a turd.'

Oliver flinched at that but continued to look Simon Kidd in the eye. 'It wasn't at all like that,' he tried, but Orlando's father was not ready to give way.

'You just dropped him in the shit when it suited you, and now you have the neck to get in touch with me because you've decided you want to pick up again…'

'It wasn't like that at all.' This time, because he

practically shouted the words, Oliver got through. 'I appreciate you may not want the two of us to be in contact again. Because of things you think you know – things you've heard – about me. I'm just hoping you'll give me the chance to put the record straight. That's why I've come here.' He paused, and Simon's momentary silence gave him the opportunity to add, 'At no small risk.'

Simon appeared to be considering this. After a second he said, 'Well, you've been brave enough to come here. That's something I suppose. For all your bravado on the phone we didn't really think you would. And I must say, you don't look like a poofter. Though neither does Orlando. Unlike the other one.'

'The other one?' For one disoriented second Oliver thought that Simon Kidd was referring to his older, barn-door, son Martin.

'What was the bugger's name? Jeremy. Theatre director and so-called artists'agent. He ran away at the first hint of trouble, that one. Left the Cat completely in the lurch. He shouldn't have been treated that way, even if it was his own stupid fault for getting involved. He's sensitive. Easily hurt. So he needs looking after. And then he meets you on the rebound.' He gave Oliver a piercing look. 'Just the kind of person he needs.' Simon underlined the irony with a snort.

'You knew about all that? Jeremy and so on. Orlando thinks – or used to think – you didn't even know he's gay.'

'Of course we knew,' Simon said brusquely. But there was a hint of tenderness in his voice when he added, 'How could we not?'

Oliver thought he saw the point. He brought to mind the image of his lover – or former lover: tall, beautiful, slender, yet muscular and masculine as well. But in the eyes of men like Simon and Martin he must have appeared fragile and fey: a little pansy of a boy. A little changeling boy. *I do but beg a little changeling boy to be my henchman.*

'All I want is to know where Orlando is,' Oliver said. 'As I told your other son just now. Nothing more. And because I want that I need to explain what happened and how we got separated. I'll own we were on a risky mission, and we knew it. But it was all quite legal. Taking Spanish wine into France under EU rules.' That drew a snort from Simon. 'It may not have been wise in hindsight. We knew there was tension about. We were told to expect trouble. That was part of the deal. Orlando's not a child and he's not a coward, and he didn't have to be talked into anything. But we didn't know there was cocaine in the fuel tank.' Only partly true, Oliver thought. But then, he'd come to explain things, not bare his soul.

Simon was shaking his head. Oliver hoped it was not entirely in disbelief. 'I don't know,' he said.

Oliver pressed ahead. 'I wouldn't leave Orlando in the lurch. Not in any situation. It'd be quite impossible for me. You said I'm not like his last …er …like Jeremy.

You're right. I'm not. I don't know how we got separated in France. We had an arrangement to rendezvous in Paris. For some reason Orlando didn't make it. Perhaps he didn't want to make it. Perhaps he wanted to get shot of me. I've no way of knowing. And if that's the case, fair enough. But that's between him and me. And I just need to know – from him – one way or the other. Can you understand that? Until I phoned you two days ago I didn't even know if he was alive or dead. I know you can understand how that felt.'

Oliver came to a stop. Simon said nothing. They stood facing each other. It seemed like a long time. It felt odd, incongruous, to Oliver to be having this confrontation in the open, in the middle of a farmyard. He who had never had his confrontations in the middle of farmyards, unlike most of the human race, who had been having them there throughout history. Even the bull ring had its origin in this place. He was surprised by the loud whinny of a horse, and turned towards the sound. A white-starred, black head had appeared in the open top door of one of the loose-boxes.

Simon's head too had turned towards the sound. 'Wychita,' he said. Then, 'Come over and say hallo.' Together they walked in silence towards the stable range. Oliver felt that he was dragging his legs over the ground like things made of wood.

He remembered, fortunately, the way to greet a horse without being bitten: by stroking it at the bottom of the bone in the nose, then letting it snuffle and catch the scent of your hand. 'Whose is he – or she?' he asked, while Wychita looked down at him with a liquid eye like darkest chocolate.

'It's she. She's Julia's. Julia, my daughter. The only horse we still keep here. There used to be three – plus a pony – when my wife was alive and the kids were young.' Simon took his turn to stroke the animal's muzzle.

'The pony for Orlando, I suppose.'

'The pony for the youngest. Passed down the line. Like bicycles.'

A thought struck Oliver. 'Which horse did Orlando ride when he came down here at Easter and went hunting?'

'This one,' Simon said. 'Wychita. He borrowed his sister's. We thought it a bit odd of him, wanting to ride out that day. He hadn't hunted for years. Actually we thought he'd rather come to disapprove of it. Town ways and town friends that he had. Not that Martin or I have ridden to hounds for a while.'

'You surprise me,' Oliver said. 'About Orly, I mean. He gave me the impression he was a very keen rider and huntsman. Gave a very spirited defence of hunting, I have to say.'

'And now that surprises me,' Simon said. 'To be honest with you, he's not that great a horseman.' He paused for a moment. 'Perhaps he was trying to impress someone.' He gave Oliver another of his penetrating, blue-eyed looks. Then he said, 'What was your job before you went off on this teaching lark? Did Orlando say something about you being a professor of economics?'

'Hardly.' Oliver smiled. 'I studied economics. But my last job was as a statistician in the Home Office. Till they had a clear-out.'

'Pity,' said Simon. Oliver thought he meant it was a pity about the clear-out, but then wasn't quite sure. 'You could teach Orlando a bit of economics. He hasn't a clue. Home Office.' A new thought appeared to strike Simon, its arrival indicated by a slight furrowing of his sunburned brow. 'Are you any good with computers?'

'Not specially. Why?'

'Come and look at this.'

Oliver found himself walking back across the yard towards another range of outbuildings, then being shown through a door, not into a realm of straw and cattle-cake, but into a well-equipped if extremely Spartan office. 'You see,' said Simon, leaning over a desk and tapping at the keyboard, 'I keep getting this pop-up and then I can't get rid of it.'

Oliver peered at the monitor, shoulder to Simon's shoulder. 'I see what you mean,' he said. 'It comes up so big, there's no room for the close button in the corner. May I?' He sat down at the desk, tweaked at the knob on the monitor front and clicked around with the mouse. 'There,' he said. 'I'm not a real expert, but what I've done is…' He took Simon through the process, click by click.

'Well, you obviously understand the thing better than I do,' Simon said, a little grudgingly. 'Perhaps there's something to be said for the Civil Service after all. We're all a bit ham-fisted with the new technologies down here.'

'Speak for yourself, Dad.' Martin had just walked in on them. 'Bolts are done.'

'Good,' said his father, looking up. 'And OK, Martin, you're not as bad as all that. Still, you didn't have any luck with that pop-up problem. Which Orly's friend's just fixed.'

'Maybe he's the sort of friend Orly needs then,' Martin said – an unexpected gesture of support that made Oliver want to hug him. 'Orly being the complete technophobe himself.'

'Well…' said his father.

'Anything that had electricity running through it, when he was a kid he'd run a mile from. Fire and all. Wouldn't dare light a gas heater till he was about twenty. Capsized a lawn-mower once. Never saw anyone run so fast. Thought the petrol would explode and send him to Kingdom Come.'

Oliver stopped wanting to hug Martin. Rather crossly, he said, 'You make him sound a right scaredy-cat.' Where had that word had popped up from? He hadn't heard it, let alone used it, since primary school. 'I've never seen any sign of that in him. He's not one for running away from things.' But even as he said this, the memory came back to him of Orlando running, panicking and in shock, from a crashed lorry and dragging himself with him. Orly had said he was afraid of the breath test and of prison. Had he been afraid the lorry would catch fire and explode as well? Something he'd never admitted to Oliver during the hours – the weeks – that followed. You never learnt to know another person completely. 'Anyway,' Oliver continued to Martin combatively, 'if he was scared of technology he certainly found ways to overcome it. Driving trucks around Spain for weeks. Isn't this what courage amounts to: being scared of things but doing them anyway? That's what he's like. That's the way he is.'

To Oliver's astonishment Simon chipped in. 'Well said.' He gave his son a look that stopped him coming back on this and turned again to Oliver. 'He may be built like a JCB,' he jerked his head towards Martin, 'but that doesn't give him the right to run his brother down like one.'

Do they know about the lorry crash in the Sierra del Chaparral, Oliver wondered? And how Orly had run away from that. If they didn't, then Oliver wasn't going to be the person to tell them. You never knew, when talking to your lover's family, exactly what they knew and what they didn't. It had been the same with Adi's family. Adi had taught him the German expression for treading on eggshells: *Eiertanz* – an egg-dance.

'I don't actually have a phone number for him,' he heard Simon say. 'I've got an address of sorts. Let me think. There's a postcard back at… No, wait. Hotel Splendor, in a place called Monte something.'

'I think it may be just Monte,' said Oliver. 'I've been there. But he's staying in a hotel?' Oliver couldn't quite get his head round this.

'Working in one, more like. He said he's doing the gardens or something.'

A cat walked in through the open door, paused a second, then darted rapidly towards a corner of the office. There was a cardboard box there that Oliver hadn't given a thought to. The cat sprang inside. Martin saw Oliver's attention follow her. 'Kittens,' he said. 'Want one?'

Oliver was shown the litter of three. They were part tortoiseshell, part tabby. Had one of them been a marmalade Oliver didn't know how he'd have reacted. 'I'm not sure that I can take one,' he said. 'I don't really have a base at the moment.' He suddenly felt sick again. He didn't want to have to tell these people he'd been chucked out of the country. Not now, when things had started to go so unexpectedly well with them. He turned to Simon. 'Do you know what took him to Madeira?' he asked. He couldn't imagine any possible answer that would be favourable to him.

'Not precisely, no,' said Simon. 'You never really know with Orly what he's up to and why. Always a bit of a smokescreen, we've noticed. Always has been. He said something about going back to Spain after you two got split up. To people he knows there.' The boys on the beach at Nerja, Oliver thought despondently, Jimmy and Dave. 'And they said for some reason he'd be better off in Portugal. But why Madeira, God only knows. You'll have to ask him yourself.'

'I will,' said Oliver. 'As soon as I get back to London. I'll track down the number of this hotel and call them up. Look – I'm really grateful to you. Both of you. I wasn't expecting...'

'Neither were we, to tell the truth,' Simon said, looking him straight in the eye. 'Look,' he went on after a pause, 'you probably want to get on your way again. Things to do and all that. And I've got to get back to my big lawn-mower. But if you wanted to have dinner with us this evening...'

*

Oliver found himself alone in Orlando's bedroom, in a state of wonder over the fact. Orlando's bedroom. The one that had been his as a boy. It would be Oliver's for tonight. Once Simon had invited him to dinner he didn't think it reasonable to expect him to drive all the way back to London afterwards. Oliver phoned the car hire company at Sevenoaks to extend the rental period by a day. He left it till he was alone in Orly's bedroom to make that other phone-call. Mountain ridge of a phone-call. But first there was the room itself.

It had the character of a room no longer used by someone, but on which that someone still had a precarious hold. Cardboard cartons were stacked along one wall. Oliver did not need to open them to see that they contained books and CDs, for the stacked contents rose higher than the tops. There was a sound system – so Orly wasn't as much of a technophobe as all that. Though no computer. An old wardrobe. A chest of drawers. Oliver wondered what the etiquette was in this situation. Orly and he had shared everything for months. They were no strangers to each other's dirty socks and underwear. The most intimate recesses of their bodies held no secrets from the other. But here Oliver was in Orlando's bedroom without the invitation or consent that had been given in respect of those other places. He didn't know if he still maintained his position as lover to Orlando. Perhaps Orlando thought of him already as an' ex'. And if so, would he appreciate that ex poking around the bedroom of his childhood? Oliver decided he would do the same as he would if offered the bedroom of a friend's absent, un-met son for the night. He wouldn't need to open the chest of drawers: his day clothes could go on the bedside chair while he slept. He'd only need to open the wardrobe to get a hanger for his jacket. He did so. It was almost empty. There were a couple of pairs of ancient trousers that Orly had probably used for farm work. But then there was a red jacket. Orlando's hunting pink. But pink was the wrong description: it was a bold scarlet, like the coat of a nineteenth-century soldier. It looked well-used, with several little mends in it. Some were neat and expert, presumably done by his mother, one more rough and ready, more recent perhaps and, if so, probably carried out by himself. The jacket shared a hanger with a pair of white jodhpurs. In spite of himself Oliver wished he could see his lover wearing them, he'd look so beautiful. And then he found that he could. As he thought the thought, he found himself visualising Orlando in his hunting togs as clearly as if he stood here with him in the room. And then he thought, he'll probably never get the chance to wear these things again, and for just a mini-second felt a bitter hatred for the vindictive or ignorant few who had engineered the hunting ban.

Oliver moved under the low ceiling towards the window, a dormer, barely two feet above the floor, around which the beams crowded down from above. It offered a view across the farmyard and of the surrounding barns, with between them glimpses of the wide flat fields, most of them white-peppered with sheep. He took out his phone and tapped out the number for International Directory Enquiries. It took a few false starts, but in the end he was given the number for the Hotel Splendor at Monte, on the island of Madeira.

Oh God, what did one say in Portuguese? He heard the phone being picked up, then two words came to him out of the blue – somehow salvaged from memories of his one visit there: *'Fala inglês?'*

'Speak to me,' said a distant voice. The sound was as brittle as if it might crack into fragments and disappear at any moment.

'I want to contact Mister Orlando Kidd who I think

482

works in your gardens. Is it possible he is there?'

'No,' said the voice, 'he is not here.' Then, 'Are you Oliver Watson?'

'Jesus,' said Oliver. 'Yes, I am.'

'We have met,' said the voice. 'In the cable car. My name is Ricardo.' He pronounced it in the Portuguese way: *Hicardo*. 'Then I saw you on television. Then Orlando came. So I was certain we would meet again.'

Oliver's head was spinning. A memory that was barely even a memory assembled itself in his mind. The attractive young man in the cable car, going up to Monte... He had to unscramble the image from that of the waiter – Joao? – with whom he'd watched the departure of the Queen Mary 2. 'You know Orlando? Where is he now?' Oliver dreaded the answer, *At home, in my bed*.

'He's not working today, or yesterday. He doesn't come every day. I expect – no, not tomorrow – the after-tomorrow.'

'Ricardo – I remember you very well. But I need to speak to Orlando very urgently. Do you understand that?'

'Yes, I understand. Orlando talks about you...'

'Will he...' Oliver could hardly get the words out. 'Will he want to hear from me?'

'Of course, of course he will. He couldn't find a way

to contact you. He wasn't sure that you…'

Oliver didn't know how he got through to the end of that phone call. He gave Ricardo the phone number of Oxford Road (how could Orlando not have hung on to that?) and the number of his new mobile for good measure, and told him also that he would be spending this night at Orly's father's house – just in case Orly should return to work earlier than Ricardo expected him. He asked if Ricardo had a number or an address for Orlando. Someone at the hotel must do – but whoever it was was not there. Oliver said he would phone again next day.

When the call was finished, Oliver lay down – or rather fell down – on Orlando's single bed and sobbed as he hadn't done since he was a child. Relief. Joy. Bitter sorrow. All mixed up. His diaphragm hurt and he could hardly breathe. He was glad there was no-one in the house to hear him, though he suspected his outburst might yet be audible to Martin working over on the other side of the yard.

*

For the remainder of that day Oliver felt he was on some new level of consciousness. The things that were happening were extraordinary enough for being so unforeseeable. But it was as if they were happening to somebody else. Because the big thing had happened already: he knew that Orlando still wanted him.

He walked as if in a dream through mown fields that

smelt of childhood summers, where self-heal and scabious flowered purple and blue along the headlands; he saw the big mowing machine – though that was nothing like anything that had existed when he was a child – patiently making its ever-decreasing circuits around the meadow; he helped Martin check and grease the attachments that would be used for turning and baling the hay over the next few days. But even as, in his euphoria, he sailed high as an eagle above the sunlit, hay-scented landscape far below, he was still conscious of the veils of cloud that had only temporarily drawn back but would soon interpose themselves once more between happiness and him. His betrayal of Michael and Carmen. Their deaths. His impending exile. He did not intend to go into any of this with Simon and Martin. But Orlando would have to know. Re-establishing contact with Orlando, even the wonderful, wrenching discovery that Orlando had been trying to contact him, these were not endings but only a beginning. It was the same as with the mountain ridges they had crossed together in their escape from the crash site in southern Spain: you made it to the top of one great crest only to see the next one rising grimly ahead.

*

Martin's girlfriend joined them for dinner. Oliver was glad he wasn't expected to meet Orlando's sister and her husband as well. He'd met enough new people for one momentous day (and he had at least met the sister's horse). They went first to a pub near the farm. Oliver found himself wondering whether this was the one where Orlando had had a wank with his old childhood friend in the gents'. Then Simon drove him, while Martin and his girlfriend went in their own car, to New Romney, the nearest town. It consisted of a pretty Tudor and Georgian High Street that seemed to be composed almost entirely of pubs, so no wonder the schoolboy Orlando had got into a drinking habit early. They were soon in the cosy dining room of the Old Ship, where the food was unpretentious, hearty and good. Simon and Martin chose a steak each, without hesitation, and Oliver went along with them.

After dinner, Martin and his girlfriend drove home and Simon drove Oliver back to Mockbeggar. He must rattle around here on his own, Oliver thought, as Simon let them in and put lights on. He's probably glad of some company once in a while. Even mine.

'I'll be off to bed in half an hour,' Simon said, showing Oliver into the living room. 'But you'll join me for a nightcap first? Obviously, you go to bed as late as you like. Ten-thirty might be a bit early for some.'

Oliver made polite noises about ten-thirty being a good enough bedtime for anybody, while Simon poured from a bottle of Laphroaig at the oak sideboard. Actually Oliver was looking forward to the novel experience of climbing into Orlando's old bed, even without the added value of Orlando's being in it. And he was more than tired.

'Orly thinks this place is going to be under water in a few years,' Simon said as he settled himself into an armchair opposite Oliver. 'I expect he's run that past you already.' Oliver nodded. 'Well, of course it's not,' Simon reassured him. 'There's towns on the Marsh here, not just farms. There's tourism. Take a look at the sea wall at Dymchurch tomorrow if you've got the time. The government's not going to let that go. Two hundred square miles of land or thereabouts. They're even going to build a wind farm halfway between here and Rye. Despite everybody's protests – including mine. But it will go ahead, for all our opposition. And they're not going to build that only to see it go under the waves in a few years.' He stopped, sipped at his whisky. 'What I'm trying to say is, there is a future here. It's not all doom and gloom, like Orly thinks. A Romney Marsh farm can still be a going concern. A family business.' He paused and looked seriously at Oliver. 'If you and Orlando do get back together – you know? – there might be an opportunity for the two of you to get involved – at some point in the future – if you both wanted it, that is. I don't know exactly – I'm spouting off the top of my head – but I'm pretty sure some sort of partnership could be worked out.'

Oliver was reeling. Yesterday he'd been given a month's notice to leave the country for ever; today he was being offered a share in a prosperous Kent farm. The craziness of life, he thought: the sweetness and the bitterness of it, the way that undreamed-of opportunities would come along at the very moment you'd lost the wherewithal to seize them. 'Well, that's… I don't know what to say.'

'Of course you don't, so don't bother trying. You don't know what Orlando would say either, and neither do I. So we'll leave it there for now. Wonder what's on the news.' Simon leaned forward to turn the TV on. Oliver took a gulp of whisky. It tasted like burnt toast, smoke, peat and honey. He had even less idea now what he was going to say to Orlando when they finally met.

When he at last climbed into Orlando's bed Oliver felt the release of a tension in his back that he hadn't even realised was there. As he laid his head down on the soft pillow he heard himself utter two words aloud. To his astonishment. 'Forgive me.' He didn't know to whom they were addressed.

*

In the morning Oliver got up early, as he imagined Orlando would have done had he been the occupant of the bed. He drank instant coffee, standing, in the kitchen with Simon. They were joined presently by Martin who also made himself a cup. Simon told Oliver they would be back indoors for some breakfast at around half-past eight. If he wanted to…

Oliver said his thank-yous, but that he'd better get going. It was a bit of an exaggeration, that, at quarter to seven in the morning, but it seemed the right thing to say and do. With warm handshakes from both Orly's father and his brother, Oliver took his leave.

He drove first of all to look at the sea. It was only three miles away. As Simon had said, it was powerfully kept back by a high concrete-and-earth-work, grass-grown on the landward side, and presided over by an old Martello Tower. From the top of the wall the sea looked far-off and unthreatening, the tide being low. Across the bay Oliver could see the White Cliffs of Dover and, seeming surprisingly close, ships sliding in and out behind the outreaching mole of the great harbour. To landward lay row behind row of bungalows, well below the level of the wall top: built presumably by people who so loved the sea that they were content to live out of sight of it, unless they climbed the wall, just so long as it was near.

Oliver got back into his car and began to retrace his path towards London. Back through Newchurch and Bilsington, taking a short-cut to the motorway junction, which Martin had told him about, via Stone Cross and Cheeseman's Green. He couldn't wait to get back on the phone to the Hotel Splendor, to root out the someone in the office who must have an address, or better still a phone number, for Orlando. But it was still not yet eight o'clock. He would have to be patient for at least another hour he reckoned. By then he'd be at Sevenoaks and returning the car. Now he thought, madly, that he wouldn't even bother to phone, but drive direct to Gatwick and get the first flight out to Funchal. He could return the car at Gatwick airport instead of Sevenoaks.

He suddenly realised that he was driving past lines of suburban semis, which he hadn't passed yesterday. Then a sign welcomed him to Ashford. He'd taken a wrong turn among the twisting lanes obviously, while lost in his thoughts, and missed the way to the motorway. He dithered for a moment. Should he turn back? But every second was bringing him nearer to Ashford town centre, and there would naturally be another motorway junction, clearly signed, on the western side of town. The next minute he was approaching the railway bridge over Ashford International station, the tracks and platforms clearly visible below. On an impulse he swung onto the station approach and down into the yard. He didn't know why. Or rather, he did, but was astonished at himself for obeying the mad, mawkish impulse in the sudden way he had. Mawkish. Was that the word he meant? Or did he mean maudlin? Back in London he would have to look them up.

He parked on a double yellow line, got out and locked the car. As if in a trance he walked into the station. The plate-glass entrance was below platform level and funnelled into an underpass from which steps led up onto the six platforms. He was heading, he knew, for platform one. He climbed the stairs. There was the rail around the glass wall of the Lemon Tree snack bar. There Orlando had been sitting when Oliver first saw him. He saw him there now. It was surprisingly easy. The thick red curls, the cute nose that almost turned up but didn't quite, the bright gentian eyes. Denim jacket and jeans; white trainers and socks. Oliver's visualisation was detailed and exact. Orlando's image seemed as solid and substantial as the real school-kids who actually sat there on the rail, joshing each other, scrapping, and changing places as they waited for the trains that would take them to their various schools.

Then Oliver realised just how many redheads there were among them. And half the others were flaxen-blond. Orlando had once said something about Viking invasions being responsible for the number of red-headed people to be found along the east coast of Britain, even as far south as here. He was right. The whole area was overrun with Orlandos – dozens of them, many of them almost as good-looking as he. Oliver looked from face to face among this lively identification parade of youth, half of them gabbling, at ease, into their mobile phones. None of them seemed to be having any trouble with the technology. Out of all of the youth of east Kent, had Oliver perhaps picked the dud? The runt of the litter? The crazy one, the no-good, incompetent one who couldn't even manage to make a simple phone call? No, Oliver quashed the unworthy doubt. Orlando was part of him; he lived in his head like a second self; they were made to be together like two intertwining, interdependent plants.

'Oli. Oliver.' The voice from just behind him was urgent and excited. High-pitched with disbelief, about to crack. Oliver turned. And there he was. Not in denim, but in a light blue short-sleeved summer top and pale beige shorts. White socks and trainers, though. His arms and legs were gilded by the sun, the freckles on them almost touching each other and merged. His eyes were Mediterranean Seas of blue. His hair was still on the short side, but it was no longer stubbly. It was even beginning to curl.

TWENTY-TWO

They slipped into each other's embrace without speaking. Speech wasn't a possibility just then. How strong and solid Orlando's body felt under Oliver's now trembling hands. The phantasm of Orlando that Oliver had conjured just a minute ago, and that he had consoled himself with alone in bed at night for the past month, had nothing on this. He explored Orly's back and buttocks, and felt Orly's big hands doing the same to him. He ran his palms down the back of Orly's farmer's-boy thighs where they emerged from his shorts. He had an overwhelming urge to get right into those shorts, running his hands up them from the front, to rediscover that absent friend, Orlando's sturdy, elegant cock. He was almost surprised at himself. But then he realised, and was flattered, that Orlando's hands were trying to restrain an identical urge. But there were still limits to what you could do on railway station platforms. Two men could embrace and kiss, and nobody raise an eyebrow – which had not been the case even twenty years ago – but hauling stiffening cocks out and fondling them in broad daylight, in front of the commuters and school kids, was still a no-no even in the sixth year of the twenty-first century. Rightly so, Oliver reluctantly had to tell himself.

Oliver again felt the stab of misery: that awful sick feeling in his stomach. He wanted to hold Orlando for ever without having to say anything. But things would have to be said – and soon. Explanations would have to be made, and listened to, by both of them. They would find themselves judging each other's behaviour. Oliver was afraid he could guess Orlando's reaction to his betrayal of Michael and Carmen only too easily. But there were other things too: mysteries to be solved, teased out. The fact of Orlando's being fortuitously here on Ashford station, where he had no reason to be, when he hadn't been at any of the places where Oliver *had* expected him, was only one of them.

Oliver was the first to speak. Banally. 'I've got a car outside. On a double yellow.' He hadn't asked where Orlando was travelling to. Presumably he had a ticket for some intended destination in his pocket.

'Let's go find it,' Orlando said, and unhooked himself from Oliver. At least he hadn't said that he'd prefer to carry on to wherever he was supposed to be going.

The last piece of the jigsaw came first – as they were walking down the steps into the underpass. 'I was on my way to Mockbeggar,' Orlando said. 'I knew you spent last night there. Hans told me. I was coming to find you.'

'It was a miracle you did,' Oliver said. 'I had no reason to be here at the station.' A bit sheepishly he explained what had brought him to stop here, once he'd found himself driving past Ashford International due to a navigational oversight. Orlando didn't say anything in reply to that. Only his lips twitched a couple of times.

Oliver pointed to the car when they emerged from the underpass and booking hall. 'No clamp, no ticket,' he said, a bit surprised. As they walked towards the car, Oliver put an arm round Orlando and squeezed him towards himself till their shoulders nuzzled.

When they were inside the car Oliver said, 'Do you want to go on to Mockbeggar now?'

'No,' said Orlando. 'I'm not expected. At some point yes, but not just now.'

'The car I rented at Sevenoaks,' Oliver explained. 'Do we drive back there and then train back to Hans's?' But Orly's lack of enthusiasm for that idea showed on his face. 'OK then, here's another idea. We enjoy the day down here. Drive around the country a bit. Do our catching up. Then decide.' A new idea came to him. 'I've got friends not far from here. David and Zara. Live at Beckley. Of course you know that. I was on my way to see them when I first saw you. And again when we first talked on the train. It was David warned me in Seville that night not to go back to England.'

Orlando said, 'And it was he first introduced you to Michael. Or Donald as you called him then.' Jarring like a gear-change from fourth into first, that name had crashed too soon into the conversation. There were other things they both needed to know before dealing with Michael.

Oliver had started the car. 'Better not hang about here,' he said, moving off. 'Which way's south?'

Orlando glanced up at road signs he hadn't seen for months. 'Er – Hastings. Left. And – er – left again at the roundabout. I do love you, you know.'

'I didn't know... I mean, at one point I didn't know. This one?'

Orlando nodded, at the same time protesting, as Oliver swung left out of the roundabout, '*You* didn't know? *I* didn't know!'

Oliver said, 'When you didn't turn up in Paris. Or phone.'

'What do you mean, I didn't phone? I phoned every day. From Spain.'

'Why Spain? I thought we agreed... You phoned every day? The British Council?'

'Consul. The British consul.'

'Counc...' The word died away. There was a silence, deep as a mirror, that seemed never-ending, as the scale of the misunderstanding was borne in on both of them. At last they both began to laugh. It was the least painful option. But the laughter didn't continue long. 'Your father said you went on to see friends in Spain,' Oliver said in as even a tone as he could manage. 'Was that Nerja?'

Orly shot him a look, of hurt, surprise and disbelief. 'You think...? Jesus, man, you thought – those two – what's their names? – Dave and... Bradford and Bingley, you called them. You thought...'

'I'm really sorry, Orly. I didn't know what to think.

495

Can we forget I thought that? Like, as from right now?'

Orlando seemed willing to do this, at least for the moment. 'I went to the farm near Logroño, where I'd worked for a summer when I left school. I told you about that. I didn't have an easy time getting away from Éringues that morning. No doubt you flagged down a TGV and got to Paris direct.'

'Orly, don't. – Please, darling. We both had a terrible day that day. We've both had a terrible time since. Roundabout ahead. Still Hastings?'

'Rye, Hastings. If that's where we're going.'

'I'll know the way from Rye. I'm just pleased you're alive. No judgements about anything, I promise. I love you too.' Oliver took a hand from the wheel and rubbed Orlando's gilded right leg, between shorts and knee.

'There were roadblocks all round Éringues,' Orlando explained. 'I hid near one, in a ditch. I saw a Spanish lorry being stopped and questioned, and then let through. It came towards me. Once it hid me from the gendarmes'view I ran into the road and stood in front of it. It hadn't got up speed yet and it stopped. It had to really, if it could. The driver's mate yelled at me through the window. I said in Spanish I was running from the Crav, who'd shot up the Spanish lorry I was driving. Could they get me away from that particular place? They were brilliant. There was one more roadblock. They folded me up in a bunk bed they had at the back of the cab. They took me all the way back across the border and went out of their way to drop me at a station near Barcelona.'

'So you never got to spend your night in Sitges,' Oliver said.

'Oh but I did,' said Orlando, poker-faced. 'Anyway, that night I thought about my friends near Logroño. I'd missed the boat as far as Toulouse was concerned. Next day was Sunday. Trains to Paris from Barcelona would go right through Carcassonne, or at least nearby – I was afraid they might still be looking for me there. But from Logroño they'd go up the other side – Hendaye, Biarritz, Bordeaux.'

'How did you contact them without a phone number?' Oliver wanted to know.

'Train. Local bus. Walk. Knock on door. It's easy when you know how.' Orlando told this all in a clipped, dry way. Now, as it became Oliver's turn to explain his escape from Éringues that day – the trip by barge, then the train to Toulouse – he realised it was the only way it could be done. You could share the events, step by step, but not the pain of separation; the agony of not knowing, not hearing what had become of the other; the growing doubt – which now he realised had gnawed at Orlando too – about whether the other wanted him back.

They were out of the town now and in open country. A turn-off was signed to Ham Street. Just to get off the main road and away from the fast traffic, Oliver took it. They stopped the car a little short of the village.

'Perhaps I'd better phone David and Zara – if we're going to look them up. See if anyone's home at least.' He paused, in the act of getting his phonet, and turned to Orlando. 'You see, I was afraid you didn't want me any more. As the days passed and became weeks. I'm sorry, but that's how I began to think.'

'That's how I began to think too. I stayed days in Logroño, phoning the consulate daily. I thought – I thought perhaps you were punishing me.'

A quick unbidden sound came from Oliver's throat: half gasp, half sob. 'Punishing you?' Oliver couldn't believe this. Tears pricked at his eyes. 'What for? Whatever for?'

'For that night I stayed out partying in Nerja – with those lads. I just thought…'

'How could you possibly – ever – ever – think that. We put that behind us the very next night. And it didn't matter anyway.' Oliver grabbed Orlando's head and kissed him roughly all over it. out of his pocke'I wanted you so much. I want you now.'

That wasn't quite possible, right where they were, in broad daylight, parked by the thirty-mile-limit sign for Ham Street, with cars passing and people strolling by on the pavement. They drove on slowly through the village and out again into open country. Orlando filled in the gaps in his tale.

After a few days on the farm near Logroño, Orlando's hosts had decided that he might not be safe in Spain.

Unlike in France, where the news of the ambush in Éringues had quickly been pushed out of the headlines by the EU referendum debacle, in Spain the story, with its element of wounded national pride, had run and run. Then another story had surfaced – of an English lorry driver who had crashed a lorry in the mountains south of Granada over a month before. That driver had a name: Orlando Kidd. Orlando expected that Felipe would come forward and say that the man who had been caught on film, wanting to go for a cigarette, was almost certainly Oliver Watson, who was Orlando's friend. But he didn't. Perhaps he had his own reasons for not getting involved.

Even so, the Logroño friends thought that the situation was getting too hot for Orlando to stay in Spain, and so they drove him to Porto, just across the Portuguese border. 'I had to stop calling the British consulate in Paris,' Orlando said. 'That was getting dangerous too. One of the people I'd been speaking to tipped me off. He said that if either you or I was in trouble with the law for any reason, it wouldn't be safe to communicate via the consulate. He gave me his home number – I guess he was gay – and suggested I phone him there every couple of days – and he'd tell me if there'd been any news of you. I did phone. Right up until two days ago. Anyway, once I was in Porto, and still with no news of you, I had no reason to stay there. I presumed you hadn't gone to Paris, so I didn't try to go there. But you'd talked about Madeira, and that you liked the place, so I thought I might try and see if you'd gone there. There are several flights a day from Porto; it was easy enough.'

Orlando went on to explain how he had got a room in the old town, and then had met someone who offered him a job gardening at the Hotel Splendor. There he'd discovered Ricardo, who had astonished him by saying that he had met Oliver back in the winter. A few days later, he had found himself walking past the Bar Zarco – and remembered the name from Oliver's account of his visit. He had gone inside. And the people there had remembered Oliver too.

It had gradually become clear to Orlando that Oliver was not on Madeira. He would surely have made himself known at the Bar Zarco if he had been. In the end it was the people at the Zarco – Maggie and Joe – who had urged him to go back to London and begin his search again at Oxford Road. And there he had arrived in this morning's small hours. He had woken Hans and his girlfriend up at dawn, only to be told that Oliver had arrived just the day before – and had then gone down to Kent. So Orlando had followed on by the first possible train. There was something else he had to tell Oliver, about Maggie and Joe, but it would keep till later...

They stopped the car on a deserted stretch of road between Appledore and Stone, and climbed over a gate into a field. It was a hay meadow still waiting to be cut, full of butterflies, flowers and bees. They lay down, hidden in the thick grass, part undressed each other, and made love as avidly as if it had been their first time. Afterwards Oliver sat stroking his lover's naked back and buttocks as he lay face down among the clover and grass. 'Listen now,' he said. 'There's things I have to tell you. Bad things. One of them is very bad indeed.'

'What sort of things?' Orlando's body stirred uneasily beneath Oliver's hands. 'If it's other blokes, I'd rather not…'

'It isn't that. And there weren't any.' If there were' other blokes'in Orlando's story, Oliver wouldn't want to know that either.' Other blokes'seemed trivial in contrast with what Oliver was going to hit Orlando with now. 'You probably wonder how I got let back into Britain. Why I'm not banged up already. Well, it wasn't easy. I was picked up at customs. Given a grilling. And though they did let me go in the end – well, there was a big price to pay. Two prices.'

'Like?' Orlando squirmed round and sat up to face Oliver. He pulled his shorts up smartly, as if his still damp private parts should not be exposed to the news that Oliver was about to impart. The reflex was probably justified, Oliver thought bitterly, and then primly hauled up and buttoned his own jeans.

'The first thing is that I've got to leave the country again within a month. Believe it or not – for good. If I ever try to come back it's almost certainly prison.''Jesus Christ!'

'Before you start thinking about how or if that affects you – Orly, my darling – you'd better hear the worst bit.' Oliver found he couldn't meet Orlando's expectant gaze, and was looking down at the flattened grass. He said, 'Michael and Carmen are dead.'

'No. Oh wow. Tell me…'

Haltingly Oliver told Orlando about the shooting; then, even more painfully, about how he had given them away – even if too late to hurt them – to the customs officer. How he had finally saved his skin by remembering the address from the envelope that had tumbled out of Michael's map.

A grey pallor came over Orlando's face, undermining his healthy tan. He didn't say anything for some seconds. Then he said, in a voice of incredulity, 'You betrayed two friends because you were scared you were going to wet yourself.' The sentence landed before Oliver like a sack of potatoes, like a dead weight.

'Of course not,' said Oliver. He tried to move a few inches closer to Orlando, which wasn't easy, sitting opposite him on the ground. But neither was it easy for Orlando to back away. 'That was a detail: whether I wet myself or not. I did it – I'm not going to say, I did it for you – I did it in order to get back with you. Because I wanted you. Because I do want you. No, I'm not proud of myself. I think it's the worst thing I've ever done in my life. But don't get things mixed up. I may have betrayed them, but that has nothing to do with their being dead. I did not cause that. And neither, if they'd still been alive, would they have died as a result of anything I said. OK, I admit this: Michael might have gone to prison.'

'Might have!'

'OK. Would have. But it was him or me. Be honest with yourself. Would you have sacrificed yourself for Michael?'

Orlando continued to stare at Oliver whey-faced, his mouth hanging open in disbelief. 'He did so much for us,' he said. 'Took us in when we were desperate. Found us a flat. Got us work. Carmen looked after us at their house for days. They were as good as friends, Oli, for Christ's sake.'

'Up to a point, yes.' Miserably, Oliver pulled and twisted a nearby bunch of grass-stalks. 'But only up to a point. It was basically a business relationship.' Oliver listened to himself saying this. He sounded as despicable in his own ears as he must sound to Orlando. 'We were useful to Michael. He employed us. You could as easily say he used us...'

'Oh fuck you, Oliver...'

'Listen.' Oliver grabbed now at Orlando's hand, but Orlando wrenched it away with surprising force. Oliver went on anyway, desperately, past caring whether he believed his own words or not. 'It suited him to look after us when we fell into his lap. I agree Carmen was lovely to us. But she was doing what she was told. Did we ever have a real conversation with her? Which one does, with real friends. All I can remember her saying was – *Los hombres: negocios, negocios; siempre los negocios.* That and, have some more wine, or chick-peas.'

'That's horrible.'

'I don't mean it like that. I'm as upset about her death – and Michael's – as you are. As upset as I could possibly be. And especially Carmen. I'm only trying to say – don't get the friendship thing out of proportion.'

'Only trying to say… Only trying to justify yourself.'

'Trying to explain. Not justify. Trying to explain to you. Because I love you. Because I want you. …Orly, I need you.' Oliver's voice shook, threatened to break.

'So much so that you let us have sex together, fucked me in the arse, before you told me…'

'You wanted sex too, just now. And it happened. As it couldn't not have done. Sorry if things don't happen in the right order all the time.' Oliver's voice was a whisper. He moved a few inches backwards and sat on his haunches. 'Stay with me, Orlando. I beg you. Don't leave me now.'

'I don't know what to do,' Orlando said. He looked, and sounded, like a desperately unhappy little boy. But then, just at that moment, so did Oliver.

'Come on,' Oliver said. He got to his feet, rather unsteadily, and reached down to pull Orlando to his. He remembered doing and saying exactly the same once before, when Orly had collapsed beside a stream and they had a mountain to climb. 'Let's get back in the car.'

*

Zara met them at the door of Lilac Cottage. It was a subdued welcome. The two visitors had clearly been rowing in the car. Even the phone call that Zara had received out of the blue from Oliver half an hour ago – back in the country, back with Orlando – had, for all its joyful content, conveyed a subliminal signal in Oliver's strained tone of voice that all was not well between them.

Zara made coffee. It was still not much past ten o'clock. She showed them the spare bedroom. If they wanted to stay the night. Or several. From the atmosphere between them at present she doubted they would. But the offer was the important thing. If they needed a place to get over things… She had been eager to meet Orlando; months ago she had said: bring him next time you come. She hadn't envisaged circumstances like this.

The morning passed. Bit by bit, Oliver managed to tell Zara his story, including the sad reason for the awkwardness between Orlando and him. As for Orlando, he skulked, or sulked, in the garden, out of their way.

David arrived at lunchtime. There was cold chicken and salad. David opened a bottle of white wine, though the atmosphere was still hardly celebratory. At first nobody thought Orlando would join them at the table, but Zara persuaded him in the end. David tried, in a no-nonsense way, to tell him, and Oliver, that they were more than lucky to have found each other again – to say nothing of having met in the first place; but his words might have been aimed at a brick wall: Orlando sat, toying with his food and drink, in dejected silence.

After lunch Oliver took Orlando out for a walk. They went up the lane towards Methersham Farm, where the view across the Rother valley opened out when you got to the top, and where Oliver had once imagined being able to see all the way to Newchurch across the Marsh.

'I dreamt of your father,' Orlando said suddenly.

'Of *my* father?' People usually dreamt of their own.

'Like a marble statue, in white robes. He kept saying,' What have you done? What have you done?'

Oliver tried to keep his tone light. 'Do you think he meant me, or you?' He thought, *the statue of the Commendatore in Don Giovanni.*

'At the time I thought… No. Now I don't know.'

'Orlando. Listen to me. I understand that at the moment you think me the biggest, most cowardly piece of shit on the planet. I understand why. But you need to look into your own conscience a little, too. You might realise you're not such a paragon yourself – of either bravery or virtue. You did once leave a crashed lorry on a hillside for someone else to find and pay for, remember, and made me go along with you when you fled the scene. Which I did, out of love for you. You and I both knew about the drug cargoes we carried afterwards, though we didn't even admit that to each other. We did it for the money, quite simply, and we were neither of us blameless in that. So don't try to tell yourself it's…'

'No.' Orlando stopped in his tracks and looked at Oliver, blue eyes and crimson cheeks ablaze. '*You* stop trying to pass the parcel of your guilt to me. I'm not in with you on this one. I never turned over a friend to the police, or customs or whoever. Never in my life. That was just you. But if you can do that to one friend, you could do it to another. You might do it to me.'

Again a sound escaped Oliver as he tried to speak. A sound that he had never made before today: this time something between a gasp and a howl of pain. 'In all my life,' he managed to say, 'nobody's said anything to me that was so cruel.' Tears sprang, and went cascading down his face.

'Well there it is,' said Orlando. 'I'm sorry but we've hit the buffers now.' Tears were streaming from his eyes too, but they did nothing to quench the red fires of his cheeks. Neither was able to reach out to touch or comfort the other. Wordlessly they turned and started to walk back the way they had come.

At the bottom of the lane, Oliver remembered something else he had to say. 'Orly: one piece of information that's no use now, but I have to tell you anyway. Your father talked to me. He said there might one day be room for both you and me as partners in Mockbeggar Farm. It's too late for me, since I can't stay here – I didn't tell him that, there was enough stuff already to sort for one day – but you need to know he said that, at least for you. He always knew about your being gay. And after he'd met me, eventually, he was fine about us. You and me. We had his blessing – for a time. Perhaps I'd been dreaming about your father too.' The day when he would play Mozart operas to Orly would never come.

'In that case,' said Orlando flatly, 'I might as well give you this piece of useless information too. I said there was something I had to tell you about Maggie and Joe at the Bar Zarco. It's this. They're going back to South Africa. They want to sell. They suggested me and you. I have to say I did dream, for a day or two…'

They had reached the main road. Lilac Cottage's garden gate stood open, just the other side. Orlando said, more gently, 'I need time to think, Oli. Time and space away from you.'

'My darling, you've just had time and space away from me. A whole month…'

'That was before.'

'Orlando, there isn't much time. I have to be out of the country in three weeks. I have to make plans and tidy my affairs. Wherever I go, I want you with me. I wish we'd never said we'd live our relationship from day to day, and take life as it came. I wish I'd said to you: be mine for ever, for better or worse, richer or poorer, the whole fucking lot. I wish I had. Wish we had.'

'I said, I need time to think. I want to go and see my father now. Can you take me to the station at Rye? Like almost right away?'

'Then let me come too,' Oliver begged. 'We can speak to him together. I'll tell him all the things I kept back from him yesterday. All the bad things I told you. There'll be nothing hidden anymore. See what he thinks, then. You can't get advice from my father. He's dead. You can still listen to yours. Then you decide.'

But Orlando shook his head. They crossed the road together and briefly went indoors. Orlando took his leave of David and Zara politely, then got into Oliver's car. They drove almost in silence to Rye station, and Oliver waited with Orlando on the hot platform till the Marsh Link train came in. He tried to kiss him as he climbed aboard, but Orlando avoided his embrace. Oliver didn't try to follow him onto the train.

*

Oliver didn't want to stay longer at Beckley after that, although his hosts tried to persuade him. They tried to reassure him about Orlando, too. 'He thinks you've let him down,' Zara said. 'But of course it wasn't you that let him down. It was an image he'd manufactured of you: the hero, the perfect man.'

'Come on,' said Oliver. 'You can't imagine he thinks of me like that.'

'Of course he does,' said David. 'He worships the ground you walk on. It's written all over his face whenever you're in the same room together. You must know that. It was probably there right from the start. It's that that makes him beautiful. He's quite an ordinary looking young man otherwise. Maybe you didn't know.'

'Oh, I can't agree about the last bit,' Zara said with a smile. 'He is beautiful, objectively so. It's not just in the eye of the beholder. And he may be beautiful all through – though we didn't get much of a chance to find out.' She turned to Oliver and, referring to her husband, said, 'He's only jealous.'

*

Oliver thought about that as he drove away. Jealous in what sense? Envious – pointlessly so – at the age of nearly forty, of the good looks of a twenty-four-year-old? Envious of Oliver for having hooked such a catch? Or regretful that it was not he, David, who had ended up in harness with Oliver when there had been the chance, so many years ago? Oliver wondered how much Zara knew, or guessed, about what almost might have been between the two of them.

Oliver drove back to Sevenoaks, returned the car and caught a train into central London. He hadn't wanted to stay in Beckley. But neither had he wanted to be anywhere else. Without Orlando nowhere had much point. He was in no hurry to return to Oxford Road, bearing his tale of joy recaptured only to be lost again at once. Instead of taking the underground or bus, he set off towards Kilburn on foot, in the late afternoon sun. Through Trafalgar Square, Pall Mall, Haymarket, Regent Street… *Not* Piccadilly, where he'd seen Orlando for the second time – and where later, unbelievably, their relationship had begun to flower. *He worships the*

ground you walk on. It's that that makes him beautiful.
Could that be, even partly, true?

Oliver was walking up Marylebone Lane when his
attention was caught by a church, a Catholic one, that he
hadn't seen before. It was a mid-twentieth-century brick
building, of indeterminate architectural style. Functional
Gothic, perhaps, if Oliver had been pressed to give a
name to it.

For no reason that he could think of, Oliver went in.
He took a seat in one of the pews. Probably he was
wanting calm: a place to think, to wonder what to do
next. Two or three other people were sitting near the
back of the church. He wondered what they were doing
there, then he realised that they were queuing for
confession. He was surprised that they should be doing
so in the early part of an evening in the middle of the
week, but then it occurred to him that it might be the eve
of some great feast. Maybe tomorrow was Corpus
Christi. Oliver didn't carry the Church calendar around
in his head, but he remembered that Corpus Christi was
a moveable feast that usually occurred some time in
June, and always on a Thursday. Today was Wednesday,
so perhaps that was it. Before he knew what he was
doing, he had got up and gone to join the short line of
kneeling figures outside the little doorway in the wall.

There was not a lot of sense in this, he thought, as he
hadn't been a believer for half a lifetime. It would
probably even be regarded as a blasphemy by the other
kneeling people if they knew. He still didn't know why
he was doing it when his turn came. But then he stood

up obediently and walked through the little door, closing it behind him.

'Bless me, Father, for I have sinned,' Oliver began, as he knelt in the dimly lit cubicle. 'It is nineteen years since my last confession…' It was nearly as many since he had believed in God.

'That wouldn't be a world record, even so,' said the voice from the other side of the gauze screen. The voice sounded friendly enough. Oliver thought that this priest might be younger than he was. That happened as you grew older. First the policemen. Eventually the priests. 'Is there something you want to tell me?' the priest prompted, and Oliver realised that he had stayed silent when it had been his turn to speak. 'You're not expected to remember everything,' the priest added helpfully.

'I betrayed somebody,' Oliver began slowly. 'Somebody to whom I owed trust.'

'Betrayed?' the priest queried. 'In what way betrayed? Are you talking about marital infidelity?'

'No. Nothing like that. Someone who employed me – but in a secret capacity. In order to save myself from going to prison. I gave his name to the customs investigators.'

'Customs investigators? Without knowing more, I'd have to hazard a guess that both you and your employer were engaged in something illegal. Perhaps I've drawn a wrong conclusion, but if you *were* in some business that the law forbade, then at least on the face of it, it would appear that you did the right thing.'

'Then why do I feel so guilty about it,' Oliver asked, 'if I did the right thing?'

'Remember,' said the priest calmly, 'I am not in possession of all the facts. You might feel guilty for all manner of reasons: some related to this matter of the betrayal as you call it, some not. What were the immediate consequences of your action?'

'My betrayal of my employer had no impact on him. He had been murdered a few days before.' Oliver heard the priest try to stifle an audible intake of breath. 'As for me, it resulted in my immediate release from detention at Stansted airport. But now I feel as bad as if I'd killed him myself.'

The priest was silent for a moment. Then, 'What kind of business had you got yourself involved in?'

'It was smuggling. Drug trafficking. I wasn't entirely sure that I was doing anything illegal.'

'You would have known, though, that drug smuggling was against the law,' the priest said gently.

'Of course, but – I wasn't sure till the very end that the articles I was carrying contained drugs. In one case the drugs were hidden in the fuel tank of a lorry I was driving.' Oliver was afraid for a moment that the priest would say he remembered the case and had seen him on television – everybody else seemed to have – but he didn't. Perhaps he didn't watch television that much.

'Then perhaps you were just – how shall I say this – a little naïve.' Oliver thought he could hear the priest smile as he said this. 'But knowingly to break the law of the land, when that law is a just law and concerns serious matters, would be regarded by the Church as a sin. You do know that, I suppose?'

'Yes, Father, I do,' said Oliver. 'I actually know quite a lot about the teachings of the Church. At least, I used to. You see, my father was a Cistercian monk.'

There was silence for a second as the priest digested this. Then he said, 'I see. We priests like to say we are surprised by nothing we hear in the confessional. Yet I must... Well, there is a first time for everything. And now perhaps, if you have a firm purpose of amendment – which means, in practical terms, extricating yourself from the criminal milieu you seem to have got entangled in (do you think you'll be able to do that?) your feelings of guilt, as you term them, about betraying your employer will disappear, and I shall be able to give you absolution. Though privately I might still wonder how a man like you, with your background, gets mixed up in such things.'

'I think,' said Oliver, 'that I was doing it to impress my partner.'

'The woman in the case, I see.'

'Man, actually.'

There was another silence. Then the priest said, 'You refer to a man as a partner. Do I understand that you use the word in its modern sense? Meaning that you have a sexual relationship with this man?'

'Yes,' said Oliver.

'And you mean to continue in this?'

'Yes,' said Oliver, 'of course. If things come right between us.'

'But you didn't see fit to include that in your confession.'

'I'm not confessing it now. I mentioned it as part of the background to the situation I've just outlined to you.'

'But, as someone with your religious upbringing must surely know, the Church's position on homosexual acts – as opposed to homosexual inclinations – is very clear.'

'Then perhaps I've been wrong about something,' said Oliver. 'I thought that, during the many years I'd been away – I mean during which I'd had no contact with the Church – it had softened its position a bit – in practice at least, if not in principle.'

'Then I'm afraid you were under a misapprehension.' The warmth had gone from the priest's voice, the man-to-man tone had disappeared. 'There is no difference between principle and practice when it comes to what the Church regards as sinful; however mindful the Church is of the immense difficulty we all have in living up to her principles, and however compassionate she is when individual people, in individual situations, fail – as we all inevitably do. But falling short of the ideal is not the same as persisting deliberately in something that the Church expressly forbids – and when you are fully aware what the Church's position is. In that case, I'm sorry but I can not give you absolution.' The priest paused. 'I'm sorry. And this has been as hard for me to say as it's been for you to hear.'

'Now I come to think of it,' said Oliver a bit uncertainly, 'I don't think I'd actually come for absolution. Or for any of the consolations of the Church. Perhaps – in fact certainly – I should have told you that from the start. You see, I haven't been a believer for a very long time.'

'Then what did you come for?' the priest asked.

'I think perhaps I just wanted to talk to someone. To tell someone what I… how I…'

*

'That is what confession means,' said the priest. 'However, since I am unable to absolve you, the fact that you have not come looking for absolution may be just as well. I would be happy to give you a blessing. If you felt you wanted that.'

'Actually,' said Oliver, 'in the circumstances I don't think that would help.'

'I thought you might say that. So, allow me simply to wish you well, and to hope that God will aid you to make wise decisions about your life, whether you believe in Him or not.'

'Thank you, Father,' Oliver said. 'I'm truly sorry if I've wasted your time. As for me, perhaps you've helped me in ways you don't know.'

'Our conversation hasn't done you any harm, at least,' the priest said. 'Now go on your way and God be with you.'

Oliver got up from his knees, turned and left the box. As he closed the door behind him the priest raised his hand in blessing toward his departing back. That could do no harm to him either.

TWENTY-THREE

As Oliver continued his walk northwards along Marylebone Lane in the early evening sunshine he really had no idea what he was going to do next. After some minutes he found himself in the Marylebone Road. The familiar cluster of buildings on the other side – Madame Tussauds, the old dome of the Planetarium, Baker Street Station – were visible through the rumbling traffic. And then it was suddenly obvious what his next move would be. At the tube station there was, he thought he remembered, a branch of Smith's. He crossed the road, went into the station and found the shop. He bought notepaper, envelopes and a first-class stamp. Then he crossed back again, bought himself a pint of bitter at The Globe and took it outside to sit in the sun at one of the pavement tables.

It was Michael – Donald – who had reminded him that when it came to communication, low-tech solutions were sometimes the best. And Orlando was nothing if not a low-tech person. Perhaps that piece of advice would be Donald's enduring legacy to them both. Oliver was about to find out. There was another thing. Letters written in the sunshine tended to go better, he had always found, than those that weren't.

My Darling... Oliver didn't hesitate but plunged right in. He wrote the story of his visit to the church, just as it had happened. When he read it through he was surprised to find it neither self-pitying nor self-justifying, but almost entertaining, as if it had been written by someone else. After that he wrote to Orlando about the two of them. He reminded Orlando of what he had said during their first day on the training course at Piccadilly: how Orly had summed up Oliver's wishes for the future, when he still hardly knew him, as,' A life in the sunshine and sunshine in his life'. Oliver was going to make sure, now that he knew he had to leave the United Kingdom for good, that he would have a life in the sunshine... *But the sunshine in my life will not return until you join me – if not at once, then at some point in the future, when you are ready. I'll be prepared to wait, my darling, but I can't take no as a definite answer.*

Sunshine you may be, and the light of my life, but I've betrayed you in betraying Michael, and I've betrayed myself as well, and that can't be undone in a month of Sunday confessions. I love you in spite of anything you may ever have done wrong, or may do in the future. I'm only (only!!) asking you to see if you can't do the same in return.

Life's a messy business – things go wrong for us and we make them worse by the things we do – the things we think we have to do – to put them right. That's what religious people call original sin and the rest of us call Sod's law. The only thing that makes any sense of all that, or that makes life worth going on with, is the thing called love. But if you can't love me, then nobody can.

Oliver read it through, folded it up, sealed, addressed and stamped the envelope. Then he put it in the post box on the corner. The last collection of the day would be in twenty minutes'time.

For the second time Oliver had the sense of dropping a stone into the deep underground lake that was his future, and simultaneously into that other one that was Orlando's. The first time had been in the Antigua Casa in Málaga, the evening they had met Felipe and had talked about coming to work in Spain. Then, Oliver had said, 'Not necessarily together', and afterwards had read the look on Orly's face. Now this letter, disappearing into the post box, had similarly dropped like a stone, plummeting down into an unknown and unfathomable world.

Oliver continued on his way in the general direction of Kilburn. He stopped off at several more pubs. At one of them he had something to eat. At another he got talking to three thirty-something men who sang in an amateur choir. They were all nice looking, and might all have been gay. Oliver didn't ask. Instead they talked about vocal technique and repertoire, about the operas of Mozart, and Rossini, and about Cecilia Bartoli's extraordinary agility of voice. Oliver thought how strange it was to be talking – and with great enthusiasm – about such things, things he hadn't had a chance to discuss with anyone in years, when the weighty matters that so preoccupied him – Orlando, the remainder of his life – were left unaired and, by the others, un-guessed at.

When that convivial little party broke up, Oliver's new acquaintances told him he'd be most welcome to join their choir. They swapped phone numbers. How odd it was, and how that oddness was the very essence of life,

Oliver thought, that opportunities came crowding in – one day a partnership in a farm, next day membership, and the friendship, of a choir – as soon as it had become too late to benefit from them.

It was late when Oliver got back to Oxford Road. He was a little the worse for drink. He told his story to Hans and Jodi – about finding Orly, then losing him again – about sending him a letter – in just a few sentences. They listened with genuine sympathy, but did not press him with questions or advice, and let him take himself off to bed in the spare room.

The next day, Thursday, Oliver's letter should, in theory, have arrived at Mockbeggar. And in theory at least, Orlando could have replied by phone. But he did not. Oliver spent most of the day walking aimlessly around London, his mind unable to focus, or take decisions about anything, despite the pressing need to take decisions about almost everything, with the deadline for his exile looming. Sometimes he didn't know where he was, and would look wonderingly about him in uncharted streets, till a corner would bring him back onto familiar territory: the Bayswater Road, perhaps, or the embankment of the Thames. Again he left it as late as possible before returning to Oxford Road. Hans and Jodi invited him to eat with them but, sensitive to his state of vulnerability, did not insist when he declined. And: no, they said, when Oliver asked them shyly, Orlando had not made contact with Oxford Road during the day.

Friday was a repeat of Thursday. At a pinch a letter

could have come back from Orlando today, but the post arrived without bringing one. Oliver roamed the hay meadows of Hyde Park, and was distantly surprised by the sight of partridges there. He inspected the Turners in the Tate. If he had felt, on betraying Michael and Carmen, that he, not they, had died, then now he felt that he was dead and gone to Hell. The sun, which had shone so warmly on his letter writing two evenings ago, made no connection with him at all; though it rose hours before he did, and poured down its rays till nearly ten at night, it left him in the dark and in the cold.

Then on Saturday among the post that arrived at Oxford Road there was an envelope written in a hand which – though it had never penned a letter to Oliver before – was as familiar to him as if the writing were his own. He ripped it open.

Oliver, the letter began. No *Darling*. No *Dear*.

Oliver, I must be a very unforgiving man. I mean, if I find it harder to forgive you for being ready to turn in Michael and Carmen than your old Church does. So that simply can not be.

I was asking myself, before your letter came, whether I'd thought I loved a perfect kind of Oliver, who didn't and could not exist. Someone I'd been looking up to, the way a child looks up to a father, and can only be disappointed.

I was knocked out by what you told me, about you and Michael and Carmen, of course. And – even if you forgive – you won't forget the awful things I said to you at the time. Like you said in your letter, things can't be unsaid or undone. But there was more. I couldn't deal with the risk you'd taken in coming back to England when you knew exactly what you had coming to you. That you did that only for me. I don't think I was ready to accept such a big gift two days ago.

So I ran away. Just as I'd been doing all my life. This time I ran away from you. I let you down at just the moment you needed me most. The opposite of what you'd always done for me. And I didn't feel I could look you in the eye again.

Then your letter came.

Oli, I've never had a love letter before – which your letter was. Not from anyone. It is a most wonderful thing to receive. I realise that it makes a present to me of your life, not just your love.

The truth is that I love you exactly as you are – exactly the way you say you love me – with all faults and weaknesses intact. Please stay with me for ever and help your Kidd grow into a man...

Oliver read on with something like disbelief. That life could be turned so upside-down in the space of half a minute. Yet with Orlando it had happened before. Time and again. Perhaps getting Orlando meant that it forever would. But for the moment, this precious moment, he felt himself rising like a bubble from the sea-bed, up into the air, and dancing, like a soul released from Hell, upon the pinnacles of Paradise. The morning air of Kilburn sparkled like a jewel, and the sun that filled the window and greened the alder trees outside began at last to warm his skin. Even the hum of traffic and voices – the car boot sale at St Augustine's, down the road – took on an exultant sound.

A simple letter, just ink-marks on a page, just words, could do all that. They told him too, those ink-marks, that Orlando would be arriving at Oxford Road during the afternoon.

*

They had dinner in the local Spanish restaurant, the Bilbao in Malvern Road. Oliver once again sat opposite those gentian eyes and saw them lit by candle flame. Here at this very table, three months ago, they had sat digesting the implications of their first mutual *I love you*. Oliver was still in a state of near disbelief – despite an afternoon's uninhibited love-making at the flat. (Hans and Jodi had very discreetly been out for the afternoon.) They had finished their starters of fresh grilled squid, and were embarked on dishes of bacalao, served in a gleaming tomato and pepper sauce, when Orlando said, 'We haven't mentioned the danger, of course.'

'Which particular one?' Oliver asked.

'You need to know that I'm aware of it. Just as you must have thought about it too. And I know that it'll never go away.'

'What are you talking about?' This was meant to be an

evening of celebration. Oliver hadn't wanted to get onto all the harsh realities of their future. Not quite yet.

'The people who killed Michael and Carmen. Who knows they may not want to come after us?'

'Darling, it's hardly likely. We were nobodies. Pawns in that game. We didn't have a patch of turf to be fought over.'

'Not just them. The guy you shopped. Michael's boss. The one you've put inside. One day... Well, just maybe.'

Oliver had thought about that. He hadn't wanted to mention it to Orly. 'Well,' he said, 'I don't know...'

'It doesn't matter,' Orlando said. 'I just want you to know that I know. And that I'm not going to run away from that. With you to the end and all. Better or worse, richer or poorer, dead or alive.'

'If that's a vow,' said Oliver, 'then it's mine too.' He wondered how many marriages had been entered into over a plate of wind-dried cod and tomatoes, then thought – with an insight that was not a Home Office statistician's – that perhaps the number was not that small. More conventionally he raised his wineglass.

*

They divided their time, over the next couple of weeks, between Oxford Road, Mockbeggar Farm and David and Zara's cottage in Beckley. For practical reasons most

days had to be spent in London. There was the sale of
the Oxford Road flat to Hans and Jodi to organise. The
opening of accounts with the Banco de Portugal, and the
transfer of funds. The sale of the flat would more than
buy the Bar Zarco – though there were some
complicated mortgage arrangements to sort out before
they went ahead. Also, they took Aids tests. It was
something they had meant to do before, but they had
never been in the same place for long enough. They
arranged for the results to be sent via a doctor in
Funchal. If they were going to be the kind of couple they
had now promised each other they would be, and if the
tests were negative (two big *ifs*, but you had to make a
start somewhere) they could at least dispense with the
condoms from now on.

André and Jérome came over from France for a
weekend to see them. Curious to see Orlando in the
flesh, no doubt, Oliver thought, but he dismissed the idea
as unworthy once they had arrived, laughing
infectiously, and boyishly clamouring to see all the
sights of London in about four hours. Other friends they
said their good-byes to by phone or letter. Adi and Bernd
would be coming to stay with them in Funchal once they
had settled in. Ditto Nicole and Jean-Marc. Oliver
thought they would have to find a better room for them
than the stock cupboard halfway up the stairs.

*

They were ready before the end of the first week in
July – about a week ahead of Jim Mahoney's deadline.
They had sent a few cases of belongings ahead of them

by freight. There were not that many belongings after all: mostly books, and the remainder of Oliver's collection of opera CDs – that part of the collection that had not been abandoned in Córdoba – and that Oliver still had hopes of playing to Orlando one day. When the time was right. So it was backpacks only that they took with them on the sixteen bus down the Edgware Road. To Oliver in his present frame of mind it looked as if the whole world was going on holiday, although it was the middle of the morning rush hour. All their fellow passengers were wearing backpacks too, it seemed: the tourists, the holidaymakers, even businessmen in suits who these days were taking them to work in preference to briefcases. Backpacks, badges of freedom, hallmarks of the traveller. Backpacks for those of all creeds, all colours, all sexual tastes. Apposite bits of kit for the likes of Oliver and Orlando, embarking on a new life.

They got off the bus and bumbled through the crowds to the tube station – the Metropolitan, Circle, Hammersmith and City one – at Edgware Road. Another hour and they would be at the airport. Soon after that, in the sky, Orlando would be wheedling extra gins and tonics out of the flight attendants – Oliver would have to talk to him seriously one day about his drinking, but not today – and then would clamber, marmalade cat-like and purring, over Oliver to point out the coast of France edging its way out from under the aircraft's wing, boyishly, absurdly, exclaiming, 'Look. Abroad! We're almost there.' It was a moment that Oliver looked forward to, and made him involuntarily smile. Yet this moment, walking down through shafts of sunlight onto the crowded tube station platform, was almost as magical, because of the promise that it held of things to come. *Life; London; this moment of June.* That was how Virginia Woolf had described the nowness of things in Mrs Dalloway. Oliver understood this morning what she'd meant. *Life; London...* Only now it was July. July 2005. July the... He looked at his watch to check the date. 'The sixth,' he said aloud.

'Wrong,' said Orlando beside him. He looked at his own new watch, a high-tech bells-and-whistles affair which Oliver had given him just last week, in a subtle bid to nudge him towards the twenty-first century. 'It's the seventh.'

'Surely it's the sixth,' Oliver began, but Orly cut him off.

'It doesn't matter, Oliver. One day here, one day there. Makes no difference. Not to us anyway.'

'Maybe you forgot there's only thirty days in June. Didn't reset. Or maybe I...' But Orlando was right, of course. It didn't matter at all. Not now. Oliver moved to touch his back, but the pack made it impossible. Momentarily he caressed his bottom instead. Their watches had agreed about the time at any rate. Eight forty-six a.m.

THE END

****

About the Author

Anthony McDonald is the author of more than twenty novels. He studied modern history at Durham University, then worked briefly as a musical instrument maker and as a farmhand before moving into the theatre, where he has worked in every capacity except director and electrician. He has also spent several years teaching English in Paris and London. He now lives in rural East Sussex.

Novels by Anthony McDonald
THE DOG IN THE CHAPEL

TOM & CHRISTOPHER AND THEIR KIND

DOG ROSES

SILVER CITY

THE RAVEN AND THE JACKDAW

RALPH: DIARY OF A GAY TEEN

IVOR'S GHOSTS

ADAM

BLUE SKY ADAM

GETTING ORLANDO

ORANGE BITTER, ORANGE SWEET

ALONG THE STARS

WOODCOCK FLIGHT

MATCHES IN THE DARK:

13 Tales of Gay Men

(Short story collection)

Gay Romance Series:

Gay Romance: A Novel

Gay Romance on Garda

Gay Romance in Majorca

Gay Romance in Paris

Gay Romance at Oxford

Gay Romance at Cambridge

Gay Romance: The Van Gogh Window

Gay Romance in Tartan

Gay Romance in Barcelona

Gay Romance: Spring Sonata

Touching Fifty

Romance on the Orient Express

All titles are available as Kindle ebooks and as paperbacks from Amazon.